1314 D0808132

FANTASY

the library
IN EAST AYRSHIRE

East Ayrshire
COUNCIL

7/12 Please return item by last date shown,
or contact library to renew

CUMNOCK

1 1 AUG 2012

2 3 OCT 2012

- 5 NOV 2013

- 2 APR 2014

2 7 AUG 2014

2 1 JUN 2016

- 5 SEP 2019

Twenty years ago Kylie Chan married a Hong Kong
man in a traditional Chinese wedding ceremony in
Eastern China. She and her husband lived in Australia
for eight years, then in Hong Kong for ten years. She has
seen a great deal of Chinese culture and come to
appreciate its customs and way of life.

Two years ago she closed down her successful IT
consultancy company in Hong Kong and moved back
to Australia. She decided to use her knowledge of
Chinese mythology, culture, and martial arts to weave a
story that would appeal to a wide audience.

Since returning to Australia, Kylie has studied kung
fu (Wing Chun and Southern Chow Clan styles) as well
as tai chi and is now a senior belt in both forms. She
has also made an intensive study of Buddhist and Taoist
philosophy and has brought all of these together into
her stories.

Kylie is a mother of two who lives in Brisbane.

Books by Kylie Chan

Dark Heavens

White Tiger (1)
Red Phoenix (2)

RED PHOENIX

DARK HEAVENS: BOOK TWO

朱
雀

KYLIE CHAN

HARPER

HarperVoyager
An imprint of HarperCollinsPublishers
77–85 Fulham Palace Road,
Hammersmith, London W6 8JB

www.harpercollins.co.uk

This paperback edition 2011
1

First published in Australia by
Voyager 2007

Copyright © Kylie Chan 2007

Kylie Chan asserts the moral right to
be identified as the author of this work

A catalogue record for this book is
available from the British Library

ISBN: 978 0 00 734980 7

This novel is entirely a work of fiction.
The names, characters and incidents portrayed in it are
the work of the author's imagination. Any resemblance to
actual persons, living or dead, events or localities is
entirely coincidental.

Set in Sabon 9.5/12 by Helen Beard, ECJ Australia Pty Ltd

Printed and bound in Great Britain by
Clays Ltd, St Ives plc

All rights reserved. No part of this publication may be
reproduced, stored in a retrieval system, or transmitted,
in any form or by any means, electronic, mechanical,
photocopying, recording or otherwise, without the prior
permission of the publishers.

MIX
Paper from
responsible sources
FSC® C007454

FSC
www.fsc.org

FSC is a non-profit international organisation established to promote the
responsible management of the world's forests. Products carrying the FSC
label are independently certified to assure consumers that they come
from forests that are managed to meet the social, economic and
ecological needs of present and future generations.

Find out more about HarperCollins and the environment at
www.harpercollins.co.uk/green

for Jason

The Serpent stirred.
Then it slept again.
It whimpered in its slumber.
There was a call.
A deep, echoing call that made
the thick black water
vibrate and shimmer.
The Serpent cried.
There was no answer.

CHAPTER ONE

I woke with a shock and stared at the ceiling, gasping for breath. Simone! A demon had us ...

No. I was safe in our apartment at the Peak. We'd escaped from the demon Simon Wong with help from the King of the Demons himself. Leo had been injured, John had lost nearly all of his diminishing energy and left us, but we'd made it with help from the God of the West, the White Tiger, Bai Hu.

I shook my head and sat up. I still felt a slight throb where some force, whatever it was, had leapt up in me and forced the Demon King out of my head during his probing mental examination of me, but apart from that I was okay.

I quickly jumped out of bed and dressed. I needed to find the others and check on them.

Five-year-old Simone, John's daughter and a little girl I loved as my own.

Leo, her bodyguard and one of my truest friends.

And John, Xuan Wu, Dark Lord of the North, God of Martial Arts, a Turtle that had lost its Serpent ... and my fiancé. It would take some time to become used to the idea of being engaged to a god, even if we wouldn't be able to marry until after he'd lost his

3

remaining energy and left us for any time between ten and a hundred years. We couldn't even touch each other until then, because he would drain out my energy and kill me. I had to trust that I would still be alive when he returned and we could have everything we wanted for each other.

I shook my head again and opened the door that joined my room with Simone's. Way to go, Emma, make your life as complicated as possible. Become engaged to a god that you can't even touch and let him give you Regency over his Empire when he's gone.

I was sure that all hell had broken loose in Heaven when the Jade Emperor had heard about this. I winced. Well, we'd soon know exactly how much trouble we were in when Kwan Yin, Goddess of Mercy, returned from Heaven with the bad tidings.

Leo and John were already in the dining room sharing breakfast when Simone and I went in. Leo was reading the English language newspaper, and John sat with his eyes unfocused, obviously talking silently to someone. When he saw Simone he snapped back, dropped his spoon into his congee and held his arm out to her.

Simone crawled into his lap and kissed him on the cheek, then pulled back to study him carefully. 'Morning, Daddy, are you okay? You and Leo nearly died.'

Leo grunted and shook the newspaper. 'Ugliest damn scar I've ever seen.'

'Better than a giant freaking hole in the back of your head,' I retorted as I sat down next to him. He smiled sideways at me from behind the newspaper then ignored me again.

John gazed intensely at me over the top of Simone's head. 'How are you feeling, Emma?'

I rested my chin in my hand and became lost in his wonderful dark eyes. 'Better and better every day.'

Leo folded the newspaper and pushed it to one side, next to the remains of his breakfast. 'Is anything up, sir? You've been "on the phone" there for a while now.'

'Wait.' John raised his hands and his eyes unfocused again. Then he snapped back. 'I've told them to leave me alone for a few minutes, but yes, there are quite a few people talking to me right now.'

I winced. 'About me and the Regency thing?'

'Amongst other things, yes.' John smiled down at Simone where she sat in his lap. 'Ms Kwan will be here soon, Simone, and after you've eaten she wants to talk to you for a while.'

Simone nodded, serious. 'About the dead people and stuff. I understand, Daddy, that was awful.'

Yes, she will receive counselling from Kwan Yin, John said into my head. *She's very clever sometimes, she knows exactly what is going on.*

'I'll ask Monica for my cereal,' Simone said, and her eyes unfocused.

'Don't talk to Monica silently,' John said quickly. 'She doesn't like it, okay?'

'Well, I'm not shouting at her like you do,' Simone shot back, and clambered out of his lap to go to the door of the kitchen. 'You're rude sometimes, Daddy. What would you like, Emma?'

'Tea and toast, thank you, Simone,' I said.

She nodded. 'I'll tell Monica.'

'Kwan Yin is on her way with a message from the Celestial,' John said. 'Hopefully not all the news is bad. Would you like to talk to her as well, Emma?'

'If you mean counselling, no, I'm fine,' I said. 'But one thing is bugging me about the day before yesterday. Simon Wong just held us, he didn't try to do anything to us. Why not? He's always said he has plans for us.'

'He kept you without food or water, yes?' John said.

I nodded. 'There was a bathroom there, but I doubt the water was drinkable, not if it was China. I wouldn't have risked it unless we were in serious trouble.'

'Coward,' he said. 'Wanted to weaken you first. I'm sure there was no water there anyway. A couple of days without water, you'd be so weak he could do anything he liked with you. And you'd probably do anything he wanted if you saw Simone suffering.'

'Bastard,' Leo muttered under his breath.

'You got that right,' I said.

Simone returned with Monica, the Filipina domestic helper, who was carrying a tray of breakfast food for us. Monica nodded to Mr Chen. 'Sir.' To me. 'Ma'am.'

I sighed with exasperation. 'Ever since we came back from Guangzhou you've called me ma'am, Monica, and there's no need!'

Monica pointed to the green jade engagement ring on my finger and grinned broadly. 'Congratulations, *ma'am*,' she said, and returned to the kitchen.

I glanced down at the ring. 'But it's not a diamond.'

'She's picked it for what it is,' John said.

'What, a Building Block of the World that's been asleep for five hundred years?'

'No, an engagement ring, silly,' Simone said. ''Cause you and Daddy are going to get married, and about time.'

'Anyway,' John straightened and became more brisk, 'you escaped, you are safe, you are going to be Regent, and we have an awful lot to do now that we are back. Gold will be here later today to talk about the rebuilding of the Mountain.'

'Can you mind Simone while we're doing that?' I asked Leo.

Leo bobbed his head. 'Yes, my Lady.'

I glared at him. 'You too? Cut it out!'

Simone giggled and I rounded on her. Her tawny eyes widened with delight over her half-eaten cereal. 'Why does Leo do that all the time now, Daddy? It really annoys Emma.'

'He's her Retainer now as well as mine and yours, Simone,' John said. 'Now that I've asked Emma to marry me, she's my Lady and Leo is her Retainer.'

Simone's eyes became even wider. 'Oh.' She glanced at me. 'That means they all have to call you that.'

'I know.'

Simone squealed. '*Uncle Bai too?*'

John nodded, serious. 'Yep.'

Simone jiggled in her seat. 'That is *so cool*, Emma.'

'But mostly,' John said casually, 'Leo does it because it really, really annoys her.'

Simone's little face lit up. 'Aunty Kwan's here!'

John concentrated. 'I told her to come straight in.'

Kwan Yin entered in her normal human form: a graceful middle-aged Chinese lady wearing a white silk pantsuit.

Leo quickly rose and fell to one knee, saluting her.

She touched the top of his bald head. 'No need, Leo, we are all family here.'

'My Lady.' He rose and towered over her; she was about five six, the same as me, and he was a good head taller than her.

Ms Kwan glanced around the table. 'Have you finished, Simone?'

'Yep.' Simone put her spoon down.

'Leo, please take Simone out. I must talk to Simone's father and Emma alone before I speak to Simone.'

Leo nodded. 'My Lady.' He held out his huge dark hand, Simone put her little one in his, and he led her out.

Ms Kwan sat at the table. Monica brought in another tea cup for her and she nodded her thanks. I poured the tea.

'What, Mercy?' John said.

'I have returned with news from the Celestial, Ah Wu. I have spoken with the Celestial One.'

'The Jade Emperor?' I said.

She nodded. 'I have news.'

John and I shared a look. Then we turned back to her.

'Did you tell them that I will resign my post if they reject Emma?' John said.

'No need, Ah Wu.' She sipped her tea. 'The Celestial is most impressed with you, Emma, and you are on probation. Your performance as Ah Wu's prospective Regent of the North will be monitored.'

I stared at her, speechless. She'd said that as if it was a *good* thing. 'Great.' I ran my hands through my hair. 'Wonderful. They're watching me. I'll make sure I screw up really badly.'

'I have complete faith in you, Emma.' John turned back to Kwan Yin. 'They are impressed?'

'She willingly followed your daughter into the nest of the most vicious demon in Hell, then negotiated with the Demon King himself to get her out,' Kwan Yin said. 'Of course they are.'

'I couldn't let her go alone, I thought everybody was dead,' I said. 'I couldn't leave her. Everybody thinks this is such a big thing.'

'You knew exactly what the demon would do to you, Emma,' Kwan Yin said. 'And you went anyway.'

'Of course I did.'

'None but my Emma would do such a thing,' John said with pride.

'It is such a shame that you two cannot marry now,' Kwan Yin said. 'The Celestial has placed some of his greatest experts in the field of energy manipulation onto this case. They are hoping to find some way around this so that you will not drain yourself completely, Ah Wu, and be gone. Or at least a way that you and Emma can touch each other, so you may marry now and share the few years you have left.'

'They are doing this for me?' John said with wonder. 'I must thank the Celestial when I see him next.'

'Of course they are doing this. Your story is becoming a legend. The Shen and the human who cannot touch but love one another anyway. Your promise to her: to return and marry. Her promise to you: to wait for you.'

John sighed and rested his chin in his hand. 'Another legend about me.'

'Hey, it's a good one. I might write it all out after you're gone and send it to a publisher,' I said.

'You do, and you are in serious trouble.' His face softened. 'It would be wonderful if we could marry now. If I could touch you now.'

I smiled into his eyes. 'I'm happy with what I have. I don't need more. I don't need to touch you. I don't need to marry you. Your company is as much as I'll ever need.'

'You are such a pair of fools,' Ms Kwan said.

'You forgot happy,' I said.

'That too,' John said.

'Happy,' I whispered.

Ms Kwan rose. 'I will spend some time with Simone now, but I don't think I will need much. She is remarkably resilient.'

'That's because she has Emma,' John said.

CHAPTER TWO

In the dining room, Emma, John said into my head
mid-afternoon.

Gold and John were waiting there for me. Gold was
in his usual human form: early twenties, slender and
jolly, with cute dimples and a kind smile under his
shock of golden brown hair. Architectural blueprints
covered the table.

Gold wore a smart tan suit, but both John and I were
dressed in our usual at-home clothes. John had on a
pair of scruffy black cotton pants with a shredded hole
in one knee, topped by a fraying faded black T-shirt.
His long hair had already come out of its tie. I wore a
pair of plain jeans and a shirt, and my hair was a mess
as well.

'Where's Jade?' I said.

'She'll be along later, to do the costing,' John said.
'Right now she's trying to find someone to reset the
seals on the apartment. They are completely blown,
anybody can come straight in.'

'What about demons?' I said.

'After the Attack there aren't that many left, but we
will have to be vigilant,' John said. 'Make sure the front
door is locked at all times.'

'Okay.' I looked down at the blueprints. 'Are these the Mountain?'

'Yes.' Gold spread them out. 'Each page covers about half a hectare.'

'Western measures?'

'We took an architectural firm from New York to the Mountain,' Gold said.

'You took architects from New York to the Celestial Plane? What did they say when they found out they were going to Heaven?'

'They thought they were in China,' John said. 'They were very impressed. Some of them went back to Hubei Province later, and were thoroughly confused. The Earthly Wudangshan is nothing like this one is. Was,' he corrected himself, wincing.

The blueprints were a mass of yellow highlighter. 'Is the highlighter the damage?' I said.

'Yes,' Gold said. 'Areas completely destroyed have a cross through them with highlighter. Partial damage is just marked.'

I checked the sheets. There were about twenty pages of detailed plans, with a single master plan showing the whole Mountain. The buildings clung to the hillside below the seven peaks, surrounded by a wall. Yellow highlighter splashed all over the plans: about two-thirds of the buildings had a cross through them, and every other building seemed to be marked. It was obvious where the demons had broken through the wall — it was covered with highlighter; with more yellow where they had cut a swathe through the buildings.

'Holy shit,' I said softly. 'This is really bad.'

'Emma!' John said sternly. 'Really!'

'What?' Then I understood and grinned. 'Leo said you'd dismiss me if you heard me using language like that.'

'He wasn't wrong,' John said. 'Most unfitting.'

'Deal with it.' I flipped through the blueprints. 'So what's first?'

'We need to get the school up and running,' Gold said. 'Right now there is no training taking place. We have lost an extensive number of both Disciples and Masters. There are insufficient Disciples to defend the Mountain if the demons attack again.'

'It will be a while before they try me again,' John said. 'Every demon in Hell was called to the Attack.'

Gold looked at John, wide-eyed. 'Every one?'

'Every single one.'

'No,' I said, and they both looked at me. 'We had four down here as well. A house demon, a Shape Shifter, a Snake Mother, and Simon Wong. Those four are the ones that blew the seals on this apartment.'

'You faced a *Mother*?' Gold said with awe.

'Leo took it down,' I said. 'I didn't have anything to do with it.'

'You looked a Mother in the face and didn't run?' Gold said.

'Run? I was protecting Simone. Of course I didn't run.' I grinned. 'Ugly, aren't they?'

Gold shook his head. 'Remarkable.'

I glanced down at the blueprints. 'We'll need a list of the remaining students, a list of the remaining Masters and their areas of expertise, and what we have left in the way of training spaces. Then we can match them up and see how we go.'

They were silent, so I looked up. They both stared at me, speechless.

'What?' I said. 'Is that wrong? Do they train differently on the Mountain to how we do here?'

John grinned. 'I'll go out and leave you to it.'

'Don't you dare! You know your students and Masters better than anyone.' I jabbed my finger at him. 'You stay right here!'

Gold's boyish face lit up and I rounded on him. 'What?'

He raised his hands. 'I don't have those lists, ma'am, the link between here and there is down. I'll have to return to the Mountain, log into the network and copy them onto a CD.'

'You have a LAN there? Wait, you have a *link* between here and there? Between Earth and Heaven? How does that work?'

'Rather complex use of Celestial Harmony. Did it myself. I put in the Mountain LAN after I was assigned to the Dark Lord, that's a standard network. Had nothing before I arrived,' he said, looking pointedly at John, who ignored him, 'but most of the hardware was damaged in the Attack. I had an off-site backup in the Western Palace, so the systems are already up and running, but the link between here and there is down, so I'll need to go myself and take a copy of the lists.'

'Go then,' I said. 'And bring back a hard copy as well, if it's not too big.'

'My Lord?'

John didn't look up from the blueprints. 'Orders from the Lady Emma are to be treated as orders from me.' Then he glanced sharply at Gold. 'Make this clear. To all.'

Gold bowed slightly. 'My Lord. My Lady.' He disappeared.

'Sorry, John, I don't mean to tread on your toes,' I said. 'Let me know if I cross the line.'

He looked at me, expressionless, then his eyes wrinkled up. 'I think you're drawing a new one.'

While we waited for Gold to return, John flipped through the plans. 'Only about a third of the buildings are useful, and none of them are training or residential.' His voice softened with pain. 'Hall of the Purple Sky, East Hall, West Hall, Dragon Tiger Hall, all gone. Some of those buildings were more than a thousand years old.'

'We'll rebuild it, John. It will be better than it ever was.'

He dropped into a seat at the table. 'I don't know what to do. It will take years to rebuild the training pavilions, and the dorms have been demolished. The White Tiger has been a true friend in looking after the Disciples.'

'How long can they stay at the Western Palace?'

'As long as they need to, he says. He doesn't mind at all — the Disciples are providing a useful exchange of skills with his Horsemen.' He sighed and tied his hair back. 'The training pavilions are gone, and there isn't any open space suitable for training Disciples because of the steepness. Only the most indestructible Celestial Weapons made it; all of the other weapons are gone. And my Disciples have nowhere to live. The Mountain is effectively out of action and nobody will be learning the true Arts for many, many years.'

'Can the Masters teach at the Western Palace?'

'Not with the Tiger's women around. The Disciples are confined to barracks.'

'I see.' I sat next to him, and pulled the plans closer. 'Monica!'

Monica poked her head in the door. 'Ma'am?'

'Tea, *tikuanyin*, and three cups, please.'

'Ma'am.' She pulled her head back into the kitchen.

'You're a mind reader,' John said.

'Will she ever call me Emma again?'

'Nope.'

'John.' I turned to him. 'Should I tell her about the situation? That I can't marry you until you come back because you're a Shen?'

'Monica has made it very clear that she doesn't want to know anything,' John said without looking up from the plans. 'When Michelle hired her she tried to explain that we weren't a normal household, and Monica said, "Don't tell me, ma'am, I don't want to know. Just tell me what to do." She's terrified of the strange things that happen, but she loved Michelle, and she loves Simone, so she stays and puts up with us.'

'We have to protect her then, and make sure that nothing scares her.'

'That's what Michelle said.'

'How long were you and Michelle married, John?'

He hesitated, expressionless.

I turned away and shuffled the plans. 'Sorry, don't bother.'

'We were about to celebrate our fourth anniversary when it happened,' he said, wistful. 'Simone was only two.'

'Oh my God, you were hardly married any time at all!' I lowered my voice. 'Does Simone remember much?'

'I don't know. She won't talk about it.'

Gold reappeared with a stack of printouts. 'My Lord. My Lady.'

John rose and pushed the blueprints aside. 'Okay, let's see what we have here.'

I stood up and riffled through the lists. 'Hey, many of these names aren't Chinese.'

'Of course not,' John said. 'I take the best, it doesn't matter where they're from.'

A good proportion of the names were Chinese, but there were some recognisably Anglo-Saxon ones, plus Japanese, Korean, and even African names. It was a complete cross-section. I scanned the Anglo names: many of them were women.

'Did you have separate dorms on the Mountain?' I said.

'For the different nationalities? No, of course not,' John said, and then, 'Oh, for men and women, of course. Except for those who are married or bonded to each other.' He saw my face. 'No, I'm not slow. I'm just cold-blooded, like you said.'

'Get out of my head.'

'I'm not in it,' he shot back. He turned over the lists. 'Let's see the Masters.'

This list was much shorter. There were only about fifteen names.

'So few, John?'

'They gave their lives for the students, Emma. Even the human Masters. They were killed by the demons.' He put his hand on the list. 'These are the Immortal Masters that have returned. And a small group of mortal Masters who were too old or frail to take part in the battle.'

'How many students died?' I said.

He sighed with pain. 'Almost half. Nearly three hundred.'

I flopped to sit. 'Holy shit. Masters?'

'Nearly all of them. About fifty.'

'How many of the Masters were human?'

He sat next to me. 'Of the ones that were killed? About three-quarters, love.'

'How will you tell their families?' I whispered. 'Three hundred and fifty people.'

He put his head in his hands. 'I don't know.'

'Do their families know where they were?'

John was silent.

'No, my Lady,' Gold said. 'Most of their families thought they were learning martial arts on Earthly Wudangshan. This is the greatest loss that the Mountain has seen in centuries. Even the Celestial Ones have become involved in dealing with this issue. A decision is yet to be made, but the consensus is that the

16

Celestial will erase the existence of the students from the Earthly.'

'They'll never have existed at all?' I said.

'It's the kindest way, Emma,' John said into his hands.

I was horrified. 'How often do you Celestials interfere with us like this?' I said. 'You just make people *not exist*?'

'This will be the first time in history, my Lady,' Gold said with remorse. 'There has never been a need for it in the past.'

John dropped his hands, but didn't look up. 'There is some argument that the Mountain should not recruit humans if they are in danger from attack like this.'

'If there are no Disciples learning, then the Celestial loses its defence against the demon horde,' Gold said. 'It won't happen, my Lord. All of Heaven needs your Disciples, they are the best.'

'But they *died*,' John moaned.

Gold sat and rested his elbows on the table. 'I carried out your orders, my Lord. I went to the Western Palace and gathered the remaining Disciples. I told them that you felt they were in danger and that they should return home. I ordered them home.'

'Good.'

'I know what they did, John. Not a single one went.' I gestured towards Gold. 'I bet they threatened to kill themselves if they were forced to return home.'

John glanced at Gold.

Gold smiled slightly.

John leaned back and put his palms on the table. 'Not a single one?'

'Not a single one, my Lord. They would rather die than discontinue the training. They love the Arts more than their lives.'

'And that's why they're on the Mountain,' I said. 'Face it. You're stuck with them.'

John sighed with feeling.

I turned back to the lists. 'Let's look at the Masters.' Most of the names had either an 'I' or an 'S' next to them. Many more of these were Chinese, but there were still some names from other nationalities there. 'I?' I said.

'Immortals,' Gold said. '"S" is for Shen.'

'What's the difference?'

'I thought you did some research,' John said without looking up from the list.

'Cut it out, old man,' I said. 'What's the difference between an Immortal and a Shen?'

Gold snorted with amusement.

'Answer the goddamn question,' I growled.

'For our purposes, nothing; we just refer to them as the Celestial Masters,' John said. 'Immortals are humans who have gained the *Tao*. We Shen have always been immortal; we are more like spirits than people. Most of the mortal human Masters on the Mountain didn't make it. There were some tremendous acts of valour witnessed that day.' He glanced up. 'Gold.'

'My Lord?'

'Are the records being made?'

Gold nodded. 'My Lord.'

'Some of them attained the *Tao* and were Raised. It was a sight to see. But it will take them slightly longer to return.'

I flipped through the list again. 'The Energy Master is a European woman?'

'Meredith was a missionary's daughter,' John said. 'She lived in Hubei Province about three hundred years ago. She was incredibly talented at *tai chi*, so I took her to the Celestial Mountain to teach her. She is one of the most talented human energy workers I have ever seen. She married one of the Immortal Masters, Master Liu, and they've been happy together for hundreds of years.'

'I'd really like to meet her.'

'You already have. She was at the ceremony where everybody swore allegiance. I didn't introduce you; you seemed slightly overwhelmed to have gods bowing down before you and swearing allegiance and obedience.'

'I wasn't overwhelmed, I was drowning.'

'You were magnificent,' Gold said. 'They are all extremely impressed with you.'

'They are looking forward to working with you as new Regent and Lady of the Mountain after I have gone,' John said.

The shock hit me when he said that. I wasn't accustomed to it; it was still very new. I was to be *their* Master.

'Are they very unhappy about an ordinary human woman taking over?' I said.

'Every single one of them is absolutely delighted that they won't have to do the job. Most of them have offered to come to the Earthly and continue your training after I'm gone. But by that time you will probably be teaching *them* a thing or two — you are exceptionally talented. A year with me is worth a lifetime with any other Master. Look at Leo.'

'They must miss your hand, without you there to teach for them,' I said.

'They were horrified when I married Michelle and decided to stay on the Earthly with her. Every time I went up there to rebuild my energy, they were waiting with a packed schedule. Eventually I told them to let me rest, so they sent students down here to learn instead. Remember, before the Attack? Young students would come down and stay in the two spare rooms here.'

I nodded as he continued. 'Sometimes I'd have so many that I'd put them in the flat below us, which is always kept vacant. But I may rent it out now, until we can organise something. You can't leave a flat empty in Hong Kong for long, it becomes very musty.'

A brilliant idea suddenly hit me out of the blue. 'John, how big is the block of flats in Happy Valley?'

'Bright Mansions? About twenty-five floors, eight flats to a floor, quite large for that area. Why?'

'What about the building in Wan Chai? How big is that?'

'About the same, my Lady,' Gold said. 'Twenty-six floors. But most of the lower floors are vacant right now, with the economic downturn.'

'The one in North Point?'

'That one's quite small, only fifteen floors, two flats to a floor. It's very old,' John said. 'I may demolish it eventually, but it's not worth it right now.'

There had to be some logistical reason why this wouldn't work, but it was worth a try. 'People in Hong Kong usually only rent a place for a year at a time, they like the flexibility,' I said. 'And most of the building in Wan Chai is already vacant. How about we move the Mountain down here?'

Gold picked it up right away. 'The students can stay in Happy Valley and go to the Wan Chai building for training. It shouldn't take much to fix up the Hennessy Road building for training — it's already offices, I'll just have to remove some partitions. I could move the administration down here too. And the Bright Mansions apartments in Happy Valley would be perfect as student residences. It won't cost us anything except the loss of income from the rent, and frankly, my Lord, the way the economy is right now, it won't be much.'

'What about language?' John said.

'Language?' I said.

'Yes, that will be a problem,' Gold said. 'Let me think about it.'

'On the Celestial Plane, language is irrelevant. All

can communicate. That will not apply on the Earthly, and could result in problems,' John said.

'No, I can fix it,' Gold said. 'Leave it with me. I'm very good with Celestial Harmony, I should be able to work something out.'

'Is the building in Wan Chai zoned for that sort of thing? We don't want to draw the government's attention.' John smiled at me. 'Have the ICAC breaking down the door.'

'Give it a rest,' I said and grinned back.

'Not an issue,' Gold said. 'If it isn't, I'll just go into the government system and fix the zoning.'

'You're a *hacker*?' I said.

'One of the best,' Gold said proudly. 'Don't do it often, but when I do, I do a damn good job.'

I glared at John. 'You said you weren't involved in anything illegal, that you would never risk Simone's happiness.'

'And I meant it. I am a creature of my word. I have not committed a single illegal act since I was Raised. The enthusiasm of my Retainers, however,' he gestured towards Gold, 'is another matter entirely.'

Gold ignored us. 'I can't think of any other reason why this shouldn't happen as Lady Emma has suggested. It's a brilliant plan.'

'Emma, you really are astounding,' John said. 'It's a perfect solution. If the Turtle can't go to the Mountain, then the Mountain can come to the Turtle.'

I laughed, but Gold was obviously horrified and made weird choking noises.

'Go and start the arrangements,' John said to Gold. 'Tell the Tiger we'll have those Disciples out of his fur in no time. Come back when you've started the process and we'll commence the rebuilding. It'll be much easier without any staff or students present, just a skeleton crew of guards. Oh. Emma.'

'My Lord.' Gold disappeared.

'What, John?'

'I can finally have you teaching. You and Leo. We are fearfully short of junior Masters. You and Leo will be perfect. He can start them on hand-to-hand and weapons, and you can start them on energy work. The senior Masters are wasted teaching the basic stuff. This is excellent.'

'Don't be ridiculous. I've been learning less than a year myself, and I have to look after Simone.'

'No, after Simone goes to school, you'll have plenty of time, and by September this year you'll be as good as any junior Master on the Mountain.' John leapt up, obviously excited.

'Wait a second!' I shouted. 'You didn't even bother to ask me! Who the hell do you think you are?'

John stopped halfway to the door and didn't move.

'Well?'

He spoke softly without turning towards me. 'For thousands of years others have been obeying my orders without question. I have precedence over nearly everybody in Creation. I've developed a bad habit of expecting to be obeyed.' He dropped his head and shook it, still turned away. 'I am so sorry, love.'

'You have precedence over nearly everybody? Don't you have any friends who are equal to you in precedence?'

He turned back to me. 'The truth? No. The Jade Emperor is my master, I serve him. Apart from that, nobody.'

'All your friends have to obey you if you tell them to do something?'

He gazed into my eyes. 'Yes. Even the other three Winds must obey me. I am their Sovereign. The White Tiger is my friend, but there is still a line there, and both of us are aware of it.'

My heart twisted. 'It must be very lonely for you.'

He snapped out of it and spoke with forced cheerfulness. 'My number is one, Emma. It is my nature to be alone.' He went to the doorway and bellowed, '*Leo*!'

I winced. 'Can't you call him silently, John? Do you have to yell like that?'

Leo immediately appeared in the doorway; he must have been in the hall. 'Keeps me on my toes, my Lady.' He leaned against the doorframe with his arms folded across his chest. '*She's* your equal,' he said to John. 'She's more than a match for you.' He gestured, palm-up, towards me. 'And she won't obey you if she chooses not to. Why don't you just *ask* her if she wants to teach?'

John turned back to me. 'Will you join my Academy as Master and teach energy work for me?'

'I'd be delighted.'

Leo didn't move from the doorframe. 'See? That wasn't hard, was it? Now feel free to ask me.'

'Leo, when the Academy is up and running, you will teach the juniors weapons and hand-to-hand, and that is an order,' John said with force.

Leo saluted with a huge grin. 'My Lord. I've been teaching on my days off for a while already. It would be great to teach students who are good enough for the Mountain.'

'I didn't know that, Leo,' I said, impressed.

'I didn't either. Well done, Leo, true initiative. Come and sit, and I'll tell you all about it.' John returned to the table.

Leo sat and leaned his arms on the table, listening attentively. 'My Lord? My Lady?'

'Oh, will you *cut that out*, Leo?' I said. 'We've been friends far too long for this.'

'Keeps you on your toes as well, my Lady,' he said with a grin.

'Leo, if I promise never to give you a direct order, will you promise to stop using the honorific?'

Leo's grin widened. 'Nope.'

'Bastard,' I hissed under my breath.

'I heard that, my Lady,' Leo said loudly with relish.

'You two can have this out later in the training room with weapons of choice,' John said. 'But no *chi*. One hole in the wall is quite enough.'

He saw my reaction and waved me down. 'And that is an order, as Master to student, Emma. Take it into the training room. Leo.'

'My Lord?'

'I don't know how much you heard while you were eavesdropping in the hallway ...'

Leo opened his mouth to protest, and John continued, ignoring him.

'...but we are moving the Celestial Wudangshan Academy here to Hong Kong while we rebuild. The Disciples will live in my building in Happy Valley, and training will take place in the building on Hennessy Road.'

'That's a brilliant solution, sir,' Leo said with admiration.

'It was Emma's idea.'

Leo glanced sharply at me. I shrugged.

'How old are the students you've been teaching?' John said.

'Kids,' Leo said. 'Some of them don't have much of a home life. I teach them the Arts, it gives them some direction and discipline. I feel I'm giving something back, I've gained so much here.'

'Are any of your students suitable to replace you?' John said. 'A young man or woman with strength and integrity, who has the talent to go far? I could take them as a student here and bring them on, and they could be ready to help guard Simone after both you and I are dead.'

'Geez,' I said softly.

'The students on the Mountain are quite old, Emma,' John said. 'They must be at least sixteen, and I prefer them to be either eighteen or twenty-one, whatever the majority is in their home state, when I take them. Having a younger student come here to learn directly from me would be ideal.'

'I've had a young man in mind for a while,' Leo said. 'Very young, very talented. American like me, half-Chinese, but his Chinese father took off and left him and his mother alone. Been drifting, a bit lost, if you know what I mean. I think he'd be perfect.'

'Is he free to take up duties with us and live-in?' John said. 'Would his mother mind?'

'I think his mother would be thrilled to have him off the streets.'

'Straight?' I said.

Both of them stiffened. 'What does that have to do with anything?' Leo said sharply.

'Nothing at all. I'd just like to know.'

'Straight,' Leo said suspiciously.

'How old is he?' I said pointedly, and now they could see where I was going. John glanced at Leo.

'Fifteen,' Leo said. 'I hadn't thought of that. Maybe I should ask around my other friends instead.'

'No, bring him in,' John said. 'Let me see him anyway. First impressions are important. If he's your first choice, then he is worth looking at.'

The ceiling was very low in the dim bathroom. I wiped my hands on the towel and turned around.

An enormous black snake, at least half a metre across, writhed across the shower cubicle and down the wall towards me. I couldn't see the head, but

I didn't bother looking for it. I didn't scream. I just ran.

I threw the door open, charged out, and slammed it shut again. There was a jade bolt on the door and I pushed it into the frame. But jade was really brittle, and if the snake wanted to come out it could.

I ran out of my room and tore down the dark hallway.

I woke up gasping.

CHAPTER THREE

John poked his head around my bedroom door. 'Simone's asleep. Want to come with me to check the work at Hennessy Road?'

I pulled away from my computer. 'Sure.' I gestured towards the book in his hand. 'How far did you get?'

He opened the book and held it at arm's length to read it. 'Eeyore losing his tail.'

'Now you know why she called her little donkey Eeyore.'

He grinned. 'I didn't realise Taoism had penetrated Western society at such an early date. Certainly when I was in England in the twenties, nobody had heard of the *Tao*.'

'I don't think the Taoist references are deliberate, the author was just a very wise man.' I pulled my copy of *The Tao of Pooh* from the shelf above my desk and tossed it to him.

He caught it easily, then opened the book and held it away to read it.

'Holy shit,' I whispered. I worked it out. It was May now; only four months since Kwan Yin had last fed him energy, but he'd been severely drained when the demons attacked us in Guangzhou a few weeks ago.

'John, could you call Leo silently for me, please?' I asked.

He glanced up from the book, concentrating. Leo appeared in the doorway behind him. 'Yes, my Lady?'

'Do you have your reading glasses, Leo?'

Leo pulled his small round reading spectacles out of his breast pocket. 'Yeah, why?'

'Give them to Mr Chen.'

'No,' John said.

I rose and leaned on my desk. 'John, you look mid-forties. Is your human form mid-forties?'

'I am four and a half thousand years old.'

'No, John. Does your human form have the characteristics of a man in his mid-forties?'

John glanced at the glasses in Leo's hand, then down at the book. He took the glasses from Leo and slipped them on, then looked at the book in his hand. His eyes widened. He removed the glasses, looked at the book, then put the glasses back on. 'No.' He sagged, took the glasses off again and handed them back to Leo.

'It's only four months since you saw the Lady,' I said.

'Oh my God,' Leo said softly.

'Do we need to take you back now?'

'No,' John said. 'This is just the human form slipping from my control. I am becoming more human as I lose energy and my characteristics as a Shen fall away.'

'Don't risk it, John. If you're running low on energy we'll go to Paris.'

'I'll last a couple more months,' he said quietly. 'We'll go in July or August, just before Simone starts school.'

I pushed away from the desk. 'Okay. Thanks, Leo. Now let's go check on the work at Hennessy Road.'

'Am I all right to drive?' John said. 'I don't want to risk you.'

'I don't wear the glasses to drive,' Leo said. 'It's only things close up you need them for.'

'Damn,' John said softly.

'I'm surprised you haven't complained of headaches from the eye strain,' I said.

John's face was miserable.

'Healing himself.' Leo sighed with exasperation. 'Take him down to Central tomorrow to buy some reading glasses before he wastes all of his energy.'

'We're going to Hennessy Road right now. Can you guard Simone for us?' I said.

'Sure.'

I stopped in the doorway. 'How come you wear reading glasses, Leo? You're too young to need them yet, aren't you?'

'It's 'cause I'm such a brainiac,' Leo said.

John drove in silence along Magazine Gap Road towards Admiralty. The city lights glittered between the trees. He carefully negotiated the winding turns as we went down the steep hill.

'It's not that big a deal,' I said.

He didn't reply.

We meandered through the highrises and took the overpass into Garden Road. Old Government House sat on the left, empty now that there was no Governor. The Chief Executive chose not to live there because of the poor fung shui. The towers of Admiralty loomed above us, still bright with office lights.

'John.'

He ignored me.

'John, you just need to guard your energy. Be careful. If you want to go to Paris sooner, tell us.' I turned in my seat to see his face. It was rigid with control.

He turned into Queens Road, four lanes both ways and still full of buses and taxis. He pushed his way through the stop-start traffic onto Hennessy Road, then eased into one of the dark, narrow side streets to enter the building's car park. One of the demon guards smiled, opened the door and waved us in. A large sign next to the entrance warned that it was private parking only.

The Hennessy Road building was perfect for our purposes. It had been built in the mid-seventies, and the external walls were covered with tan tiles. Each floor was about two hundred square metres, and there was a floor of shops on the ground level, with two basement car park levels. We'd kept the shops; they provided the building with camouflage. A fashion boutique and a stationery shop leased the ground floor units, both run by friendly Shen who lived as humans.

There was only one van left in the car park; all the other human workmen had gone home. John didn't even bother parking in a space; he just left the car in the middle.

After we'd climbed out of the car I stopped him with my hand on his sleeve. 'Are you embarrassed about needing glasses?'

He sighed with feeling. 'It was one thing having clothing bought and made. It was another dealing with human weaknesses and needs. But this ...' He pulled his arm away, turned and looked into my eyes. 'This is my effectiveness as a warrior. If I can't see well, how can I defend you and Simone?'

'Okay,' I said. 'Easy. If you closed your eyes and worked blind, what's the highest level of demon you could take down?'

'I could take down the King himself without needing to see.'

'How many Snake Mothers could you take down blind?'

He smiled sadly. 'You're right, Emma. You're always right. I don't need my eyes.'

'See? It's not that big a deal. And when we're in Central tomorrow, you are not going to give me a hard time. Instead, you are going to sit quietly and let them test your eyes.'

'Yes, ma'am.'

'Now let's see Gold about your Academy.'

He turned and gestured for me to lead. '*Our* Academy, Emma.'

'Do you have any idea how good that sounds?'

He grinned. 'Yes.'

Gold met us at the lift lobby, smiling and jolly as ever. He wore a tan polo shirt and a pair of tan slacks, setting off his golden-brown hair. 'Come up to the fifth floor. We're nearly finished there.'

Like most Hong Kong buildings, the Hennessy Road tower didn't have a fourth floor. 'Is there a fourth floor at all?'

'Nope, fourth is skipped,' Gold said. 'Do you want to renumber the floors? We can have the lifts altered.'

'Not worth the effort,' I said. 'And when we have Western kids coming in, they'll learn that "four" sounds like "death" in Cantonese, so it's bad luck.'

We exited the lift at the fifth floor. The lobby was plain brown tiles, with a single door leading directly ahead.

'This will be a training floor,' Gold said. 'Two training rooms, ten by twelve metres each. For large classes of juniors.'

We went through the door to a small hallway with two more doors. Gold opened the one on the left and guided us in. There were several workmen still there.

'And I said to that fucker, you watch your shit, because if you don't, you'll find it shoved up your ass —' The workman speaking saw us and fell silent.

'They've nearly finished painting the ceiling,' Gold said. 'After that we can put the mats in, and the lowest ten floors will be ready for the juniors to commence training.'

John dropped to one knee and inspected the mats piled in the corner. *How many Immortal Masters have returned?*

All but three, my Lord, Gold said. *They are in the Western Palace, ready to assist in moving the students down here when Bright Mansions is ready.*

'Are the workmen human?' I whispered.

Yes, Gold said. *Can you understand them?*

'What? You mean they're speaking Cantonese and I can understand them?'

Gold grinned. 'Good. It's working. And it's Fukien, not Cantonese.'

I had a sudden evil idea, and called out to the workmen. 'How long before you'll finish painting the ceiling?'

They stared at me with their mouths open. One of them snapped out of it. 'About an hour, miss.'

'Thanks.' I turned to Gold. 'What's next?'

'We'll meet with Jade in the sixth-floor common room and talk about the budget.'

'Oh, damn. Budgets.'

'Miss?' one of the workmen called.

I turned back to them. They grinned at me. 'How come you can understand our dialect?'

'Magic.' I grinned back. 'Come on, let's talk to Jade and have this over with. I hate dealing with accountants.'

After Jade had gone, I tapped the papers into a stack. 'I need a folder to put all this stuff in.'

A black manila folder materialised in front of me. 'Thanks, Gold.'

I leaned on the table and looked at John. 'You'll need to rewrite the orientation material. The students will probably appreciate some information on the new location, and they'll need help adjusting to life in Hong Kong.'

Gold grinned broadly. John glared at him.

'What?' I said.

Neither of them spoke.

'You'd better tell me before I start shouting, guys.'

Gold gestured towards John. John grimaced. 'Gold has been harassing me to write orientation material for years, and I've never done it. No time. But nobody else can do it; it has to be me.'

'That's his Lordship's decision, not mine,' Gold said, his boyish face cheeky. 'I think anybody could do it. But the Dark Lord disagrees.'

'I'm the only one with the expertise to prepare the material,' John said. 'Nobody else has the knowledge to do it. Not even you, Gold.'

'John, after we've been to Central tomorrow, we'll sit down together, and you can tell me what you want to say, and I'll write it,' I said. 'We can do it together.'

John hesitated, then put his hands out. 'Oh, all right. You're the only one with the brains to do it anyway.'

Gold's face lit up with a wide grin of triumph, making him look even younger, barely out of his teens.

Three days later we sat together in the dining room at the Peak for a follow-up.

'Do we have a nomination for a chair for the meeting?' Gold said.

'No, we don't,' I said. 'And if you pull that "voted and seconded" and "minutes of the last meeting" crap ever again, I'll take your head completely off. I don't have time — I have an assignment due next week, and Simone's only going to sleep for about half an hour.'

John made a soft sound of amusement. I ignored him.

'Very well, my Lady,' Gold said, unfazed. 'First matter: housing the Disciples in Happy Valley. About a quarter of the flats are vacant now, but we need to make arrangements for who goes where.'

John explained. 'The barracks on the Mountain housed a large number of juniors together with a senior supervising: standard military style. As they moved up through the ranks they received more private accommodation. We can't do that here; the walls have to stay put, they're supporting walls.'

I flipped through the papers in my black folder. 'I don't have a copy of the floor plan, Gold. Do you have a spare?'

Gold waved one hand and a floor plan appeared in front of me. 'Thanks. Four three-bedroom, four two-bedroom units to a floor. That's nineteen to a floor with one supervisor. Too many; we need a common area and some study rooms.' I thought for a moment.

'You think so?' John said.

'What we'll do is give the supervisor one of the three-bedroom units, make the other two bedrooms study areas, and the living room a common room for all of them.' I scribbled on the paper in front of me. 'How many students to a floor?'

'Seventeen students, one supervisor to a floor,' Gold said. 'Twelve floors will handle two hundred and four. Enough.'

'What's the cube root of six thousand, seven hundred and fifty-three?' I said.

'To how many decimal places?'

'Ten.'

'Eighteen point nine zero one six one five one five eight —'

'Stop. How come you can do that?'

'Do what, my Lady?'

'I've noticed that. You can do enormous sums in your head.'

'Not in my head, and it's part of my nature, my Lady. Can we return to the logistics of the accommodation?

I'd like to finish it before Simone wakes and starts pestering you.'

'Simone can go to Leo,' John said.

'Use your super Shen mega-powers, John, and see that Leo's taken Monica out to the market,' I said. 'When Simone wakes up she'll be right in here annoying us.'

'Mega-powers. You make me sound like something out of a Japanese superhero show.'

'You are ten times weirder than anything on those shows, and that's saying something.'

Gold grinned. 'Even the Beetle Boys?'

'It's close, but even them.' I checked my notes. 'Okay, junior Disciples, twelve floors. How about we give the seniors their own units, or let them share? Is that acceptable?'

'Quite acceptable,' John said. 'It will be smaller than the Mountain, but that's Hong Kong.'

'How many floors, Gold?'

'Probably about ten; plenty of room.'

'There will still be room for you and Jade?' John said.

'Yes, my Lord. That leaves the top four floors.'

'The mortal human Masters can go there,' John said. 'I'll take the walls out; they're not supporting walls at the top. We'll make some big penthouses for them.'

'I'll get right onto it,' Gold said. 'I'll move in some tame demons to clean up the empty units and prepare them. Next item.' He checked the agenda in front of him. 'Armoury. My Lord?'

'That's your area of expertise, John.'

John sighed, pulled his glasses off and rubbed his eyes. 'Only a handful of the most robust Celestial Weapons made it. Some of them are very special. I don't like the idea of them staying on the Mountain without the Celestial Masters to guard them.'

'Do we have room here for them?' I said.

'The seals are set. The answer is: yes,' John said. 'Gold.'

'My Lord.' Gold nodded and scribbled some notes. He glanced up at John. 'Seven Stars?'

John leaned back. 'Seven Stars is the most destructive weapon ever forged. But it was forged for me. It will not shine for another. Leave it where it is. Only my most trusted lieutenants have access. It is safe.'

Gold was silent for a moment. Then he spoke softly. 'I really am most profoundly honoured, my Lord.'

John waved him down. 'The forge is undamaged. Gather the forge staff and put them to work. I want them replacing weapons as soon as possible.'

Gold nodded and scribbled some more. 'My Lord.'

'Also, go shopping for me. Hunt around the Earthly suppliers. I don't want anything too poor in quality, it would be a waste of time teaching with rubbish. See what you can turn up.'

'My Lord, I'll see what I can do. I'll go to Japan, they have always made quality blades. Don't expect too much though. The art of crafting a fine weapon that isn't a firearm is becoming lost.'

'I know. Search out the antique weapons markets as well; there are some excellent old blades that could serve us well. We may even be able to pick up some more Masamunes — anything from that school would be worth having. Don't worry about the expense, the cost is worth it. If you're not certain about authenticity, let me see the blade. How is work proceeding in Hennessy Road?'

'Very quickly. The demons work day and night. Only noise restrictions are holding us back.'

'This really is working out very well.'

* * *

Four weeks later we met in the new conference room on the ninth floor of Hennessy Road.

'Happy Valley,' Gold said without any preliminary meeting nonsense. 'The residents are complaining about the noise of the renovations. They are cancelling their leases and moving out.'

'Good,' I said. 'Offer the remaining residents a reward to leave.'

'I already did,' Gold said. 'The building should be ours by September.'

'That fits perfectly,' I said.

'We need to employ people to look after the units,' Gold said. 'Cook, clean, things like that. I thought at first the Disciples could do it themselves —'

'Of course they can't,' John said. 'They're exhausted at the end of the day. And some of them are studying as well. We can't expect them to cook and clean for themselves on top of that.'

'The Dark Lord is quite correct,' Gold said. 'So we need to hire people to help out.'

'You can't employ domestic helpers,' I said. 'It wouldn't work.'

'Why not?' John said.

'Have you seen those women on a Sunday in Central? They all meet there. There must be thousands of them —'

'About eighty thousand, last time I counted,' Gold said.

'You were there on a quiet day,' John said.

I continued, ignoring them. 'And they're all discussing their employers. They'd find out in no time flat —'

'About the unusual nature of the residents of Turtle's Folly,' John said. 'And how everybody seems able to speak Tagalog, regardless of where they're from, because of the language charm Gold put in.'

Gold and I stared at him, speechless.

Eventually I found my voice. 'How the hell did you know I call it that?'

John took his glasses off and leaned over the table to glare at me. 'I know everything that happens on my Mountain.' He leaned back. 'I think it's a good name for Bright Mansions. Very bad move, buying it at the top of the market like that. I'm doing a nice piece of calligraphy. Took me a long time to find a correct translation for the word "folly".'

'You're not.'

'I am. I'll have it done in brass and put it over the door.'

'You're joking,' I said.

'Deadly serious. I'll buy a couple of stone tortoises and put them on either side of the entrance as well, just to make the point.'

Gold's mouth flopped open.

'The Chinese Disciples will refuse to live there,' I said.

'They won't have a choice.'

'Xuan Wu Xuan Tian Shang Di,' I said very severely, 'Celestial Highness, Dark Emperor of the Northern Heavens, if you do this stupid thing your shell is in very serious trouble.' I glared at him. 'Simone will have to go in there sometimes, and I *do not* want to have to explain this to her, particularly about how it relates to your true nature.'

'My true nature as the egg of a turtle, or my true nature as a motherless bastard?'

Gold made a quiet choking sound.

'Both!'

'Oh, all right.' He leaned back, slipped his glasses on and gave it up. 'But only for Simone. And I will definitely do it when I come back and she's old enough to understand.'

'You will be the one to explain it to her then. Which are you anyway? Turtle or tortoise?'

Gold sounded like he was strangling.

'Same thing, same essence,' John said without looking up. 'Turtle in water, tortoise on land. The Tiger is the essence of all the great cats.'

'And the Phoenix is bird essence. I understand. What about the Dragon?'

'Essence of arrogant bastard.' John gestured with one hand. 'Gold.'

Gold flipped frantically through his notes. 'Where were we?'

'Staff for Turtle's Folly,' John said. 'Emma's right. Overseas or local domestic helpers are out of the question — they'd find out too much about us. I'll send some of the Masters out demon-hunting and see what they come up with. Should be okay to put newly tamed low-level demons in there with so many senior Disciples and the Masters to keep an eye on them.'

'Very good, my Lord,' Gold said, taking notes.

'We need to buy a couple of buses to carry the students between Wan Chai and the Valley,' I said.

'Easily done, my Lady.' Gold looked up and shrugged. 'I have nothing else to do.'

'I'll talk to the Masters about a demon-hunting expedition,' John said. 'And I'll need to put that calligraphy in a safe place so you won't find it and destroy it before I come back.'

'The Disciples will be out of the building and back on the Mountain by the time you come back,' I said. 'There won't be any place to put it.'

John took his glasses off and put them in their case. 'I'll find somewhere.'

CHAPTER FOUR

About ten o'clock Saturday morning I put the finishing touches to the first draft of my assignment and set it to print in John's office. I jumped when he spoke into my ear.

I'm going to call you on your mobile. Ready?

I put my hand on the phone and picked it up when it rang. 'Yeah?'

'Do you have time to come down to Hennessy Road with Leo and Simone? There's something we all need to do together.'

'Sure. I need a break from this anyway. Give us twenty minutes.'

'You'll need longer than that, I have the car. Gold will drive it up for you. Leo can bring you down.'

'Okay.' I hesitated, then changed my mind about mentioning the transport situation. Maybe when Simone started school. 'See you soon.'

'You forgot to put your hands on the wheel again,' Leo said as Gold pulled up in the car.

Gold just grinned and disappeared.

At Hennessy Road, Leo and I took Simone up to the large training room on the fifth floor. Mirrors covered one of the long walls, and vertical blinds shaded the windows on the short wall. John and Gold were waiting for us.

The room was prepared for demon training. The Academy's demon jar sat in the corner, full of large black beads. Black hand towels were stacked neatly on shelves under the windows.

'Simone, go with Gold to the top-floor conference room and wait for us there,' John said.

'Okay, Daddy.' Simone took Gold's hand to leave the room.

'Now.' John linked his hands behind his back. 'Have either of you warmed up?'

Leo and I shared a look, then turned back to John and shook our heads.

'Good. You are to do this cold, without any preparation. We'll start at level ten.' John pulled a black bead out of the jar and threw it onto the floor under the mirrors. 'Leo.'

The demon grew into human form: a Chinese man in his early twenties, wearing jeans and a plain T-shirt.

Leo moved to the middle of the room, faced the demon and readied himself. He nodded without looking away.

The demon threw itself at Leo. He ducked under it, turned, twisted, and threw it over his shoulder onto its back. He rammed his fist through its face and it dissipated into feathery black streamers.

'Good,' John said. 'Towels on the side.'

Leo collected a towel from the shelves and wiped his hands. He tossed the towel into the wicker laundry basket next to the shelves, then returned to stand next to me.

John pulled another demon out. 'Emma.'

'Am I limited to physical?' I said. 'If I am, hold off releasing it. I'll take my ring off.'

'No limit on what you do,' John said. 'Energy, physical, anything. Just take it out.'

I raised my hand and transferred my ring from my finger to the chain around my neck anyway. Then I readied myself in the centre of the room and nodded.

John threw the demon to the floor and it took the form of an elderly Chinese woman in a bright green *cheongsam*. She lunged forward to attack me and I took her out with a ball of *chi*.

'Good,' John said. 'Obviously not a challenge for either of you. Let's try something bigger.' He shuffled inside the jar. 'Level twenty.' He glanced up. 'Call if you're not confident.' He stopped and spoke more fiercely. 'I mean it. This is not a competition. *Call if you're not confident.*'

'Yes, sir,' Leo and I said in unison.

'Good.' John threw the bigger demon and it formed under the mirrors. 'Leo.'

Leo took it easily. John pulled out another level twenty and I took it just as easily with energy.

'Level thirty.'

'Once we're higher than this I'll need a weapon, my Lord,' Leo said. 'They're much faster than me and I need an edge.'

'Emma?'

'Me too. I can't generate enough energy without the weapon to take them out.'

'I've seen you take a level twenty-five bare-handed,' John said.

'I prefer to use energy. Don't get my hands dirty.'

'Against humanoids?'

'Oh, come on, you know that physical is the only way to go with them.'

'Very well,' John said. 'Take the level thirties, and then we'll move to weapons.'

'Is this a test?' I said.

'Of course it is. A simulation.'

Leo and I shared a look, then shrugged. Whatever. He was the boss.

John tossed the level thirty to the floor under the mirrors. It took True Form: a massive humanoid, seven feet tall, with black scales and tusks.

'Nice one,' I said.

Leo hesitated. 'You want it?'

'Nah, you can have it.'

Leo stepped forward, readied himself and nodded.

The demon came alive. It looked at each of us in turn, then quickly saluted John. 'Dark Lord.' It nodded to Leo. 'Black Lion. I am honoured.' It saw me and stopped. 'What are you?'

'Perfectly ordinary human female. What, you've never seen one before? I find that hard to believe.'

'Not like you.' The demon turned its three red eyes onto Leo. 'Lion.'

'A second chance,' John said.

The demon threw itself at Leo, clawed hands raised. Leo ducked beneath its hands and sliced at its abdomen as he went through. His hands glanced off.

The demon stopped and turned. Leo took two steps back, leapt, and ran a jumping high kick straight through its head.

He landed lightly on his feet and the demon dissipated.

'Leo!' John shouted.

Leo didn't reply. He just turned to face John and held his hands out from his sides.

'How many rules did you break just then?'

Leo hesitated. 'I think at least five, my Lord.'

'It is possible that it could have been a higher level disguising its speed. What if it had been a level fifty and you performed a stupid move like that?'

Leo didn't reply.

'You know the drill; you *teach* it! Treat all weapons as if they were sharp. Treat all demons as if they were Mothers. *And never take both feet off the floor.* When we return you will face five demons of random levels, and if I see you do *any* more stupid moves like that you will be restricted from weapons for three weeks.'

'My Lord.' Leo wasn't fazed. 'How many more? I need a shower now.' He gestured towards his slacks, which were covered in black demon stuff. 'Another pair ruined.' He grinned at me. 'I see what you mean.'

'Not much longer,' John said. 'If it burns let me know and I'll dismiss you. You should be fine for a while.' He turned and threw a bead onto the floor. 'Emma.'

The demon took female human form. She came straight for me.

I quickly bound her, and she stood frozen, her face a mask of loathing.

'Move back, Leo, this is going to be big.'

Leo backed away.

I used the chi I had drained from her when I bound her and made it into a huge ball, a good metre across. I threw it at the demon and she exploded.

'That was a foolish thing to do,' John said. 'You are pushing your reserves too hard.'

'I can handle it.'

'Not only was that a dangerously large amount of energy to throw at the demon, the energy you received when you destroyed her was an even more dangerous amount.'

'I need a larger reserve. I need to be able to take out much bigger demons with energy. Is there any other way to enlarge my energy reserve?'

He sighed with resignation. 'No. I understand. But please be careful; we need you.' He gestured towards the weapons rack. 'Your weapons are there; collect them and we'll move up to level forty. And that means no more stupid grandstanding from either of you.'

'Can you take one that high, Emma?' Leo said as he selected John's sword, Dark Heavens, from the rack.

'With the sword, yes,' I said as I collected my own. 'Bare-handed, probably another year and I'll have it.'

'Sooner than that if you continue to work this hard with the energy,' John said. He shuffled in the jar. 'Damn, not many that high a level. Wait.' He closed his eyes and held his hand over the jar.

'No!' Leo shouted.

'You are in serious trouble!' I yelled.

Two beads slid to the top and flew into his hand. He opened his eyes. 'There are only about ten left.'

'For heaven's sake will you guard your energy, John.'

'If Ms Kwan saw you do that she'd have your shell for breakfast,' Leo growled.

'Too late.' John threw one of the beads onto the floor. The level forty took human form, a tiny ancient Chinese man. 'Who wants it?'

Leo stepped forward. 'I remember this little bastard. I was there when you took him. He's mine.'

He readied himself and nodded.

The demon didn't move but something changed in its eyes. It scowled. 'I will not face something as worthless as you,' it said, and spat on the floor at Leo's feet. It looked at me then. 'Disgusting,' it sneered. 'A lowly female.' It turned to John and gestured angrily towards us. 'Is this what you held me for? A gay-lo nigger and a little girl? I will not face *women*,' it said, glaring at Leo.

'I see what you mean, Leo,' I said softly. 'Please, my friend, take your time with this one.'

'Do you like the taste of *turtle*, gay-lo?' the demon said viciously.

Both John and Leo stiffened.

'Do you like the taste of *turtle egg*?'

John's face went rigid and his eyes burned. 'Take this one out before it speaks again, Leo, or I may be forced to do it myself.'

Leo gestured a come-on to the demon. 'With a great deal of pleasure, my Lord.'

The demon didn't move.

'Come and get me.'

The demon smiled slightly and shook its head.

'To hell with it,' Leo said, and swung the sword at the demon's head.

The demon backed, avoiding the blade, but didn't fight back. When Leo swung at it again, it backed again. Eventually it reached the wall and turned away from Leo.

Leo lunged after it and it jumped back out of his reach. 'You will need to do better than that, gay-lo. You have not even touched me.'

Leo's face went rigid and he lunged to run the demon through before it could escape. It looked down at the sword piercing it with surprise, then smiled up at Leo and exploded.

'Enough, Leo,' John said. 'I can see the level you are at. Shower, change, meet us in the top-floor conference room. Dismissed.'

Leo went to the weapons rack and collected Dark Heavens' scabbard. He stopped at the doorway and saluted both John and me. 'My Lord. My Lady.' Then went out.

'Your turn, my Lady,' John said. He threw the level forty onto the floor.

It took True Form: a greyish-green humanoid with tufts of red hair and two bulging eyes.

I moved to the centre of the room, readied my sword and nodded. Physical was the way to go with this one.

The demon was unbound and studied me curiously. 'What are you?'

'Why do you things keep asking me that? Haven't you seen a perfectly ordinary human woman before?'

'Not like you. You are different.' The demon turned and saluted John. 'Dark Lord.' It saluted me. 'Lady.' It threw itself at me.

I ducked under its outstretched arms and spun around it, hitting it on the back of the head with the pommel of my sword as it went through; I couldn't move my arm around quickly enough to use the blade. It was knocked down by the blow, but turned a neat somersault and landed on its feet facing me, arms outstretched.

'Nice move,' I said.

'Thank you.'

It went for me again, this time throwing a swinging fist at my face. I ducked under the fist and swung at its abdomen with my sword, but it wasn't there. It had pivoted on our mutual axis and was beside me. It swung at my head but I ducked under the blow, flipped over forwards, rolled, and jumped up facing it. I didn't lose momentum as it tried to keep up with me; I swung the sword straight at its neck.

It blocked the blow with its forearm and pushed my sword hand back. It was stronger than me and I couldn't stop it from pushing my sword backwards.

I went with the movement, spun, and used my foot in a roundhouse kick into the side of its chest.

My foot went in with a satisfying crunch. I was through it. I carried my foot through the middle of the black stuff, then spun and leapt back as it exploded.

Not fast enough. Black stuff completely covered me from head to toe.

'Damn.'

'Well done,' John said with satisfaction. 'I can see the level you are at. Good.' He didn't move from the other side of the room. 'Shower. Change. Meet me in the conference room.' His voice became fierce. 'Excellent!'

Everybody was waiting for me in the conference room. Simone had drawn brightly coloured dragons on the whiteboard; one of them was recognisably Jade and the other was Qing Long, the East Wind. She even had their size difference nearly accurate; he was about five times bigger than Jade.

'Gold, take Simone to my office. I want to speak to Emma and Leo alone.'

Simone scowled.

'Last time, sweetheart, I promise.'

Simone took Gold's hand and led him out.

'Good.' John leaned his arms on the table. 'Emma, what we just did is confirmation of something I already knew. You can both take up to level forty without too much difficulty.'

I stiffened as I understood. I was at the same level of expertise as *Leo*.

'News, Emma?' Leo said softly.

'I didn't think too much about it before, Leo. You've always been better than me at hand-to-hand. But with a weapon and energy, I can take the same level as you.'

'You realise what this means?' John said.

Leo and I shared a look, then turned back to John and shook our heads.

'You can take turns staking out the school. You can share the guardian duties. You're just as good a guard as Leo now, Emma.'

'Oh *no*!' I shouted. 'Is that what this was about? You want to make me bodyguard as well as nanny? You must be joking! My thesis is due in five months and I haven't even found a topic for it.' I ran my hands through my hair. 'No *way*. I have enough to do as it is.'

'When Simone starts school, you'll have plenty of time,' John said. 'You and Leo can share guard duties, and spend time teaching here. It will work out very well.' He leaned over the table to me, his eyes sparkling. 'Dear Lady Emma, I formally request of you. Will you assist Leo in the guarding of my beloved daughter?'

'This is brilliant, my Lord,' Leo said. 'We can rotate the time. Some spent guarding, some spent teaching. A good balance.'

'I want a pay rise,' I grumbled. 'I cannot believe you are doing this to me.'

'Wait.' John pulled a folded chequebook out of his hip pocket. He flattened it on the table, opened it, scribbled on a cheque, tore it out with a flourish and handed it to me.

'How much?' Leo said.

'Ten million.' I tore the cheque into tiny pieces. 'But you forgot to sign it.'

'You can sign it yourself, you know that.'

'You both hate me. This was a setup from the start.' I sighed with feeling. 'I'll be fiercely busy until she starts school, John. The rebuilding, the management of Hennessy Road and Turtle's Folly —'

Leo broke in. '*What*?'

'She calls it Turtle's Folly,' John said.

I ignored them. 'The management of the school and the residence is a huge job. I can't possibly teach until Simone returns to school and frees up some time for me.'

'We can hire someone to help look after Simone,' John said.

'No *way*!' Leo and I said in unison.

'She's far too special to give to anybody else,' I said. 'She stays with either Leo or me.'

'How about I bring Charlie over from London to help you out until school starts?' John said. 'She can mind Simone while you're in meetings, and care for her at the Peak so you can finish your thesis. I promised she'd be able to come over and brush up her cooking skills here in Hong Kong anyway. James can mind the house in London by himself for a while.'

'That's a great idea,' I said, and Leo nodded agreement. 'Simone loves Charlie dearly and would really enjoy seeing her. Perfect.'

My footsteps echoed eerily through the tunnel leading out of the MTR station. There wasn't anybody else in the tunnel with me. Most unusual for Hong Kong.

A scraping sound came from the tiled area behind me. Loud enough to echo through the tunnel. It sounded like scales dragging along the ground.

I glanced back and saw it. It was enormous; at least six metres long, black and shining. It flicked its forked tongue at me.

I spun and ran. I raced through the tunnel, but my feet slipped on the tiles. It closed on me, the sound of its scales on the tiles a wet, shining slither. Louder and louder . . .

It crashed onto me, pinning me under its enormous, slick body. I couldn't move.

It wrapped its body around me, but didn't squeeze. It just held me.

Then it was gone.

I pulled myself up and walked out through the tunnel. Well, it was *about time*. What a wonderful feeling of satisfaction. I was complete. I was whole. And it felt so good, because I was so very, *very* dangerous. Now. Who would I kill first?

I woke and stumbled out of bed, then collapsed on the floor, panting and drenched in sweat.

John must have felt my distress because he came in. He wore his plain black pyjama pants and his long hair had come almost completely out of its braid. He knew better than to approach.

I knelt on the floor, gasping.

'If I could hold you right now, I would. Do you want me to call someone?'

I raised my hand. I took a deep gulping breath and pulled myself to my feet, then sat on the bed. 'I'm okay.'

He sat on the other side of the bed. 'That must have been a hell of a nightmare.'

I glanced into his eyes. 'I dreamed I turned into a snake. No, that's not right. I dreamed that a snake turned into *me*.'

He was taken aback. 'Really?'

I dropped my head. 'A really big black snake.'

'I would love to see that,' he said, his voice intense.

'What?'

'I'm sure you would be spectacularly beautiful. Black?' He smiled slightly. 'Wonderful.'

I looked away. 'Go back to bed, reptile man.'

'Are you sure you're all right?'

'It was just a freaky dream. That's all.'

'If you're sure . . .'

'You need your rest. Go back to bed.'

'As you wish, Emma. Good night.'

'Night, John.'

It took me a long time to go back to sleep after he'd gone.

CHAPTER FIVE

I met my friends April and Louise for lunch in the Thai restaurant in Wan Chai. It had been a long time.

April was a lovely Australian Chinese who I'd met working at Kitty Kwok's kindergarten before I went to work full-time for John. Her pregnancy was already well along and she had a cute bulge in front, accentuated by her lime-green maternity dress. The dress was an awful concoction of frills, bows and ruffles, and made her seem bigger than she was. Her face had filled out with the pregnancy, but she looked healthy and happy.

Louise was still herself, blonde, bony, and full of freckles and mischief. We'd shared an apartment in Sha Tin before I'd moved in to work as a live-in nanny for John, and I hadn't heard from her since we'd run into the White Tiger while having lunch at Sha Tin shopping centre and she'd fallen for him on the spot. I'd ferociously warned him off her otherwise she would have ended up as a member of his extensive harem.

'When's the baby due, April?' I said.

'September. Mid-September,' April said. 'It's a boy.'

Louise glanced up from her menu. 'You had it tested already?'

'Sure,' April said. 'Every month, when I visit the doctor, I have an ultrasound. They found out last appointment. Andy's very happy. He says he wants to keep it now.' She leaned back and smiled with satisfaction. 'We're a family. I knew it would all work out.'

'That's so wonderful, April,' I said. 'So you're all together now?'

'Yes, but not living together. He doesn't have time, he needs to be on the Island to be close to work. So he lives on Hong Kong Island, and I'm at Discovery Bay with the domestic helper. He comes and sees me once every few weeks, and tells me how happy he is.'

'What about the other wife?'

'She doesn't matter,' April said with a dismissive wave of her hand.

Louise and I shared a look.

'Is he still in the same work, April?' I said, carefully not mentioning Andy's underworld connections in front of Louise.

'He says he's not involved any more,' April said, obviously happy. 'He's working in Aunty Kitty's business. Mostly in China.'

'I'm pleased for you,' I said, and I meant it.

Louise looked up from her menu. 'Soft-shell crab. Want some?'

'Can't eat crab while I'm pregnant,' April said.

'Why not?' I said.

'It will make the baby a criminal. Scuttle sideways, like a crab.'

'What else can't you eat?' I said, trying to keep the disbelief from my voice.

'Lots of stuff,' April said. 'Have to be careful. Not make my blood too hot or too cold. The Chinese doctor keeps an eye on me. I drink Chinese medicine, to stay strong. Aunty Kitty is looking after me very well, she has doctors who are looking after me.'

'Kitty Kwok?'

'She says she misses you from the kindergarten, Emma. She says you should go and visit her at her house. She keeps asking me to take you over there.'

I didn't say anything. Kitty Kwok still called me, and approached me at charity functions, and I still carefully avoided her. I was sick to death of the woman. But at least she was helping April with the baby.

'I'm not going through that when I have a baby,' Louise said grimly.

'What?' I hesitated. '*What*?'

'Oh, didn't I tell you?' Louise said with an evil grin. 'I'm off to get married at the end of the month. Say bye bye, ladies, I'm marrying a king.'

'No!' I shouted, and heads snapped around to look at me. I lowered my voice. 'Don't you dare go off with that bastard!'

The waiter approached and we ordered quickly.

After he had gone I turned to Louise. 'If you go off with him nobody'll ever see you again. For God's sake, Louise, *don't do this*!'

'A king?' April said, trying to keep up.

'Yep,' Louise said with satisfaction. She eyed me sideways. 'Watch this, Emma, this is really good.' She turned back to April. 'I'm marrying an Arab sheik. A king. Filthy rich. I'll be moving to the Middle East at the end of the month. Say ta-ta.'

'You're marrying one of *them*? You have to wear those veils and things, you know,' April said, explaining. 'You can't go out in public. And they sometimes have more than one wife. If he's really rich it might be worth it, but if he's not then it's a waste of time.'

'Oh my God, you are so mercenary sometimes, April.' I leaned forward to speak intensely to Louise. 'This is such a bad idea. You *do* know how many wives he has already?'

'They're great. I've met some of them,' Louise said. 'They came with him to explain. They all help each other, look after each other, great friends. Can't wait.'

'Don't let his . . .' I hesitated. I chose my words. 'His *prowess* cloud your judgement, Louise. Once you're over the novelty, you have to live with him, and share him.'

'You know him too, Emma?' April said. 'He has wives already?'

'Prowess?' Louise said still grinning. 'Wouldn't know, the guy hasn't touched me.' The grin widened. 'He is a perfect gentleman; you have to marry him and go with him before he'll do anything. Like I said, can't wait.'

I put my head in my hands. 'Oh *God*.'

Louise dropped her voice to a low purr. 'Soft white fur.'

I folded my arms on the table and dropped my head on them. I wanted to bang my head on the table. 'Oh *God*! I am going to *kill* that bastard when I see him!' I glared up at her. 'He promised me he'd stay away from you!'

'Oh, that explains it,' Louise said. 'I had to chase him around for ages. Took a long time to finally make him give in.'

I buried my head in my arms. 'I am going to *kill* him.'

The waiter came back and I lifted my head. He placed four jelly coconut milk drinks and a pineapple rice on the table, and turned away.

I stopped him. 'We didn't order this.'

He froze, then his face stiffened. He picked up the drinks and the rice with disdain and stomped away.

'What did your family say when you told them?' I said.

'They're not speaking to me.' She changed her voice so that she sounded very stern and spoke down her nose. 'I *cannot* tell you how *disappointed* I am.' She grinned. 'Makes it easier, really.'

'You're throwing your whole life away to be one of a hundred,' I said.

'One hundred and seventeen. But the first fifty or so are really old and ugly. No competition. He just keeps them around 'cause he has to.' Her eyes sparkled. 'Like you can talk, anyway. I hear yours has *scales*. Yuck.'

'What *are* you talking about?' April said, completely bewildered.

The waiter came and plonked some dishes onto the table. He glared at me. 'We ordered some drinks too,' I said. He stomped off.

'Scales?' April said softly. 'You have a man, Emma? Not this Chen man, is it?'

'Yep,' Louise said with satisfaction. 'Engaged to him.'

'You going to marry *John Chen*?' April turned away. 'Lucky you. When's the wedding?'

'Not for a long time, April. A lot of problems. May never happen at all.'

'Lighten up, Emma,' Louise said. 'The Tiger says it'll happen.'

I didn't say anything.

'Why did you say he has scales?' April said.

'He's a *turtle*,' Louise said with relish.

I glanced up quickly. April inhaled sharply, her eyes very wide.

'You say that about Emma's man? You insult Emma too? What a horrible thing to say!'

'What?' Louise said, not understanding. 'What did I say?'

April leaned across the table towards Louise. 'You said he's a *turtle*,' she hissed.

'That's a shocking insult, Louise,' I said.

'Is it? No wonder the Tiger says it all the time.' Louise grinned. 'What does it mean?'

'Man who cannot satisfy wife,' April said, very softly. 'Wife turns to other men.'

'Cuckold,' I said.

'Whoa.' Louise's eyes widened with delight. 'Cool. Good one.'

'Same thing as wearing a green hat,' April said.

'Why turtle?' Louise said. 'Why is that particular animal the insult?'

I didn't want to discuss it. 'I have no idea.'

'I don't know either,' April said. 'Just turtle is very offensive animal. Lot of insults attached to it.'

I studied them. April: living in dreamland, believing she had a family when she only saw her man every few weeks. Louise: willing to share a man with more than a hundred others. And me.

I was probably the most pathetic of us all.

'Will I still be able to see you, Louise?' I said.

'Since you know all about it, you might be able to talk to me occasionally,' Louise said, still obviously happy. 'Don't count on anything; usually when we go there we're gone for good. Never seen again.'

'What?' April said. 'You don't mean that, do you? I don't understand.'

'Your poor family,' I whispered.

'Thoroughly worth it.' Louise glanced down at the dishes. 'Is this what we ordered?'

I looked at the dishes as well and sagged. 'Nope.'

'The economic downturn hasn't affected this place at all,' Louise said as she tried to catch the waiter's eye. 'They still act as if they're doing us a favour by letting us eat here.'

'I'm glad everything turned out for all of us,' April said. 'We'll all be happy married women.'

I really did feel the need to bang my head on the table.

I tapped on John's office door and opened it a crack. 'Free to talk?'

'Just let me save this file,' he said, studying the computer, then turned and leaned his elbows on the pile of papers on his desk. 'What?'

'It's May fifth. The festival's started. And you haven't done anything.'

'*Aiya*,' he said, and I giggled. 'What?'

'That's an extremely Cantonese sound coming from you,' I said, still smiling.

'I've heard you say it too. You can pick people who have lived in Hong Kong for any length of time, even expats. They all say it.'

'Cheung Chau,' I said, bringing him back to the point.

'*Aiya*,' he said again. 'It's already started?'

'The buns are up, John. The three effigies have already been built.'

'When's the big day?'

'Three days from now. May eighth.' I sighed with exasperation. 'Why don't you ever look in your diary?'

'I have a secretary and I have you,' he said. 'I don't need to.'

'You forgot your own birthday, Pak Tai.'

'You know it's not my birthday,' he said impatiently. 'It's the Buddha's birthday. They just lumped me into the holiday because it was convenient.'

'Did you know him?'

'Who?'

'The Sakyamuni Buddha.'

He hesitated, watching me, then, 'No.'

'What about the teachings?'

'What about them?'

'Are they true? The Buddhist Precepts?'

He sighed. 'You know better than to ask me that, Emma. You know you have to find your own way.'

I shrugged it off, it was worth a try. 'Okay, so when's your birthday?'

'You know I have no idea,' he said. 'After four and a half thousand years I'd challenge anybody to have an idea. I doubt if I was ever actually born, anyway. I just *am*.'

'Well then, Eighth Day of the Fourth Moon it is. May eighth this year. Three days from now. Thursday.'

He leaned back and retied his hair. '*Aiya.*'

'I've already cancelled all your classes, and booked the boat to take us over. We leave at ten in the morning. Okay?'

He grinned broadly. 'You already arranged it?'

'Of course I did. You don't think I'd leave it to you, do you?'

Cheung Chau was a dumbbell-shaped island about an hour's boat ride from Central Pier. The island was only three hundred metres wide at its narrowest point and hardly any height above sea level. The two 'weights' on the dumbbell stretched to either side, and were slightly higher.

The island was completely packed with people for the festival. John carried Simone so that she wouldn't be crushed.

The air was full of the noise of shouting, drums and gongs, and the smells of food and sweat. A thick pall of incense smoke hung over the entire island.

We stopped for lunch at one of the small restaurants near the pier before we went anywhere. The restaurants usually specialised in live seafood, held in tanks next to the kitchen. Diners could select exactly which fish and shellfish they wanted, how they wanted them served, and the restaurant would oblige. But for the week of the Bun Festival the entire island of Cheung Chau went vegetarian in Pak Tai's honour. The butcher shops closed for the holidays.

After lunch we wandered through the packed streets to the Pak Tai temple. The bun towers stood proudly outside the temple, enormous ten-metre-high bamboo cones held by a bamboo scaffold. The buns were strung around the outside of the cones.

The tradition was that at the end of the festival, after midnight on the final day, young men would climb the towers to retrieve the buns for the crowd; a good-luck race. But in 1978, one of the towers had collapsed and some of the bun racers had been killed. Since then the buns had been distributed to the island's residents by the clergy of the temple.

John wouldn't talk about what had happened in '78. Apparently he hadn't been present that year; normally he would have been there to make sure that nobody was injured. But in '78 he hadn't been able to make it, and wouldn't say why. It may have had something to do with him losing the Serpent about that time, but with a creature as strange as him it was impossible to tell.

Three enormous effigies had been constructed out of bamboo and brightly coloured paper, about five metres tall. They were of a black-skinned demonic-looking deity with horns; a benign elderly scholar with a flowing white beard and traditional robes; and another demonic-looking red-skinned figure. They were Dei Ching Wong, Ruler of the Underworld; Do Dei Gang, the Kitchen God; and Shang Shan, the God of Earth and Mountains.

There was no effigy of Pak Tai; he was far too awesome to be shown like that. But he would have his chance later.

* * *

After we'd lit some incense at the temple and John had bought Simone a brightly coloured good-luck pinwheel, we wandered back to John's house on the island. No motorised vehicles were permitted on Cheung Chau, so the streets could be very narrow.

We stopped at a plain concrete three-storey village-style house on the main thoroughfare. John pushed the door open.

The lower floor of the house was paved with pale green tiles and had bare concrete walls. The living room was minimally furnished with old-fashioned rosewood furniture and a stained coffee table, with a folding mah jong table. A set of rusting metal bunk beds with faded silk quilts folded at the feet stood against the wall on one side. It appeared to be a typical island village house, like many rented out for holiday weekends. John led us up the stairs to the second floor.

The second floor was plushly decorated with smooth cream Italian floor tiles and textured wallpaper. A comfortable leather lounge and a wide-screen television stood to one side and a rosewood six-seater dining table to the other. A well-fitted kitchen was at the back of the house, and Monica was already busy in there.

John opened the French doors onto the balcony. The balcony overlooked the main street of Cheung Chau, a perfect location for watching the parade. John gestured for me to sit at the outdoor table there, on one of the comfortable plastic chairs. Simone climbed into John's lap and leaned on the railing. Monica brought us iced lemon tea; the day was already very warm and humid.

A lion dance led the procession, with three lions: one gold, one black and one red. The drummer did his best to bring down the houses, banging for all he was worth. A martial arts troupe followed, performing acrobatics as they passed us on the street.

'Any of them ours?' I said.

John shook his head.

A small altar followed, carried by four proud young men. I peered down to see inside; it held an effigy of a god seated on a throne with his hands on his knees, his black robes flowing around him and his long hair over his shoulder. His face was square and dark, and his bare feet perched on a snake and a turtle.

John squeezed Simone. She whispered in his ear and he nodded. She leaned back to stare at him, incredulous, and he nodded again. She collapsed over his lap laughing.

John and I shared a smile.

About twenty people followed, all holding lanterns with good-luck characters on them.

The next altar contained a serene goddess sitting on a lotus flower, wearing flowing white robes and holding a small bottle in her hand.

'Aunty Kwan!' Simone yelled, pointing.

'That's right,' John said.

The next altar contained a goddess with colourful flowing robes and a benign smile. She wore a hat with a square brim with beads that hung in front of her face.

'Tin Hau?' Simone said, naming the Goddess of the Sea.

John nodded.

'Do you know her?' she said more softly, barely audible over the noise of the drums and gongs.

John nodded again.

Simone turned back to the parade and jiggled with excitement in John's lap.

The final altar contained Guan Di, the red-faced God of Justice, holding a huge halberd and glaring fiercely.

'He's actually a very nice man,' John said into Simone's ear. 'But he doesn't come for this. This is mostly for me.'

'Why you, Daddy?'

'A long time ago, a vicious band of pirates was attacking this island. The peaceful fishing folk here had no defence against them. The pirates attacked again and again. So I came down and had a small chat to them about their behaviour. They went away, and the people of the island built the temple for me, and hold the festival every year.'

'I heard you cured a plague,' I said.

'That too,' John said, smiling. 'I'm not sure if any of us remembers the exact origin of the festival. There were a few things. But the talk with the pirates is the one that sticks in my mind the most.' He gestured over the balcony railing. 'Here come the Floating Children.'

'Floating Children?' Simone squealed, standing to see better.

The five- or six-year-old children wore elaborate costumes and make-up. They were poised on the end of long steel poles, making their feet level with the heads of the crowd. But the poles were invisible, camouflaged by complicated accessories that matched the children's costumes. The children appeared to be standing, but it was obvious that they sat on chairs inside the costumes.

The costumes depicted traditional mythical characters as well as modern celebrities and politicians. One little boy dressed as a fireman sprayed water into the crowd from his miniature fire hose, making the audience scream with delight. Many of the girls were dressed as fairies and spirits in flowing robes.

'Uncle Sun!' Simone yelled, pointing to a little boy who was dressed as the Monkey King.

It was dusk by the time the procession ended. Simone yawned furiously. We moved inside and Monica presented us with a vegetarian meal that we ate at the dining table next to the upstairs living room.

Later, as we shared a pot of tea and discussed the parade, a chorus of thumps echoed on the door downstairs. John nodded to Monica, who went to open it.

John rose and stood to one side, his face fierce. He gestured for me to stand next to him, and I did.

Monica led a Taoist priest up the stairs. He wore the full regalia of a senior practitioner: vividly coloured robes with yin-yang symbols on them, and a high, square black hat. The face under the hat was mid-forties, with a kind, jolly expression, and I liked him immediately.

When he reached the top of the stairs he took two steps into the room and then fell to his knees and touched his forehead to the floor. 'Man shui, man shui, man man shui.'

'Hei sun,' John said, his voice clipped.

The priest rose, then bowed slightly from the waist, very serious. 'Celestial Highness. Welcome.'

John gestured towards me, still very formal. 'This is my chosen, Lady Emma.'

The priest bowed slightly to me as well, saluting. 'Ma'am.'

Simone didn't bother with the formalities; she ran to the priest and raised her arms. 'Uncle Ming!'

The priest lifted her, sat her on his hip, and kissed her on the cheek. He reached into the folds of his robe and pulled out a bun for her, which she accepted with delight. It was one of the buns from the three bun towers outside the temple; it had been stamped with a red good-luck motif. He carefully lowered Simone.

John gestured towards the couch and we all sat. Monica brought tea, and the priest poured. John nodded as he was served. Now the formalities were over we could all relax.

'It's a tremendous honour to have you back here with us, Highness,' the priest said. 'It's been a while.'

'Circumstances are quite difficult right now,' John said. 'Even worse than '78. But in a couple of years I will be gone for a very long time.' He lifted his tea cup and gestured towards me with it. 'Emma will be Regent.'

The priest was obviously taken aback. 'The Celestial will permit a wedding in these circumstances?'

'No. But she will be Regent regardless.'

'You always were one for breaking the rules, Highness,' the priest said, shaking his head with disbelief. He smiled at me. 'Did you have any idea what you were getting into?'

'No idea whatsoever, until it was too late.' I shrugged. 'And now it's definitely too late.'

'Kwan Yin herself has sponsored the Lady Emma,' John said. 'She is one of the most talented practitioners of the Arts I have seen in centuries. She loves Simone as her own. She is my chosen.'

I glanced at John, but he concentrated on the priest.

The priest bowed his head slightly to me. 'I will be honoured to serve you, my Lady.'

John relaxed almost imperceptibly. He'd obviously been worried about the way the priest would receive me, but there didn't seem to be a problem. I was relieved as well.

'Come up to the temple after the noise has died down and we're not so busy,' the priest said. 'Say hello to the acolytes. The renovations are finished, as well.'

'Do they know too?' I said.

The priest smiled. 'I'm the only one who knows, my Lady. It is a trust handed down to each senior priest of the temple as they take the post.'

'One of the most fun parts of the job,' John said with amusement.

'Oh, definitely,' the priest said. 'My Master took a photo when the Dark Lord revealed his true nature to me, and had it over his desk for a long time.'

'That was the look I normally get,' John said.

I was dying to ask about the arrangements that John had with the temple but it wasn't the polite time to talk business yet. Small talk for a while, still.

'How go things on the Celestial?' the priest said.

'All is well. But,' John leaned back slightly, 'there is a particular Demon Prince, number One Two Two, who has decided to make a bid for my head. His human name is Simon Wong.'

The priest's face went rigid as he thought about the consequences.

'I will give you an identikit photograph that Emma has created, and we will reset the seals on the temple every six weeks. I don't want any of you held as hostages.'

'My Lord,' the priest said, nodding. 'How powerful is this particular demon?'

'Right now, not a threat,' John said, raising his tea. 'We will have to wait and see what his plans are.'

Okay, now I could talk business. 'Exactly what arrangement do you have with the Dark Lord regarding the management of the temple?' I asked. 'I'll be helping out after he's gone. You said the temple had just been renovated? It looks terrific, they did a great job.'

The priest smiled with appreciation. 'I think I *will* enjoy working with you, Lady Emma. Let me tell you about the management of the temple, and what your part will be.'

John sipped his tea, his eyes sparkling over the rim of the tea cup as we talked about administration and funding.

Simone was still heady with excitement as we took the boat back to Hong Kong Island. It was well past midnight, but she was full of nervous energy.

She eventually couldn't hold it any longer and whispered in my ear, 'Now?'

I nodded and she wriggled with delight. She went to the galley of the boat, opened a cupboard and pulled out a red-wrapped gift.

She took it to her father and held it out to him.

'Happy birthday, Daddy,' she said, very serious, then kissed him on the cheek.

John shot me a delighted glance and then grinned broadly at the gift. 'I think this is the first time for me.'

'Open it now, Western-style. We want to see your face,' I said.

Simone came and sat next to me to watch. 'Yeah, Daddy, open it.'

I quickly pulled a camera out as John proceeded to undo the tape that held the gift wrap. He pulled the wrap away, held the box up, turned it the right way up, then stared at it with shock.

I took a photo just as he lit up with a huge delighted grin and then roared with laughter. Got it.

'Do you like it, Daddy?' Simone said. 'You can put it on your desk next to your computer monitor.'

'Was this your idea?' John asked Simone, still grinning broadly.

Simone glanced at me then back to her father without saying anything.

John turned the Ninja Turtle figure around so that we could see it. In Hong Kong the Ninja Turtles were called the Hero Turtles; the word 'Ninja' had too many unpleasant connotations. It meant 'assassin' in Japanese and was associated with stealthy murderers with no honour, completely at odds with the Western image of the powerful Ninja fighter.

'Two swords,' he said. 'I only have one sword.'

'You have two,' Simone said. 'Seven Stars and Dark Heavens.'

'I suppose I do.' He turned the box back around and studied the turtle figure. 'It looks just like me.'

'That's the idea.' I couldn't hold it any more. Simone let go as well and we clutched each other and giggled with delight. That photo was very, very precious.

The minute we were home John took the turtle out of the box and put it carefully next to his monitor. It stayed on his desk, guarding his mess, for a long time.

CHAPTER SIX

John tapped on my bedroom door.

'I'm in the middle of something,' I growled loudly. 'Can't it wait?'

He poked his head around the door. 'I have something to show you.'

I glared suspiciously at him. 'Not *another* priceless antique weapon.'

'No. Something for you.' He gestured with his head. 'Come and see.'

I pushed myself away from my desk. 'Oh, all right. But I need to finish this tonight.'

'Don't worry, it won't take long.' He opened the door for me. 'It's downstairs.'

He couldn't control his expression as we went down in the lift together. I had never seen him looking quite so smug.

'What have you bought?' I said.

'You'll see.'

We went out of the ground-floor lift lobby and into the car park that surrounded the building.

He raised one hand towards the mid-size black Mercedes parked next to his.

'That's for you.'

I stopped dead, then spun to face him and pointed at it. 'I don't want this. Why didn't you ask me first? This is totally unsuitable.'

He was taken aback. 'What's wrong with it? Is it too small?'

I sighed with exasperation and dropped my hand. 'No, John, it's much too big. I'd really prefer something much smaller, that's easy to drive around and park. And black is too hot, a nice light blue would be much better. And not a Mercedes, that's too much of a target. A cheap little Japanese hatchback would have been much better.'

'You want a *small, blue, cheap* car?'

'That would be perfect, yes. If it's small enough, Leo won't fit in it to drive it. And if it's not black and luxurious, you wouldn't be caught dead in it. I'd have it all to myself.'

He grinned broadly. 'You're quite correct.' He eyed me sideways with delight. 'You are very evil sometimes, Emma.'

I bowed slightly. 'Thank you, Dark Lord.' I gestured towards the car. 'So can you swap this monstrosity for something more suitable?'

'If you really want me to, I will. But Leo will be sharing it with you. Both of you will go to the Academy to teach, and to the school to watch Simone. Will you really force him to squeeze into such a tiny car?'

I sighed. 'Okay. I'll put up with this monster if I have to. But please don't make me drive the other one; it's enormous.'

'Very well, my Lady, I thank you.' He handed me the keys, very careful not to touch me. 'Go up and find your Australian driver's licence, and take it out for a run. Once you've had a drive in it, you may find you like it.'

'I can drive with that licence?'

'Yes. You just need to sign a statutory declaration to

apply for your Hong Kong licence. Gold can organise that.'

'Do you own the Mercedes dealership or something? Why only Mercedes?'

'One: it's the most common luxury car in Hong Kong and therefore less of a target, despite what you said. Two: I may not own the dealership, but I am very good friends with the Tai Pan of the company that does.'

'Okay, whatever you say. Want to come with me?'

His face went expressionless.

'Oh my God, you are such a typical male sometimes. Bad driver, and worse passenger.'

'I have been driving automobiles for nearly seventy years,' he said stiffly. 'During the 1930s the Tiger and I took European form and raced each other on the Grand Prix circuit. He kept winning because it was easier for him to stay white. I had to concentrate to keep the shape, and it ruined my performance. We only stopped because the competition became too professional. I am *not* a bad driver.'

I turned away. 'Leo has a completely different opinion on that.' I wondered what he looked like as a European. Probably not nearly as attractive.

'Leo thinks that everybody else in the world is a bad driver,' he called as I walked to the car. 'He will never let you drive him anywhere.'

Simone jumped up and down with excitement as we waited at the arrivals hall for Charlie. She fell over and I helped her up.

'Try to stay on your feet, Simone.'

'There she is!' Simone squealed, and raced to Charlie who stopped, crouched and threw her arms out to catch her.

Charlie rose with Simone held tightly in her arms and smiled over the top of the little girl's head. She

71

hadn't changed at all; her cheerful soft face was still rosy, round and smiling. Her greying light-brown hair had come out of its bun but she didn't seem to care. She rocked Simone in her arms. 'I missed you, Princess.'

Charlie lowered Simone and pushed her trolley as I led her towards the car park. 'I love this new airport.' She bent to speak conspiratorially to Simone. 'Have you been on the little train inside yet?'

Simone shook her head, eyes wide. 'We're not allowed in there. We have to take the *silly* small plane.'

Charlie laughed. 'I missed you, darling.' She patted my shoulder. 'I missed you too, Emma.'

'Let me take your trolley.'

'No, Leo can do that.' She looked around. 'That's not like Leo to leave you alone, Emma. Where is he?'

'Leo's teaching at the Academy.'

'What Academy?'

'Oh, dear Lord, John hasn't told you anything, has he?'

'John?' She continued without waiting for an answer. 'All Mr Chen said was to come to Hong Kong, help look after Simone, and brush up on my cooking while I was here. That's all, Emma.'

'It's *Lady* Emma now,' Simone said with relish.

'No it isn't, Simone, not for Charlie.' I saw Charlie's face. 'Don't worry about it, Charlie.' I paid the parking ticket and guided Charlie to the car. 'We need to talk. But we should wait until we have you settled in.'

When we reached the car Charlie stopped.

'Daddy bought it for Emma,' Simone said proudly.

Charlie glanced sharply at me.

'I needed it,' I said. 'Simone starts school soon, and I'll be taking her. I'll be sharing it with Leo.'

Charlie nodded, but she was obviously unhappy. We put her bags into the boot and she sat in the back of the car with Simone. 'How are you, my little Princess? You've grown so much. Starting school soon, eh? You're a big girl already.'

'I'm really good, Charlie. I'm learning energy work with Emma. Emma's teaching the Disciples. She's really good too. She'll be in charge.'

'Don't worry about that, Simone,' I said, not wanting to take the conversation in a difficult direction. 'We'll talk about that later.'

Charlie appeared very uncomfortable.

'Charlie, I'll tell you all about it when we're back at the Peak. In private,' I said pointedly, and she nodded. But I could see she was concerned.

When we arrived at the Peak I took Charlie into one of the student rooms behind the training room. 'Is this okay? If it's not good enough, you can go in with Simone, or you can have my room. I don't mind.'

'You can't do that, Emma,' Simone squeaked. 'You can't give Charlie your room, it's not fitting.'

Charlie didn't miss that. 'This will be fine, Emma, I've had this room before.' She put her bag down and folded her arms over her chest. 'Please tell me what's going on.'

'Simone, could you go to Monica for a while?' I said. 'Call me if you need me, I'm right here.'

'Okay, Emma.' Simone waved one hand as she went out.

'She's very grown-up for such a little girl,' Charlie said.

'She's been through a lot lately. We all have.' I gestured for her to sit on the bed and I sat on the student chair next to the desk. I leaned my elbow on the desk and rested my chin on my hand.

'I heard about the Attack,' Charlie said. 'I heard that most of the Mountain was destroyed. It's awful. I hope Mr Chen is okay.'

'We nearly lost him, but the White Tiger helped and managed to pull him back. It was a very bad time for all of us.'

'How is he now?'

'He's fine. We moved the Wudang Academy from the Mountain to here in Hong Kong. The students are staying and learning in buildings that he owns here.'

'That's wonderful! It's fantastic he can teach again.' She became serious. 'He's teaching you?'

'Apparently I'm very talented. He already has me teaching energy work to the juniors, as if I didn't have enough to do already.'

'Well, a nanny's job is never easy,' she said cheerfully.

I stopped and thought about what to say. This would be hard. I dropped my head and didn't look at her. 'I'm not the nanny any more, Charlie. He asked me to marry him.'

'He can't marry you. He can't marry anyone.'

'He promised to come back for me. And I promised to wait for him. When he comes back, we'll be married.'

'And in the meantime?'

I dropped my head even lower and mumbled, 'I'll be Regent, Charlie. I'll be in charge of the Mountain, of Simone, everything.'

Charlie's face screwed up with fury. 'I *knew* it!' She threw herself out of her chair and stood over me, shaking with rage. 'You *cow*! I knew you were after his money!' She stormed into the hallway. 'I don't know what you did to him, but I'll find out!'

I rushed to follow her. 'Wait!'

She ignored me. She charged straight out the front door and slammed it behind her.

I poked my head into the kitchen. Simone sat at the table with Monica. 'Simone, could you call Jade or Gold for me?'

Jade appeared behind me in the hallway and I closed the kitchen door. 'Jade, you know Charlie? The housekeeper from London?'

'Yes, ma'am.'

'She just raced out the front door, furious with me. Could you follow her and make sure she's okay? Don't let her know you're there. If she doesn't come home by herself, bring her home in about an hour, but she needs time to think so leave her alone.' I hesitated. 'Also, could you ask Lord Xuan to come home? I think I need him.'

Jade bowed slightly. 'My Lady.' She disappeared.

I sagged. Nothing I could do now except wait. I went back into the kitchen. Simone and I could read a book together or play with Lego until Charlie came back.

I understood completely how she felt. I would have been that protective of him as well. John was so insensitive sometimes; he hadn't even considered what Charlie would think, or warned her about the situation. He'd just expected her to follow orders.

Half an hour later Simone and I had nearly built a complete castle on the living room floor when my mobile phone rang. It was John.

'I'm going to be late, Emma, I'm stuck in traffic at the bottom of Stubbs Road. There's some construction work at the bottom here and the traffic is banked back to Ruttonjee.'

'That's fine, John, whenever you're here is okay.' I dropped my voice. 'This is all your fault. You could have at least told her what was going on.'

'I know.' He sounded sheepish. 'I'll make it up to her. I keep forgetting that Westerners need to be treated differently.'

'What, with a reasonable amount of respect and care?'

'Exactly,' he said with a smile in his voice, and hung up.

About half an hour later I heard arguing outside the front door and sent Simone into the kitchen with Monica. The front door opened and Jade entered, holding Charlie's elbow.

'She's hypnotised all of you!' Charlie said. 'I don't know what she's done, but I'll get help!'

Jade wore her usual pale green tailored suit but her hair had come out of its tight bun and fell over her shoulder. 'Charlie, it's true. Everything I've told you is true. She's worthy.'

'Worthy my eye.' Charlie saw me and glared.

'Come into the dining room and talk, Charlie,' I said. 'I really do have everybody's best interest at heart.'

Charlie didn't move.

'Go with her,' Jade said gently. 'Let her explain. It's true.' Her voice softened. 'She loves him, Charlie, a truer love than any love I've ever seen before. And you know how old I am. She loves our Lord and his daughter more than her own life.'

'Thanks, Jade,' I said.

Jade smiled slightly. 'Go with her, Charlie. Listen to her. Ask what she did in Guangzhou.'

I gestured towards the dining room. Charlie sighed with resignation and went in.

'Good luck, Emma,' Jade said, and disappeared.

I followed Charlie into the dining room. She sat stiffly at the table and glowered at me.

'Please believe me, I'm only doing this for them,' I said. 'This was all John's idea.'

'John!' she said sarcastically. 'Lovely.'

'It was his idea. I didn't want to teach, I don't have time.'

'I'm sure it was his idea about you taking over everything as well.'

'I don't want this at all.' I looked her right in the eyes. 'You have no idea how hard this has been for me.'

'It wasn't hard for you to order Jade to come and get me.' Charlie leaned back and folded her arms over her chest. 'You had her follow me around without any trouble at all.'

I sighed. She had a point. I put my elbows on the table and my chin on my hand. She glared at me as if I was some sort of demon.

'Charlie, listen to me. I love Mr Chen more than my life. I love Simone more than that. All I want is for us to be happy together. But you know the situation.' This was very hard; normally I didn't talk about how I felt for John. 'He can't even touch me. But he's promised. And I've promised. And that's the way it is. He wants me to mind everything for him while he's gone. I don't know why, there are so many people who would be much better at it than me —'

'No, there aren't,' John said. He was leaning on the doorframe and listening, holding a teapot and some tea cups. He came and sat at the table, and poured tea for Charlie, who tapped the table in thanks. 'You are absolutely the best person for the job.'

'Oh, give it a rest, John.' I wanted to slap his arm, but I saw the way he looked at me.

Charlie studied John carefully. He smiled at her.

'Did you tell Charlie what you did in Guangzhou, Emma?'

'What, the energy work? The sword stuff?'

John leaned back. 'Charlie, while we were in Guangzhou, we were attacked by a demon. It was the same demon that killed Michelle.'

Charlie gasped and her eyes went wide.

'You know how Michelle died. You know how her family died. The same demon broke into the White Tiger's stables in Ireland, and raped and mutilated two of his women. Emma heard the Tiger describe what had happened.'

'That's awful, sir,' Charlie whispered.

'The demon took all of us down, and went into the house to kidnap Simone.'

Charlie's eyes were huge. 'No. How did you stop it?'

'We couldn't stop it. It took Simone into its nest. Do you know what Emma did?'

Charlie glanced at me, her eyes still wide.

'Emma went with them. Into the demon's nest. She knew exactly what would happen to her if she went, but she went anyway. To be with Simone. To the very end.'

Charlie stared at me. 'You willingly went into that demon's nest?'

'I don't know why everybody is making such a big deal of it,' I said. 'Anybody would have done the same. I couldn't let Simone go with that monster alone.'

'The King of the Demons himself went in and tried to take them for himself,' John said. 'Emma negotiated with him to release them instead.'

Charlie gasped. 'The *King*?' She turned to me. 'You faced down the *King*?'

'If she hadn't had the courage and intelligence to negotiate with him, it is quite likely that Emma would be dead, Simone would be in the Demon King's hands, and my head would be gone,' John finished.

Charlie studied me appraisingly for a long time. She didn't move at all and her face was rigid with restraint. I waited, mystified, to see what she would do.

She rose, and John smiled.

I just watched her, wondering.

She carefully lowered herself to one knee before me. 'My Lady. I pledge allegiance.'

I threw myself to my feet. 'Will you people stop doing that!' I banged the table with frustration. 'John, will you *please* tell your staff to stop doing that. It drives me completely nuts!'

Charlie rose and threw her arms around me, tearful. 'I'm your staff too, my Lady.' She smiled at John with her arms still around me. 'Congratulations, my Lord, you have chosen well.'

John put his hands out. 'I didn't choose her, Charlie. Fate chose us for each other.'

I gently pulled myself out of Charlie's arms. 'I have had absolutely enough of this.' I gestured impatiently. 'Go and unpack, Charlie. Have a rest and settle in. You can start helping with Simone tomorrow, if you're not too jet-lagged.'

Charlie bowed. 'Yes, my Lady.'

'Dammit, will you people stop doing that!' I shouted, and stormed out.

They laughed as I went out. They were all enjoying this *far* too much.

'May I use the phone and call London, my Lord?' Charlie said behind me. 'I would love to tell James and my mother.'

'Be my guest,' John said. 'Tell everyone you know.'

'You all hate me!' I yelled over my shoulder.

CHAPTER SEVEN

I checked the phone number: Leo. 'Hello?'

'I know it's Sunday, my Lady, but I was wondering if you and Mr Chen would like to see the kid. I have him here at the martial arts school in Causeway Bay, and his mother's out of town. Can I bring him up for you to meet him?'

'John's not here, but bring him up anyway. John'll be back soon, he went out with Simone. What's the kid's name?'

'Michael. Michael MacLaren.'

'Bring him up.'

Just as I put the phone down the front door slammed. I went out to the hallway. John and Simone had just come in and were kicking off their shoes in the entry.

'Leo's bringing his student up for us to see,' I said.

'If they're here before I'm out of the shower, look at him for me,' John said.

'You don't need a shower every single time, Daddy,' Simone said patiently.

'Yes I do,' he said, and headed past me towards his room.

'He really hates the summer,' Simone said. 'He hates being all sweaty like that.'

'He's probably not used to it,' I said. 'Shen don't get sweaty in summer.'

'He does. He's a Shen.'

'He's in human form. He's human all the way through.'

'He hates it.'

'Too bad for him, he's the one who has to wear black all the time,' I said unsympathetically. 'He's a big wussy boy.'

She grinned. 'Yeah. He's so weak!'

I can hear both of you, John said into our ears. Simone and I giggled together.

The door opened and Leo came in, guiding Michael.

Michael was tall for a fifteen year old, about five eight, and obviously still had some growing to do. He moved with muscular grace as he kicked off his shoes, but the first thing I noticed was his hair; he had dyed it blond.

'Michael, this is Miss Donahoe,' Leo said pointedly.

Michael bobbed his head. 'Ma'am.'

I nodded back. 'Mr MacLaren. Leo's told me good things about you. How about we go into the dining room together and talk?'

'I'll take Simone,' Leo said. 'Where's Mr Chen?'

'In the shower,' Simone said. '*Again.*'

Leo grinned. He held his hand out to Simone. 'Come on, Simone, let's play on the Playstation while we wait for Emma and your dad.'

'It's your day off, Leo,' Simone said, concerned. 'You don't have to work.'

'This isn't work, sweetheart,' he said. He nodded to Michael. 'You'll be fine.'

'Come with me, Michael.' I opened the dining room door and took him in.

He sat at the table, carefully serious and respectful. He was obviously very nervous. His half-Chinese heritage gave him golden skin under his blond hair. His eyes were a light shade of brown, and his Eurasian features were stunningly good-looking.

I sat across from him. 'Leo tells me that you might be suitable for an opening we have here. We're looking for a trainee bodyguard, full-time, live-in. Could you do that?'

'Yes, ma'am.'

I leaned back. 'Tell me about yourself.'

He paused and looked down at his hands where he had them clasped on the table. 'I finished third form, and I don't want to go back to school. I want to do something with martial arts.'

'Well, you've come to the right place. Why do you dye your hair blond?'

He grimaced. 'I don't. Sometimes I think I should dye it black or brown instead. It's natural.'

'You're a natural *blond*?'

He nodded.

'Well, that's not unheard of, I suppose. I've seen other blond half-Chinese kids around. Have you been looking for work? Have you had any previous jobs?'

'I wanted to work at Mr Pak's martial arts studio when I was able to leave school, but times are tough and he can't pay me. My mom won't let me work for nothing, otherwise I would. I go in there and help anyway, but Mom says I have to find a real job that pays.'

I didn't say I agreed with her. 'Have you asked your mother about moving in here?'

He shrugged. 'Not yet.'

'I suppose we can cross that bridge when we come to it. How good are you at the Arts?'

Michael shrugged again. 'Leo says I'm good.'

'How about we see.' I rose and gestured. 'Come with me, I'll try you out.'

'*You'll* try me out?'

I smiled grimly.

When Michael reached the training room he stopped and stared at the weapons on the wall.

I moved to the centre of the room and gestured for him to face me. 'I'll try you. Ready?'

He moved about a metre away from me and stood uncomfortably. 'I'm not sure about this, ma'am.'

I straightened. 'Are you worried I'll hurt you?'

He grinned, he was confident. 'No, ma'am.'

'You're worried you'll hurt me?'

He nodded and his blond hair flopped over his forehead.

'Good.' I moved into a standard short defensive stance, left guard. 'All I want you to do is pin me. See if you can have me immobile on the floor. You're taller than me and stronger than me; if you have a reasonable amount of skill it shouldn't be a problem. If you can do it you have the job.'

He hesitated, unsure.

'Don't worry about hurting me. If I'm injured I'll take full responsibility.'

He shook his head. 'I won't hurt a woman, Miss Donahoe.'

'If you're a good student of Leo's then you can probably best me.' I waved a come-on. 'Try me.'

He was lightning fast. Leo had taught him well. He dropped to perform a spinning kick, trying to take my feet out from under me.

I just stepped over it.

I rose and he hesitated, then lunged and tried to grab my arms. I twisted my arms up and away and stepped back out of his grip. I dropped and spun and took his feet out from under him. He fell on his behind with a thump.

He flipped back onto his feet; strong abs. Good. He was obviously feeling inadequate, because for the next move he just threw a fist at my face.

Extremely bad idea. I grabbed his wrist, twisted it, and threw him over my shoulder onto his back, knocking the wind out of him. He lay on the mats and panted for about half a minute.

'All you have to do is pin me, Michael.'

He grimaced and flipped onto his feet again. He performed a roundhouse kick at my head. I ducked underneath it. 'I don't think Leo taught you that. Roundhouse kicks are useless against somebody who has a decent amount of skill.'

He ignored me and performed a series of roundhouse kicks, forcing me back as I ducked underneath them. Eventually I tired of it, grabbed the foot as it sped towards my head and tipped him over onto his back again. 'Enough, Michael. I can see where you're at. You're very good.'

He lay on his back on the floor and stared up at me. 'Who taught you, Miss Donahoe? You're incredible. I've never seen anybody as fast as you.'

'Leo's better than me at the physical stuff,' I said. 'If you learn diligently from him, then you'll probably eventually be able to best me.'

'Leo taught you?' he said with new respect. 'Hold on, *physical* stuff? What other stuff is there?'

I ignored the second question. 'Leo and I learned from the same Master. Up you get, Michael, and we'll see how you do with weapons.'

He rose, brushed himself off, and saluted me. I nodded back, Master to student. He didn't miss that.

'Who's your Master? He must be really famous.'

'You'll find out if we decide to take you, Michael. For now, prove yourself.' I stepped back and gestured

84

with one hand towards the weapons on the wall and the racks on the floor. 'Anything here you can use?'

He pointed. 'Sword. Staff. Chucks. Spear.' He moved closer to one of the more esoteric weapons. 'What the hell is that?'

'Don't worry about that for now. Choose a sword.'

He lifted a few swords from the rack, then selected one. It was one of the Celestial weapons, a white and gold Japanese-style *katana*. An elegant weapon, well-balanced and sharp, and wrought with demon-killing essence.

'Good choice.' I picked my own sword from the rack, pulled it from its scabbard, and readied myself. 'Tell me when you're ready.'

He took the sword from its scabbard and stopped dead. 'No way, Miss Donahoe, I chose the wrong one.' He tested the edge with his thumb. 'Wow, this is really sharp. It's real, not a training weapon. It shouldn't be on the rack at all, it belongs in a display case.' He moved forward to return the sword to the rack. 'I'll get something else.'

I raised my hand. 'No need, Michael. They're all real. They're all sharp. We don't mess around here.' I raised my own sword. 'If you're not up to sparring with real weapons, then just say the word.'

He hesitated, then returned the sword to its scabbard. 'I'm sorry. I don't think I'm up to sparring with real weapons. I don't think I'm good enough.' He shook his head as he returned the sword to the rack. 'Thanks for talking to me, though. I appreciate it. Maybe another time.'

'Good.' I put my own sword back. 'You know your limitations. Instead of a spar, how about you just perform a set for me? Anything you like, any weapon you like. I just want to see how you move.'

'Can I use this?' he said, raising the white *katana*.

I nodded. 'Sure. Nobody's using that one right now.'

I leaned against the short wall and watched as he performed a very elegant level four Shaolin long sword set. He finished and saluted with the sword in his hand.

'Did Leo teach you that?'

'Yes, ma'am.'

I smiled; this time he'd called me 'ma'am' with real respect. 'How long did it take you to learn the full set?'

'About six weeks, ma'am.'

'That's exceptional.' I pulled myself away from the wall. 'Come and have a chat to Mr Chen, the Master. I think you're perfect. Leo's chosen well.'

He grinned broadly, then became shy as he returned the sword to its scabbard. 'Thanks, ma'am. Mr Chen?'

'That's right. Come with me.'

'I don't know of any famous practitioners named Chen. Chen or Chan?'

'Definitely Chen,' I said with amusement. 'And you probably have heard of him. Come with me.'

I led him to the dining room and sat him at the table, then went into the study to find John. He sat in front of the budgeting spreadsheet, his noble face intent on the work. He looked up and smiled when he saw me.

I leaned on the back of his chair and checked the sheets over his shoulder. 'You forgot something. Remind me to go through these with you later. You men have no idea how to budget for female needs.'

'Too close, Emma.'

I moved slightly away.

He grinned over his shoulder. 'And?'

'Oh. Yeah. The kid's in the dining room. He's only first or second grade black belt in anything, but he has a lot of talent and Leo's started him well on the right path.' I heard myself. 'I sound like an expert, and I've only been learning myself for about a year.'

'A year with me is worth a lifetime with any other Master. You *are* an expert, Emma.'

I shook my head. 'I'm just a beginner. Anyway. Michael. He has a lot of talent. He can't best me at hand-to-hand —'

'I doubt if anyone who has learned from any other Master could best you at hand-to-hand,' John said.

'— and he turned down weapons when he saw how sharp the blades are. Very sensible, lot of discipline, and smart. I like him, he's a good kid.'

'That's enough for me.' John pulled himself to his feet and pushed his big executive chair away from the desk. 'Let me see him.'

We went into the dining room together. Michael rose and shook John's hand, obviously intimidated, but still trying to work out who John was.

When he took Michael's hand, John stopped and concentrated, having a quick look inside. Then he dropped Michael's hand and roared with laughter.

I watched him with bewilderment; I'd never seen him react like that before. Michael shot a querying look at me and I shrugged.

John gestured for us to sit and flopped into a chair, still chuckling. He leaned his elbow on the dining table and rubbed his chin. 'I know your father. He's one of my best friends.'

Dear God, that explained the hair. And it made the kid an even better choice for the job; well done, Leo. But also a riskier choice, if Michael followed his father in other directions as well.

Michael stiffened. 'How do you know my father, sir? My mother won't tell me who he is.'

John stopped laughing and studied Michael intently. 'You don't know who your father is?'

'No, sir.'

'Do you know where you were born?'

'Somewhere in China, sir. My mother left when I was two. She didn't go back to the States, she stayed here.

She won't say why. I've been to school here, but I want more.' He hesitated, then grimaced. 'Sometimes I think there has to be more than just this. This life in Hong Kong.' He glanced up at John. 'Something more, you know? I think my dad may be someone important, and I want to know who he is. He provides well for us, we have plenty of money. I've asked Mom about it, but she won't tell me. I looked for him for a while, tried to trace the finances back, but I hit a dead end and gave up. Then Leo said you wanted someone to work for you and learn martial arts, so here I am.'

'You have no idea who your father is?' John said.

'No. But you do?' Michael said, his intelligent face full of hope.

'If his mother doesn't want him to know then I think we should respect her wishes,' I said.

'I want to know!' Michael looked from me to John. 'I'm old enough to decide for myself, and I want to know!'

'I think he should know,' John said. 'He may have abilities beyond the norm that we could bring on before I go. It will make it easier for him to fit in, being the same as Simone, half Shen. Besides, the Tiger said that none of his women ever wants to leave, and I would love to rub his wet pink nose in this one.'

Both of us laughed quietly at that. Michael looked from one of us to the other, bewildered.

'How could she have left?' I said. 'You said they're content to serve him forever.'

'This one must be exceptional. It would take a tremendous act of will. Both of Michael's parents are exceptional, Emma. Leo really has chosen very well.'

'Do you think the Tiger would like to come down and meet him?' I said. 'He may be interested in seeing his son after so many years.'

'Is the Tiger you're talking about my father?' Michael said.

Both of us nodded.

'He wouldn't come anyway,' John said. 'The Tiger doesn't care one way or the other about his offspring, past ensuring they're fed and housed. If they stay in the West they may learn the Arts and join the Horsemen. Or they may come down to the Earthly and have a normal human career. The ones at the Guangdong house were probably all his sons. He calls them by number.'

I remembered how Bai Hu had called one of the grooms by number when asking how many horses he had. That was son number two hundred and something. I inhaled sharply. 'All of them died in that attack and he didn't even bat an eyelid.'

'If you mean he didn't care, that's correct,' John said. 'He has hundreds of children; they mature, grow old, die. He's used to it. He's really past caring.'

Michael was obviously confused by the whole exchange.

'Some of his children have special abilities,' John said. 'Others are ordinary humans. This one is interesting: he has a great deal of chi and ...' He eyed me meaningfully. 'A huge reserve of ching.'

'Normal for his age, though,' I said.

'Could be, could be.' John nodded. 'You are showing remarkable restraint, Michael, and I am impressed. We are discussing your father, who you have waited so long to find, and you remain silent. We are discussing you, and you also remain silent. We have said things that you obviously don't understand, but you have the discipline not to ask. This sort of discipline will suit you well in the training, you should go far.' He rose. 'I'll take him, Emma, he is eminently suitable. Swear him to silence first, then tell him all: about me, about his father, everything. After that we'll see if he's willing to serve as Retainer. I want him to swear allegiance before I begin training him. I leave this in your capable hands.'

'Yes, sir.'

'Emma.' John sighed with exasperation. 'When will you stop calling me "sir" outside the training room? It is entirely not fitting.'

'Sorry, John,' I said. 'Force of habit when you boss me around like that.'

He bowed slightly. 'If it *pleases* you, my Lady Emma.'

I rose and bowed slightly back. 'With a great deal of *pleasure*, Lord Xuan.' I grinned. 'And speak English.'

'I was.'

Michael looked at us, from one to the other, with complete bewilderment. Time to put the poor kid out of his misery.

John went out, and I sat again. 'Now, Michael, where to begin?' I suddenly remembered a conversation I'd had with Leo and Ms Kwan what seemed like centuries ago. 'First,' I said, 'I need you to swear on your honour that you won't tell anybody what I'm about to tell you. Nothing is to travel beyond the walls of this room; you are not to share it with anybody unless they know already.'

He looked me right in the eye and I could see that he meant it. 'I swear.'

'Good. Now, how much do you know about Chinese culture in general?'

He was carefully obedient and answered my weird question. 'Enough.'

'Do you know the names of any of the Chinese deities?'

'A few.'

'Have you heard of Pak Tai?'

'God of Martial Arts? Sure. We have an altar for him at the studio.' He opened his mouth and then closed it again.

'Did Leo put that altar there?'

'How did you know that? He won't talk about it. He even puts incense on it. It's really weird.'

'How much do you know about Pak Tai?'

The kid was good. He patiently let me lead him through my pointless series of questions. He really wanted the job. 'God of Martial Arts, always in black. Controls water. Destroys demons. They hold the Cheung Chau festival for him.'

'Do you know his name in Putonghua?'

He grimaced. 'My Putonghua is terrible. My Cantonese is passable, but not great. It's all English at home, my mom doesn't speak much Chinese.' He seemed about to say something then changed his mind.

'Pak Tai in Putonghua is Xuan Wu, Xuan Tian Shang Di, Dark Lord of the North.'

His face began to betray him. He waited for me.

'Have you ever heard of Kwan Yin? Gwan Yum?'

'Of course. Goddess of Mercy.'

'White Tiger God of the West?'

He nodded, then scowled, beginning to lose patience. He'd done well to let me take him this far without becoming irritated at the seemingly pointless nature of the questions.

'Okay.' I leaned back. 'They're real. They're all real.'

'Of course they're real,' he said. 'People put altars up for them all over the place.'

'No, Michael. They're extremely real. In fact, you just met one of them.'

He went completely still.

'Mr Chen, the gentleman you just met? Your prospective employer? He's Pak Tai. He's Xuan Wu.' I smiled. 'That was the God of Martial Arts.'

His expression didn't shift. The kid was good.

'Lord Xuan Wu married a human woman, and had a child with her. That child is the little girl you saw. Her name's Simone. Her mother was killed by demons, and they're after her as well. We will teach you the skills you will need to protect her against demons. You should be very good at it with some training, considering who you are.'

'I don't think . . .' His voice trailed off. 'What's who I am got to do with it?'

'You are the son of the White Tiger of the West, Michael. You are half god yourself. You are also half tiger. Let me tell you about your father.'

He stared at me. He gave me rope and I took it.

'Your father has a palace in the Western Desert, in Heaven. He has a great many women there. Your mother fell for him and he carried her away to join his harem. She obviously grew sick of sharing him and left. She's highly unusual in this regard, because he's claimed, in my presence, that none of his women ever leave. Your mother must have a very strong will.'

'She does. But —'

I cut him off. 'There's more to it than that, Michael, but I think that's enough for now. Let me summarise. Your employer will be Lord Xuan Wu, God of Martial Arts, Dark Lord of the Northern Heavens, the North Wind. He will teach you to use your skills to defend his daughter, Simone, against demons. Your father is Lord Bai Hu, the White Tiger God of the West, the West Wind.' I wondered how much had gone in. 'Any questions?'

Michael rose. 'I'm sorry, Miss Donahoe. I appreciate the attention, but I don't understand why you're doing this. It's obvious you're good, but there's really no reason for you to spin this story. And I can assure you,' he said sharply but politely, 'that I am *not half tiger*. That's a slur on my mother, you know, but you're obviously crazy, so I'll let it pass.'

I clapped my hands with delight. The kid was perfect. He hadn't believed a word I'd said. 'You are truly very impressive. Come with me, I'd like to show you something.'

He eyed me suspiciously.

'Would you trust me if I brought Leo along?'

He nodded. He trusted Leo. Good.

I took him to the training room. Leo was there already, working with Dark Heavens, the sword that resided in clips next to the front door. As soon as we entered Leo fell to one knee and saluted me.

I sighed with exasperation and Leo grinned as he pulled himself back to his feet.

Michael glanced sharply at me.

'Leo, do you know who Michael's father is?'

'No, my Lady,' Leo said. 'No idea.'

Michael didn't miss the honorific and glanced at me again.

'Lord Xuan says that he is the son of Bai Hu.'

Leo reeled back. 'Whoa. What a good choice. Half Shen. Half tiger. Son of the West Wind. I couldn't have chosen better.' He glared at Michael. 'Why didn't you tell me?' He raised his hand and grinned. 'No, don't worry, of course you didn't know that I'm familiar with Shen.'

Michael looked as if he was about to fall over. His face was ashen.

'He didn't know who his father was until about five minutes ago,' I said. 'His mother never told him. He has no idea about anything, and didn't believe me when I just told him.'

'Even better.' Leo studied Michael appraisingly. 'I can't believe what a good choice I made here.'

'How about we pull out the demon jar? Could you get it for me, please?'

'Yes, ma'am.' Leo grinned at Michael and put Dark Heavens back on the rack. 'Don't worry, you'll believe the Lady Emma soon enough.'

Poor Michael just stood there, stunned, and watched Leo go out.

'Remember, Michael, you are sworn to secrecy on this,' I said. 'Don't bother trying to tell anybody, anyway. Nobody would believe you.'

'I stand by my word,' Michael said absently.

Leo came back with the jar. I took it from him and put it in the corner of the room. 'You guide him, I'll get the demons out.'

'Demons?' Michael said.

'Lady Emma told you everything, didn't she?' Leo said.

Michael nodded.

'Well then, select a weapon.' Leo picked Dark Heavens from the rack.

Michael's face was full of scepticism, but he took the white *katana* from the rack anyway.

Leo snorted. 'Did Lady Emma tell you to take that one?'

'No,' Michael said, 'I chose it myself. Is it the wrong one?'

Leo glanced at me. 'You know that sword's name?'

'Nope.'

Leo grinned broadly. 'That sword is the freaking *White Tiger.*' He gestured for Michael to stand next to him in the centre of the room. 'Here.'

I opened the jar and the air hissed. Michael's expression was priceless. He didn't know whether to believe us or not, but he was beginning to worry.

'Don't be concerned, you are in absolutely no danger here,' I said.

Leo readied himself. Michael did too, obviously just in case.

I threw a low-level demon onto the floor in front of the mirrors and it formed into a twenty-year-old Chinese man wearing plain slacks and a shirt.

Michael took a step back, his eyes wide.

'What level is that, my Lady?' Leo said.

'Four. It's bound right now, Michael. I can release it if you like. It will attack you if I do. Do you want me to?'

Michael took a step forward and studied the demon carefully. 'That's a demon?'

'Yes.'

'I've seen them before. I wondered what they were. They look like ordinary people, but they're different somehow.' He grimaced. 'I thought something was wrong with me; the minute I see one I want to tear it to bits.'

'Good God, he can spot them already,' Leo said with awe.

'You are a true son of the White Tiger,' I said. 'You will be extremely valuable to us. I'm glad you came, Michael, we can help you to realise your full potential.'

Leo turned to Michael, full of approval. 'You're more than an ordinary human, Michael. You'll probably be able to do some amazing things with training from Lord Xuan. What a stroke of luck for all of us.'

Michael grinned. 'Really?'

'Do you want to try the demon?' I said. 'I can release it, and it will attack you.'

Michael hesitated, then relaxed and put the sword away. He shook his head with remorse. 'I don't know if I can take one. After seeing what you can do, I'm probably not up to it. I think I'll leave it to you.' He shrugged. 'Sorry.'

'I can't tell you how proud I am of you, Michael. That was exactly the right thing to do,' Leo said.

Michael grinned again.

'I can't put it back, guys. Once it's out somebody has to take care of it. Lord Xuan's too weak to put it back into the jar.'

'Show him energy work,' Leo said. 'That will prove it beyond a doubt.'

'I know what chi gong is,' Michael said.

'What?'

'Chi, energy. Gong, work. He's right, Leo,' I said. 'Michael, the chi gong you see in the park is a very low level of the real thing. Let me show you some high level chi gong — some real energy work.'

I held my hands out and generated a ball of chi about the size of a basketball.

Michael's mouth fell open.

I moved the chi off my hand and floated it around the training room just for fun. The look on Michael's face was absolutely precious. I called the chi back and reabsorbed it.

'Dragon Ball,' Michael said.

Both Leo and I laughed softly.

'I suppose you could say that,' I said. 'I'll release the demon and destroy it with chi. Stand back, Michael, and if it goes for you, don't worry. Either just move out of the way or let us handle it. This won't take long.'

I released the demon and it hesitated, looking from one of us to the other. Eventually it lunged towards Michael and he leapt back.

I hit the demon with a big ball of chi and it exploded, dissipating into black feathery streamers. I received the demon's energy with my chi as it returned; what a rush.

'Did any of that stuff hit either of you?' I said. 'Did any of that black stuff get you, Michael?'

'We're okay,' Leo said. 'Missed us entirely.'

'How did you do that?' Michael whispered.

'Would you like to learn how to do that?' I said. 'There's a good chance that you could.'

'Hell, yeah,' Michael said, grinning. 'Can you do it too, Leo?'

I cut him off before he could embarrass Leo. 'Would you like to stay and learn from the Dark Lord?'

Michael stopped and put it together in his head. 'That really was a demon.'

I nodded.

'You really blew it up with a ball of energy, a ball of chi.'

Leo and I both nodded. Leo began to smile.

His voice filled with wonder. 'That was Pak Tai, God of Martial Arts.'

'In human form, yes,' I said. 'You can just call him Mr Chen.'

'My father is Bak Fu, the White Tiger God of the West.'

'In Cantonese, yes.'

'And that means,' he said with disbelief, 'that I really am *half goddamn tiger*.'

'Half Shen as well,' I said. 'He's more than just a tiger, he's the West Wind. Your father's a good friend of ours, and comes over all the time. You'll meet him very soon, I'm sure. Don't expect too much, though; he's an irresponsible bastard.'

'Lady Emma!' Leo said, shocked. 'I owe him my life!'

'Look me in the eye and tell me he's not an irresponsible bastard.'

Leo hesitated, then turned to speak to Michael. 'He tried to run off with Lady Emma the first time he met her. He is something of a womaniser, to say the least.'

'I believe it. My mother won't talk about him at all. Miss Donahoe.' Michael was clearly curious. 'How do you fit into all of this? You're obviously trained, but what's your role here? I know you told me that Mr Chen has a daughter, and that Leo's her guard, but where do you fit in? You didn't mention yourself. Are you his wife?'

'No,' I said. 'It's complicated. I'll tell you more later, but there's a few things we need to do first. After I talk to your mother, that is. It would be wrong for us to take you into training without her permission; you're too young. The first will be to swear you in. The second is to move you in. The third is to put you back in school.'

Leo nodded agreement.

'I don't want to go back to school, Miss Donahoe,' Michael said. 'I don't think it has anything to offer me.'

'It will be part of your job,' I said. 'We'll send you to the same school as Simone, and you can keep an eye on her. You can call us if a demon turns up, and help us to handle it.'

'Brilliant, Emma,' Leo said softly.

'Caught you not using the honorific,' I shot back as quickly as I could.

'Brilliant, *my Lady*,' Leo said pointedly, and bowed very deeply.

'Not good enough.' I saw my chance to rub it in. 'You will perform twenty-five level one sword katas immediately as punishment. Return the demon jar and put the weapons away. Come with me, Michael, we'll talk about the job.'

I slapped Leo lightly on the arm as I passed him to go out.

He tried very hard not to laugh, and bowed even deeper. 'With a great deal of pleasure, my *honoured* Lady.'

Michael followed me out, and glanced back at Leo with bewilderment. He had no idea what he was getting into. The demons were the least of it.

CHAPTER EIGHT

After I'd seen Michael out I went into John's office and sat across the desk from him. He turned away from the computer and leaned on his mess. Some of the papers slid off the desk onto the floor and he ignored them.

'Friday afternoon,' I said. 'But I think I need more than half a day for this lot. You've done exceptionally well this time.'

'Am I free?'

'Yep.'

He shrugged. 'Okay. I'll take her ice skating.'

'In the air conditioning.'

'I am *not* weak.'

'If you wore another colour you wouldn't be so hot.' I leaned back and sighed.

'Is there a problem?'

I straightened. 'His father is totally rampant. Are you sure you want a son of the Tiger in such close proximity to your daughter? It won't be long, you know. They grow up so fast.'

'I know,' he said, almost a moan of pain. 'And I won't be around to see it. Maybe that's not such a bad thing. I've never raised a child and I'd probably mess it up badly. You'll be better to guide her through her growing years, you're so much wiser in the ways of humans.'

'Don't be ridiculous, you're her *father*. She needs you more than anything.' Then I heard what he'd said. 'She can't be the first child you've ever had, you've been around for centuries. You can't expect me to believe that Simone's your first child. Really! You think I'm stupid?'

'I know you're not.' He smiled slightly. 'She really is. She is the first human child I have fathered. The White Tiger was delighted; he's been harassing me to have a human child for ages.'

'*Human* child? What other children have you had?' I said, then raised my hands to stop him. 'Don't answer that, I don't want to know. Just tell me if I've ever met any of them.'

'No.'

'Okay, then. Anyway, back to the point. I'm not sure this is a good idea. Something will probably grow between them as she gets older. It's inevitable. Michael will understand what she's going through; they'll have had similar experiences.'

'That's why the Tiger has been harassing me,' he said with grim humour. 'He's wanted me to have a human child for a long time so that we could formally seal the union between our Houses. The minute Simone was born he tried to talk me into arranging something with one of his sons. When he finds out about Michael he'll be thrilled.'

I glared at him. 'Don't you *dare* promise my little Simone to anybody, Xuan Wu. She will choose her own partners, and your politics will have absolutely nothing to do with it.'

He grinned. 'Yes, my Lady. I agree with you, anyway.' He sobered. 'But I want you to know something. I trust you to guide her. If she chooses somebody while I'm gone, and you approve, then I won't have a problem with it. And if it's Michael, it's Michael.' He paused, thinking. 'There's quite an age difference, though. He's nine years older than her.'

I collapsed over the desk, silently laughing.

'Which is absolutely nothing,' he said with amusement, 'compared to the more than four thousand years between us. I see your point.'

'I suppose I'd better call his mother then,' I said. 'She and I have a lot to talk about.'

'Humph.' He rose with fluid grace and pushed his chair back. 'Human women comparing notes on how you survive living with male Shen.' He spoke with mock dignity as he retied his hair. 'I will be in the training room meditating, and I do not wish to be disturbed.'

Monica knocked, then poked her head around my bedroom door. 'American lady, Ms MacLaren, here to see you ma'am.'

I rose. 'Thanks, Monica. Is Simone okay?'

Monica smiled and opened the door wider for me. 'She's making cookies with Charlie and me.'

'I hope she hasn't trashed the kitchen too much.'

'Not a problem.' Monica hesitated, unsure. 'The office is very bad, ma'am.'

I patted her shoulder. 'I know. He's taking Simone out Friday afternoon, and I'll tidy it then. You can come in and dust before they're back.'

She smiled with relief. 'Thanks, ma'am.'

I leaned in to whisper. 'It drives you crazy too?'

She nodded, still smiling.

I stopped at the entry to the living room and studied Rhonda MacLaren. She saw me and returned the look, sizing me up, and obviously wasn't impressed; I wore my usual scruffy jeans and shirt, and my hair was a mess.

She was immaculately groomed and wore a smart navy business suit. She had her blonde hair neatly pinned back from her attractive face. No wonder the Tiger had gone for her; her intelligence and strong will shone through her beauty.

Monica brought some Chinese tea and I served. I was curious about Ms MacLaren's history, but decided to tackle the matter at hand first. If I gained her trust then she would be more open with us. Michael hadn't told her about John; he really was very impressive. Any other kid would have stormed home and confronted his mother. Michael had left it to me.

'Please just call me Emma, Ms MacLaren. I know Michael's told you he wants to come and work here live-in. But he's very young, and I wanted to make sure it's okay with you first.'

She sighed. 'Just Rhonda, Emma. I appreciate you talking to me like this, and asking me first. I don't want him to move out, but I really can't stop him if he's determined. And if he's going somewhere good, it may be better than having him sit at home being miserable. He's not doing anything right now, not going to school, no job, and he'll get into trouble if I don't do something. I'm in and out of Hong Kong all the time for my business, and I leave him at home alone with the domestic helper quite often. I just thank God Leo has taken him under his wing. Without Leo, I think Michael would already be in jail.'

'You're probably right. Michael's very talented at martial arts, and that makes him a target for recruitment by some unsavoury groups.'

'What are the details of Michael's job, if he comes to work here?'

'Let me tell you the situation.' I leaned back, working out where to begin. I decided to tackle it head-on. 'Leo works as bodyguard for a little girl by the name of Simone Chen. Michael will be training to replace Leo.'

Rhonda nodded.

'Simone's mother is dead. Simone's father, John Chen Wu, is really Xuan Wu, Dark Lord of the North.'

She went completely still.

'Michael would be working for the North Wind, Rhonda. We know his father is the White Tiger, the West Wind. We already told him that.'

'You had no right to do that.' Rhonda rose stiffly. 'You're probably one of them as well. I want nothing to do with you creatures any more. Don't ever contact me or my son again, you cause nothing but misery. I'm going.'

'Wait.' I jumped up and put my hand on her arm. 'I'm not a Shen. I'm just the nanny. Well, I used to be. I know what the White Tiger is like; he tried it with me too. I don't blame you for falling for him. But Xuan Wu is completely different. He's only ever been married to a single human woman in his whole history, and he only has one human child, and that's Simone.'

She stared at me. 'Is he really that different?'

'Yes I am,' John said from the doorway. He came in and sat on the couch, stretching his long legs in front of him. His torn black cotton pants were really starting to fall apart and I made a mental note to throw them away and send Leo shopping. 'Monica, another tea cup!'

Monica rushed in with a tea cup for him, then disappeared back into the kitchen.

'Sit down, Ms MacLaren,' he said. 'Let me tell you about myself, and what I can do for young Michael.'

After we'd explained the situation for about ten minutes, Simone came out of the kitchen with a plate of chocolate chip cookies. She served them around, then put the plate onto the coffee table and crawled into John's lap. He wrapped his arms around her and kissed the top of her head. Rhonda didn't miss that.

He concentrated.

Charlie poked her head out of the kitchen across the hall from the living room. 'Of course you can eat them, sir, completely vegetarian. Simone made them for you.' She smiled around at us and returned to the kitchen.

John reached around Simone to try one of the biscuits. Simone watched him carefully as he took a bite.

'Good,' he said through a mouthful of biscuit. He raised it to see it. 'What's this black stuff?'

'Chocolate,' Simone said. 'Chocolate chip.'

'Oh. I thought it was red bean. Needs milk with it, it's very sweet,' he said, still through the biscuit. 'Soy milk would be good.'

'Don't talk with your mouth full, Daddy. That's rude for Westerners.'

'Okay.'

Simone leaned back to put her head on his shoulder and snuggled into him. He pulled her tight and took another bite of the biscuit.

Rhonda's face softened.

'Will you let Michael come and work for us, Rhonda?' I said.

'Let me think about it,' she said. 'I'm not sure I want him to follow in his father's footsteps too much. I was hoping he would just lead a normal life, away from all of this.'

'It's his birthright, Rhonda,' John said softly.

Rhonda snorted with disdain. 'His birthright is to be completely ignored by his father, who is too busy chasing women and horses to care for his mother.'

'The White Tiger always tells his women the

situation before he takes them,' John said. 'You knew what you were getting into.'

Rhonda sighed. 'I thought I was different. I thought I could change him. I thought I was so special that he wouldn't need anybody else.'

'You all think that,' John said sadly. 'Every single one of you. But the others stayed. You left.'

'I was wasting my time. I was surprised that he let me go, but in the end I think he didn't give a damn one way or the other. He has provided well for us, I don't need to worry about money. It's a sad episode of my life that I want to forget. But I did gain a wonderful son out of the whole sorry mess, and that's made it sort of worthwhile.'

'What are you doing with yourself now, Rhonda?' I said.

'I started a business with the money he gave me. I deal in antique furniture from China. It's quite lucrative. I don't actually need the child support money now, but it's nice to hit him where it hurts, so I still collect. I suppose if Michael moves in with you, I'll tell the Tiger not to worry any more.'

'I can see where Michael gets his spirit,' John said. 'He is a very impressive young man. I hope you'll let us take him on.'

'Will you be teaching him martial arts?'

'Yes. It will be part of his job.'

'Another part of his job will be to go to the same school as Simone and guard her,' I said. 'And I will expect his grades to be good as well.'

Simone looked at me. She hadn't known that. She didn't say anything.

'He shouldn't have left school, but he's old enough to choose for himself,' Rhonda said. 'If you can make him go to school, then it will be worth it. Does the Tiger ever come here?' She turned to John. 'You're one of the Winds, too.'

'He's over here all the time, Rhonda,' John said. 'He's one of my best friends. Michael will see him quite often.'

'He doesn't seem to have any romantic notions about his father,' I said. 'In fact, when he does finally see him, he may break his nose.'

'Take a photo for me if he does, please.' Rhonda rose. 'Well, I think that settles it for me. Michael can move in here whenever it suits him.'

'Sit back down, Rhonda,' I said. 'There's one more thing I have to tell you, and it's about Leo. John, take Simone out for me, will you?'

'I'll be right back,' John said, and carried Simone into the kitchen. Simone didn't protest.

Rhonda watched them leave, then turned to me. 'Did you just order around one of the Four Winds?'

'I just ordered around the Sovereign of the Four Winds, Ruler of the Northern Heavens, and Right Hand of the Jade Emperor Himself,' I said. 'It's a long story, and sometimes even I can't believe it. I must tell you the whole thing one day.'

Rhonda sat and shook her head. 'What else do you want to tell me?'

'Leo has AIDS, Rhonda. As long as he stays with John, the virus is dormant. As soon as John leaves us, the virus will become active, and Leo will probably have less than a year. That's why we're bringing Michael in; we'll need a bodyguard for Simone when both Leo and John are gone. I hope that doesn't change your attitude about Michael working here.'

'If you're suggesting that Leo and Michael are more than friends, you're wrong. Michael has already had a few girlfriends.'

'I'm not suggesting anything of the sort,' I said. 'I just want you to know. I want to be completely open and honest with you about this, and want you to feel that we're not hiding anything.'

John came back in without Simone, sat and poured himself more tea. 'Yes, young Emma here is very big on being completely open and honest.'

'Give it a rest, old man.'

He chuckled good-naturedly.

'I don't think that's a problem, Emma,' Rhonda said. 'Leo is terrific, and it's a shame this had to happen to him. I suppose I have to trust you and John.' She studied John. 'How long do you have?'

John smiled sadly over the top of his tea cup. 'Not more than three years. You know how hard it is for us to stay in human form. This is one of the most difficult things I have ever done.'

'And you're doing it for your little girl.'

He nodded.

She looked from John to me. 'Are you two married?'

'No, it's a long story,' I said. 'It may happen one day if we're both very lucky, but at this stage it's not possible. It's mostly to do with the fact that he is a Shen. And that I'm completely nuts.'

John nodded agreement and I glanced at him impatiently. He saw that I wanted to thump him and grinned.

Rhonda watched with wonder. 'You must tell me the whole thing later. But I have to go. Michael's waiting for me to let him know my decision.'

'You will be welcome up here any time,' John said. 'Feel free to come and check on Michael whenever you please.'

I rose. Rhonda stood as well, and I showed her to the door. 'Give me a call sometime, Rhonda. We'll meet for lunch and share a good moan about the trials of living with male Shen.'

'I heard that,' John called from the living room.

'Good,' I said loudly without turning back. 'It's even worse living with a reptile. At least the Tiger has nice fur.'

'A reptile?'

'I'm a Turtle,' John yelled.

'Yes, you damn well are,' I shouted back. I grinned at Rhonda. She didn't seem to understand the insult.

Rhonda shook her head. 'He really is different. You're very lucky.'

'I know.'

He's here, Emma. At the door.

The doorbell rang and Monica answered it; I heard the voices.

I went out to the hallway. Leo and Michael were kicking their shoes off at the door. Michael had a duffel bag.

'Don't worry, ma'am, I'll take care of him,' Leo said. 'I'll show him around, introduce him to everybody, stuff like that.'

I want him to come into the training room and swear allegiance at the same time, Leo.

'Yes, sir.'

Michael's face went completely blank.

'Oh, you heard him,' I said. 'He was on broadcast mode, everybody in the household heard him. I wish he wouldn't do that. And he's not supposed to be listening anyway. If he does it again he'll be in serious trouble.'

Sorry.

'You're still listening.'

Ma'am.

Michael grinned, then tried to control his face.

'Leave it with me, ma'am,' Leo said.

'Okay.' I went back to my room and my thesis.

Later, there was a tap on the bedroom door.

'Come.'

Leo poked his head around. 'Charlie grabbed him off me and told him the whole story. Right now they're in the kitchen and she's trying to see if she can feed him so much he explodes.'

'Did he swear allegiance?'

'Yep.'

'Did he understand what it means?'

Leo opened the door and came in. 'Yeah. He knew. And he did it anyway. He's a great kid.'

'I don't know what we'd do without you, Leo.'

'Neither do I.' He went out.

CHAPTER NINE

A few weeks later John, Gold and I sat around the dining table and studied the student lists.

'How many do you think we need to recruit?' I said.

'Gold?'

'We should bring on another three hundred to guard the Mountain when the demons have returned to strength,' Gold said, 'but we don't have room for them. Bright Mansions is full. There's plenty of room in Wan Chai to train them, but nowhere for them to live.'

'We could buy another residential building in Happy Valley,' John said.

'Good idea, my Lord,' Gold said. 'The market is down, there are some good buys. We could buy an older building, demolish it, and construct something purpose-built. We could even do that with the North Point building, put up something with more space.'

'At the current rate of construction, Gold, how long before we can start moving students back to the Mountain?' I said.

Gold's boyish face went pensive. 'I think about five years, my Lady.' His face cleared. 'I see your point.'

'Yes,' John said. 'It will take that long to build to

purpose anyway. Forget it. We'll buy something in the Valley and put them there. See to it. Dismissed.'

'My Lord,' Gold said, and disappeared.

John turned to me. 'I don't know how I managed without you, Emma.'

'Neither do I.' I glared at him. 'It's August already.'

He leaned back and put his hands behind his head. 'I don't have *time*, Emma.' He threw himself forward again and rubbed his hands over his face, then tied back his hair.

'You'll have all the time in the world if you fade out and leave us. But we won't be able to defend Simone.'

'Simone can call a Celestial Master now. You don't really need me any more. I could go now.'

I shot to my feet, horrified. 'Don't you dare leave us, Xuan Wu!' I shouted. 'We *need* you! You can't go!'

He sat unmoving, his face expressionless.

'Don't go, please, John.' I fell to sit. No. He was right. He could go. Simone would be safe if she could call a Celestial Master.

'You wouldn't be safe though, Emma. I need to stay near you.'

'My safety is beside the point. Simone's the one we need to protect.'

'I need to protect both of you.'

I crossed my arms on the pile of papers in front of me and put my chin on them. 'We need you here. Please don't go yet. Wait until you can't stay any longer. We *need* you. *I* need you.'

He smiled gently. 'If I'm going to stay around then I'd better see Mercy.'

I leaned back and sighed with relief. 'You gave me a terrible fright just then, John. Please don't do that again. Promise you'll stay absolutely as long as you can.'

'I promise you, Emma. Of course I will stay as long as I possibly can. I want to be with you. I want to be with both of you. I was just teasing.'

'You'll be teasing on the other side of your shell next time,' I growled. 'I'll clear our diaries for the week after next and we can all go to Paris. We'll need to have it done before Simone starts school. Michael should come as well; some travel will open his mind, and he can meet Kwan Yin. We can return Charlie to London while we're in Paris. How's that?'

He spread his hands across the table. 'Whatever you organise is fine with me. I am in your capable hands.'

'I wish,' I said with feeling, and he went expressionless again. 'Call Kwan Yin and tell her you're coming.'

He remained unmoving.

'Do it right now, Xuan Wu.'

He pulled himself upright. 'Is that an order?'

'Damn straight it is.'

He leaned across the table and glared at me. I leaned forward as well and glowered back. We faced off across the table. I was about to shout at him when Ms Kwan appeared next to me. 'Don't worry, Emma, he called me. I will be waiting for you, Ah Wu. Look after yourself and your family.'

He nodded to her but she had already disappeared.

'Happy?' he growled.

'Not until I have you in Paris and locked up with her,' I growled back. 'Go and meditate. Guard your energy. You're probably running on empty.'

He grinned and pushed his chair away from the table. He was.

A week later Charlie came in to clear the dishes from the family dinner.

'Sit, Charlie, Monica can do that,' I said. 'Meeting time. I've arranged for us to go to Paris next week.'

Simone wriggled in her seat. 'I want to go to the Eiffel Tower!'

'You always want to go to the Eiffel Tower,' John and I said in unison, then shared an indulgent smile.

'I've made the arrangements,' I said. 'Out of Macau, as usual ...' I hesitated, then shook my head. 'It feels very strange to be the one saying this.'

'Get used to it,' Leo said softly.

I ignored him. 'Out of Macau, as usual, next week. When we arrive in Paris, we'll pop you on the train to London, Charlie, and you can organise the house in Kensington for us.'

'My Lady.'

'Oh, come on, Charlie, please,' I said, exasperated. 'There's really no need for that.'

She just smiled.

'We're going to London too?' Simone squeaked, eyes wide. 'I want to go to —'

'The Science Museum,' Leo finished for her.

'Well I *do*, silly Leo.'

Michael sat quietly. I understood: he was listening carefully and didn't want to mess up. At least he knew the situation. When I went to Paris, I hadn't even known why we were there until we'd been attacked by demons. Then I realised that Michael didn't know why we were going to Paris either.

'Stay here after everybody's gone, and I'll explain for you, Michael.'

He nodded appreciation.

'We'll be staying in Paris for five days ...' I turned to John. 'Are you sure five days is enough? We can spend the whole week in Paris if we have to. You needed a good ten days after the Attack.'

'Five days is sufficient.'

'Okay. Five days in Paris, then two days in London, then back here to prepare these young people for school.'

Leo and Michael scowled and I glared both of them down.

'Everybody happy?'

Charlie opened her mouth, then closed it again.

'Go on, Charlie, this is family.'

'My Lady.' I sighed, but she continued anyway. 'My Lady. Before we go, may I take some time to shop for my relatives? I'd like to go to the markets, Stanley and maybe Temple Street, to buy gifts for them.'

'Temple Street!' Simone said, excited again.

'You want to come too, Princess?'

'Ooh, yes please, Charlie, I love Stanley and Temple Street. Can I go with Charlie, Daddy?' She stopped and thought. 'I have some money I can spend too.'

'You can go, Simone. When is a good time, Emma?'

'How about Saturday?' I said. 'Temple Street will be really buzzing. I don't have anything on at the Academy.'

'That would be perfect, my Lady,' Charlie said.

'I'm teaching all day Saturday, Emma, I won't finish until six,' Leo said. 'I can't come to Stanley during the day, but Temple Street night market I can do.'

I considered the options. Both locations were extremely busy and full of people. Demons usually preferred to attack us when we were isolated. 'I should be able to guard Simone with Michael as backup in Stanley. We'll have dinner here, pick you up and go to Temple Street. Can you come as well, John?'

'I have some of the Generals coming on Saturday, looks like it'll be a long one. Leo, yourself, Michael — I think that's sufficient.'

Simone scowled; she didn't want Michael along.

'Give it up, Simone,' I said. 'I think you're right, John, the three of us will be plenty.'

Everybody went out, leaving me to talk to Michael. Monica brought in some tea.

Michael's face was intense. 'Why does he have to

go to Paris, Miss Donahoe? What's the big deal with this?'

I sighed. This was hard.

'Mr Chen has to retain human form to stay and guard Simone. It's a tremendous drain on his energy to stay in human form for such a long time; normally Shen like him shuttle between a number of different forms. What he's doing in staying with us is extremely difficult.'

'How many forms does he have?'

'Three that I know of, including the human form that he has now. We'll probably never see the True Form.'

'True Form?'

'Animal. I've never seen it. I think Leo has. If he changes to the animal form, then he'll be gone for a long time; he won't have the strength to return to human form.'

'What animal is he?' Michael paused, thinking. 'North Wind. I know that the East is a Dragon, and of course the West is a Tiger. But I don't remember. What animal is Mr Chen?'

I nearly choked on it. 'A Turtle.'

His jaw dropped and his eyes went wide. Then he lit up into a huge delighted grin. 'You know that calling someone a turtle is slang for calling them a —'

'Michael.' I cut him off. 'I understand every single insult attached to the turtle. I've heard them all. I know what the poor beast's head and neck resemble. I know that the Ancients thought that the male turtle had no sex organs. I know that turtles are notorious for their ...' I hesitated, searching for the right word. '*Behaviour*. I know about the egg business. I know it all. So does Mr Chen. So watch your mouth. Okay?'

His mouth snapped shut and he nodded. He could see that he'd pushed it too far.

'Mr Chen's True Form is even stranger than that. He's a combination of two animals, a snake and a turtle. He claims that right now he's lost the Serpent part of him and doesn't know where it is.'

'He's lost part of himself? How could that happen?'

'Even he doesn't know how it happened. He really is extremely weird. Compared to him, your father is almost normal.'

'What about my father?' Michael said. 'He has different forms too?'

'Yep. Simone likes to have rides on his True Form, his tiger form. It's enormous.'

'He's really a tiger?'

'He really is. Anyway, back to Mr Chen. He's constantly draining his energy by staying in human form. He's really weak while he's like this. He goes to Paris and meets Kwan Yin. She helps him by feeding him energy for a few days — tops him up, so to speak — so that he can retain the form and stay with us.'

Michael nodded silently, listening carefully.

'You have to understand something.' I ran my hands through my hair. This was very tough. 'As soon as Simone is able to defend herself, Mr Chen will revert to True Form and leave us. He'll be very drained. It will take him a long time to come back. Maybe more than a lifetime. Ms Kwan, Kwan Yin, says something between ten and a hundred years. I'll look after Simone, and all the other stuff, when he's gone.'

Michael's face didn't shift. 'How long before he goes?'

I swallowed it. 'He thinks probably when Simone's about eight years old.'

'She's nearly six now, Miss Donahoe.'

'I know. I know every minute of the day. We have to keep him here until she's able to defend herself.'

'I understand. Is that why you two never married? Because he has such a short time left?'

'No, it's not, Michael.' Something inside me really began to hurt. 'The fact that he'll only be around for a short time makes no difference to either of us at all.' He opened his mouth but I cut him off. 'You notice that we never touch each other?'

'Yeah.' He grinned. 'You two are really old-fashioned.'

'No, we're not.' I smiled through the misery. 'Exactly the opposite, in fact. Which is funny, considering how old he is. The reason we never touch is because if he touches me, he could kill me.'

He went completely still.

'If we were to physically share our feelings, even with just a touch, we would share our energy as well. And he is very drained. He would suck the energy out of me, suck the life out of me, and kill me. We have to be extremely careful.'

Michael gestured with one hand across the table. 'Then how come you wear his ring?'

I glanced at the ring, a small square piece of very green jade on a plain gold band, with three studs on either side. It was supposed to be sentient, but I had been wearing it non-stop for months now and it still hadn't woken to me. I wondered if it ever would.

'If he ever comes back in my lifetime we will be able to touch. Then we can be what we want to be for each other. He's promised to come back for me. I've promised to wait for him.' I looked up at Michael and smiled. 'And that's the whole story.'

'I hope it happens for you, Miss Donahoe,' he said quietly.

'Thanks, Michael, you don't know how much I appreciate it.' I shrugged it off and spoke more briskly. 'So that's why we're going to Paris. It's a long way from the demons' power centre, so it's a good place to do it. Mr Chen will be locked up with Kwan Yin, and the three of us will take Simone sightseeing. I think you'll enjoy it.'

'Sounds like fun. I'm looking forward to meeting the real Kwan Yin.'

'She's a wonderful person. She's very special. You'll love her when you meet her.'

'Why are we going from Macau, and not Chek Lap Kok?'

'Oh, you'll like this. We're going on Mr Chen's private jet.'

'A *private jet*! That is *so sweet*! Wait until I tell my friends about it!'

'Remember, you have to be careful what you tell your friends, Michael. Don't give anything away, please.'

'Yes, ma'am. Don't worry on that account. I have to be careful what I tell people, 'cause no way would they believe the truth.' He hesitated; he'd obviously thought of something. 'Will Simone be okay when she starts school? It's sort of really normal for her; she may say something she shouldn't.'

'I sincerely hope she'll be all right. If she gets into trouble I hope you can help her out.'

He nodded. 'Yes, ma'am.'

'Anything else?' He shook his head. 'Okay, dismissed.'

Michael went out. I sat and drank the tea.

Are you okay?

'I'm fine.'

He brushed over my hair. It was like a hand touching me with nobody there. He dropped it onto my shoulder.

'Don't do that. It's a waste of your energy and you're close to empty. Don't risk it.'

The touch disappeared. I sipped the tea.

'Are you still there?'

Yes.

I sighed.

It breaks my heart to do this to you.

'I have never been so happy in my entire life.'

You are a fool, Emma Donahoe.

'So are you, Xuan Wu.'

It will happen for us.

'I know. I'm okay, you can stop watching me. Guard your energy, stupid turtle.'

Yes, ma'am.

I sat in the dining room alone for a while after his presence left me.

CHAPTER TEN

'And a *Snake Mother* came in and said it wanted Leo's skin,' Simone said from the back of the car. 'And he told it to come and get it, and then ...' I couldn't see her from the driver's seat, but her voice became breathless. 'And then Leo *pulled its tongue out* and *killed* it.'

'That must have been very scary,' Charlie said.

'Leo looks after me. Emma looks after me too. They protect me. I'll be okay.'

'Of course you will, dear,' Charlie said.

Michael glanced at me from the front passenger seat.

'I'll tell you later,' I said softly. 'But believe me, you don't want to know.'

'Michael would probably run if *he* saw a Mother,' Simone said.

'That was a very nasty thing to say, Simone, I'm surprised at you,' I said. 'Michael's sworn allegiance, he's a Retainer, he'd never run. Tell him sorry.'

'Sorry,' Simone said, sullen.

Michael snorted with derision and looked out the window.

'It's so pretty,' Charlie said, watching the scenery of Hong Kong Island as we travelled down Stubbs Road.

Everywhere there was even the tiniest square of flat land, there was a highrise. Kowloon, on the other side of the harbour, was a mass of tall buildings of different sizes and shapes, mostly residential blocks. Hardly anyone lived in a house in Hong Kong; there wasn't the space.

'But the pollution is bad, isn't it?' she went on. 'You can hardly see the other side of the harbour.'

'When it's very hot like this, there's an inversion layer,' I said. 'The pollution's trapped.'

'I see.'

We came to the bottom of Stubbs Road and topped out over Wong Nai Chung Gap. As we passed the ridge, the scenery of the south side opened up. There were fewer highrises here, less densely packed, with more greenery. Some of the residential blocks were only three or four storeys tall.

We drove through Shouson Hill, a prestigious enclave of low-rise apartment blocks built around the gently undulating hill, then rounded the curves of the south coast of the island to Deep Water Bay.

The usual Saturday crowd packed the beach and people filled the water within the shark net. Rubbish floated at the end of the beach; it broke my heart. John could never swim in this water, in his own element. I had an inspiration: I would take him back to Australia when it was warmer there. I could visit my family, and he could swim in the sea. It would do him so much good. And then I realised: my family would see everything. Maybe not such a good idea.

'Ocean Park, Charlie,' Simone said, pointing across the bay to the peninsula on the other side. Deep Water Bay gave a good view of the cable car that wound around the peninsula of Ocean Park.

'Would you like to go there with me? Before I go back to London?' Charlie said.

'No,' Simone said. 'I don't like Ocean Park. I went with Leo and Monica before Emma came, and bad things happened. I don't like it.'

'What happened?' Michael asked me softly.

'One of the dolphins was sick and talked to her,' I said, matching his low tones. 'It cried for her help, and she couldn't do anything.'

'I *hate* Ocean Park,' Simone said.

The road outside the car park at Repulse Bay was blocked with people queuing to go into the car park, even though it was full.

'If queuing ever becomes an Olympic sport, Hong Kong will win all the medals,' Michael said.

Simone giggled. 'That's funny.'

The traffic jam finally cleared and we passed the beach to the far south side of the island. Fortunately Stanley wasn't too packed; everybody was at the beach. I found a place to park and we all piled out.

'You know your way around, Charlie?' I said.

'I haven't been here in a while, ma'am, but I think I remember. The market isn't very big, anyway.'

'Let's just wander around and see what we find. Stay close to Simone, Michael.' I glanced around at them. 'While we're in there, guys, can we drop the "Lady" and "ma'am" stuff, please? It'll attract unnecessary attention. Just Emma, okay?'

'Yes, ma'am,' Charlie and Michael said in unison, and I sighed.

'Can I call you Mummy?' Simone said brightly.

I felt like I'd been hit in the stomach.

I knelt on one knee and took both Simone's hands in mine. 'Simone, darling, I'm not your mummy. Your mummy was married to your daddy. She died. I'm not your mummy, so you can't call me that. It wouldn't be right.'

'Okay.' She wasn't fazed; it obviously wasn't an issue

for her. 'When you marry Daddy, can I call you Mummy then?'

I brushed some hair from her eyes. I would love her to, I really would. I doubted I'd ever have children of my own; I'd probably be too old when John returned for me. If he *did* return for me. She was the closest thing I would ever have. 'No, Simone. It wouldn't be right.'

'Okay, Emma.' Her little face was serious. 'I would like to, you know. But if you don't want me to, that's fine.' She threw her arms around my neck and kissed me on the cheek. She released me and took Charlie's hand. 'Let's go.'

I rose. 'One more thing, Simone.'

She smiled up at me.

'If you sense any demons, let us know straightaway, okay? Just say "bad people" or something.'

Simone dropped Charlie's hand and put her little hands on her hips, tilting her head with impatience. 'Of course I will, silly Emma.' She took Charlie's hand again. 'Let's go.'

I saw Michael's face. He had watched Simone's little performance with something approaching contempt. He noticed me and nodded, professional again.

We walked down the narrow hill to Stanley market, which was a maze of narrow laneways winding through the village. Each stall had an awning, and the awnings stretched from one side of the lane to the other, giving the impression of being indoors.

'I haven't been here in a long time, Emma,' Charlie said. 'I think it was better when I came before. Everything seems more expensive now.'

'It's still cheaper than London for this sort of thing, though, isn't it?' I said.

'You can't even buy this sort of thing in London. And everything's cheaper than London, Emma,' she said. 'London's nearly as expensive as Hong Kong.'

'Nowhere's as expensive as Hong Kong,' I said. 'Everything costs more here.'

'Not Chinese vegetables,' she shot back, and we laughed together.

Charlie bought some touristy T-shirts for her nieces and nephews back in London, and some little Chinese toys. She found some nice handicrafts for her other relatives: cloisonné and ceramics. One stall had some delightful Chinese papercuts under a pile of old magazines and she bought them all.

'You should go to China Products in Central as well,' I said. 'No, hold on, there's one in Wan Chai. Next time I go down to the building in Wan Chai, I'll drop you at the China Products there. You'll be able to find some really good stuff.'

'That's a good idea, Emma. Whenever it suits you should be fine.'

'I'm teaching Monday. Come with me. I'll take Simone to the Academy and drop you at the store. You should be fine by yourself. No danger if you're not with Simone; they know you're not trained and it's not honourable to go after you.'

'Thanks, Emma.' Charlie reached out and squeezed my hand. 'I appreciate it.'

'Not a problem.' I stopped at a raised step outside one of the shops. 'Sit here and have a drink of water, it's very hot.'

'I'll buy some cold water, ma'am,' Michael said, and trotted down the hill to a hole-in-the-wall shop selling drinks and snacks. He returned with some mineral water for everybody. The water bottles were already soaked with condensation from the humidity. Charlie lowered herself to sit on the step and fanned her face, then placed the bottle of water on her flushed cheek.

'It's not the heat, it's the humidity,' she said.

'Take your time. Rest. You have a drink too, Simone.'

'At least it's cloudy,' Charlie said. 'If the sun was out it would be impossible.'

I shrugged. 'That's summer in Hong Kong.'

'You're used to it?'

'I don't think anybody ever gets used to it.'

'So what do you do?'

'Be like Daddy,' Simone said cheekily. She waved her bottle of water. 'Stay inside in the air conditioning, and if you go out, have a shower straightaway when you're inside again.'

We had dinner at home before Leo took us to Temple Street.

'Sir on the phone, ma'am,' Monica said through the door between the dining room and the kitchen.

I put my chopsticks down, went into the kitchen and took the call on the phone next to the door.

John sounded close to the end of his patience. 'I could really use you down here, Emma. The Generals are being particularly difficult; there are some major problems in the Northern Heavens because I never go there any more. It's like taking the battery out of a toy or something. No energy up there. All the trees are dying.'

'We're going to Temple Street, John. I'm needed to guard.'

'It will be very busy, you won't be at much risk from demons.'

'It's not just demons I'm worried about. You know the sort of stuff that goes on down there.'

He sounded amused. 'That's just an excuse and you know it.'

'Simone needs me.'

'All right, you're out of it just this once. But next time they're giving me hell you're coming to help me out. You can't avoid this forever, it will be your responsibility too. Okay?'

'Yes, my Lord. And speak English.'

'Damn,' he said softly, and hung up.

I sat in the back of the big car with Charlie and Simone. Michael rode shotgun next to Leo. Temple Street market was in Kowloon, across the harbour in Yau Ma Tei district.

Leo drove us down the hill between the highrises of Wan Chai and into Causeway Bay. The road flanked the north shore of the island, four lanes each way. At Causeway Bay we entered the Cross-Harbour Tunnel. Two more lanes merged with the existing four, then everybody had to take turns to enter the two tunnel lanes. Leo inched through the traffic and poked the nose of the Mercedes into the next lane to grab his space; it wouldn't be handed to him. Anybody who sat back and waited for someone to politely let them into a lane could quite easily become a target of road rage. Everybody pushed; but as John had said, there was method in the madness.

As soon as we entered the tunnel the traffic accelerated to the speed limit. We shot through the autopay toll gate on the other side and we were in Kowloon.

The scenery opened up on Kowloon side. There was more room to move here, but all the buildings were still highrises. The expressway continued north and we exited at Mong Kok onto Nathan Road, the main thoroughfare through Kowloon. People packed the sidewalks and the shops were all open, their lights blazing. Typical Saturday night in Hong Kong.

The Mercedes' windows fogged up on the outside from the humidity and Leo used the wipers to clear them. He didn't even have the air conditioning on terribly cold. The humidity was close on a hundred per cent, and the temperature was still blistering.

'If it's too much for you, let me know, Charlie,' I said. 'The temperature doesn't vary much from day to night. It's still awfully hot.'

'I'll make it,' Charlie said cheerfully. 'There are still some things I need to buy.'

'If you can't do it, just say so. I'll go out later and collect anything you want,' Leo said.

Charlie's voice softened. 'Thanks, Leo. I think just a cold electrolyte drink when we get there, and I should be okay.'

'Pocari Sweat,' Simone said.

'What, Simone?'

'Pocari Sweat,' Simone repeated patiently.

'Japanese electrolyte drink,' I said, and waited for it.

'They have a drink called *sweat*?'

'Actually it's not too bad,' I said.

'I have to try some,' Charlie said with enthusiasm.

We entered Shanghai Street. Temple Street was next, but the road was blocked for the market. We parked in a large car park at the entrance to Temple Street.

Fortune tellers lined the narrow road to the car park. They worked from small folding tables with folding stools, their spaces on the pavement carefully marked by the government. Large banners hung above the tables describing their skills, some in both English and Chinese. Some read heads and faces. Others read palms. Some used tortoise shells and the *Yi Ching*; John would have been horrified. A large number of people wandered from stall to stall and sat to have their fortunes told. Charlie watched, fascinated.

Leo carefully eased the car up the ramp into the car park and took a ticket from the gate. A few suspicious-looking young men loitered at the entrance and eyed us curiously, but a large black Mercedes was one of the most common types of car in Hong Kong.

'Any of them demons, Simone?' Leo said.

'Nope,' Simone said.

The car park started at the third floor after a very long ramp. We went left and up again.

'Look, Charlie,' I said. 'This is an unusual building. The expressway goes right through the middle, at about the fourth floor.'

Charlie watched out the window as we went past the expressway. The road went in one side of the building and out the other. Leo drove up a ramp inside the car park to pass the road.

It was a long way up before we found a parking space; obviously a busy night in Temple Street. Leo gingerly edged the car backwards into the space. The space was so narrow he had to fold in the side mirrors to avoid the pillars.

'Why does the road go through the building, Emma?' Simone said.

'The building was already here when they built the expressway,' I said. 'It would have cost a lot of money to knock it down, so they just put the road right through.'

'What's it like to drive through the building?' Charlie said.

'Like a little tunnel. You don't even realise you've been through the building until you're out the other side.' I opened the door to help Simone out. 'Let's go and see how much Hello Kitty stuff Simone can buy in one night.'

Charlie was obviously not impressed when we entered the lift; it was filthy and smelled of urine. The buttons were black with dirt. At the ground floor the lift stopped with a lurching jerk, and Simone squeaked and grabbed my hand.

'Don't worry, sweetheart,' I said. 'This lift always does that.'

'You come here often?' Charlie said.

'Not really. I used to come here to buy toys for my relatives in Australia, but I saw them at the beginning of this year, so they'll be happy for a while.'

The smell of urine was even stronger when we left the lift; the building had public toilets on the ground floor outside the car park entrance. We hurried past.

A middle-aged Chinese couple sang Chinese opera under a makeshift marquee across the road. A trio of musicians on Chinese instruments accompanied them. A small crowd of passers-by had gathered to watch them.

'Sounds like someone's torturing a cat,' I whispered to Leo.

Leo bent to speak into my ear. 'I like it. But then again, I hate cats.'

During the day, Temple Street was a normal Kowloon thoroughfare, lined with shops on both sides. In the evening, stalls were set up, leaving a narrow passageway down the middle. The large number of people moving between the stalls caused a crush.

Leo walked in front of us and cut a swathe through the crowd. Michael brought up the rear, very serious and professional.

'Mind your bag, Charlie,' I said quietly. 'There's a lot of pickpockets here, targeting the wealthy tourists. This is something of a gang centre.'

Charlie nodded. 'Don't worry, Emma, I've been on the Tube in London.'

Charlie passed the stalls selling T-shirts printed on the spot, and didn't bother with any of the flashing mobile phone accessories. She bought some small cheap toys for her nieces and nephews, but didn't want any laser pointers. She hurried Simone past the stall selling luridly coloured sex toys and the stall with the suspicious-looking movies. But she stopped at a stall selling ties.

Leo stood behind us, folded his arms and glowered. A magic space appeared around us as people avoided him. He was having a great time.

Charlie selected a number of outrageously inappropriate ties from the hangers.

'Who are they for?' I said. 'Check the illustrations before you buy them — some are really crude and offensive.'

'I know exactly what I'm doing,' Charlie said with a small, evil smile. 'I have a cousin in his late twenties. He loves these disgusting ties and always asks me to buy some for him when I'm here.'

'Typical.'

Michael looked unhappy, but remained completely professional as he helped Simone at the stall across the road. She bought two Hello Kitty bags, three T-shirts and a pair of Hello Kitty sunglasses, every single item pink. He helped her with the bargaining and then returned her to us.

Leo and I shared a look. He was impressed with Michael too.

At the end of the market we moved from the middle to the side of the street, between the back of the stalls and the closed shopfronts. There were fewer people and we could walk back to the car in relative peace.

We stopped to buy some Pocari Sweat at a small shop selling drinks.

'It's not bad,' Charlie said. 'Lemony.'

'It's horrible if it's not cold,' Simone said.

'I wonder if I can buy it in London.'

'Overseas it's just called Pocari, they leave out the Sweat,' I said. 'You can probably buy it in Chinatown.'

'But I won't need it nearly as much back home,' Charlie said.

We walked further and reached a *dai pai dong*, a small open-air restaurant specialising in fresh seafood.

The restaurant had a number of flimsy folding tables on the pavement displaying plates of live seafood.

Charlie was fascinated. 'What are those?' she said, pointing at some shellfish that had six legs and large spiked claws. They were a pale creamy colour, with large abdomens and unusual triangular-shaped heads. Most were about ten centimetres long, but big ones were double that size.

Michael opened his mouth to answer but I stopped him with a raised hand. 'They're mantis prawns.'

'That's quite appropriate for them, really,' Charlie said. 'With those front claws and the heads like that, they do look like praying mantises.' She saw Michael's face. 'What?'

'Oh, go on, Michael,' I said. 'I can see you're dying to tell her.'

Michael leaned closer to Charlie. 'In Cantonese they're called "pissing prawns",' he said with quiet satisfaction.

Charlie's eyes went wide with delight. 'No, really?' She grinned broadly. 'Why on earth are they called that?'

'I have no idea,' Michael said with a shrug, and suddenly he was the image of his father.

The car park shroff office was right next to the public toilets and the smell was still bad, so Leo sent us on ahead while he paid the ticket.

The lift lurched to a stop at the seventh floor, and Simone squeaked again and grabbed my hand. Michael made a soft sound of disdain.

The seventh floor was almost deserted; most of the shoppers had already gone home. Our car was one of only three left on the floor and the other two had a thick layer of dust on them, apparently abandoned.

I unlocked the car using the remote. 'I'll start the engine, Charlie, and run the air con so you can sit in there and cool off.'

'Thanks, Emma,' Charlie said, her voice weak.

Michael grabbed her shopping bag off her and she didn't protest.

'You should have said something,' I said.

'We're finished anyway.'

Just as we reached the car I heard a shout and turned. A large group of young Chinese men charged around the corner of the car park towards us. Most of them were shirtless and covered with elaborate tattoos. Many had dyed hair, blond and red. They all carried machetes and choppers, the weapons of choice for Hong Kong gangsters.

'Why didn't you tell me, Simone?' I hissed. I quickly unlocked the boot of the car and pulled out my sword, pleased that I'd thought to bring it. I took the white Japanese blade as well and turned to throw it to Michael, then I saw his face.

Simone stood completely still, her eyes wide, staring at the young men.

These weren't demons.

I put the swords back into the car boot, closed it, locked it and pocketed the keys.

Charlie took Simone to the shelter of the back of the car alongside the wall of the car park. I nodded to let her know I approved; if she tried to take Simone out of the car park it would draw attention to them. They were safer over there.

The young men came to within about three metres off us and stopped. One of them stepped forward to talk to Michael. He was much better dressed than the others and slightly older, in his thirties. Quite good-looking in a rodent-like way. He seemed relaxed and confident.

I stood next to Michael, facing the leader. 'I cannot tell you how disappointed I am with you, Michael,' I said ferociously without looking away from the gang.

'They recruited me when I was twelve. I thought it was pretty cool at the time, but it didn't take me long to realise I'd made a huge mistake.' Michael sounded tired. 'I left them a long time ago, but they keep trying to get me back.'

The leader of the gang leered at me. 'You his new boss?'

'Yes.' I tried to project an impression of being very calm and unafraid. I wasn't afraid, but I certainly wasn't calm. I was furious with Michael. I crossed my arms in front of my chest. 'Leave him alone.'

The leader put his hand on his hip and posed. 'You stop me?' He eyed me up and down, leering. 'How much? I give you hundred dollar.'

The lift doors opened behind us. I didn't need to see him to know it was Leo. All the guys except for the leader inhaled and took a step back.

Leo stood on the other side of Michael. 'I thought you were out of this,' he said.

'I am, sir. They keep coming after me.'

'Well, here they are,' I said. 'This should be an interesting experience. They're armed. It'll be hard to take them down without killing them. Any suggestions on how to avoid this?'

'I'll go with them,' Michael said. 'They want me, not you.'

Leo shot Michael a quick, impressed glance.

'You will stay here with us, Michael, and that is an order,' I said.

Michael hesitated. Then he said, 'Yes, ma'am.'

Leo made a soft sound of approval. The kid had sworn to obey and he was as good as his word.

'If the weakest of us can take the strongest of them, I think it'll be over.' I stepped forward, pointed to the leader, then at myself. 'You, me, one-on-one. You win, you get him *and* me. I win, you go away and leave him alone.'

The gang leader looked me up and down again, this time more calculating. He was average height for a Chinese, about five eight, but he was a wall of solid muscle and from his build it was obvious he was a Master of the Arts.

'What Arts has this guy done, Michael?' I said.

'Just about all of them, Lady Emma. For God's sake, be sure about this.'

'Is his word good if he agrees?'

'Yes. These guys have a twisted code of honour.'

The leader said something loudly in Cantonese that I didn't understand. The rest of the guys laughed.

'That was too crude to translate, my Lady,' Michael said.

'I guessed that.'

The leader nodded. He told the other guys the deal; I could understand that much. The others moved back. Some of them grinned with anticipation, but others seemed concerned. I was obviously confident.

'No need to translate, Michael, I get it.' I stepped forward to face the leader.

'Get him,' Leo said softly without moving.

I didn't turn. 'That's not like you at all, Leo.'

'I think Leo's met this one before,' Michael said.

The leader grinned broadly at Leo then kissed the air loudly. A chorus of kissing sounds echoed from the other guys.

Leo didn't move a muscle.

'Are you okay back there, Charlie?' I called without moving.

'Charlie fainted, Emma,' Simone said, sounding unconcerned.

'That's all we need,' Leo said. 'Get him out of the way quickly, Emma.'

I nodded. We couldn't help Charlie until this was sorted.

'I am so sorry about this, my Lady,' Michael said, full of remorse.

'I will deal with you later,' I said in a voice so ice-cold it rivalled John.

The gang leader waved a come-on, still leering.

I watched him as I worked out what to do. This wasn't a spar; this was full-on. I would have to hit him hard to defend myself and anything physical I used could easily kill him. It would take a great deal of skill to disable him without seriously injuring or killing him and I really didn't have the time to mess around. I wanted him out of the way in a hurry.

Energy was absolutely out of the question.

I had a sudden brilliant idea. If I did this with enough hubris then the whole thing would be quickly sorted without anybody being hurt at all.

I moved close and smiled up at him. He leered back, confident, but didn't make a move to attack me. I strolled around him, and he turned to follow my movement. I stopped when we were side-on to the rest of the group and they could clearly see what was happening. I raised my right hand with my index and middle fingers out and the rest in; it must have looked like I was pretending to hold a gun. He still stood there grinning, waiting and confident.

Stupid bastard. They probably wouldn't even hang around long enough to take him along with them.

I very quickly and lightly tapped the five points. Forehead, throat, shoulder, above the heart, solar plexus. Five little taps.

He went perfectly still. He was paralysed. His face smiled but his eyes were terrified.

The other guys gasped. I turned to face them. I raised my index finger towards the leader without looking at him and casually gave him a little push right between the eyes.

He fell like a dead tree with the smile still on his face. I was right. The rest of them just took off.

I raced to the back of the car. Charlie lay on the concrete next to the rear wheel, her face ashen. Simone crouched over her, holding her hand.

'Leo,' I said, but he was already there. He felt for a pulse with one hand and put his other hand on her forehead.

'Her pulse is weak and thready, but she's still breathing. She has a fever. Looks like —'

'Heatstroke,' a benign voice with a very crisp English accent said at the same time as Leo. 'Take her to a hospital immediately. Ask the Princess to call Jade or Gold; one of them can take Charlie to the hospital, front door of the nearest emergency ward. Then Leo can drive the rest of you there and meet up.'

'Do what he said, Simone.'

'What?'

'Call Jade or Gold, like he said.'

'Nobody said anything,' Simone said.

'Call them anyway,' I said.

Jade appeared.

'Charlie has heatstroke, Jade. Take her to the nearest hospital, front door of the emergency ward. We'll meet you there.'

Jade crouched next to Charlie, took her hand, and both of them disappeared.

I rubbed my hands over my face.

'Come on, Emma, don't stand around, move yourself! She's in the hospital already and you need to be there,' the voice said.

'He's right,' I said. 'Let's go.'

'Where?' Leo said, confused.

'Tang Shiu Kin. Waterloo Road,' the voice said.

'Did you hear that?'

'I didn't hear anything, Emma,' Leo said. He bent to study my face. 'Are you okay?'

'I'm hearing voices. But the voice is helping. Tang Shiu Kin Hospital, Leo.'

'What the hell's going on?' Leo said.

'Voices?' Simone said. 'Is Daddy talking to you?'

'Just go, we'll discuss it later,' the voice said.

They all stared at me with bewilderment.

'We don't have time to stand around here looking stupid, guys, let's go. We can discuss whatever new weirdness we have to deal with when we're in the car.'

'Excuse me, madam, but I am *not weird*.'

'Did anybody hear that?' I said.

They all just stared at me as if I was completely crazy.

'Maybe I am crazy.'

'You have no idea,' the voice said.

'Stop doing that!' I jumped into the car. 'Leo, is the parking ticket still good?'

'We have five minutes.'

'Then let's move.'

CHAPTER ELEVEN

'Can you hear it now, Emma?' Leo said as he manoeuvred the car through traffic.

I listened. 'No.'

'What does it sound like?'

'An English man.'

Leo shook his head with incomprehension.

'I thought that move was a myth, ma'am,' Michael said. 'The Five-Point Push. Incredible.'

'The move *is* a myth. No such thing.'

'But I just saw you do it!'

'All of that was for show. Only the push on the solar plexus, the central dan tian, is really necessary. You just have to use exactly the right amount of chi to disable them without killing them. It's about a level ten energy move. I don't normally teach it; it doesn't work on demons, only humans. Mr Chen taught it to me just in case.'

'How long will he be paralysed, Emma?' Leo said.

'About six hours.' I smiled grimly. 'I hope none of them go back for him, he'll be really stiff when he regains control. And I *really* hope he had a lot of beer before he decided to pay us a visit.'

'You are very nasty sometimes, you know that?' Leo said with delight. He pulled the car into the lay-by at the front of the hospital. 'Here we are. Everybody out, I'll find a space. Michael, stay close to Lady Emma. I'll be a while. There aren't many car parks around this part of Kowloon.'

'Who'll take Simone?' I said.

'She'll be safer in the hospital than on the streets around here, Emma. You and Michael take her.'

'Okay.' I stepped out of the car and helped Simone out.

The English voice spoke into my ear. 'Jade's already taken her in. She's in examination room three. In through the main doors, down the corridor, fourth on the right.'

'Who are you?' I followed his directions, gesturing for Michael to follow me. 'John?' But it didn't sound like John.

We marched down the hallway and nobody tried to stop us. The room didn't have a door, just a curtain. Charlie was sitting on the bed; she smiled when she saw us. She was on a drip. Jade stood beside her, talking to a kind-looking young doctor and a middle-aged, dour-faced nurse.

I went in and stood next to the bed. 'How is she, Jade?' The doctor and nurse looked at me. 'I'm her employer,' I explained. 'She's my domestic helper from England.'

They nodded; that made me as good as next of kin.

'I'll take the children out and watch them,' Jade said. 'Where's Leo?'

'Parking the car; he'll be here soon,' I said.

Jade took Simone and Michael out, Michael glaring at her.

My mobile phone rang. It was Leo. 'Where are you? I'm at the front door.'

'Straight ahead, you should see Jade and the kids,' I said. 'Take them and guard them.'

I leaned into the corridor and saw him come into view. He waved to me, then took Simone and Michael into the waiting room.

'Can I speak to you privately?' the doctor said.

I studied him carefully: ordinary human. Simone would have said something otherwise. I let the doctor lead me out of the room into the empty examination room next door.

'I am Doctor Au Yeung.'

'Emma Donahoe. How bad is she?'

'Not bad at all. Actually it was more like a fainting fit than heatstroke. Did she have a fright of some kind? She's borderline diabetic and her blood sugar was very low. We've put her on an IV, but she should be all right to go home after we've performed a couple more tests.'

I sagged with relief. The voice was wrong; she'd really just fainted.

'I wasn't wrong,' the voice said. 'She also has a mild dose of heatstroke and needed to be put on fluids. This was the easiest way to make you move yourself.'

From his face the doctor hadn't heard anything.

'How long will this take?' I said.

'Not long. Please wait here. We have a small procedure to perform, then you can see her. Take a seat, this won't take a minute.'

'Okay.' I sat on the chair next to the wall.

The doctor flipped the curtain up and went into Charlie's room. He quickly returned holding a hypodermic and approached me with it. 'You look like you could use some fluids as well. How about a vitamin injection?'

I shot to my feet and moved into a defensive stance.

He approached me carefully and grabbed my arm with his free hand. Bad move. I performed the Push with my other hand and he went down, falling on his own needle.

I heard a soft sound in the hallway. Simon Wong flipped the curtain up and stood in the opening, watching me. I stared at him, then my breath caught with horror. *Simon Wong.*

He glanced down at the doctor on the floor, then grimaced and disappeared behind the curtain.

'He's making a try for Charlie! *Quick!*' the voice shouted, but I'd already charged after him.

I raced into the next room. Wong stood behind Charlie with his hand over her mouth. Her eyes were wide with fear. He grinned at me over the top of her head and they disappeared.

I fell to lean on the bed. I couldn't support my own weight. Simone charged into the room, followed by Leo, Jade and Michael. They stopped dead when they saw.

The grim-faced nurse came in behind them. She held up a clipboard. 'Miss Donahoe.' She glanced up at me. 'Go home and talk to the Dark Lord. He has been contacted.' She spun on her heel and went out.

Simone threw her little arms around me. 'The bad demon has Charlie!'

I pulled her into my stomach. 'I know, sweetheart.'

'No,' Leo whispered.

'That nurse and the doctor weren't demons, were they?'

Simone shook her head into my stomach. Her shoulders quivered. 'Charlie.'

'This is very bad,' Leo said. 'Let's get home to Mr Chen right now.'

'Should we grab that doctor and nurse and take them with us?' Michael said.

'That wouldn't be a good idea,' the voice said. 'You can't go around kidnapping drugged human doctors.'

Simone jerked her head away from my stomach and stared up at me. Everybody's mouths flopped open.

'It *does* sound like an English man,' Michael said. 'Who is it?'

'Don't worry about me!' the voice snapped. 'Just get yourselves home! Jade, go directly and brief the Dark Lord. Everybody else, *move*!'

'By your leave, my Lady,' Jade said.

'Go.'

Jade dropped her head and disappeared. Leo guided the rest of us out and followed us down the hallway.

'If you do not tell me who you are *right now*,' I said furiously as I stormed down the corridor, 'I will be very, very cross.'

'I'm not a who, I'm a what, and I'm on your engagement ring.'

I stopped dead.

Leo pushed me forward. 'Move, Emma.'

I raced out the front doors of the hospital, Leo following. 'You're the stone?' I said, stunned.

Leo ran to collect the car. Michael and Simone stood with me, watching me as if I was completely bonkers.

'You were wondering when I'd wake, weren't you?' The stone's voice was cheerful. 'Well, now you know. I am extremely displeased with the Turtle for keeping me locked up for so long. He should have known better. Even though I was unaware, I honestly feel I deserve better treatment than that.'

'Maybe he was waiting for someone worthy?'

'You think you're worthy of something as precious as me?' the stone said with delight.

'I don't know. Am I?'

'Are you talking to the voice, Emma?' Simone said.

'Yep. It's the stone —'

The stone cut me off. 'Here comes Leo. He managed to find a meter not far away. Now *there* is

142

someone worthy. Shame this setting wouldn't fit on him.'

'If you want me to give you to Leo, just say the word,' I said. 'You are very precious, you know.'

'More precious than you could possibly imagine. But I think I'll stay with you for now, and see what you do.' Its English accent made it sound like a BBC newsreader. 'You are a very interesting person, you know. A great deal of hidden depth to you. And most of it isn't even there.'

'What the hell is that supposed to mean?'

Leo brought the car around and I opened the door for Simone.

'What do you mean?'

But the stone didn't reply.

I was quiet in the car for a while, and everybody kept sneaking glances at me. Eventually I thought I'd better reassure them.

'I haven't gone crazy, guys. The stone in the ring that Mr Chen gave me woke up and started talking to me. It helped out. That's what you heard.'

'Let me see, Emma,' Simone said.

I showed her the ring. She touched it and squeaked.

'Did it do anything to you?' I said.

'Of course I didn't,' the stone said. Its voice became kind. 'Hello, Princess.'

Simone's eyes went wide. 'Hello.'

'That jade ring?' Leo said over his shoulder as he drove. 'That little green stone?'

'Yep.'

'Do you have a name?' Simone said.

'I am far too important to have anything as mundane as a name,' the stone said. 'I am thoroughly above such boring inanities.'

'O...kay,' Leo said without looking away from the road.

143

Michael grimaced.

'Yes, it just gets stranger and stranger, Michael,' I said. 'Sometimes it's more the House of Weird than the House of Chen.'

He shook his head. I'd read his mind.

CHAPTER TWELVE

We sat around the table and looked at each other. Leo, Michael, John, me. We'd included Michael; he was a part of this now. I didn't have the energy to tell him off. He'd genuinely tried to leave the triads.

'How did Wong contact you?' I asked John.

'On my mobile. Perfectly normally. How did he manage to take Charlie?'

'He separated us,' I said. 'He probably wasn't expecting us to have Jade, though. He didn't try for Simone while Jade was with her.'

Michael snorted with amusement. 'He's scared of your *accountant*?'

'My accountant is a dragon,' John said. 'One of the fiercest on the Celestial. She would protect Simone with her life.'

'Oh. Sorry.'

'Anyway,' I continued, 'he separated us. Leo was out parking the car. Simone and Michael were alone, but we were lucky, we had Jade, and Leo found a meter, so Simone was protected quickly. He separated me from Charlie using a freaking *human* doctor —'

John's face went very grim as I continued.

'— and the doctor tried to sedate me so he could take me. I Pushed him and he went down. Wong himself didn't want to try me without sedation, so he took ...' I hesitated, searching for the right way to put it. 'He took Charlie as second prize.'

'He knows Simone can sense demons,' John said. 'So he's using humans to work around it.'

'I am so glad you taught me the Push. He used humans right up to the last minute. Oh, and the stone woke up and helped.'

'Good evening, stone, good to see you awake,' John said.

The stone was silent.

'I think it's cross with you for keeping it locked up for so long,' I said. 'It has the most incredible English accent, it sounds like somebody reading the news on the BBC.'

'Well, if I'm forced to speak English I may as well do it properly,' the stone said. 'You have more important things to deal with right now, Turtle.'

John rubbed his hands over his face, then pulled his hair out of its tie, tidied it, and tied it back again. He sounded helpless. 'I don't know what to do.'

'Tell Emma,' the stone said gently.

'He wants me for a one-on-one.'

I fell back. 'No.'

'I'm very drained, and I don't know how strong he is right now. There is a chance he could take me down. If I face him, win or lose he'll give Charlie back unharmed. He's a Demon Prince, he'll stand by his word. If I don't face him, you have an idea of what will happen to Charlie.'

'Holy shit,' I said softly. 'This is really bad.'

'I know,' John moaned.

'Simone can call a Celestial Master; she'll be safe even if you lose. You have to go and face him, and get

Charlie back. He can't kill you if he wins, and he won't be able to get Simone. He'll just take your head to his dad, receive a nice little promotion, and you'll be out of their way slightly sooner than we'd planned.'

'You will still be at risk, Emma,' John said, looking into my eyes. 'You can't call anybody for help. If he wins he'll come straight after you. You know the King wants you.'

'He's right, Emma,' Leo said, his voice full of misery. 'Simone might be okay, but the Demon King wants you and you know it.'

'Simone is the important thing, Leo.' I looked John in the eyes. 'Simone and Charlie. We must get Charlie back.'

'Why do they want Mr Chen's head?' Michael said. He bobbed his head. 'Sorry. My curiosity gets the better of me sometimes.'

'No, Michael, you're quite right to ask,' I said. 'Always ask if you need to know. We might not answer, but we'll never tell you off. Where to start?' I ran my hands through my hair. 'The King of the Demons has put a price on Mr Chen's head. Any demon that brings him the Dark Lord's head will be promoted to Number One.'

'Like Number One son?'

'Precisely,' John said. 'Number One is second in precedence only to the King; all the other demons must obey it. It is an immensely powerful position.'

'One particular Demon Prince, the One Hundred and Twenty-Second son, has decided to make a bid for it,' I said. 'He's been at us for a while, either trying to take Mr Chen's head directly, or kidnap Simone or me to swap for it. He appears in human form most of the time, and his human name is Simon Wong.'

Michael's head shot up and his eyes went wide. '*Simon Wong?*'

'You know of him?' John asked sharply.

'He's the Big Brother of all the Big Brothers.'

'Somehow I'm not surprised,' I said. The idea of that creep being in charge of all the underworld activity in Hong Kong wasn't much of a leap.

'He's notorious,' Michael said. 'They keep bringing girls over from the mainland for him, all the time. They say he does things to them that you wouldn't believe. The girls have even started refusing to come to Hong Kong, because they've heard what happens if he gets his hands on them.' His voice softened. 'Boys too. Even young ones. I left when someone warned me. He wanted me. They were coming to take me.'

'He worked out what you are, Michael,' John said. 'I'm not surprised he wanted you.'

Michael gestured towards Leo. 'Leo helped me. If it wasn't for him, I think I'd be dead.'

'You should have told me that was who you were running from,' Leo said. 'I would have brought you in a long time ago, son of the Tiger or not. You should hear what he has planned for me.'

Michael glanced sharply at Leo. Leo smiled slightly and shook his head.

'He has Charlie, Michael,' I said very calmly.

'Oh my God,' Michael said.

'He wants a one-on-one with Mr Chen, so that he can take his head and present it to his father. And become the second most senior demon in Hell.'

'Holy shit,' Michael said.

'That's what I said.'

'If he takes your head, what will happen to you, my Lord?' Michael asked. 'Can he kill you? Can you even kill a Wind?'

'No, you can't,' John said. 'But I would revert to my True Form and be gone for a long time, leaving Simone and Emma without my protection. The demons would

148

have a chance to hold my two most loved people in the world, and through that gain control over me.' He rubbed his hands over his face. 'Now you see why Simone is my first human child, Emma. I always knew this could happen. You are my weakness. If they have you, then they have me, and without me to defend it all of humanity would be at their mercy.'

'He will never take me alive,' I said. 'I'd fall on my own sword before I let that monster have me. Don't worry about Simone; she can call a Master.'

John dropped his head and spoke quietly to the table. 'I want to be absolutely sure that she is able to defend herself.'

'What will you do, my Lord?' Leo said, full of despair. 'If I were Charlie I know what I would want you to do. All of your Retainers understand the situation. We would rather die than put you or your loved ones at risk.'

'And you all know that I would never leave you in a demon's hands if I could do anything about it,' John said. 'You are my family. I love you all. I will fight to the end to protect you.' He raised his head and looked me in the eyes. Suddenly it was just him and me. 'Leo, Michael, go out. I need to speak to Lady Emma alone.'

Leo didn't move. 'Don't risk yourself. Don't risk your loved ones. Charlie wouldn't want this.'

John didn't look away from me. 'Leo, go out and take Michael. That is an order.'

'My Lord,' Leo said hoarsely. He and Michael rose and went to the door.

'Leo,' I said.

He stopped and turned back.

'Please don't tell Simone what's happening. Until it's all over. Guard her for us.'

Leo nodded and he and Michael went out, closing the door quietly behind them.

'Just go, John,' I said. 'I agree with your decision. We must get her back. It's your duty as her Lord. Go.'

'He wants to meet me on the top floor at Hennessy Road. I'll have to let him in past the seals. His presence will blow every seal on the building.'

'Clever. Two birds with one stone. You, and broken seals on Hennessy Road.'

'And perhaps *you* as well if he wins, dear one.'

'Never. I meant it. That thing will never get its hands on me.' I knew what I had to do. 'I'll come with you, and bring Michael. Leo can stay here and guard Simone. Win or lose, we'll have Charlie back, and Michael can escort her home.' I tried to control my voice. 'If you lose, I'll end it there. You won't have to worry about me. Charlie and Simone will be safe.'

'No, Emma.'

'There's no other way. You won't have to worry about them having me. If you lose, we can both die in peace. Simone will be safe, and that's all that's important.'

He looked down at his hands and didn't say anything for a long time.

'It's the only thing we can do, John.'

He looked up at me and smiled. 'No. I have a better idea.'

I heard the quiet jingling of a wind chime and snapped open my eyes. The geometric carvings on the ceiling were picked out in gold. The fringes on the blue silk light fitting fluttered in the warm breeze.

I sat up. There was barely room for me on the couch with all the cushions. The main colour around me was purple, with peacock blue and gold. Brilliantly blue late afternoon sky filled the large arched windows in the red stone walls. I appeared to be in some sort of Middle Eastern or Indian palace; what looked to be priceless Arabian rugs covered the floor.

'Where the hell am I?' I demanded.

'Snow White said that differently,' the stone said dryly.

'Tell me where the hell I am *right now* or I will take you off my finger and throw you down the nearest toilet.'

'You are safe in my palace in the Western Desert,' the Tiger said from the doorway. 'Who are you talking to?'

'My engagement ring.' I pulled myself around to sit on the edge of the couch. I felt dizzy; it must have been from the travelling. I rubbed my hand over my forehead. 'It seems to think it's a BBC newsreader.'

'The weather will be very dry today,' the stone said in its very best announcer voice.

'Shut the hell up,' I said. 'I meant it about the toilet.'

'Typical of the Turtle.' Bai Hu leaned against the wall and folded his arms over his chest. 'Never does anything by halves. Not a diamond, oh no. Has to give his Lady a Building Block of the World.'

I ran to him and threw myself into his arms. He held me gingerly and kissed me on the cheek. His golden face lit up with a huge smile and his tawny eyes sparkled. He wore his usual old-fashioned white cotton pants and jacket trimmed with gold.

'Why am I here, Tiger?'

'No demon can get you here.' He shrugged. 'You're completely safe. He doesn't have to worry about you.' His voice changed slightly. 'Whatever happens.'

I stepped back and sagged. I fell to sit on the couch, put my head in my hands, then ran my hands through my hair.

'No.' I glanced up at him. 'Did he win?'

'If he wins he will tell me. Until then he has requested that he not be disturbed, as he needs to concentrate.'

'I was taking him to Paris next week, Bai Hu. He's almost completely drained.'

The Tiger came and sat next to me. 'It will all be over soon, Emma, one way or another. Have faith in your Lord; he will defeat this bastard, and then you can take him to Paris. Remember . . .' He smiled sadly. 'This is the God of Martial Arts we're talking about here. He is the best there is, even drained and in human form.'

'What are his chances, do you think?'

'About fifty–fifty, my Lady.' He put his arm around my shoulder and squeezed me affectionately. 'Would you like to take a look around the palace while you wait? Louise would love to see you.'

I hesitated. 'If you don't mind, Tiger, I think I'll stay here and meditate. Alone. I'll just wait for him. However long it takes.'

'Very well, Emma. If you need anything,' he pointed at a small brass gong on the intricately carved teak coffee table, 'sound the gong. A servant will come. I am nearby. Would you like tea?'

'Yes, please. But right now I'd just like to be alone and wait.'

After he'd gone I settled to sit on one of the rugs to meditate. But for the first time since I'd gained the skill I couldn't do it. Wonderful. If I couldn't even do this now, then I'd be completely incapacitated when he left, and I would have duties to perform. Not good enough.

I rose and performed a Yang-style tai chi set, to set my body in motion and clear my mind at the same time. This was more effective. I had to concentrate on the moves and I couldn't think about John. I phased out and relaxed.

I made it. I was freed from the anguish. My mind and body moved in harmony, becoming the moves themselves. I moved the chi around very slowly and deliberately, following it with my eyes as it glowed in my hands, pure shining white.

I stopped mid-move without losing concentration. My chi was white. It wasn't chi, it was shen. This was incredibly wrong and very dangerous. I had my *soul* out there on my hands. I didn't even know I could *do* that.

I maintained the harmony and very slowly completed the set. It didn't feel wrong; in fact I felt absolutely wonderful, glowing and relaxed. It felt like Ms Kwan was with me, filling me with complete peaceful serenity. I looked around for her, but she wasn't there. 'Kwan Yin?'

'No, that was all you,' the stone said. 'You are on the Celestial Plane, where it is possible to work with *shen*. But even here, what you just did is exceptional. Thank you; that was a wonderful feeling. If the Turtle returns for you, you should tell him about it. I cannot wait to see his reaction.'

'I'm on the Celestial Plane?' I went to the window and looked out. I wished I could enjoy it.

The window was high up in the wall of the palace. Gardens spread below me. They were desert gardens: red soil holding mostly succulents and cacti, with cycads and ferns. The paths between the gardens were paved with golden yellow bricks, and a climbing plant with bright golden flowers hung from a blue-tiled pavilion with a red-tiled roof. A network of ponds and fountains meandered through the gardens, joined by blue-tiled channels of splashing water. Beyond the gardens stood a very high red-brick wall, and beyond that was the desert.

The desert was a rich tapestry of different shades of red and gold, the colours so intense they were almost dazzling. The sky was a brilliant crystalline blue, bluer than any sky I had ever seen, without a single cloud. Crinkled red mountains lounged on the other side of the wide red and gold plain.

Brightly coloured tents flapped in the breeze. Banners snapped on top of the tents, some of them bearing the motif of a white tiger. The sun had nearly set and the tents made long shadows over the red desert plain.

The wind chime hanging above the window made a gentle musical sound.

Riders practised manoeuvres on the plain. They rode Arab horses, decked out with colourful blankets and flowing ribbons. The riders tore over the desert with spears and impaled pegs on the ground.

'That's tent-pegging,' I said. 'I did that in pony club.'

'At full gallop on a pure-bred Arab?' the stone said.

'I wish.' I began to warm to the stone. It was good company.

I sighed. 'This is so beautiful.'

'The Mountain was even more exquisite,' John said behind me.

I turned. There he was. He still wore the black cotton pants and T-shirt he had worn to the meeting earlier, and appeared uninjured. His hair had come completely loose and fell around his shoulders. He smiled gently, the golden skin of his face glowing. It was all I could do to stop myself racing to him and throwing myself into his arms.

'Is that really him?' I asked the stone.

'Yes, my Lady, it really is,' the stone said.

I sagged against the window frame with relief.

The Tiger, in True Form, padded out from behind John. He went out the door and it closed softly behind him.

'What are you doing here?' I said.

'The Tiger brought me here. He is a complete fool. It will take him at least a day and a night to recover from the exertion before he can carry us back. He is completely incapacitated. He can't even take human form.'

'I'll have to rearrange the Paris travel plans. What a nuisance.'

'I think Mercy will understand.'

We sat together on the couch and I poured the tea. He was far too close to me; I could feel the warmth from him. His T-shirt was damp and crumpled from the exertion of battling the demon. Now he was closer I could see tears in the fabric where Wong had made some near misses.

'Are you hurt? He made it through you a couple of times.'

'He didn't touch me.'

'Will everyone be okay while we're stuck here for two days? Will Simone be all right?'

'Monica, Leo and Michael are minding her for us. A Celestial Master is also guarding. It's a shame Simone can't travel to the Plane.' He glanced out the window. 'But I'm sure she'll like it when she can come.'

'How old will she have to be before she can come?'

'Fully grown.' He shrugged. 'I will know, but I will not be here anyway.' He smiled and I became lost in his eyes. He really was sitting far too close to me. His eyes studied my face, his voice warm and low. 'But while I am here there's something I can do.'

More duties to perform. 'What's that?'

He reached to take my hand, pulling me closer. 'I can touch you.'

My heart leapt to my throat. 'Oh dear Lord, no.'

'Oh dear Lady, absolutely yes.' He put his hand gently around the back of my neck, pulled me in and kissed me.

I pressed hard into him. I threw my arms around his neck and dug my fingers into his hair. His hands stroked over my shoulders and down my back. He pulled my shirt free and shoved his hands inside, running them along the bare skin of my back and making me moan into his mouth.

I couldn't be close enough to him. The blood pounded in my ears. He breathed heavily, his chest heaving against me. His grip tightened, then he pulled away to study me, his face very intense. He glanced down and worked at the buttons on my shirt, making me tremble.

Then he stopped and his face went rigid. A black shutter rolled up over his eyeballs. No whites, no irises, nothing. Just black.

He shoved me backwards on the couch and threw himself on top of me. He held me down by the throat. I nearly panicked but I tried to control it; he wasn't choking me, he just held me.

'John. John. What are you doing?'

He didn't hear me, his face had twisted into a fierce grimace. I didn't struggle; he could easily snap my neck. I tried to lie very still but my heart raced.

He grabbed the front of my shirt, pulled it upwards and ripped it off me, chafing the skin of my back. He shifted sideways slightly and did the same to my jeans; grabbed, pulled, ripped them away. His black eyes didn't focus on me.

He released my throat but I didn't move; I didn't risk fighting back.

I touched his cheek, trying to snap him out of it. He grabbed my wrist, thrust it over my head and pinned it to the couch. He held it, grabbed my other hand, and put it over my head as well. He pinned both of my hands in one of his, his grip like steel. He breathed heavily, his eyes hard and black and glittering above mine. His hair hung like a curtain around our faces.

He shifted on top of me and pinned me with his body. He tugged at his pants using his free hand.

He pushed himself hard onto me and forced his knee between my legs. He moved his forearm across my throat to hold me down. His other hand held my hands above my head. I was unable to move and barely able to breathe as he forced himself on me, black eyes glittering, face fierce and terrible.

I didn't try to move. I didn't try to fight him. I couldn't move. I couldn't do anything. I was completely defenceless. He had me.

When his eyes returned to normal he pulled back to study me, his face expressionless. He threw himself off me, fixed his clothes, and stalked to the window. He brushed his hair out of his face to watch the desert.

I rose as well. I didn't bother with my clothes; they were ruined. I shrugged off the remains and went to him. I stood behind and slightly to one side of him, leaned into him and put my arm around his waist.

He silently leaned on the window frame, looking at the desert for a long time. I held him and waited.

Finally he spoke, his voice very soft. 'Did I hurt you? Are you injured?'

'I'm fine. You didn't hurt me at all.'

He banged his palms on the stone of the window ledge, stalked back to the couch and threw himself to sit on it. He bent forward and put his elbows on his knees and his face in his hands. I followed and stood over him, waiting. He rubbed his hands over his face and looked up at me. He saw me without my clothes and his face went intense again. He looked away.

I sat next to him and took one of his hands in both of mine. 'You completely lost control, didn't you? Both you and Ms Kwan said that could happen.'

He studied his hand where I held it. 'It's been more than three years.' His face went fierce. 'I should have better control than that!' He looked into my eyes. 'I am so sorry, Emma. I could have hurt you.'

I squeezed his hand. 'Will it be like that every time?'

'No, not every time. But sometimes ...' He hesitated. 'Perhaps. I don't want to hurt you. This is such a bad idea; having a human wife has always been a bad idea.' His voice gained a very slight edge of despair. 'I would understand if you were to change your mind now.'

'So it won't be like that every time?'

'No. But sometimes it may be.'

'Good,' I said firmly. 'Because if it was like that every single time, it would definitely be too much of a good thing.'

His face went blank. Then he heard what I'd said and it filled with wonder. 'You really are amazing sometimes.'

'You're pretty damn amazing yourself.'

I levered myself over him so that I straddled his lap, and threw my arms around his neck. I moved my face very close to his and looked him in the eyes. 'I want to see your eyes go black again. That was cool.'

He wrapped his strong hands around my bare waist and his face became intense. 'I'll see what I can do.'

'So soon?'

He just smiled.

I woke with a start. Someone lay next to me, facing away. Long, black shining hair. Smooth, muscular golden shoulders. I vaulted out of the bed and nearly brushed the ceiling as I somersaulted and landed lightly on the carpet nearly seven metres away. What the hell?

He rolled over to see me. His eyes sparkled in the moonlight as he smiled. 'That move needs some work, Emma. You have been concentrating far too much on the energy work lately and letting the physical training fall beside the way. You are even becoming slightly soft in the middle.'

I looked down at myself. He was right.

He threw the covers open. 'Come back to bed.'

He was teasing me. He'd deliberately thrown the covers off so that I could see him. He was magnificent. His long black hair had come completely loose and fell over his shoulders and neck in wonderful disarray. He was solid muscle under smooth golden skin, shining in the moonlight.

'You really need to go to Paris,' I said. 'You look nearly fifty years old yourself.'

He laughed softly. 'I'm an old man.'

I climbed back into bed and he pulled the covers over us; the desert night was cold. I snuggled next to him and ran my hands over his strong back. He wrapped his arms around me and I felt the muscles of his back move beneath my fingers. His hands were cool, but his chest was warm. I stuck my face under his chin and he nuzzled the top of my head.

'Not where it counts.'

It became very warm under the covers. One of his hands trailed up my back and buried itself in my hair. He gently rolled me so that I was on my back and he was above me. He lowered his face to mine.

I could tell his eyes didn't go black, even though I couldn't see them. He took his time.

CHAPTER THIRTEEN

We didn't shift our eyes from each other as we ate our noodles in the shade of the pavilion. The Tiger lounged under the table and noisily tore apart the haunch of a large ungulate. The fountain splashed next to us and the breeze wafted cool, moist air off the water.

The clothes the Tiger had given me were much too elaborate for me to be at ease. The flowing golden yellow cotton pants and Indian-style long top with black embroidery had been in the way when John and I had practised some hand-to-hand that morning. But the silk slippers were delightfully comfortable, and I wondered if he could bring me some to Hong Kong later.

The Tiger had provided John with his usual black training gear: a pair of cotton pants and jacket similar to what the Tiger himself wore in human form.

'Did you destroy Wong?' I asked John. 'Tell me it's gone.'

'It ran, as it usually does, as soon as it saw I was winning,' John said. 'It really is the most tremendous coward.'

'Damn,' I said quietly into my food.

The Tiger crunched the bones under the table.

'Must you do that, Bai Hu?' I said patiently. 'It sounds revolting, and I'm trying to eat here.'

'Sorry, my Lady.' He picked up the remains of his meal in his mouth and carried it, exactly as a cat would, a short distance away from us. He dropped it and lounged next to it. 'Is this okay?'

'Whatever,' John said. 'As long as we don't have to look at you.'

'Good coming from you,' Bai Hu said, amused. 'You should see him eat in True Form, Lady Emma, it is a sight to behold.'

'Turtles are cute when they eat,' I said, smiling into John's eyes. 'I would love to see that.'

'I'm not talking about the Turtle, I'm talking about the Serpent,' the Tiger said. 'It eats pigs whole, and takes its sweet delicious time about it.'

John's head shot up. 'Have you seen it?'

'No, my friend, and nobody else has either. I wonder what happened to it.' The Tiger glanced up from the carnage of his meal. 'It has been gone for a very long time. Does it answer when you call?'

'No,' John said quietly.

'You are a very strange creature, Xuan Wu.'

'I know,' John said, still very quietly.

Bai Hu returned to crunching the bones.

'We need to go back tomorrow,' John said. 'There are things we need to do, and I don't want to leave Simone alone for too long.'

'I understand, John. This was more than I could have asked for. It's more than I ever expected.' I took his hand. He put his other hand on top. I became lost in his eyes. 'Thank you so much, Tiger.'

The Tiger said something unintelligible through the meat.

'Charlie wasn't too upset?' I said.

John stiffened and his face went expressionless. The Tiger stopped crunching the bones.

I ripped my hands away. 'That *bastard*! You said the word of a Demon Prince was *good*!'

'That demon is one of the most disgusting pieces of scum it has ever been my misfortune to encounter,' John said evenly, 'and I have seen some fine pieces of work over the past two thousand years or so. He killed her the minute he knew he would lose.'

I clutched the table. 'She's dead?'

John nodded, his face still expressionless.

'I am going to rip the arms and legs off that bastard, tear out his innards and feed them to him,' the Tiger said with quiet menace.

'No you aren't, because I am,' I said.

The Tiger made a soft sound and I turned to look at him; he studied me intently, his tawny eyes glowing.

I crossed my arms on the table and dropped my head onto them. 'No. Charlie.'

John moved closer and put his arm around me. 'She didn't suffer, Emma. He hadn't laid a hand on her until he saw he was losing. Then he took her head off and ran. I was honestly not expecting it. It is the first time I have ever seen a Demon Prince go back on his word.'

'We will be ready for him next time,' I said fiercely into my arms. 'We will get that bastard.'

'Call me if you see him,' the Tiger said. 'Let me help. I have a score to settle with him as well.'

'Very well, Tiger, we will get him together.' John squeezed my shoulders. 'We can't go home for another day, love. Try to enjoy this short time we have.'

The Tiger wandered back to us and threw himself to lie beside the table. He proceeded to wash himself, his tongue rasping over his fur. He turned one of his front paws over and licked the pads, then nibbled delicately between the toes.

'Go and have a screw,' he said between licks, his eyes half-closed. 'It will make you feel better. Worry about the rest of the world when you return.' He stopped licking and twitched one ear. 'Actually, that's good advice, and I might take it myself.' He winked. 'Later.' He lazily pulled himself up, stretched like a big cat, flicked his tail and padded away.

John watched the Tiger go with amusement. 'He is absolutely incorrigible.'

'And very wise. Up for it?'

'I am a Turtle.' He smiled gently. 'Don't you know about us?'

'What?'

His eyes crinkled up. 'We always are.'

He brushed his hand over my back as we lay silently side by side. His hair had come completely out and I twisted it through my fingers. The dark purple silken bedcovers were exquisitely comfortable and I dozed in his arms. Despite the warmth of the afternoon, the room was shady and cool. A fountain splashed outside the window and a bird sang some distance away.

'Tell him about the shen,' the stone said.

'You are not supposed to be listening,' John said. 'Go back to sleep.'

'I really will flush this thing down the toilet and ask you for a diamond instead,' I said. 'Imagine. A little green voyeur on my finger.'

'I am not a voyeur,' the stone said crisply. 'I am not at all interested in what you animals get up to —'

'Animals!' I squawked.

'I am,' John said, amused.

'— but you really should tell him about the shen,' the stone said, ignoring us. 'It is quite important.'

'Which Shen?' John said.

'I did a Yang tai chi set while I was waiting for you last night. I thought I was working with chi, but then I saw I was working with shen.'

'You did shen work?' John pulled himself up and threw his long legs over the side of the bed. 'Show me.'

I hesitated; then, what the hell. I went to the middle of the room, moved into position and began.

It happened again about halfway through the set. I didn't need to see it to know; he went very still. It felt absolutely marvellous. I was one with the universe; all of history stretched before me. His presence shimmered dark and cool behind me. The warmth of the desert smouldered outside the window. It was exquisite.

I finished the set, moved my hands through the final position, and put the shen back. Then I took a deep breath and stood still for a moment, revelling in the wonderful feeling.

'You should not have been able to do that,' John said quietly.

I turned to see him. 'What?'

'Only Immortals can work with shen, my love.' His voice went strange. 'Come here.'

I went to him and sat next to him.

He put his hands on my face. 'Open up, love.'

I relaxed and let him in.

He shuffled through all my feelings. He looked in all my corners. It was much easier this time; I was accustomed to the feeling of him inside my head. I relaxed and enjoyed it.

He sighed when he felt the after-effects of the shen work. 'That really does feel wonderful, doesn't it? I haven't been able to do that in a long time. I miss it. But why can you work with shen?'

I imagined myself holding my hands out. I hadn't even known ordinary humans couldn't do it.

He hunted through me. 'Same as before, nothing

special, ordinary human.' He hesitated for a moment, then said, 'Stone.'

'Yes, Turtle?'

'I looked inside her before, she is an ordinary human being. Something dark emerged when the Demon King saw inside her; it was enough to push him out. It must have been something very powerful, but when I look now, I see nothing. But she just worked with shen, which ordinary humans can't do. Why is this?'

'To tell you the truth,' the stone said in its best BBC voice, 'I have no idea either. All I know is that you have chosen a most unusual female —'

'Female!' I squawked again.

'— and that she has talents that will only grow with time. There is a great deal of hidden power in this one. Immense destructive capability. It is a shame you will not be around to guide her to full realisation of her potential. When you return, you will be astounded.'

'Destructive capability?' I said.

'Immense. When you realise your potential, I think you will be the most destructive thing the Dark Lord has ever seen, and he is the power of yin himself.'

'Is she dangerous?' John said quietly.

The stone hesitated. I heard it hesitate.

'Answer the question, stone. Am I dangerous?'

The stone didn't reply.

'Tell me right now,' I said. 'I don't want to be a danger to Xuan Wu, Simone, or any member of the family.'

The stone still didn't reply.

I took John's hands from my face and put them on my throat. 'Kill me now, John, please.' I looked straight into his horrified eyes. 'Kill me!'

'No!' the stone shouted. 'There is absolutely no need for this.'

We sagged against each other.

'Am. I. Dangerous,' I said very slowly and clearly.

'Yes, you are,' the stone said.

We snapped our heads up and gazed into each other's eyes.

'But not to your family, Emma. I should have made myself clearer,' the stone said.

John visibly relaxed. I put my hands on his shoulders. He brushed his hands over my back. We touched foreheads and sat motionless.

'What the hell are you talking about, stone?' I said, quietly exasperated. 'You make absolutely no sense whatsoever.'

'Let me elaborate,' the stone said. 'You are very unusual. Very talented. Right now you are an ordinary human being. That will change as time passes —'

'Of course it will. I will Raise her when I return,' John said.

'Don't interrupt me!' the stone snapped. 'You may not need to. She is a long way there herself already. Look what she just did. She is extraordinary.'

'That's what Ms Kwan is always saying,' I said.

'*I will stop talking if you keep interrupting me,*' the stone said. 'Lady Emma Donahoe, I don't know quite what you are or where you're going, but I would like to come along for the ride. Lord Xuan Wu, Dark Lord, listen to me.'

'I'm listening,' John said.

'Teach her as if she is Immortal. See how far you go. Don't push her too hard, you could kill her. Until you leave her. When you return, you will be astonished.'

John raised his head to gaze into my eyes. 'I'm looking forward to it.'

'And now I think I will stay quiet and watch. Except when you're doing your animal thing, because then I'll be asleep. Understood?'

'I love you, Xuan Wu, and I wish I knew what the stone was talking about here.'

'I love you too, Emma, and so do I.'

'Animals!' the stone snapped, and went quiet.

'I think you should talk to somebody about this death wish that you seem to have,' he said.

'Excuse me, doctor, could you help me, please? When my fiancé, who is a turtle that I can't touch because it would kill me, went to fight this demon, I offered to fall on my sword rather than into the demon's hands. And then later, when my engagement ring said that I might be dangerous to my family, I asked the turtle — who, by the way, is missing his snake half — to kill me. Oh, and all of this happened at the house of our best friend, who is a tiger.'

'I see your point.'

'Maybe an animal psychologist would be more help.'

'I think the Tiger has one or two here in the palace,' he said, perfectly serious. 'Would you like me to make an appointment for you?'

I giggled and pushed him over. He grinned and pulled me on top.

'Not again *already*.'

'Emma, I thought you did some research on me. If you knew about the nature of turtles then you would not be surprised.'

'John Chen Wu, you never cease to surprise me, every day of my life.'

'Good.' He ran his hands over my back and his face became intense.

CHAPTER FOURTEEN

After we'd changed into the swimwear the Tiger provided for us, John led me out of the room and into the long outdoor hallway. He took me down carved wooden stairs to the ground floor, and along the breezeway through the gardens. The demon gardeners looked up and smiled as we went past.

'How much time did you spend here before?' I said. 'Were you here often?'

'I honestly miss it.' He stopped and looked around. 'When I wasn't on the Mountain, or in the Northern Heavens, I spent quite a lot of time here. The Tiger and I shared some good times.'

'He misses you.'

'Yes, he does.' He took my hand. 'Come on, let's go for a swim.'

We continued through the gardens. 'I have not seen a single one of these notorious women that you both carry on about,' I said. 'I'm beginning to think it was just pure bravado on his part, and a careful scheme by you to keep me out of his paws.'

'You have found me out. I just didn't want him to have a chance with you.' He smiled sideways at me. 'Not even I am permitted into the women's quarters. He's probably hunted them away from the pool as well. He's very protective of his females.' He nodded. 'Here we are.'

It was more like a country club than a swimming pool. Palm trees and red rocks surrounded the freeform lagoon; a couple of demon servants waited attentively next to the deck chairs that flanked the pool bar.

'Geez, this is the life.' I looked around. 'This is like a five-star resort.'

'He's a tiger. He likes his swimming.'

'With his women, as well. Shades of the Playboy mansion.'

John laughed softly. 'You are very perceptive sometimes.'

'You can't swim though, John, it's chlorinated.'

'It's not. It's kept pure by some sort of Celestial thing. I can go in.'

'Some sort of Celestial thing? Is that a scientific term?'

He stopped, his face completely blank. Then he spun, grabbed me and tossed me over his shoulder. He ran to the pool and threw me in, towel and all, then jumped in after me.

I lay back on the deck chair with the crossword on my knees. I sipped the rich, ice-cold fruit drink, then returned the glass to the table and the demon waiter refilled it for me. John was at the bottom of the pool; he'd been there for some time. The occasional bubble rising from his dark shape was the only sign he was alive.

'Damn if he hasn't gone and fallen asleep at the bottom of the pool again.' The Tiger strolled over to me and sat down next to the deck chair. 'He does that every single goddamn time.'

'Is that what he's doing? I was wondering. How come he can stay so long under the water? He's in human form, doesn't he need to breathe?'

'He's in his element. Even drained and in human form, it's his element. Even when I'm drained I can still do things with metal.'

'That's right, your element is metal. What can you do?'

'Just about anything.' He looked around. The spoon lifted out of my drink and floated to him. He sat up, held it in front of his face and closed his eyes.

The spoon changed to gold.

'Take it,' he said.

I plucked the spoon out of the air. 'Really gold?'

'Yep. Not worth anything here on the Plane, but on Earth it's quite handy. I have to be careful not to do it too much, don't want to upset the world economy. Let it go, I have it.'

The spoon lifted from my fingers and I released it. It floated in front of his whiskers again. 'Note, my Lady Emma, nothing up my sleeve.' The spoon changed to copper. He concentrated, and the spoon folded up into a ball slightly smaller than a golf ball. He changed the copper ball to gold, then to silver, then it changed shape again until it was a little silver tiger.

'Stop.' I took the tiger out of the air. 'This is really sweet.'

'You like it? It's platinum.' He concentrated, and the little tiger floated off my hand. A tiny loop grew out of its back. Another spoon floated off the table next to me, went shiny, and turned into a matching chain. The chain threaded itself through the loop, and the platinum tiger drifted back down to settle on my hand.

'It's delightful,' I said. 'I'll give it to Simone. She'll love it.'

He was speechless for a moment, his tawny eyes glowing. 'I'll make one for you as well if you like. It would flatter your pale skin.'

'No need. One for Simone is enough. I don't need anything.' I glanced at the bubbles rising from John's dark form. 'I have everything I could possibly want in the whole world.' I had an inspiration. 'Is Louise here?'

'Nope. You just missed her. About twenty of them went shopping in Paris this morning. Not to worry, you'll see her there. Look around Rue du Faubourg St Honoré. They always go crazy in there, costs me a fortune.'

'You should buy shares in the fashion houses, if the others are anything like her. She won't buy anything for months, then go berserk and spend a fortune on clothes and shoes.'

'I already did. Bought a couple of hotels for them to stay in, as well. Wherever they are, they stay with me.'

'You said they never want to leave. You lied to our faces.'

He looked blank for a moment, then understood; his mouth opened to reveal his gleaming fangs. 'No, my Lady, I said they never *want* to leave.'

'Why would Rhonda leave if she didn't want to?'

'Because she is quite remarkable.' He glanced at the pool. 'He'd better get his shell into gear, I have a big dinner planned for you two. And I want you both looking halfway neat.'

'Oh no, Tiger, please, you know that neither of us does neat.'

'Not a single hole in any of the clothes that you wear. And try to keep your hair tidy for at least the first five minutes.'

'Yeah, why is his hair always coming out? It's like it has a life of its own. And he hates wearing shoes, he'll always go barefoot if he has the choice.'

'Ask him. It's a long story.' He pulled himself up and stretched, his tail shivering. He yawned widely, making his whiskers stand out from his face. 'Time for the Turtle to move his shell.'

He loped to the pool, jumped in and disappeared under the water.

The water swirled, exploding into a huge whirlpool with the Tiger at its centre. The water expanded and rose like a water spout with the Tiger on top, a look of horror on his tiger face.

The column of water carried the Tiger to the edge and unceremoniously tipped him off. He landed gracefully on his feet at the edge of the pool.

'You *bastard*!' he yelled. 'This is the thanks I get for looking after your Lady while you sleep your ass off in *my* pool! You are a lazy piece of shit and should get your fucking shell *moving*!'

'I think you are in big trouble, Tiger.' I rose from the deck chair, still holding my drink. I leapt, somersaulted, and landed lightly on the roof of the pool bar about twenty metres away. I knew what was coming.

'Would you like me to freshen your drink for you while you're up there, ma'am?' the demon servant said from the bar below.

'No, thank you,' I called down. 'I think we'll be leaving soon.'

The entire contents of the swimming pool lifted like a huge watery brick. It rose in a single glistening transparent lump and hovered over the Tiger. John stood on the bottom of the empty pool and grinned.

'Holy fucking *shit*!' the Tiger roared, but it was too late.

John dropped the entire pool of water on the Tiger. The Tiger crouched like a cowed house cat as the water poured over him. The noise was incredible; it seemed to go on forever. Finally the deluge stopped, and there was complete silence except for the thin noise of the water trickling back into the pool.

Suddenly the water on the paving rushed together and cascaded back into the pool where it formed watery steps. John casually walked up the stairs and stepped out. He saw me on the roof. 'Told you that move needed work. That was much more like it. Did you spill your drink?'

That was it. I fell off the roof laughing.

We walked back in the glowing late afternoon sun. 'I like that swimsuit. You should keep it,' John said.

'I won't keep it because you like it. I dress for me, not for you.'

'I can tell. Most of the time you dress like a street sleeper.'

'Oh, that's *very good* coming from you,' I shot back. 'You didn't even know I threw those awful old pants away.'

'I found them in the trash and took them back. I like them. They're comfortable.'

'I found where you'd hidden them and threw them away again. Face it. You will never see those awful old pants again.'

He stopped with his hand on the doorknob. 'I may put a hole in one of the new pairs that Leo bought me, just to annoy you.'

Two smiling demon servants waited for us inside with a portable rack of clothing. We immediately sent them out.

'Most of this is designer gear,' I said as we flipped through the rack. I handed him a plain black cotton shirt, and he swapped it for a black *cheongsam* embroidered with silver good-luck bats. 'He hates us.'

'He loves us.' He took the plain black slacks from me and pulled his swim shorts off. 'Thanks.' He reached around the rack, grabbed me and pulled me in for a lingering kiss. 'Let's do it Japanese-style.'

'I hope you mean have a bath Japanese-style.' I released myself and pulled my swimsuit off. We went into the bathroom together. 'Can you fill the bath quickly?'

'Right now I can only work with water once it's there. When I'm not drained I can make it rain in a focused area, but it's too hard right now.' He threw our swimsuits into the linen basket and they disappeared. 'We'll have to fill the bath normally.'

'Damn. That bath's enormous. It'll take a while to fill up. Having it Japanese-style is a good idea.'

'Not washing here.' He started the water into the bath. 'This bathroom isn't set up for it. Have a shower first.'

He pulled me into the shower. 'I should have shown you this in the pool, but I fell asleep. Hold your head under the water and breathe it.'

I tried it. He was right. I could breathe the water. It was a most remarkable feeling.

Then he washed me and that was an even better feeling. He took his time, soaping me all over. He pressed himself against me as he did it, then pushed me forward out of the water to wash my hair.

I rinsed my hair, then turned, put my hands behind his neck and pulled his face down to mine. We stayed under the water together for a while. I breathed the water as I kissed him; the water was sweet in our mouths and flowed deliciously between us.

I pulled away. 'Let me wash you. Turn around.'

His long hair took a great deal of shampoo. When wet it went down to the tops of his thighs. I lingered, enjoying the sensation of his silken hair running through my fingers. I pushed him to sit in the shower and massaged his scalp. He leaned back into me and closed his eyes.

I bent to speak into his ear. 'Remind me to give you a massage later. All over.'

'You are absolutely on,' he said, his voice a low rumble.

I squeezed the water out of his hair and pulled him up. 'The desert's making your hair very dry. It needs a treatment.'

'It's because I'm so drained. After Paris it will be okay again.'

I brushed the grey at his temples. 'I like this though. It makes you look distinguished.'

He smiled over his shoulder at me, then his head shot up and his face went blank. He quickly jumped out of the shower.

The bath had overflowed.

He turned the water off, then moved the excess from the bath to the shower in a floating shiny blob. He dried the floor at the same time, then reached into the shower and gently guided me into the bath.

We stepped in together. We watched each other as we sank into the steaming, crystal-clear water. It was Japanese-style, breathtakingly hot.

His face remained expressionless as he dropped his head into the water and his long hair floated around him. He reached to me and took my hand, then tugged it gently.

I dipped my head under the water as well. I took a deep breath, trusting him completely. I could still breathe the water. He pulled me into him so we touched all over, breathing the water together.

Our mouths met and we floated together. The water was sweet and pure and hot.

We stayed under for a very long time.

He sat with his arms draped over the side of the bath and I lay on top of him with my arms folded across his chest. The water was beginning to cool but neither of us was eager to move.

'Your eyes haven't gone black since,' I said with a touch of disappointment.

His chest moved under me as he laughed softly. 'You are so different.'

'Different?'

He didn't say anything, he just smiled down at me. I heard what he'd said and pulled myself up so that my eyes were level with his.

'What did Michelle do the first time? I hope she wasn't too frightened.'

He still smiled, but I could see he was hesitant about what to say.

'It's okay, I understand,' I said. 'I'm just interested. It must have been terrifying for her.'

'It was.' He unfocused, remembering. 'She didn't take it nearly as well as you have. In fact she nearly left me on the spot.' His eyes wrinkled up. 'I can't believe we're talking about this.'

'I like to think that there's nothing we can't talk about.' I dropped my chin onto my arms where they lay on his chest. 'What did she do?'

'She said if I ever did it again, she'd kill me. So I let her.'

I went completely still. His smile didn't shift.

'I gave her a little revolver, and showed her how to use it. She put it beside the bed. If my eyes went black, she'd shoot me. Right between the eyes. One minute I'm seeing the rich brown eyes of my love, the next minute it's the ugly face of the Judge.'

'Judge?'

He shook his head, still smiling. 'Your eyes are a very bright shade of blue, you know that? The first time I saw blue eyes I thought the European was blind.'

'They're more grey than blue.' I pulled him back to the point. 'She'd *shoot* you?'

'I took the human form with me so there wouldn't be a mess. I'd be gone for at least a day, sometimes more. I think she enjoyed it.'

I dropped my forehead onto his chest; I'd had a sudden horrible thought. 'If they come at us with guns we're defenceless, aren't we?'

'No. I just fill everything with water, change the cartridge to water. Makes them useless. Never had a chance with her though; when I'd lost control I wasn't thinking.'

'Can you still fill them with water? Even now?'

He nodded, and his body moved underneath me. 'One or two, not a problem. There are other ways to disable them as well. Simone will learn a few tricks that will stand her in good stead against them. Don't worry.'

I relaxed. 'When you come back I want to have a go too.'

'You are welcome to try. If you can take me I will give you anything you desire, which is within my power to give.'

'Not fair. You know I don't want anything in the world right now.' I pulled myself upright with delight. 'Except an answer! I have you.'

He glanced down to where I sat on him. 'You certainly have me.' He smiled back up at me. 'What?'

I fingered his hair. 'Why the hell does it keep coming out all the time? And what's the thing with the bare feet?'

He laughed gently and I shook on top of him. 'I thought you did some research on me.'

I slapped him lightly on the chest. 'Tell me.'

He wrapped his arms around my back. 'Is the water too cold?'

'No. Tell me!'

His eyes sparkled for a while. I was ready to slap him again when he smiled. 'It's a very simple story.'

I leaned forward on his chest so that my face was right next to his and gazed into his eyes. 'Tell me.'

Bad move. He stopped to kiss me first and I couldn't concentrate for a while. The water warmed up. Steam rose.

He pulled back, still smiling. 'When an Immortal is Raised, they are Raised as they stand. I was Raised directly after an enormous battle. My hair,' he stopped and moved it to one side out of the way, 'was in the standard style of the time, long and tied on top. But it was a mess after the battle; it usually is. My shoes were gone. So that was that. Stuck like it.'

'That is totally ridiculous.'

'That's what happened. You've seen Iron Crutch — he was even worse off. I don't have to keep the form; you know I can take any form I want. But despite myself, I keep reverting.' His eyes sparkled even more. 'It's a damn nuisance.'

'But you're a *Turtle*. How can you be a human Raised Immortal as well?'

'That is not for one such as you to know,' he said sadly, but he still smiled. 'Later you will know. Now is not the time.'

I didn't push it. 'Give me plenty of warning before you Raise me. I'll put some make-up on and make sure my hair is tidy.'

'Doesn't work like that. Sorry.'

'I don't think you are. I think you want us to be the scruffiest Immortals on the Celestial Plane.'

He brushed his hands over my back. 'You have found me out.'

'Took your sweet time,' the Tiger said. Dinner was set out on a long low table with a large number of cushions scattered around it. 'I know what you two were doing.'

'You know I hate Western food.' John eyed the dishes with contempt. 'You are doing everything you possibly can to annoy me because you know it will be a long time before I can get you back with the thorough and detailed cruelty that you deserve.'

'Can't you two grow up?' I said. 'It's not Western food, John, it's definitely Chinese.'

'Western Chinese,' the Tiger said. 'Lots of chilli. Spicy.'

'I hate it,' John moaned.

'How about a beggar's chicken for the Lady, and some vegetarian buckwheat noodles and a selection of Northern-style steamed buns for the Lord?' The Tiger's voice was amused but his face didn't show it.

'Now you're talking. Monica can't do Northern food.' John grinned. 'I was there, you know.'

'Where?' I said.

'When the beggar was caught with the chicken. I was riding past the palace with my guards.'

'You are a lying bastard,' the Tiger growled.

'I saw him do it. It was already wrapped. He covered it with mud and buried it next to the little fire he'd built. I told my guards, silently, to leave him, as he'd already ruined his dinner. I changed my form and went back later to check on him.' John smiled, remembering. 'He was a great guy.'

'That's not vegetarian, John. I can't eat the chicken.'

'Beside the point on the Celestial Plane. You can let your hair down here.'

'Don't you dare,' the Tiger said. 'I am very careful not to get any fur in the food, and you will be too. Mao tai?'

'Now you are really talking,' John said with grim pleasure.

'Yuck,' I said. 'Mao tai tastes like donkey urine that something died in.'

'It's an acquired taste,' John said. 'After a couple of hundred years I think you'll probably like it as much as we do.'

'I sincerely hope I'll have the chance.'

'You will. Here's the chicken,' the Tiger said. A servant brought a large covered platter. 'My Lady, would you like to do the honours?'

'Sure, where's the hammer?'

'I usually make one on the spot.' The Tiger looked around. The lid of the serving platter twisted and went shiny. Part of it separated and formed a tiny golden hammer. The hammer floated in front of me, and I picked it out of the air and nodded to the Tiger.

The servant removed the remains of the platter's lid to reveal a large lump of baked dough. 'I have to be careful not to hit it so hard that I completely destroy it,' I said, almost to myself.

'Look inside the dough, see where its weakness is,' John said. 'It will have points in its structure where a single firm tap, not too hard, will crack it open.'

'How do I look inside it?'

He took my hand and showed me. He opened his consciousness and studied the dough. He released my hand. 'Now you try.'

I did the same thing he had. I opened my inner sight and peered inside the dough. I could see its structure, the way it was put together. The dough had been made slightly unevenly and there were parts where it was strong and other parts where it was weak. There were points where the strong and weak parts met, making clearly visible fracture lines. I studied one of the lines and followed it, searching for the place where a single light tap would crack the dough open. I found it.

I drew my consciousness back, remembering the location of the weak spot. I put the hammer down; I wouldn't need it.

I reached with my index finger and lightly tapped the dough on the weak point. It fell open like a flower, revealing the steaming chicken wrapped in lotus leaf. A wonderful warm aroma of wine and chicken and lotus leaf spread around us.

'You should not have been able to do that,' the Tiger said with awe.

'She did *shen* work this afternoon as well,' John said.

The Tiger pondered for a while, then spoke. 'There is something seriously weird going on here, Xuan Wu. Lady Emma is an ordinary human. Why is she able to do this? It's worrying.'

'Please let's just enjoy the meal and not freak me out,' I said with a calmness I didn't feel.

'Good idea, Emma,' John said briskly. He lifted his chopsticks and eyed the buns impatiently as they were brought in. 'I haven't had this in a while and I don't think I'll leave you any.'

'How will you eat, Bai Hu?'

'Very messily,' the Tiger said. 'Looks like I get all the chilli peppers.'

Familiar music began to play. It was soft enough for us to talk and seemed to come from all directions. The Tiger pointed with his head. 'They're over there.' An alcove on one side of the room was covered with a gauzy curtain. 'I had them come over and play specially for you, since I know you like them. They sound different when they're unplugged, but we need to be able to talk.' He nodded towards the Szechuan food. 'Fits the generally spicy theme. Peppers for the food, Peppers for the music.'

'How do you know what music I like?' I demanded. I glared at John and he shook his head, innocent.

'I had Leo go through your CDs.' The Tiger's golden eyes sparkled with amusement. 'He said you have one of the most distressing collections of trash that he's ever seen.'

'That can't be right,' John said through a mouthful of noodles. 'Leo said that *my* CDs were the most distressing collection of trash he'd ever seen.'

'No, Turtle,' the Tiger said patiently. 'That was your *vinyl* he was talking about.'

'You are quite correct,' John said. 'Shame I threw away my eight-tracks. Leo is quite incapable of appreciating the subtle harmonics and delicate nuances of truly fine Western heavy metal.'

'But do you have to play it so damn *loud*?' I said.

'Nuances.' He grinned. 'Wait till we have Simone off to school and I can turn the bass up to where it belongs.'

'You are very scary sometimes, you know that?'

He just grinned over the noodles. But I knew what he was thinking: good.

It was very late when we returned to our room. We quickly changed out of the fancy clothes and into something much more comfortable; him in his black cotton jacket and pants, me in a flowing long top and matching trousers.

The desert sky was full of a million brilliant stars. We sat on the balcony together and warm candlelight flickered in the room behind us.

'How long have we known each other, Emma?' he said quietly, his arm draped around my shoulder and his other hand holding mine.

'I don't know, let me think. I started part-time with you end of the year before last. I changed to full-time beginning of last year. Just over a year and a half. Is that all? It feels like forever.'

'It does, doesn't it? It seems like there's never been a time when I didn't know you.' He pulled me into his lap. I leaned back and put my head on his shoulder. He wrapped his strong arms around me. 'It's as if we've known each other forever.'

'I know how you feel. I feel the same way. Maybe we're soulmates or something.'

'Could be.' His voice vibrated through his chest. 'That was one of the toughest battles I have ever faced.'

'What was?'

'Simone and Leo wanted you to come full-time almost immediately. Simone particularly made my life complete hell. She wanted you there all the time. I should have listened to her.' He ran his mouth over the side of my neck, then pulled away slightly to speak softly into my ear. 'We could have had more time.'

'I don't want to go back. I want to stay here forever with you.'

'That is the fate of the ruler,' he said, his voice soft and sad. 'Our own happiness always comes second. We have so many people who rely on us. We must care for them first.'

'You're right. There are people relying on us. We are so lucky to have had this short time together. I am so privileged. Not only have I met you, but I've gained your trust, and your love, and your promise.' He kissed the back of my neck and I shivered. 'There isn't a thing in the world that I want for myself right now.'

He unbuttoned my shirt, gently pulled it over my head and threw it aside. He put his arms back around me and his grip tightened. He kissed the side of my throat, then over my shoulder.

I turned on his lap so that I was side-on to him. I gazed into his dark eyes; they glowed in the starlight. I ran my fingertips over his high cheekbone and over the edge of his jaw. He watched me without moving. I reached behind his neck and pulled his long braid towards me. I undid the tie holding it and combed it free with my fingers. I nibbled lightly along the edge of his jaw then ran my mouth down the silken skin on the side of his throat. I pulled away slightly to speak into his ear.

'I changed my mind. There *is* something I want for myself, right now.'

He studied my face intensely. 'I have no idea what you are talking about. Please come inside with me and explain in complete and accurate detail exactly what you would like for yourself, and I'll see what I can do.'

He moved his face closer to mine and our lips met. We pushed into each other. I wrapped my arms around his neck and pulled him in. He rose and carried me inside, which was a very good thing. My legs weren't working at all.

CHAPTER FIFTEEN

The warm desert sun shone through the window but we ignored it. I straddled his lap and ran my fingertips over his face. We didn't have much more time.

I took his hands and moved them onto my bare breasts. His face went strange and he shifted his hands to my shoulders.

I'd noticed that. I tried it again, moved his hands onto my breasts. He slid them around to my back.

He saw what I was doing and watched me, expressionless.

'Tell me,' I said.

He didn't reply.

I bent and kissed him for a long time. I pressed myself against him and felt him stir.

When I came up for air, I moved his hands again and he shifted them away. I grinned, and he smiled slightly in response. 'You're not upset?'

'More curious than anything.'

He put his hands on my shoulders and drifted them down my back. This what he really liked; it was easy to tell.

I bent and spoke into his ear. 'I like you touching my back better too.'

He jerked his head back to see me. 'You're joking.'

'It seems we like the same thing.'

'That can't be right,' he said, bemused.

'Why not?'

He laughed quietly and shook beneath me.

'Don't do that again,' I said more loudly, 'or I'll have to stop talking.'

'Laughing? Or ...' He brushed his hands lightly over my back and I wriggled in response.

'Both! Why can't it be right? It feels perfectly right to me.'

'This,' he said as he brushed his hands over my back and shoulders, 'is something to do with my true nature.'

'Oh my God.'

'Right here, all yours.'

'It's because you're a *reptile*, isn't it? You aren't a *mammal* at all.'

His face froze. 'I am a mammal in this form,' he said grimly. 'I am one hundred per cent human.'

'You're worried I'll be freaked out.'

He was silent but his face said it all.

'Did it freak her out?'

He hesitated, his face still expressionless, then nodded once, sharply.

'Sit up.'

He didn't move.

'Do it!'

He pulled himself upright. I shifted to let him move but remained on his lap.

I brushed my hands over his shoulders and down his back. He shivered and his eyes went very dark.

I loaded my hands with a tiny amount of *chi* and did it again.

He closed his eyes, arched his back and quivered into my hands. Yes.

I pressed myself against him and ran my loaded hands up and down his back, then brushed them over his shoulders. He stiffened under my hands and his face became a mask of rapture. A low sound of pleasure floated from deep within him.

Then he completely lost control. His eyes went black. He threw me onto my back and forced himself on top of me.

'Yes!'

When he came back he fell beside me and watched me.

'Listen to me,' I said firmly.

He didn't move but his eyes studied my face.

'I am not freaked out. In fact I am so turned on I cannot believe myself. This ...' I ran my hand over his back and watched his response with delight. '... is the coolest thing I have ever experienced in my entire life. *God* but I am glad we had this time before you went.' I kissed him and sat up. 'I'm starving. Do we have time for breakfast before we go?'

'With or without another mutual back rub?'

'I'll skip the breakfast for the back rub.'

I came around on one of the couches in the living room of the Peak apartment.

John and Leo sat on the other couch, watching me with concern. The Tiger was stretched on the carpet in front of them in True Form. Simone reclined on his back and stroked his fur.

I rose, slightly dizzy, and saw them. I suddenly wanted a photo of them all together like that. My family.

'Before we do anything, guys, could you all stay like that so I can take a photo? Please?'

'Monica can fetch the digital camera,' John said. 'Monica!'

Monica hurried out of the kitchen, then fell back against the wall and clutched her chest, her face ashen.

'Damn!' I yelled and rushed to her.

'Damn!' John shouted at the same time. 'I completely forgot.'

Everybody crowded around Monica. We took her into the dining room and sat her down. I fanned her face. John patted her hand. Leo hovered, concerned.

'Get her some cold water, please, Leo.' I sat next to her. She gasped for breath and clutched her chest. 'Monica, it's all right, it won't hurt you.'

Monica stared at me with her mouth wide, still gasping for breath.

Leo returned with the water and I held it for her to take a couple of sips. 'Breathe, Monica. You'll be fine. Relax. Breathe.'

Monica nodded, took some deep breaths, and then another sip of water. Colour returned to her face.

'Everybody out except me,' I said. 'John, tell the Tiger to stay right where he is. I still want that photo. And Monica will need to get used to it. Now is as good a time as any.'

'You sure about that, Emma?' Leo said.

I turned and spoke softly to them. 'If she doesn't see for herself that he's harmless, she'll be living in constant fear of what comes in the front door.'

'I'll go and find the digital camera,' John said. 'Come on, people. Emma knows what she's doing.'

I sat with Monica for a while, letting her settle, holding her hand. Her breathing returned to normal, but her eyes brimmed with tears and I gave her some tissues.

'All right now?' I said.

She nodded, wiping her eyes.

'Monica, you know that Chinese man with the white hair who comes over sometimes? Bai Hu?'

'Yes, ma'am, I know him.'

'That's him. He's a tiger.'

'I don't want to know, ma'am.' She winced and looked down. 'I don't want to know about it.'

'You have to know, because he's Michael's father.'

Her head shot up to look at me and her eyes went wide.

'Yes, that's right, Michael's father is a tiger. Many of the people who come through here are strange, you know that. You'll just have to be ready for it. And not be frightened, because nobody who comes in here will ever hurt you.'

She was silent, her face full of misery.

'He's stuck as a tiger right now. Come out and say hello to him. He won't hurt you; in fact his fur is very nice. You can touch him. You saw Simone, you know we wouldn't let anything ever hurt Simone.'

'I think I'll just stay in here, ma'am. I don't want to. Please don't make me.'

'If that's what you want, then I won't force you.' I moved closer and put my arm around her shoulders. 'I just don't want you to be frightened. It would be better if you came out and saw him. I can come with you, I won't let him hurt you.'

'I can really touch him?' she said, still frightened but becoming curious.

'You really can. Come and see. You know him already; you've seen him come and go. He's just the same person.'

'What about the others, the blue man and the red lady? Are they tigers too?'

'No. The blue man is a dragon, and the red lady is a phoenix, a big bird. Monica.' I spoke more firmly. 'Mr Chen is an animal too.'

'Sir is an *animal*?'

'Yes, he is. Are you scared of him?'

'No,' she said, her eyes wide. 'I'm not scared of him. Sir is a *good man*.'

'So is the Tiger. He's a wonderful man as well. Come and say hello. I promise he won't hurt you. Did you know that he can talk? A talking tiger, how about that? Come and see.'

Monica thought about it, then nodded and rose, still clutching my hand. I kept my other arm around her shoulder. 'Don't be afraid.'

We went out of the dining room together, Monica still holding my hand. I eased her slightly into the living room, and let her stand for a moment and become accustomed to it.

The Tiger stretched out on the carpet with Simone draped casually over his back and rubbing the sides of his head. He lay with his eyes half-closed, obviously enjoying it. Leo and John sat on the couch waiting for us.

Monica pointed at the Tiger. 'That's where the fur comes from. I'm vacuuming it all the time. I thought it was coming out of the carpet.'

'Sorry, Monica,' the Tiger said.

She stiffened and clutched my hand.

'It's all right, Monica.' I rubbed her arm and squeezed her around the shoulders. 'He won't hurt you. Remember, you know him already. It's Mr Chen's friend, Bai Hu.'

'I'm sorry I scared you, Monica,' the Tiger said, his voice gentle. 'I won't hurt you, I promise.'

'Uncle Bai is great, Monica,' Simone said without moving from his back. 'He gives me rides.'

'Do you want to touch him?' I said softly into Monica's ear.

She remained unmoving, pondering. Then she straightened. 'No, thank you, ma'am.' She pulled her hand free from mine. 'Do you need anything? Sir? Ma'am? Mr Tiger?'

'Tea, tikuanyin,' John said.

The Tiger chuckled.

'Off you go, Monica,' I said. 'Don't be afraid.'

'Can I ask you something inside, ma'am?'

'Sure.' I shrugged and followed her into the kitchen.

'Hurry up, Emma, if you want to take a photo,' John said.

'I'll be right out, don't be so impatient.'

'Humph,' John said, and the Tiger chuckled again.

I went into the kitchen and closed the door. Monica rinsed the teapot for us.

'What did you want to ask me, Monica?'

'Ma'am,' Monica said without stopping or looking up, 'what animal is Mr Chen?'

'He's a turtle.'

Monica collapsed over the sink and howled with laughter. I had never heard her laugh like that before. Tears sprang from her eyes. She shook her head, speechless.

I just smiled and went out. Obviously she knew.

'One more,' I said, fell to one knee and lined them up. Before I pressed the button I stopped and glared at the Tiger. 'Put that tail *back*.'

The Tiger grinned and covered himself with his tail again.

'What's he doing, Emma?' Simone said from his back.

'Nothing,' the Tiger said, but the minute I'd taken the photo he moved his tail away again. 'Good thing it's a digital camera.'

'I forgot once before and had some photos taken out and processed,' John said. 'Family photos at a banquet. The staff asked me a lot of questions. They recognised us as the Four Winds. I told them it was a movie set.'

'I'd love a photo of all four of you Winds in True Form,' I said.

'Bai Hu?' John said.

'You're on,' the Tiger said with a smile in his voice. 'What a good idea.'

'As soon as I'm back, we'll do one for you, Serpent and all,' John said.

'Not eating,' I said.

Monica came out of the kitchen holding the tray of tea things. I didn't push her; I went to her to take the tray.

'No, ma'am, I'm fine.' She walked calmly around the Tiger and put the tray on the coffee table. She returned around the Tiger as if he was a big cat, carefully stepping over his tail, and proceeded into the kitchen as if absolutely nothing was amiss.

We stared at each other. Leo grinned like an idiot.

'Every single member of my household staff is a treasure beyond compare,' John said with wonder.

'I don't know how you do it, Ah Wu,' the Tiger said. 'I have hundreds, and not a single one can hold a candle to anything you have. And you have less than a dozen.'

Michael had heard our voices and came down the hallway. He stopped dead when he saw the Tiger. The Tiger gently eased Simone off his back, then rose to face Michael. He stood completely immobile, but the tip of his tail twitched.

Simone moved to John's lap and he wrapped his arms around her.

We all waited quietly to see what would happen.

'Is this him, my Lady?' Michael said.

'Michael MacLaren,' I said loudly, 'this is your father, the White Tiger of the West, Lord Bai Hu.'

'You are Rhonda's boy?' the Tiger rasped.

Michael nodded and his blond hair fell over his forehead.

The Tiger's voice was still a low rasp. 'How is your mother, boy?'

'My mother is well, my Lord.'

'She remarried?'

'No, sir.'

The Tiger sat on his haunches and flicked one ear. 'You are working as a Retainer for the Dark Lord, Xuan Wu?'

Michael nodded, his hair flipping over. It was an even match. The kid was totally unafraid.

'Ah Wu.' The Tiger spoke to John over his shoulder. 'If the kid ever wants to leave your service, let me know. I have a place for him with the Horsemen.' He turned back to Michael. 'Serve the Dark Lord well, Three One Five. If you wish to leave his service, I will take you.' He paused, then dropped his voice. 'Say hello to your mother for me.'

He turned and bowed to John, lowering his head over his front legs. 'My Lord. I think I should return and recuperate. By your leave.'

'Bai Hu,' John said kindly.

The Tiger bowed similarly to me. 'My Lady. I suggest that you permit me to offer my services and my palace one more time before the Dark Lord departs. It is the least I can offer the two of you.'

'I don't think that's a good idea, Tiger,' I said, my heart breaking. 'We need you strong.'

'I understand. But I'll see what I can do.' He bowed again. 'By your leave, my Lady.'

'Go home to your palace, Tiger. Come back soon. I like having you around.'

He gazed at me with his golden eyes, then he was gone.

Michael stumbled to the couch and dropped to sit on it. John saw what was up and took Simone out, gesturing for Leo to follow him. Michael didn't even notice.

I sat on the other couch and waited for him to recover and start asking questions. But he just sat for a long time, staring at me without saying anything. I sighed. Two in one day. Maybe I should make a set of signs to hold up. 'No, it won't hurt you.' 'Yes, this is a strange household.' 'A turtle.'

I suddenly understood: this was why John never told anybody anything. He always asked somebody else to tell people the truth about him. It wasn't just because it wasn't fitting, him being who he was. It was because he was bored to death of telling people the same things over and over and having to explain the truth patiently to them.

I wondered if I could delegate the job to somebody else after he'd gone. Maybe Jade could do it.

Monica came to collect the tea things. She saw Michael's face and smiled.

'Thanks, Monica,' I said. She nodded and took the tray out.

'What did he call me?' Michael said softly. 'Three One Five? What's that?'

'You're son number three hundred and fifteen.'

'He doesn't even know his own kids' names?'

'Frankly, Michael, I don't think he cares very much.'

'Where were you, my Lady? Leo said not to worry, you were fine. What happened?'

'The Tiger took us to his palace in the Western Desert.' I paused, remembering that beautiful place. 'It's on the Celestial Plane. I finally made it there.'

Michael's eyes went wide.

'The Tiger wanted to make sure that I'd be safe, so he took me there, where the demons couldn't get me. When the demon ran from Mr Chen, the Tiger took Mr Chen there too. He is a complete idiot. Mr Chen obviously takes a lot of carrying and now the Tiger has to stay in True Form and recuperate.'

'And that was it?' Michael said. 'True Form.'

'Yes, it was.'

'What was the palace like?'

'Wonderful. But we didn't see that much of it, we were busy.' Michael didn't seem to hear me; he was obviously deep in thought. 'If you ever want to go there, you can. He has an army there, the Western Horsemen. You heard what he said. You can go and join any time you like.'

'I think I'll stay here and learn from you and Lord Xuan. But I'll think about it.'

'Give me plenty of notice if you do decide to go. You're really very good, and I'd have a hard time finding someone good enough to replace you.'

He lit up with a genuine grin of delight. 'Thanks, ma'am.'

CHAPTER SIXTEEN

Leo brought Michael into the dining room and they both saluted John and me, then sat.

'Okay,' I said. 'Before we discuss the revised trip, there's something I'd like to talk about first.' I sighed. 'John, while I was talking to Monica, I assured her that Bai Hu wouldn't hurt her. That's true, but I also told her that she was safe. After what happened to Charlie, we know that's no longer true.'

John's face went expressionless. 'You're right, they're not safe any more. None of them. This is the first time in my history I have experienced this. I have encountered a demon that is so without honour that it will attack defenceless Retainers.' He rubbed his hands over his face. 'Time to do it. I hoped this day would never come. I will dismiss everybody.' He looked down at his hands, then up at me. 'I'll sell the house in London, it's too far away. With no staff to manage it, it won't last until I return. We'll trim back to bare essentials. I can't afford to put anybody else at risk. I'll dismiss all the household staff and you can go to the Western Palace. We'll leave it as just me and Simone.'

'I'm not going anywhere,' I said. 'Don't be ridiculous.'

'I want you safe, Emma.'

'We've had this discussion before, John. I'm staying with you and Simone, and there's nothing you can do about it.'

'Me too,' Leo said. 'You can't fire me.'

'What, because you quit?' I said.

'No, because I just won't go,' Leo said. 'I'll camp out on the doorstep if I have to.' He gestured towards Michael. 'Michael is safer here with us. The minute he walks out the door he's a target. Doubly so. If he doesn't stay here he should go to the palace.'

'They're all targets,' I said to John. 'He knows you can't protect your staff now. I think if you dismiss them he'll just go around and pick them off one by one.'

'Shit,' John said, very calm. 'I must move them all somewhere safe. Everybody should go to the palace.'

'Give me the choice, my Lord,' Leo said.

'Stay or go, Leo?'

'Stay.'

'Very well. Done.'

Leo sighed with relief.

'Michael,' John said. 'I would understand if you chose to leave. You would be completely safe in the Western Desert.'

'Stay,' Michael said.

'Are you a hundred per cent sure, Michael?' I said. 'This could be rough. Please take some time to think about it.'

'I've sworn allegiance. That was more than just words.'

'Whoa,' Leo said under his breath.

'I will teach Michael to call immediately we return from Paris,' John said. 'We will have another energy session as soon as he is ready. We must have you up to speed as quickly as possible, Michael, so that you are able to call for assistance if you need to.'

'I don't want to mess around when it comes to Monica and James though,' I said. 'We need to move them somewhere safe right now. Will the Tiger take them?'

John's eyes unfocused, then he snapped back. 'Yes.'

'Who'll mind the house for us?' Leo said.

'Ah Yat,' I said before John could say something stupid. 'She can teleport, she can sense them coming. She'll be safe. All the demon staff will be safe, wherever they are.'

'I'll tell James, you tell Monica,' John said.

'Good. Next item: Charlie,' I said. 'Do you still have her?'

'Yes. She's in the morgue on the twenty-fourth floor of Hennessy Road,' John said.

'You have a morgue in the Academy?' Michael said.

'Accidents happen,' John said. 'All students and Masters are aware of the risk. Learning about the facilities will be part of your induction when we return.'

'Has her body been prepared, John?' I said.

'All taken care of.'

'Do the police know?'

'No. Fortunately no complications there. But I need to …' His voice changed slightly. '… contact her family in England and tell them, and move her over there. There is a Chen plot at a cemetery in London, where all Retainers are interred. But we'll need to inform her family.'

'We can do that while we're there,' I said. 'How will we move her over there without customs knowing?'

'Jade can probably carry her.'

'And if she's too big, Jade can just put her on the plane.'

John nodded. 'Either way, we take her with us.'

'If we take her on the plane, we'll need to make sure that the hold is cold enough to keep her in good condition.'

'I can tell the pilot. Hopefully we'll have Brian again; he's usually very careful about that sort of thing.'

'Good. Will the family want a viewing? Is she in good enough condition for that?' I smiled slightly. 'If Wong's blade was very sharp, it will be a neat cut, easy to fix. But I wouldn't put it past that bastard to use a blunt blade that made a huge mess of her.'

'If you don't mind, my Lord, my Lady,' Leo said, his voice forced, 'I'd prefer Michael and myself not be involved in these arrangements.'

I suddenly heard what I'd been saying and dropped my head. 'Am I being extremely cold-blooded, Leo?'

'Yes, you are.' Leo studied me, his face strange. 'I don't know how you do it sometimes.'

'She has to be, Leo,' John said. 'It will probably be worse before it is better. Dismissed.'

Leo and Michael rose and left the room together. Leo shot another very concerned look at me as he went out.

I crossed my arms on the table and dropped my head onto them. 'I didn't even realise, but Leo is quite right. I don't believe myself sometimes. I'm just sitting here discussing what to do with poor Charlie's body as if it was the most natural thing in the world. The thing I'm most worried about is how easily we can sew her back together!'

'And that is what will make you the perfect Regent when I am gone,' John said.

'John ...' I hesitated, then rushed into it. 'The stone saw something about me. I can do stuff I shouldn't be able to. This dark thing inside me came out for the Demon King, but not for you. I have these dreams about snakes. There's something wrong here, I know it. I amaze myself sometimes, I'm so cold-blooded. Look at when we were at the palace: you told me Charlie was dead and I didn't even grieve for her. I just continued as if nothing had happened —'

'That was the right thing to do,' he cut in evenly. 'You grieve for those you love when you have the time. Grief is a luxury that often we cannot afford.'

'— And now I'm just sitting here joking about how neatly Wong took off her head!' I cried, distraught. 'What the hell is wrong with me?' I put my head on my arms again, my heart full of misery. There was something terribly wrong with me. Was I even human? 'It's like I'm some sort of dark heartless monster.'

'I am exactly the same way and you do not question me.' I looked up desperately. He gazed into my eyes. 'I have been as cold-blooded about this as you have. And yet you all still love me.'

'You have more than one good excuse,' I whispered.

'Wake up, stone.' John tapped the stone on my finger without touching me.

'Yes, Turtle?'

'Is Lady Emma a dark heartless monster?'

'Yes she is,' the stone said without hesitation and with absolutely no emotion whatsoever.

John jerked back. That was obviously not the answer he was expecting. He glanced sharply at me.

'I knew it.' I closed my eyes with anguish. We remained like that for a while. I had a few options, none of them very pleasant, but at least I knew the truth.

'I have looked inside her and she is an ordinary human being. You said yourself she is an ordinary human being,' John said.

'She is,' the stone said.

'Will she ever hurt any member of her family?' John said with a slight edge of despair.

'I think you have asked me that before, Turtle, and the answer is still no. Of course not. She loves you more than her life. Look at her; right now she is pondering whether you would be safe if she were to leave forever.

She thinks that's not good enough, and wants to kill herself to be absolutely sure that none of you are in any danger. You really should talk to somebody about this death wish, Emma. The Dark Lord is quite correct.'

'But I'm a dark heartless monster, stone,' I said.

'My Lady, of course you are. But *so is he*,' the stone said. 'You are a perfect match. Dark and heartless together.'

Both of us sat back with relief. He *was* a dark heartless monster. And the Tiger was a white heartless monster.

'We're all monsters together,' John said with amusement.

'I think what the stone is trying to say,' I said, 'is that I've been around you far too much, Xuan Wu, and some of your monstrosity is rubbing off on me.'

'No, Emma, it is quite the other way around,' the stone said. 'You are at least twice as monstrous as he is.'

That sobered me. I had an awful thought. 'Am I a demon in human form?'

The stone hesitated again.

'Answer me!' I cried, mortified.

'You cannot be, Emma,' John said. 'I would know immediately.'

'I could be very well hidden, and you're very drained.'

'What you are is beside the point,' the stone said. 'You are what you are. You are devoted to your Lord and your family and would give your life for them. That is what is important.'

'The stone is right, Emma.'

'What am I, stone?' I said, miserable. I was thoroughly tired of its games.

'You are a perfectly ordinary human being, Emma.'

'But I'm a dark heartless monster.'

201

'That is quite correct. Your true nature will probably emerge over time. The Dark Lord, as I said, will be astonished. You are well on the way to Immortality. Live. Love. Continue your duties. And please leave me alone. I was in the middle of a lovely dream, I dreamed I was a mountain.'

'Go back to sleep, stone,' John said with quiet tolerance. 'You are quite useless.'

'That is why I was never used.'

'You are not a demon, Emma. I would know immediately,' John said. 'Don't be concerned. You are not a danger to anybody. It will be fascinating to see how you grow. Trust the stone, it is very ancient and wise. It is even older than me. We all love you, and you love us. That's what's important.'

'I wish I could believe you, John. I hate to think that I'm a danger to anybody.'

'You will be Regent, Lady Emma, and you will do a wonderful job. And you will be here when I return, and I will Raise you and marry you. We will be happy together on my Mountain. I promise you.' He ducked his head to see into my eyes and smiled.

'I only hope I'm worthy,' I whispered.

'Would it make you feel better if Kwan Yin looked at you when we're in Paris? She could examine you and clarify for us. Would you like that?'

'Yes.'

'Come on, Emma, snap out of it. We have a lot to do. You need to talk to Monica, and I have to phone James. Get a move on.'

We smiled and sighed together. Things to do, worry later. We rose almost in unison and he hung back to let me through the door first. I went into the kitchen to find Monica. He went into his study to phone James.

Poor Monica. She'd only just become accustomed to the idea of the White Tiger and now she had to live with him for a while. I made a mental note to warn him to keep his paws off her.

I stopped in the hallway. I was being completely cold-blooded again. The thought made me feel slightly ill. But John and the stone were right. I had too much to do to worry about it. Provided everyone was safe, it didn't matter what I was. And besides, I had parents. I had a family. I'd grown up normally. I was a normal human being.

Wasn't I?

CHAPTER SEVENTEEN

Two days before we left for Paris, Leo drove me, Michael and Simone to the school to buy their uniforms. We wouldn't have time to buy them when we came back. Leo waited outside while I took the kids in. Several domestic helpers already had children there trying on uniforms.

One of the volunteer mothers helped Simone find the right size in her little dress.

Michael slumped, miserable, as I selected a uniform for him. When I held the PE shorts up he backed away and raised his hands. 'Oh no. No way. This is stupid.'

I pushed the shorts at him. He stood his ground.

I moved closer and hissed in his ear. 'Try these on, and that's an order.'

He glared at me, snatched the shorts out of my hand, and thundered to the change room.

'You know I don't need PE anyway,' he grumbled as he moved inside the room. 'You know what I can do.'

'Shut up and try them on,' I said loudly.

'They're all like that,' one of the assistants said as she came out of the change booth with Simone.

Simone clapped her hands with delight and twirled in her uniform.

'You look adorable, darling,' the assistant said. 'You and your brother are really cute together.'

Simone scowled and put her hands on her hips. 'He's *not* my *brother*.'

'Cousins,' I said. 'Large Chinese family.'

Michael came out and shoved the shorts at me. 'They're okay.'

The assistant looked from Michael to me, then moved closer to me to speak softly. 'He won't be able to dye his hair. He'll have to dye it back to its natural colour.'

Michael snorted with disdain and stomped away.

'That *is* his natural colour,' I said. 'He's a natural blond.'

'You'd better tell his teacher then, otherwise he'll be in trouble for dyeing his hair.'

'Thanks.'

She nodded and returned to the counter.

A Chinese woman entered the shop with a small boy. Simone stiffened and squeaked, then scurried to me and hid behind me. Michael also came swiftly to me, very alert, and I knew what was up.

'Michael, go to the door, poke your head out and tell Leo to get in here *right now*,' I whispered.

The female demon ignored me completely, talking to the little boy about what uniform to buy. The boy behaved like a normal child. They paid no attention to Leo and Michael as they came back in.

'What do you think they're up to?' Leo said softly into my ear.

'I have no idea. You have more experience than I do,' I said, just as softly. 'What should we do?'

'They can't do anything with so many people around,' Leo said. 'Keep Simone close, buy the rest of the stuff, and let's get out of here.' He stationed himself against one of the walls and watched the demons.

I took Simone into the booth to change out of her uniform. Michael posted himself outside and guarded, completely professional.

We went to the counter to pay. Simone stayed very close and quiet. Leo didn't move or speak as he leaned against the wall and watched.

I paid for the uniforms and nodded to Leo. He opened the door for us and I guided the kids out.

The demons dropped what they were doing and followed.

It was still school holidays and the school was deserted. We passed the school cafeteria next to the uniform shop, then stopped. A large open balcony overlooked the playing field. A deserted play area next to the playing field would be a good place to face them.

'Emma, take the kids down to the car,' Leo said. 'I'll deal with them.'

'No, there might be more of them at the car.'

'No more right now,' Simone said.

'But they might appear any time. We should stick together, deal with these first, and then go to the car,' I said.

'You're right, my Lady,' Leo said.

'Let's go down to the play area,' I said. 'Nobody around, and room to move.'

We went down the steps to the playground. Simone clutched my hand. Michael was tense and prepared. The demons followed us, talking to each other as if nothing unusual at all was happening.

When we reached the play area we stopped and turned to face them. Leo and I put Simone behind us. Michael stood beside Leo, ready. The demons stopped pretending. They retained the form of a mother and child, but went very still and watched us impassively.

'What are you waiting for?' I said.

The mother looked around. There was nobody nearby who could see us. They both fell to their knees and touched their foreheads to the rubber matting covering the ground.

'Dark Lady, I pledge allegiance,' the mother said. 'I plead. Allow me to serve you. Protect me. I am yours.'

'I pledge allegiance,' the child said in an adult's voice. The deep voice coming from the child was a chilling sound. 'I am yours. I vow to serve you. Do not destroy us, we beg you.'

'Sweet mother of all the demons, Emma,' Leo said. 'You just tamed them.'

'How could I have tamed them? I didn't do anything.'

'You don't have to do anything. It's a choice they make themselves. Mr Chen always gives them a chance to plead before he destroys them, if they don't attack immediately. Like you just did. You waited for them to go for you, and they took the opportunity.'

'Why did she call you Dark Lady?' Simone said.

My blood ran cold.

'Because she is the Lady of the Dark Lord, of course,' Leo said.

'Oh.' Simone moved to lean between us and studied the demons. 'What are you going to do with them, Emma?'

'I have absolutely no idea. All suggestions welcome. We can't even fit them in the car.' I paused. 'And I'm not sure I even trust them after what Wong did. This could be a trick.'

'It could be quite easily,' Leo said. 'We could destroy them anyway, you know.'

Simone and Michael stiffened at that. The demons didn't move.

'That would be totally wrong, Leo, and you know it,' I said.

The woman demon exhaled with relief.

'Mr Chen will know what to do,' Leo said. 'Let's send them to Wan Chai and he can meet us there.'

'You know the Academy building in Wan Chai?' I asked the demons.

The woman raised her head and nodded, full of hope.

'Meet us in the car park,' I said. 'We'll go in the car. You go directly. Wait about half an hour before you go. If you're there first, somebody will probably come out and take your heads off.'

The demons smiled up at me.

'Are there any more demons around here besides these two, Simone?' I said.

'No,' Simone said. 'Just these two.'

'Wait here,' I said to the demons. 'We'll meet you in Wan Chai in half an hour.'

They rose together. Leo braced himself. They bowed to us, then went to the play equipment. The woman sat to watch the child as he proceeded to play on the equipment like a perfectly normal little boy.

We returned to the car park. 'That was extremely weird,' I said.

'You should be used to it by now, Emma,' Leo said.

'Has that ever happened to you, Leo?' I said.

'Nope.' He grinned. 'I've seen Mr Chen do it a few times. I wish I knew how you do it.'

'I wish I knew how I did it too.' The whole thing had many unpleasant connotations for me. Particularly being called Dark Lady.

John and Gold were waiting for us in the middle of the Academy car park.

'Hi, Gold,' the stone in my ring said as we approached them. 'Still stuck, eh?'

'Hi, Dad,' Gold said cheerfully. 'Yep, still stuck. 'Bout time you woke up.'

'You've grown,' the stone said.

'Three millimetres in the last hundred years, Dad, and I've put on three whole grams.'

John saw my face. 'Forgot to mention that, Emma. The stone is Gold's father.'

'We prefer the term "parent", my Lord.' Gold's smile disappeared. 'Here they are.'

The demons appeared at the end of the car park and approached carefully.

'Leo, Michael, take Simone upstairs,' John said. 'There is an advanced hand-to-hand class on the sixth floor right now. You should be safe with them. Gold, you too. Let's see what the Lady Emma has gotten herself into this time.'

Leo and Gold herded the kids towards the lift.

'Gold,' John said loudly without turning away from the approaching demons.

Gold stopped. 'My Lord?'

'Arrange for the seals to be reset on the school. And have the Master who set the original seals come to my office first thing tomorrow morning.'

'My Lord,' Gold said.

'Sixth floor,' John said, still watching the demons.

They went into the lift lobby.

I tried to control my voice. 'They called me Dark Lady, John.'

'That is perfectly natural and nothing to be concerned about.'

'That's easy for you to say.'

'Don't worry about it, Emma. Kwan Yin will look at you in Paris. Until then, don't be concerned. It is of minor importance. You are a perfectly normal human being, just very talented. Now let's have a look at your new pets.'

The demons stopped about two metres away and fell to their knees. 'All hail the Dark Lord. All hail the Dark Lady.'

Damn. I shrugged it off. He was right. 'You think it's a trick?'

'Could be. Rise.' The demons didn't move. 'Good; first hurdle overcome. If they are truly tamed then at this stage they will obey only you. Tell them, Emma.'

'Rise,' I said, and they both pulled themselves to their feet.

'Take True Form,' John said. Once again they didn't move. 'Good. Tell them, Emma.'

'Take True Form.'

They were small humanoids in True Form. Nearly two metres tall, red, with smooth skin instead of scales. They had bulging horns and huge bulbous eyes. The one that had appeared as a boy had small tusks.

'Yuck.'

'Not too bad, could have been worse.'

'Yeah, I suppose,' I said. 'Could have been worms.'

'You know worms don't take human form.' He straightened and spoke briskly, suddenly the teacher. 'What level are these?'

'Three, very low level. I could bind them easily.'

'Yes. Good. I wonder why they were sent.'

'Me too.' He was right. These low-level demons weren't a danger to any of us. 'Go back to human form.'

They complied immediately. This time they appeared as a Chinese couple in their mid-thirties.

'Final test,' John said quietly. 'If they can do this then they are truly tamed. If they can't, they will attack immediately.' He held his hand out and the demons eyed it suspiciously. 'Tell them to come and take my hand. One at a time.'

'What are your names?' I said.

They didn't reply, they just watched me.

'These low-level ones don't have any names, they never do,' John said. 'You can name them later if you like. I ran out of names a long time ago.'

'Is that why you just give them numbers?'

'Yes. Much easier anyway.'

'You.' I pointed at the woman. 'Come and take the Dark Lord's hand.'

She hesitated, watching John's hand as if it was something highly toxic.

'Be ready, Emma,' John said quietly without moving.

The woman sidled towards John. This was obviously very difficult for her. I had seen what Simone could do when she touched a low-level demon; something much worse would probably happen to this one if it touched John.

'You won't kill it?' I whispered.

'I could quite easily kill it,' John said, loudly enough for the demon to hear, 'but it must take my hand anyway.'

The demon inched to John, reached out gingerly and touched his hand, its face completely expressionless. The other demon flinched.

Nothing happened to the demon and its face filled with wonder. It moved forward with more confidence and clasped John's hand. It dissolved into True Form and stood holding John's hand with awe.

'Well done, Emma,' John said with quiet satisfaction. 'You have tamed your first demon. Now you need to work out what you will do with it. Order it back, let's do the other one.'

'Let go and move back,' I said. It nodded and complied. 'Oh, for God's sake, take human form.'

It changed into a Chinese woman again. She smiled and bowed slightly. 'My Lady.'

'You.' I pointed at the other one. 'Come and do the same thing. Take the Dark Lord's hand.'

The other demon moved towards John, its face rigid with terror. John waited calmly with his hand out.

Just as the demon was within touching distance it went for him, swinging its arm around in a vicious slice at John's neck.

John blocked the attack with his left hand and caught the demon's hand in his own. The demon dissolved into True Form and its mouth fell open.

'Duck, Emma,' John said. The demon exploded, covering both of us with black stuff. 'Too slow. Damn. We'll need to take a shower now. Ask the other demon if it knew that its partner wasn't tamed.'

'Did you know that it wasn't tamed?'

'No, my Lady, on my honour,' she said. 'I honestly thought that he had turned. But he was more hesitant about coming, he knew that this might happen.'

'Good enough,' John said. 'We can shower upstairs. Not together.'

'I dunno, together sounds like a good idea.'

'Yes, it does.' He shrugged. That was enough for both of us; we had more important things to do than brood. 'Let's go up and work out what to do with your new little toy.'

I opened my mouth to protest that it was a living thing, not a toy, then closed my mouth again. Low-level demons weren't really alive. They were more like animated black stuff. Automatons, programmed to take orders, and really only mildly sentient — unless they had a flash of free will, decided to take matters into their own hands, and joined us in an attempt to attain humanity.

'Come on,' I said, and the demon followed us to the lift. 'Why were you following us? Were you ordered to attack us?'

'My Lady,' she said, 'we escaped.'

'Who was your master?' John said quickly.

'One Two Two.'

We shared a look. Simon freaking Wong.

'Why did you escape?' John said. 'Such an act of disobedience is highly unusual. You know what will happen to you if you are caught?'

'I know,' she said, miserable. 'But One Two Two is completely without honour. He treats his thralls worse than he treats his victims. I have already lost fifty nest mates to him. I would be next. Coming to you was my only, slim hope.'

'Why did your partner change his mind?' I said.

'I honestly don't know. I think he panicked at the idea of touching the Dark Lord.' She stared at John with awe. 'Why could I touch you, Highness? It felt ...' She hesitated. 'I don't know how it felt.'

'I will explain that later, after you have truly proved your worth,' John said.

'You are a legend, my Lord. I have touched you. I serve your Lady. You have no idea what this feels like, for a small thing such as I.'

'Why did you call me Dark Lady?' I said.

'Because your essence is dark,' she said. 'Dark, and pure, and beautiful. Same as his.'

'You have tamed a poet,' John said with quiet delight. 'She has described you in a nutshell. Dark, and pure, and beautiful.'

I suddenly felt a million times better.

We stopped at the ninth floor to shower and change into some training gear we kept at the Academy. The demon waited patiently outside for us.

Back on the sixth floor, one of the Celestial Masters was taking an advanced group through hand-to-hand. Leo and Michael practised the moves at the back of the class. Michael had some trouble, the moves were slightly too complicated for him, but he tried valiantly anyway with Leo's help. Gold and Simone sat to one side and watched. When we entered everyone stopped, fell to one knee and saluted us, then rose and continued.

Simone ran to her father. He hoisted her to sit on his hip and they watched the class.

I saw my opportunity. I gestured for the demon to stay put, then went to John and cuddled into him, wrapping my arm around his waist. He put his free arm around my shoulders and rubbed me affectionately. The three of us, him holding Simone, watched the students together. It was delightful.

Leo saw us out of the corner of his eye and his face went rigid. He spun and rushed towards us, but stopped halfway. His eyes turned inward as he listened. Then he smiled, nodded, raised his hand in understanding, and returned to Michael.

'Which one of you told him?' I said.

'Me,' Simone said.

'I didn't know you knew, Simone,' I said.

John smiled affectionately down at Simone. 'I never told her.'

'You did, Emma,' Simone said. 'You said Daddy could never drain me. And that means that while he's holding me, he can't hurt you.'

'You are a very clever little girl, you know that?' John said, delighted.

We enjoyed the closeness as we watched the students.

'I think a couple of these are ready to move up, Emma,' John said. 'What do you think?'

'Matthew, definitely. Yong Xin, maybe. I'd give her more time if it was me.'

'Whatever you say, my Lady. You're the boss.'

'Not here. When it comes to the Arts I think you have the tiniest bit of seniority on me. Being God of Martial Arts and all.'

'Oh, yes, I am too.' He glanced down at me and

squeezed me around the shoulders. 'I keep forgetting, the way you boss me around all the time.'

'You need bossing around, Daddy,' Simone said. 'You're hopeless at everything except martial arts.'

'You think so, Simone?' he said.

She nodded, her little face serious.

'I think I must be the happiest old Turtle in the whole wide world,' he said with a sigh and a huge grin. 'But I'm afraid a couple of these students could use my hand, so I'll have to let both of you wonderful ladies go.'

'Let me move away first before you put Simone down,' I said, and he released me.

'Go and talk to Gold,' he said. 'I saw that look on your face.'

'What look?'

He gently lowered Simone. 'The look that says you have to find something out *right now* or somebody will be in big trouble. Go and ask him.'

He was right. I told the demon to stay at the back of the class, then went to Gold.

'How can the stone in my ring be your father, Gold?'

He smiled cheerfully and it made him seem very young. 'Come with me, out of the room, and I'll show you.'

John moved through the class to give the students individual attention. Simone sat down cross-legged against the back wall and the demon stood next to her. The demon nodded and smiled, and I nodded back. Looked like she would be a good one.

'This way, ma'am,' Gold said, and led me out.

He stopped in the lift lobby and grinned at me. 'Don't worry, this doesn't hurt a bit.'

He held his hand out and flicked his wrist like a magician. Then he plunged his hand straight into his chest. He pulled out a stone about the size of his fist and held it out to me.

I took it gingerly, expecting it to be wet and disgusting, but it was warm and dry. It was a gorgeous piece of clear quartz shot through with shining veins of gold.

'That's me,' he said, his eyes sparkling.

I nearly dropped the stone. 'You're a *rock*?'

'Yes. Gold isn't my name, it's what I *am*.'

'Pretentious,' the stone in my ring said. 'You are less than twenty per cent pure gold. Your correct name is Quartz.'

'Give it a rest, Dad,' Gold said, still smiling. 'Go back to sleep, old rock.'

'Humph,' the stone said, and went silent.

I studied the stone in my hand. 'You are very beautiful, Gold.' I turned it over and ran one finger over the veins of gold. It was smooth and warm, quite delightful to touch.

Gold shivered and inhaled sharply. His eyes went wide and dark.

I rubbed my palm over the stone, enjoying the smooth texture.

Gold breathed heavily and became very flushed. 'Uh, my Lady ...'

I stopped and felt my face redden. 'Sorry,' I mumbled, embarrassed. 'I didn't know.'

He pulled himself together. 'Not a problem. I should have told you. Better give me back, my Lady, I can't hold human form well unless I am inside it.'

'Oh, wonderful,' the stone in my ring said. 'You know she rubs me sometimes when she's thinking. Now she knows, she won't do it any more.'

Gold's grin didn't shift. 'You are a dirty old man.'

'And I won't be rubbing you any more,' I said.

'Damn,' the stone said softly.

'Your father said you were stuck, Gold.' I handed the stone back to him. 'What did he mean?'

'Not my father, my *parent*.' Gold shoved the stone back into his chest. 'Like Jade, I displeased Heaven, and I am stuck in human form, serving, until I have atoned.'

'What did you do?'

He looked sheepish. 'I would prefer not to say, my Lady. If you order me, I will tell you. But I would prefer not to.'

I changed the subject to spare his feelings. 'If the stone in my ring is your parent, I really don't think it's appropriate for me to be wearing it around. Do you want to take it?'

'It is honoured to be an item of jewellery. It is the highest honour a stone can attain, to be treated as something truly precious. And the fact that it symbolises the bond you share with the Dark Lord gives my parent a great deal of distinction.'

'Oh. I never thought of it that way. You are pretty enough ...' I stopped. 'I mean your stone is pretty enough ...' I was lost for words. I didn't know how to say it.

'I think I understand what you mean, and I am sincerely flattered. When I am freed, I would be honoured to become an item of jewellery for you. I could shrink myself to any suitable size.' Gold grinned broadly. 'What a truly gracious lady you are.'

'Let's go back to class,' I said. 'Sounds like they're finishing.'

'Very good, my Lady,' Gold said cheerfully.

CHAPTER EIGHTEEN

John drove me and the demon back to the Peak building and the others followed in the second car. When we reached the front door to the apartment, my tame demon stopped.

John went in, turned and gestured. 'Come in.'

She hesitated.

'Go in. Trust him,' I said.

Her face screwed up with fear and she closed her eyes as she walked through the door. When she was on the other side she took a deep breath, opened her eyes and smiled.

Monica came out of the kitchen. 'The new helper is here, ma'am.' She hesitated. 'May I speak to you alone, ma'am?'

'In the dining room, wait for me there.'

I indicated for my demon to follow me, and took her into my bedroom and pulled out the book of baby names. 'Choose a name from here, then wait and we'll decide what we want to do with you.'

The demon took the book and looked at it. She smiled and shook her head.

'What?'

'I never thought I'd have anything as wonderful as a name.'

I patted her arm. 'Just choose one, and wait for me. I'll be right back.'

Monica was in the dining room, her face full of misery.

I sat next to her. 'What's the problem, Monica?'

'It's the new helper, ma'am.'

'Ah Yat? I thought you'd like her. She's very good, she's from the house in Guangzhou.'

Monica dropped her head and spoke softly. 'She lies, ma'am.'

I leaned back, relieved. 'She told you about herself.'

'She says she's more than a thousand years old, ma'am.' Monica appeared even more miserable. 'I know you say she's good, and Sir trusts her, but she *lies*. I don't know why she says these things.'

'It's the truth, Monica. She's twelve hundred years old.'

Monica's head shot up and her eyes went wide. 'She's one of *them*?'

'She's a tame demon. Same as the woman I just brought in.'

Monica stared silently at me, her eyes wide. Then she grimaced. 'Can you trust her with Simone?'

'She's served Mr Chen faithfully for six hundred years. I think we can trust her.'

Monica appeared to come to a decision and nodded. 'If you and Sir are okay with it, then I am too.'

I patted her arm. 'Good. Hurry up and get organised, the Tiger will be here soon to take you to the palace.'

'Will I be able to say goodbye to Simone before I go?'

'Of course. She's on the way home with Leo and Michael in the other car.'

She nodded and we both rose. She hesitated at the door.

'What?'

She quickly spun and embraced me. 'I'll miss everybody.'

I held her close. 'We'll miss you too. Hopefully you'll be able to come with the Tiger when he visits sometimes.'

She pulled back, tearful. 'I hope so too, ma'am.' She smiled through the tears. 'There are still a few things I need to show the demon.'

I squeezed her. 'Mr Chen says that you are a treasure beyond compare, Monica, and I agree with him.'

She nodded, speechless, and went out.

I sighed and went back to my room. John was already there, holding the demon's hand and studying her.

'Well?' I said.

He didn't look at me; he continued examining the demon. 'One Two Two has been doing some interesting things with his demon-breeding. I would be fascinated to see the Mother that produced this one.'

'My Mother is terrifying,' the demon said. 'And she is one of the smallest in the nests.'

John released her hand and snapped back. 'And now we need to work out what to do with you.'

'Have you chosen a name yet?' I said.

'The Dark Lord says I am the first demon you have tamed, my Lady, so I have chosen Alpha.'

'Go through the Greek alphabet and name them, easy,' John said.

'You sure?'

The demon nodded. 'Yes, ma'am.'

I shrugged. 'Okay.'

'You'll probably run out of Greek letters before the end of the year,' John said.

'Oh no. No *way*. No way do I want a horde of tame demons trailing after me.'

'I do not think you will have much choice, ma'am,' Alpha said. 'I have already told my remaining nest mates about your kind heart.'

'Oh *no!*'

John chuckled. 'So where will we put you, Alpha?'

Alpha bowed slightly. 'I am content to serve wherever you put me.'

'She can help run the house in Guangzhou while Ah Yat's here,' I said. 'Sixty-eight can manage, but he could really use another pair of hands.'

'Good idea,' John said. He took Alpha's hand. 'Go here, report to this demon. Do this.'

Alpha's face lit up. 'This is one of your residences?'

'Yes. You can help maintain it.'

Alpha glanced from John to me. 'Thank you!' she said, breathless with delight. 'I am profoundly honoured.'

I smiled back. 'Go.'

She released John's hand, bowed slightly, and disappeared.

'What are you doing with a book of baby names in your room?' John said.

'April gave it to me to hand on to Louise, now that Louise is married,' I said. 'I'm hoping to see her in Paris. The Tiger said she'd be there.'

'Oh.' He opened his mouth and closed it again.

'It's too early to tell, John. It's only been a few days.'

He sighed and sat on my couch. 'We should have taken precautions.'

I laughed softly. 'We never had a chance. Besides, the timing was wrong. I don't think we need to worry.'

He looked up at me, his eyes full of pain.

'Yes, John. I hope it happened as well.'

* * *

I stood quietly outside the uniform shop waiting for the kids to come out. Leo was inside with them, they were fine.

I looked down at the football field. There was a demon there.

More appeared. Many more. Dozens of them. They filled the field. They approached the stairs to come up to the uniform shop. I studied them carefully: they were mostly humanoids, but some worms too. Not too much of a problem; mostly low-level stuff, level two or three, biggest about level five.

Damned if they would get near *my* family.

I let my breath out in a long hiss.

I went to the top of the stairs and waited for them to come up. I wasn't worried at all; in fact I was looking forward to this.

As the first ranks of them reached the top of the stairs, I raised myself on my black coils, opened my mouth and struck.

I woke and shot upright, panting. I looked around. My room. The lights from Central leaked through the curtains covering the large picture window above the bed.

I threw myself down, turned over and tried to go back to sleep.

John poked his head around my bedroom door about mid-morning the next day. 'What time do we leave tomorrow?'

'Flight leaves at ten. Early start tomorrow.'

'I haven't even packed yet. Can you control all the emergencies for the next hour or so?'

'No, I'm having lunch with Rhonda, and I'd better move.' I sighed with exasperation. 'She wanted to go for yum cha and I can't.'

He was amused. 'You can't eat meat at all any more, can you.'

'I know I don't have to be vegetarian any more, but if I eat meat I feel awful afterwards.'

'I'll need to arrange some pine nuts and spring water for you in the near future, I think.'

'What the hell is that supposed to mean?'

'Where's Leo? He can mind Simone while I pack.'

'Leo's in your room packing for you right now.'

He went still and his eyes unfocused as he looked into his room. Then he snapped back and raced to the door. 'If I let him pack I won't have a single black shirt to wear the entire time we're there!'

'That's the idea!' I called to him as he ran out, his long hair flying behind him.

I'd arranged to meet Rhonda MacLaren for lunch at Central. I needed to talk to her about Michael before we took him to Paris with us the following day. My car's alarm popped and I climbed in. I wound my way out through the car park to the gate. I smiled and waved to the guards as they opened the gate for me, and they waved back.

I went slowly down the drive and stopped at the end. An English guy further up the hill drove his Porsche like a bat out of hell down the hill sometimes, and never checked to see if someone was coming out of our drive. Nobody there. I turned out onto the road and drove down towards the Peak Tower.

There weren't many tourists on the viewing platform and the fountain in the tower's forecourt had been turned off again to save money. The clouds descended onto the Peak, and would probably engulf us in the afternoon. John had made such a mistake buying that building, it was so damn damp all the time. And then I understood: up high. On a mountain.

I headed for Magazine Gap Road, and turned on the CD player.

Freddie Mercury attacked me from all sides.

I turned the volume down and changed to the next CD in the box in the back, silently cursing Leo.

Freddie Mercury again. *Best of Queen.*

I flipped through all six CDs in the box. All of them were *Best of Queen.*

That bastard. He hadn't just been through my CD collection, he'd been through my goddamn *books* as well and obviously been *reading* them.

I smiled at the deliberate irony. *Best of Queen.* Cute.

I quietly contemplated revenge as I wound my way down the hill. Gold must have helped with this one; Leo wouldn't have been able to copy the CDs himself. It would take me a while to think up something suitably cruel to get him back with. Maybe Michael could give me a hand. Yes.

I turned left at the bottom into Connaught Road and crawled through the traffic of Central. Lunchtime crowd; but I was adding to it. I went past the Star Ferry terminal on the right. I wasn't parking there today, although it was the most convenient car park for John's building in Central. He had a small office in the building to manage the tenants, and I made a mental note to drop in there after lunch and talk to them about occupancy. We needed to keep the building completely leased out, even if it meant dropping the rent.

I continued along Connaught Road, under the huge overpass that carried pedestrians to the Star Ferry. The office workers in their business suits and smart shoes bustled from one side to the other. I still hadn't bought any suits. Miss Kwok would definitely dock my pay. I smiled. I had come such a long way since she'd asked me to spy on John Chen and I'd resigned on the spot.

Kitty Kwok still called me. She had been a total bitch to me at the first charity function I'd attended with

John, but after that had suddenly warmed up and kept asking me to lunch or to visit her house. It was obvious I made an excuse every time, but she still kept at me. She'd probably worked out what the ring meant, and was trying to keep me onside. She even had April harassing me about visiting as well. April's baby was due in another month. I made a mental note to give her a call and check on her.

I turned left and meandered up a tiny one-way street. The sidewalks overflowed with people and many of them walked on the road. I sounded my horn to let them know I was coming and they looked at me blankly then moved to let me through. Normal working day in Central.

I turned right and went down the ramp under the shiny new building, The Centre. Spectacular neon lines marked out its floors, making a rainbow of colours that moved slowly up its sides at night.

I grabbed a ticket on the way into the car park and parked at the bottom of the casual area away from the other cars. One of the reasons I'd chosen The Centre: the car park was large and convenient to where I was going, but even better it often had areas that were empty of cars. I stepped out, locked the car, and waited.

Gold appeared next to me and quickly saluted. I nodded back and we went to the elevators together.

We exited at the ground floor. Huge silver-clad pillars supported the building over the open paved area at ground level with small gardens and fountains. A large-screen television to one side displayed the latest stock prices.

Central Market stood on the other side of the road. It was old and blackened from the car exhausts, and reeked of blood and ripe meat from the butcher stalls inside. The pigs were delivered in the morning, butchered and the meat hung in the heat without refrigeration for the whole day. A public toilet under the market at the end of the street added to the aromatic mix, making the walk past quite unpleasant.

As usual for a summer's day it started to rain. I pulled out my umbrella and opened it, and Gold huddled underneath it with me. Eventually he gave up, turned towards me and made a large umbrella appear in his hand. He moved away and opened it. The road was awash and we skipped over the puddles to the market.

We stepped onto the escalator outside the market and turned onto the walkway at the bottom of the Mid-levels escalator. We were under cover now; I folded my umbrella and put it away. We stepped onto the long moving ramp, and Gold turned towards me and made his umbrella disappear. Neat trick: I wished I could do that. Sometimes I would accidentally leave the umbrella at home, drying, and be stuck without it in one of Hong Kong's massive rainstorms.

Gold peered at the water gushing from the sky. 'May get an amber rainstorm warning.'

'If it keeps up like this, we'll get a red or a black warning and all the kids will be sent home from school. Anybody able to carry me and my car back home so I can miss the traffic?'

He grinned. 'Not that I know of. You'll have to put up with the traffic.'

'Damn.'

It was only a short distance to the prestigious apartment blocks of the Mid-levels, but the vertical nature of Hong Kong meant that it was too steep to walk. The government had built a continuous series of escalators that went up the hill, allowing office workers to travel up and down without needing to take the bus. The escalator travelled down until ten in the morning, then changed direction and went up for the rest of the day. Very convenient.

'Where's Ms MacLaren's store?' Gold said.

'Halfway up Hollywood Road. Between one of those tiny shops selling trash and an antiques store that sells the real thing. She specialises in furniture bought on the Mainland and restored in Shenzhen.'

We stopped halfway up the hill outside the restaurant. Hollywood Road was a steep narrow street lined on both sides with stores selling antiques and furniture. Since the construction of the escalator, a number of Western-style restaurants had also sprung up along the corridor, catering to the expat crowd riding the escalator home.

I steeled myself, then opened the restaurant door.

'You'll be fine, ma'am. She'll understand,' Gold said softly behind me.

Rhonda smiled and waved to us from a small table near the windows. Good, I could talk freely over there, nobody would hear us. I winced inside. I didn't want to tell her this.

I was ready to shake her hand as I approached, but when I was close enough she embraced me instead. I was thrilled. I had a great deal of respect for Rhonda and really liked her, and was delighted she thought of me as a friend. It made it even more unpleasant, though, thinking of what we were about to discuss.

Gold shook Rhonda's hand and we sat.

'Rhonda, have you met Gold?' I said, trying to remember if she had.

She shook her head and smiled kindly. 'No, I haven't. Hello, Gold, unusual name.'

'He's one of *them*,' I said pointedly, and she nodded without losing the smile.

'I should be offended, my Lady,' Gold said, his boyish face full of good humour.

'Why? I was about to say that you're a *lawyer*,' I said, and Rhonda laughed quietly. 'He's a Shen as well, by the way.'

Gold's grin widened. 'Two strikes against me already, ma'am, and I haven't even said a word to Ms MacLaren.' He turned to Rhonda. 'I'm very pleased to meet you. I handle the Dark Lord's legal matters here.'

Rhonda blanched. 'Is Michael in trouble? He's not in trouble with the police?'

I waved my hands in front of me. 'No, no, nothing like that.' She relaxed. 'But we do have some things we need to discuss. No problem with the police,' I reassured her quickly when I saw her face. 'But let's order something to eat first, I'm starving.'

The waiter presented us with menus. I ordered some mineral water and Rhonda asked for a basket of bread.

It was an upmarket Western restaurant with an interesting fusion of East and West, and from the descriptions on the menu possibly well done, which was unusual. There was even a varied vegetarian selection for me.

'Are you vegetarian, Gold?' I said, wondering what stones ate.

'Human form, I can eat what I like,' Gold said. 'I love ice-cream. Strawberry. But I feel weird ...' He hesitated. 'Eating the flesh of animals. Not really keen on the idea at all.'

'I am so glad I don't have to put up with that any more,' Rhonda said as she eyed the menu. She put it down. 'There's obviously something up for you to bring your lawyer, Emma. How about you just tell me?'

'If we're ready to order I think we should do that first,' I said, pretending to study the menu. 'I'm ready. Gold?'

Gold called the waiter over and we ordered. The vegetarian ho fan with fungi sounded good. Gold ordered a vegetarian pizza-type thing and Rhonda had a chicken Caesar salad.

When the waiter had taken the menus and moved away, I buttered some bread and sighed. 'This is hard, Rhonda.'

Gold dropped his head without saying anything. Rhonda shifted impatiently.

'We've been under attack quite a lot recently, and last week someone was killed,' I said.

Rhonda's eyes went wide but she didn't say anything.

'Michael obviously had some friends in very unpleasant places. He'd left them a long time ago, but they came after him.'

'I'm sorry, Emma, I honestly didn't know,' Rhonda said. 'I knew he had some nasty friends, but I didn't know he was that caught up in it. I'll *kill* him!'

'We handled it.' I didn't elaborate. 'But John's housekeeper from London was visiting, and fainted from the stress. We took her to the hospital. A particularly nasty demon took her as second prize when he couldn't get his hands on Simone or me. He used her as a bargaining chip, and when she was no longer useful, the slimy little bastard killed her.'

Rhonda's face didn't move.

'Michael's learned his lesson. They know who he is, what he is, and they want him for that. The demon who killed our housekeeper,' I said, and took a deep breath, 'is the Big Brother of all the Big Brothers. And he wants Michael for his own amusement.'

'Shit!' she exploded quietly, and banged the table softly. 'I'm going to *kill* him!'

Gold jumped, but didn't say a word. His face said it all.

'Rhonda.' I tried to keep my voice even. 'Michael is in big trouble. This guy wants him. Michael is an enormous target. He's the son of the West Wind, and they know that.

He's a Retainer of the Dark Lord, and they know that too. They want him very badly.'

'Is he safe with you?'

'He is safer alongside the Dark Lord and the Dark Lady than he is anywhere else on the Earthly Plane,' Gold said.

Please don't call me that, I begged Gold silently.

The food arrived. All three of us sat and looked at it miserably, without touching it.

'Why did you bring your lawyer, Emma?' Rhonda said softly. 'You want me to sign a release? In case something happens to him?'

'I want a witness,' I said, trying to stay calm. 'I don't want a release from you; I know you trust us, there's no need for that. What I *do* want is your permission to move him to the Western Palace if things get out of hand. We have control of the situation right now ...' I tried to sound confident. 'But if it appears that Michael is in real danger, and we can't protect him, then we'll move him to the West where he'll be completely safe. If he refuses to go, Gold will be able to back me up that it's your wish as well.'

The noodles were going cold. Ho fan were absolutely no good cold, they went stiff. I didn't care.

'Would you like us to move him to the palace now?' I said. 'I asked him if he wanted to and he refused, but you're his mother and it's your decision as well.'

'Don't you *dare*,' she said fiercely. 'Not unless you absolutely have to. I do *not* want my son spending all his time with his father, I don't want him learning anything off that man. Only move him if you have to. I'd much prefer he stayed with you and John, as long as you think you have it under control.' She leaned back. 'I trust you not to put him in danger. I leave the decision up to you.'

'What if he wants to visit the palace and have a look?'

'He can go for short stays, maybe school holidays or something. But I don't want him spending all his time there. He'll learn too much of his father's attitude.'

'His father asks about you all the time,' I said.

She didn't say anything, but her face spoke volumes. She hadn't remarried after leaving the West.

'You ever think about going back?'

'Not as long as I'm one of a hundred.' She straightened, picked up her fork and stuck it into the salad. 'I think I deserve better than that.'

'You definitely deserve better than that,' I said. 'I think you're the only one who ever left him.'

Her face said it all.

'Getting involved with Shen is always an extremely bad idea,' I said, trying to cheer her up. 'Look at me.' I became serious again. 'You still okay about Michael going to Europe tomorrow?'

'Sure. From what I understand, they're at their most powerful near the centre of China. Europe is a long way away, and they'll be weak. It'll be good for him to see a bit of the world. Take him, show him around. Just make sure he rings me now and then so I can keep track of him.'

'I'll make sure he does. Every day.'

The apartment was quiet when I returned. I poked my head into the kitchen. 'Where is everybody, Ah Yat?'

Ah Yat's eyes unfocused. 'Master Leo and Master Michael have taken Miss Simone to the park. The Dark Lord is in his room, resting.'

'Any messages?'

'No, ma'am.'

'Thanks.'

I went down to my room and called April.

'*Wei?*'

'Hi, April, it's Emma. I'm just checking. How are you? How's the baby?'

'Not long to go now,' she said with satisfaction. 'You should see me, I'm huge. I'm not going out until the baby comes, it's too embarrassing.'

'And it's due mid-September?' I said.

'I've already chosen a good day.'

'What?'

'A good day for the baby to be born,' she said patiently, explaining.

'Oh God, April, you won't have a caesarean just so the baby's born on a lucky day, will you?'

'Of course I will. But they won't do it in Hong Kong any more, they've gotten stupid about it. They want all the babies to come naturally; the rates of caesar here were very high or something, and it made them look bad. So Aunty Kitty's arranging something for me in China.'

'Aunty Kitty? Kitty Kwok?'

'Yes,' April said. 'You should go and visit her, Emma, she really wants to see you.'

I didn't say anything.

'September twelfth, the baby will be born. I'm going to China just before that. Aunty Kitty says the clinic is very nice. She owns it. Like a private hospital. I was worried that the baby wouldn't have Hong Kong right of abode, but since I'm Australian and both me and Andy have right of abode, it's okay.'

'How are you feeling?'

'Fine,' she said. 'The doctors that Aunty Kitty sends me to are very good. Give me lots of medicine, lots of tonics to keep me strong. I'm feeling really good. A bit tired sometimes, but that's normal.' She laughed quietly. 'I just don't seem to be able to eat enough food. I'm so *hungry* all the time!'

Her voice dropped out, then returned. 'I have another call,' she said. 'Probably Aunty Kitty, she checks me all the time, and Andy does too. Better say goodbye, I'll talk to you later.' She sighed. 'I'm very happy, Emma. I hope you're as happy as me one day.'

'So do I, April.'

But not for the same reason.

CHAPTER NINETEEN

Simone and Michael sat in deck chairs on the open-air back of the boat and chatted about the scenery. John and I read books in the air-conditioned lounge.

Leo sat cross-legged on the couch with us, obviously trying to meditate and failing miserably. I wondered what had happened in the past to freak him out about being on the water. But if he didn't want to tell me, it was his choice.

I decided to leave it and annoy John instead. 'I thought you were planning to buy a bigger boat.'

'Haven't had time,' John said. 'I'm only good for a few more trips now anyway. Hardly worth it.'

'Oh for God's sake, John, don't talk like that. Do you have to keep reminding me?'

'Sorry. Feel free to go shopping for a new boat for me. You'll have it when I'm gone.'

'You're doing it again. And don't you dare tell me to read the *Tao*.'

'I think you're past that stage. Look at what the stone said.'

I ran my hands through my hair and sighed. 'God, but you hate me, Xuan Wu.'

Leo snapped out of it. 'What did the stone say?'

We shared a look and decided to tell him. We didn't need words. Leo was family.

I put my book down and closed the door to the back of the boat. Simone and Michael didn't notice. I sat next to Leo, and he uncrossed his legs with relief, then shifted over for me.

'You don't need to sit like that if it's uncomfortable,' I said. 'It's best just to be comfortable to meditate. Remind me to show you some techniques when we get back.'

'Thanks, Emma.' He stopped and looked pointedly at me, waiting.

I sighed. 'Exactly what did the stone say, John? I can't remember. Most of what it says is stupid, anyway.'

I fully expected the stone to butt in with some acerbic remark but it remained silent.

'Leo,' John said, 'the stone said that Emma is well on the way to Immortality without my assistance to Raise her. It said there is something unusual about her, but it didn't know what. It suggested that she is dangerous, but not to her family. It said that she was a dark heartless monster. It also said that she is a perfectly normal human being. It is absolutely infuriating.'

Leo remained silent on the couch next to me and watched John. He didn't look at me at all.

'While we were at the Western Palace,' John continued, 'Emma did some things with energy that only Immortals should be able to do. I have never seen a mortal do that in my entire history. I had a close look at her and she is an ordinary human. There is something going on here, and I would dearly like to know what it is.'

'I'd like to know as well,' I said. 'I don't *feel* different. I didn't even know I wasn't supposed to be able to do it. It just happened.' My throat tightened. 'I don't want to be a monster. I want to care for all of you. I want to make sure that Simone is safe.'

'That explains it,' Leo said with satisfaction.

'Explains what?' I said.

Leo pointed at John. 'He is incredibly cold-blooded sometimes. Look at him: he was just talking about leaving his family as if he was discussing a shopping list. It's not because he's a reptile, it's because he's an Immortal.'

'Say the word, Leo,' John said without smiling.

'Oh, all right. *Turtle*,' Leo said. 'You see? Cold-blooded. You somehow get, I dunno ...' He searched for the word. '*Detached* from the world or something. And now you're getting like that too, Emma. You're getting dark, like him.' He turned back to John and spoke with conviction. 'Emma will be Immortal without your help.'

'Could be,' John said.

Leo quickly wrapped his arms around me and pulled me into a huge hug. 'That's *great*! I am so goddamn glad for you two. This is wonderful.'

I held him and buried my head in his chest. 'Leo,' I said, muffled by his shirt, 'you are the most wonderful man it has ever been my privilege to meet. If anybody deserves Immortality, it's you.'

Leo pulled back to smile into my face. He ruffled my hair affectionately, making me giggle. 'You go, girl. Do it. Then you'll be here for sure when he comes back.' He pulled me back in and hugged me so tight he just about killed me. 'This is *great*.'

'Leo, you're in serious danger of cracking my ribs,' I said into his chest.

He released me and put his hands on my arms with a huge, honest grin on his face. 'Damn, but you have just made my day. You should have told me before, my Lord. This is the best news in the world.'

John spread his hands. 'We shall see when we shall see.'

*   *   *

It was our second-last day in Paris. John was with Kwan Yin, replenishing his energy levels, and Leo, Michael and I were sightseeing with Simone. The driver dropped us outside the Madeleine when we'd finished in the Luxembourg Gardens. We proceeded towards the Place de la Concorde; Simone wanted to see the obelisk again.

Afterwards, as we walked along the narrow tree-lined Rue du Faubourg St Honoré, I heard someone call my name. I turned, but didn't see anyone.

'Over here,' called a female voice with an Australian accent.

'Why are they dressed like that?' Simone said.

It was a group of six Muslim women, all wearing traditional dress: long straight skirts, long-sleeved large tops, and veiled faces, only their eyes showing. Three burly male bodyguards holding a large number of glossy shopping bags escorted them.

'Emma!' one of the women shouted again. She waved, then dashed across the narrow busy street to us. One of the bodyguards quickly followed her.

It was Louise.

'Why are you dressed like that?' I said. 'Does the Tiger make you?'

'No.' She giggled and pulled the veil from her face. She looked exactly the same: blonde, bony and full of mischief, but I'd never seen her wear quite so much make-up before. 'We choose to do it ourselves. Isn't it *fun*?' She looked around at us. 'And here's little Simone. Remember me?' She crouched in front of Simone. 'I hope I have a little girl just like you.'

'You're pregnant?' I said.

She rose. 'Not yet. Won't take long though — I see him nearly every second or third week. Apparently I'm

237

a big favourite.' She shoved me playfully on the arm. 'God, Emma, this is so much *fun*!'

One of the women in the group across the road called out with an English accent, 'Come on, Louise, Chanel will close soon.'

'I'll be right there,' Louise called over her shoulder. 'You go on. Josh can bring me.'

'Okay,' said another woman with an Indian accent. 'Hurry up.'

The bodyguard with Louise was a half-Chinese in his late twenties or early thirties, with very light brown hair.

'Are you a son of the Tiger?' I asked him.

He didn't smile. 'I'm number Two Seven Nine.' He studied Michael. 'Are you Three One Five?'

'My name is Michael.'

'I've heard about you.' The bodyguard nodded to Leo. 'Black Lion.'

Leo hesitated, unmoving. Then he nodded back.

'What have you heard about me?' Michael asked stiffly.

'We'd all give our right arms to learn from the Dark Lord.' The bodyguard grinned broadly, and when he smiled he looked completely different: kind and good-natured. 'Name's Josh.' He held his hand out to Michael. 'Pleased to meet you.'

Michael moved forward and shook his hand. 'I suppose we're brothers.'

'That's right. All in it together.' Josh nudged Louise. 'Gotta look after the pride.'

'Cut it out, Josh.' Louise giggled. 'Want to come up to the hotel later, Emma? We're having a fashion show for the Tiger.' She leaned over to whisper. 'I've spent upwards of twenty thousand US dollars on clothes and shoes alone. Just *today*.'

The bodyguard sighed loudly.

'You were never much into fashion before,' I said.

'Hey, Chanel, YSL, all of it — how can you say no?' Louise said with a huge grin. 'I look so *great* in some of this stuff, you should hear what the Tiger says. It's just so much *fun*! Come and see the show. We've set up a runway in the ballroom of the hotel.'

A fashion show. I couldn't think of anything more boring in the whole wide world.

Leo rescued me. 'Lady Emma, I don't think it will be possible for you to visit this evening. The Golden Boy and the Jade Girl have arranged a meeting with you and the Dark Lord.'

'You are Lady Emma?' the bodyguard said quickly.

I nodded.

He fell to one knee and saluted. 'Profoundest apologies for not recognising you sooner, my Lady. I am most honoured.'

'What the hell are you doing?' I hissed. 'Get the hell up! We're in the middle of goddamn *Paris* here!'

Leo made some amused sounds behind me and I nearly rounded on him, then changed my mind.

The bodyguard pulled himself to his feet. 'I have heard of you, my Lady. It is an honour to meet you.'

'Hey,' Louise said loudly. 'You don't do that for *me*.'

'You're not the chosen of the Dark Lord,' the bodyguard said.

'Can I visit you tomorrow, Louise?' I said. 'During the day? Leo and Michael can take Simone for me.'

'I'm off to Milan tomorrow,' Louise said with a huge grin. 'I'll come and visit you in Hong Kong later. How about that?' She shoved me on the arm again. 'If I'm not pregnant, that is. If I'm pregnant I can't leave the palace. I want a girl, but the Tiger is really old-fashioned, and he's close to breaking four hundred with the sons.'

The bodyguard put his hand to his ear. I hadn't noticed before, but he wore an earpiece. 'Time to go,

Miss Louise. The others are nearly finished, and we'll be heading back to the hotel.'

'You can't talk silently?' I said.

The bodyguard shrugged. 'Most of us didn't inherit anything. No special abilities whatsoever. Perfectly ordinary human beings.' He held his hand out to Michael, and Michael shook it. 'Hope to see you again soon, Michael. Pleasure to meet you.' He quickly saluted me, shaking his hands in front of his face. 'Lady Emma.' He bowed to Simone. 'Princess.' He nodded to Leo. 'Lion.' He put his hand around Louise's back, guiding her. 'Let's go.'

Louise let him steer her away. She pulled the veil over her face and waved cheerfully. 'Ta ta, Emma, see you in Hong Kong.'

'Bye, Louise. Come and visit,' I called, but she was already across the street and didn't hear me.

I wandered back up the busy Montmartre street, enjoying the sights and sounds around me. I went past the roundabout with its elaborate sculpture, then along the boulevard towards the house. The plastic shopping bag bounced against my leg.

After we returned from Place de la Concorde I'd gone down the street to buy a few bits and pieces from a pharmacy. The stone that Gold had given me was in my pocket and worked perfectly; I could understand everything that was said to me and reply in the same language. I had even spoken what was probably an Indian dialect to a couple of exchange students in the pharmacy. Their faces had been priceless.

A typical Parisian café sat on the corner, dark wood and big windows. A bright canvas awning hung over a large number of small, round, metal-topped tables with old-fashioned wooden chairs facing the pavement. Some people had already set themselves up with their pre-dinner glass of wine, watching the crowd go past.

A couple of leathery old men sat with glasses of red wine on the table in front of them and cigars in their hands. They watched me appreciatively as I walked towards them.

'Face of an angel,' one of them said quietly.

'Grace of a tiger,' the other one said.

I couldn't help it; I smiled. One of them raised his glass to me and I nodded back, still smiling. I had a spring in my step as I walked around the corner and back to the leafy lane that held Ms Kwan's imaginary house. She might even have finished with John, and I could do a tai chi set with him before dinner. Life looked very pleasant.

I pushed open the door, stopped dead, and dropped my little bag.

Simon Wong stood in the middle of the large entry, at the bottom of the sweeping stairs. Stood over John's headless body. Holding Simone with one hand. And that damned *Wudang* sword in the other.

Simone tried to pull away from Wong, but he held her. He ignored her and smiled at me.

I sized up the situation. First: John was dead. Fine. Deal with that later.

I cast around for help. Leo? Michael? Leo's body lay in a pool of blood under the stairs. No. I grabbed myself and shook. Breathe. Deal. Remember: Simone was there, alive.

Michael? There, behind Leo. I could see the blood staining his lovely blond hair. No. Incongruously: the Tiger and Rhonda would both kill me.

Concentrate. Simone.

I examined Wong's chi level, already knowing what to expect. Yep: any energy work I used on him would kill me.

'Help me, Emma,' Simone said, still trying to pull away, still being ignored.

'Stay strong, darling,' I said. 'I'll get you free.'

Wong stayed perfectly still and ignored Simone's struggles. His smile widened. His voice was like a razor. 'You. Are. *Mine*.'

He reached with his mind and unlocked something inside me.

Something huge and dark and monstrous emerged from deep within me. It recognised Wong. It bowed to him. 'Master.'

'NO!' I didn't care any more. I would destroy that monster if it was the last thing I did, regardless of what happened to me.

I struggled to generate the energy. The thing inside me blocked it. I couldn't do it.

It grew and took hold of me. It took control. I fought it, but I was losing. It covered me and drowned me in the darkness. I struggled, but it forced me down and took control.

Then ... No. You do not have control over me. There is nothing like that inside me. I am Emma, one hundred per cent, all the way through, and I will protect that little girl with my last breath.

The dark thing disappeared.

I knew it: a trick. You bastard.

But my energy abilities were still blocked. He had taken down everybody else, so I was no match for him physically. No problem. He held Simone with one hand and his sword with the other. I could use that against him. Simone would be okay with Kwan Yin.

I ran straight at him and his face went slack with shock.

I threw myself onto his sword.

The blade went straight through me with hardly any

force; it must have been razor-sharp. It scraped past my spine on the way through.

I grabbed his wrist with my left hand. There, demon, try getting around that. One hand was locked with the sword through me; the other hand was holding Simone. He didn't have a free hand to do anything.

I thrust my other fist through his face. I just needed to survive long enough to kill him ...

He exploded all over me. Thank God that monster was finally gone; I didn't need to worry about him any more. But it would have been nice to be clean and dead instead of covered in black stuff like this.

The ground hit me like a wall, smashing into me from the side. The sword twisted inside me as I landed, adding to my agony.

I struggled to speak. 'Are you all right, Simone?'

I thought I heard her say, 'I'm okay,' but she faded. Everything faded. It all disappeared.

CHAPTER TWENTY

'I didn't know you were capable of something so cruel,' John's voice said in the darkness.

Of course I was capable of something that cruel. I felt a stab of pain. Goodbye, love. Heaven and Earth didn't move for us.

'It needed to be done,' Ms Kwan said. 'She needed to face her fear, and realise that it is simply not possible.'

I may have been able to speak to them. It was worth a try.

'Is Simone okay?' I surprised myself; my voice was just a dry croak, but it was there.

A cool, callused hand held mine.

'Open your eyes, Emma,' John said.

I opened them but I couldn't see very much. Then two figures swam into view. John on my left, holding my hand. That proved it: definitely dead, otherwise he wouldn't have been able to touch me. Ms Kwan on my right, holding my other hand, with the most anguished expression I had ever seen on her face.

John helped me to sit up, and I had a moment of dizziness. I expected the sword to twist inside me again, but it seemed to be gone. Thank heaven for small mercies. John's hand came around the back of my head to lift me. They both watched me, concerned.

'Simone,' I said. 'Simone.' I tried to get more words out. My throat was too dry to speak properly. 'Is okay? Alive?'

'Simone is fine, my love,' John said. 'We all are. Mercy just showed you how wrong you are. Look at you. Even now. You think we are all dead, and your first thought goes to Simone.' His voice thickened. 'You truly love her as if she were your own.'

I didn't really hear him. 'Where's Simone? Is she all right?' I jerked my hands free. 'Oh my God! Leo! No. No! Leo. Michael. John.' I peered up at him. 'John?'

Kwan Yin put her hand on my forehead. 'I am so sorry, little one, but it needed to be done. Sleep.'

'Contact the Hall of Records,' Ms Kwan was saying. 'There may be a lost Shen, and it may be her. The stone is right: there is something there.' Her voice softened. 'But it was wrong of the stone to frighten her so. She does not deserve that sort of treatment. You will be dealt with appropriately when the time comes, I can assure you, stone.'

'Do you think I should take the stone back and give her something slightly less troublesome?' John said.

'I vow to cause you less trouble, my Lord,' the stone said. 'I apologise. I told only the truth. I beg you, do not take me back. I am profoundly honoured by my role. Please leave me here. I promise to behave.'

'See what Emma has to say about it,' Ms Kwan said. 'She may still want to flush it down the toilet.'

'I do.' I opened my eyes. There they were.

'Please tell me Simone's okay.' My voice sounded really strange, hardly anything at all, just a hoarse whisper.

John dropped his head and shook it with wonder. He looked back up and gazed into my eyes with an expression of such adoration that my throat tightened. 'Everybody is absolutely fine,' he said.

'Can you sit up, Emma?' Ms Kwan said.

'I can try,' I said, but it came out a whisper.

Both of them pulled me up and I managed to stay there. I looked around. I was on the couch in the study of Ms Kwan's imaginary house. I had no recollection of arriving there. The last thing I remembered was coming home after taking Simone to the Obelisk, then slipping out to buy a few things at a pharmacy down the street.

'How come you can touch me?' I said.

He raised his other hand, which was holding Ms Kwan's. I understood; she shielded me.

'Did you do that to me?' I whispered. 'Ms Kwan? You made me live through that?'

'I'm sorry, Emma, but it had to be done,' she said. 'Do you understand now?'

A great many unpleasant words hit the back of my throat. I swallowed them all.

I thought back. I did that. I threw myself onto Wong's sword to save Simone. There was nothing inside me he could control. I was just being paranoid. Of course I would never hurt Simone. John was right: I did love her as if she was my own. Nothing else mattered; not John, not Leo, not me. As long as Simone was okay, everything else was just detail.

'Lady Kwan Yin,' I whispered, 'thank you so very much.'

Both of them sighed with relief. They probably thought I was about to leap up and chop their heads off.

'Did you say I could be a lost Shen, Ms Kwan?' I said.

'I think that is a remote possibility,' Ms Kwan said. 'But I think it is more likely that you are just a very talented human being who is in love with her Dark

Lord and is learning from him in many more ways than one. You have shared your minds and your bodies. Of course you are becoming more alike all the time.'

'That actually makes sense,' I said. 'That's the most sensible thing anyone's said to me in quite a while.'

'Do you understand now that you could never hurt any of us?' John said.

'Of course I could never hurt anybody. I can't believe I thought that.' I should have looked into my heart straightaway and seen the truth, instead of letting the stone make me so worried. Dark heartless monster.

'Humph,' I said. 'Of course I'm a dark heartless monster with hidden depths. I'm your Lady. I'm rapidly turning into a smaller version of you.'

He smiled intensely into my eyes. 'You say that as if it were a bad thing.'

'You're damn right it's a bad thing. I'm my own woman here and the last thing I want to be is another you. I'm *me*.'

'You are quite extraordinary,' Ms Kwan whispered.

'I'm going to make you pay me money every time you say that,' I snapped. 'I'll be very wealthy indeed.'

She smiled, reached into the pocket of her white silk pantsuit, and gave me a gold coin in the traditional round shape with a square hole in the middle. 'Here, but I think it is a drop in the ocean compared to the riches you already possess.'

'I think you are quite right, Lady.'

John dropped his head to kiss me and I stopped him with my hand on his chest. 'John, please. I need to see them. Can we go out and see them right now? I need to prove to myself that they're still here. I need to see Simone and give her a big hug, right now. Just to make sure.'

He smiled. 'Let me help you up.' He carefully didn't let go of Ms Kwan's hand.

The next morning, our last in Paris, Simone dragged Leo along the Champs-Élysées from the Jardin des Tuileries. I followed, with Michael next to me.

Michael stopped. We continued walking, but he didn't catch up. I turned back to see what his problem was. He was staring into the park at the side of the road, his face rigid with emotion.

I looked in the same direction, and Leo stiffened beside me.

The Tiger sat on a park bench, smiling and talking to a blonde woman, holding her hand. He put his arm around her shoulders and she leaned into him. She turned and rested her head on his chest, bringing her face into view.

It was Rhonda.

Michael stormed towards them.

The Tiger saw him and grinned, then they both disappeared.

Michael stood and glared at the park bench, then shook himself and returned to us. 'Let's go.'

'You wanna talk about it?' Leo said softly.

'No,' Michael said. 'Let's get out of here.'

He called her later that evening, after dinner. We left him alone, but everybody could hear him shouting at her. He still refused to talk about it afterwards.

After we'd shown the London real estate agent out, John called Michael and Leo to bring Simone down from the top-floor nursery.

'Are we going to the Science Museum now?' Simone yelled as she clattered down the stairs.

'Yes, we can have lunch there,' I said.

'Good!' She threw herself at John. 'I want the chicken.'

John lifted her and sat her on his hip. 'Michael, with us. Leo, you have things to do. Take the rest of the day.'

Leo was tremendously relieved. 'My Lord. Where's the list?'

'On my desk.'

'Buy him some more like this,' I said, pointing to the black straight-cut jeans and black T-shirt Leo had picked up for John in Paris. 'He looks like a Chinese rock star on holiday.'

'You like it?' Leo said, grinning.

'Buy Emma some matching ones,' John said.

'Oh no. No way. I buy my own clothes.'

'You'll have to wait until we're in Paris again for jeans,' Leo said. 'I buy the more formal stuff here.'

'Buy anything for me and you are in *serious trouble*,' I said.

John focused on Leo and spoke silently to him.

'No, you don't! Out loud!' I shouted.

Leo nodded to John, then touched Michael on the arm. 'Michael, stay close to them and guard them well. I want a good report when I see you later.'

'Don't you dare buy me anything,' I growled.

'Come on, Emma, hurry up,' Simone said. She wriggled out of John's arms and took my hand. 'I wanna go to the Science Museum.'

CHAPTER TWENTY-ONE

John held one of Simone's hands, I held the other, and we bounced her along the street to the Science Museum. John sparkled with energy and appeared slightly younger than me, in his late twenties. He really did look like a rock star on holiday wearing his new jeans.

It felt wonderful to walk together down the leafy Kensington street on a crisp, bright London summer's day. Michael followed, very quiet.

When we arrived at the Museum Simone dashed inside, then stopped. 'Sorry, Daddy.' She returned to us, took John's hand, and we entered together.

After we'd been through just about every display, we had lunch in the new wing with its computerised displays at the far end of the Museum. The second floor housed tremendously annoying interactive musical computers, but Simone really liked them so we stayed there for a while.

'Does she have to see *absolutely everything*?' Michael asked me, weary.

'Yes, she does. You saw Leo's face when we let him off.'

Simone dragged us to the top floor of the new wing. Each floor was smaller than the one below, allowing us to see all the way to the ground. Two round tables with projected computer images were the only display on the top floor. Six people could stand around each table and interact with the computer.

Michael, Simone and I took a place each and played games about the future of technology, genetics and space exploration. Michael and Simone competed fiercely to see who could win the most points. John stood and watched with his arms folded over his chest; he was too fast to give anybody a fair chance and the kids had thrown him off.

John tied back his hair.

The Museum fell completely silent, then a silent noise boomed through the whole structure. A vibration shuddered from my feet to my head. Without changing temperature, the air went very hot, then very cold. Something was very, very wrong.

The expression on John's face probably mirrored my own. Simone and Michael hadn't felt it. I went to John. 'What was that?'

He didn't need to reply. A large school group were visible on the ground floor of the Museum, running around and talking loudly. A minute ago they hadn't been there.

John was very calm and spoke softly. 'There are about fifty of them. We need to get out of here.'

'Why here, just after you've been to Paris? You're at your strongest.'

'They know Simone comes here every single damn time,' he said placidly. He concentrated. 'This is a really big one.'

'We're ready for them,' I said, much more calmly than I felt.

'I still think we'll need some help. We're pinned on the top floor.'

The demons were clearly audible coming up the levels towards us, talking loudly and shrieking as if they were normal children. John looked around, then gestured. 'Fire escape. Let's go.'

I went behind Simone and Michael and quietly spoke to them. 'We have to move. Leave it. Let's go.'

Michael appeared bewildered, but Simone's eyes widened. 'There's a lot of demons coming, Emma,' she said, breathless.

'How many, ma'am?' Michael said as we approached the door.

'Lord Xuan says about fifty.' I tried to control my voice. 'You can hear them coming, they've taken the form of a school group.'

John waited at the fire escape. I moved to open it, but he raised his hand to stop me.

The demons spread out, still talking noisily to each other, on the floor below us. They were looking for us. They would be on our level soon.

Gold appeared next to John. He examined the door and smiled grimly, then put his hand on the latch and concentrated. He became completely transparent, as if he was made out of clear plastic, with his stone self clearly visible in the middle of his chest.

Michael gasped.

Gold returned to his normal human form and pushed the door open for us without setting off the alarm. He smiled and waved us through.

We went through the doors to the top of an external set of metal stairs, a standard fire escape. No stairs led further up, and I had the incongruous thought: oh, what a shame. We couldn't do the typical action-movie thing of stupidly running up to the roof and pinning ourselves with no way out.

We quickly and carefully took the stairs down. The Museum's back loading dock was at the bottom. It was nearly deserted; it was almost closing time. Damn. If it had been busy then the demons would have stayed away.

When we were about halfway down Jade appeared, flying over the roof in dragon form, whipping through the air. She landed lightly on the ground of the loading dock. She checked the location, her gold claws making metallic clicks on the pavement as she moved. She glanced up to us and nodded.

Gold vaulted over the edge of the railing, and splattered like goo when he hit the ground. He quickly re-formed and stood next to Jade.

A couple of Celestial Masters appeared next to them: two of the most senior Masters on the Mountain. The Shaolin Master, in his tan jacket and pants, and the Energy Master, in a plain black cotton pantsuit with white cuffs.

The Shaolin Master, Master Liu, was a tiny ancient Chinese man with a completely bald head, a long flowing white beard and matching white eyebrows. His eyes twinkled merrily as he smiled up at us. He held one hand in the traditional Shaolin greeting of a half-prayer and bowed slightly.

The Energy Master, also Master Liu, was a tall, elegant European woman with short dark hair and an intelligent, angular face, appearing in her mid-forties. She saluted us Chinese-style, hand on fist.

'Hi, Emma,' she called in her delightful English accent.

'Hi, Meredith,' I called back. I really liked Meredith, she was the only Master who didn't give me a lot of grief about calling me 'Lady Emma'.

'What do we have here, my Lord?' the Shaolin Master said as we neared the bottom of the stairs.

'About fifty of them, only small ones, taking the form of English schoolchildren,' John said.

'Always knew English schoolboys were right demonic little bastards,' Meredith said cheerfully.

As soon as we were all together, the Immortals stopped and looked at each other. Then they turned as one to face the exit of the loading dock where it met the street.

'Goodness me,' Meredith said evenly. 'South Kensington is Demon Central today.'

John faced the alley. 'Here they come, and the ones from inside are coming out as well. Attacked from both sides. Put the children and Emma in the middle —'

'Oh no you don't,' I said loudly. 'Put me next to Meredith and I'll use energy. She can help me when I fill up.'

John opened his mouth to say something and I glared him down.

'Permission to fight, my Lord,' Michael said. 'Let me at them.'

'Let him,' I said. 'It's his job.'

'Very well,' John said.

'And I'm not a *child*,' he said under his breath.

'I know,' I whispered back. 'But both of us are, compared to them.'

Jade remained in dragon form. She sharpened the golden claws of one foreleg against the claws of the other with a metallic rasping sound.

Gold froze and concentrated, then his whole body turned into the same stuff his stone was made of: quartz gleaming with veins of gold. He still moved fluidly, even though he was made of stone.

The door at the top of the fire escape opened and the children came down the stairs. They dropped the childlike act as they came, becoming very quiet and serious, their little feet moving in unison like a zombie army.

'Emma, Meredith, Michael, Liu,' John said, and pointed behind him. 'Me, Jade, Gold,' and pointed next to him. 'Simone between us.' He cracked his knuckles loudly. 'Count them as you take them. The one who destroys the fewest is buying dinner.'

'I'll lose then,' Meredith said cheerfully over her shoulder as she moved into position next to me. 'My Art is the slowest. But that's okay, I know an excellent family-friendly pub over near Oxford Circus. The little Princess will love it.'

'Not Western food,' John moaned. More demons appeared at the end of the alley. These looked like ordinary European men and women. 'You women hate me.'

Meredith and I shared a smile. Then we turned to face the demons.

'Look sharp, Emma,' Meredith said. 'If you fill up, just point the energy in my direction and let go, or throw it into the ground. Please don't blow yourself up, dear. If you do, the Dark Lord will be totally impossible for absolutely bloody ages.'

The demons moved into range and I threw balls of chi at them, making them explode with a satisfying thump. 'You mean *more* impossible, Meredith.'

Shaolin Master Liu ran into the middle of the demons and cut through them with hands, fists and feet. He was so fast he was a tan-coloured blur. Demons exploded around him as he shredded them. He took the time to bounce off the wall and throw himself back into the middle of them.

'Show-off!' Meredith yelled as she blew up demons with a devastating destructive rhythm. She stopped using energy and went in next to Master Liu, using the tai chi moves with deadly speed and accuracy, her hands glowing with energy as she struck. The Lius positioned themselves back to back and cut down every demon that approached them.

My energy neared a dangerous level as I absorbed the demons' chi. 'Heads up, Meredith!' I shouted, and shot a large ball of chi straight at her. She caught it, broke it into tiny balls, and scattered them around her, hitting about twenty demons at the same time.

Michael faced the demons one at a time and was more than a match for them. His face was a grim mask of fury as he destroyed them hand-to-hand. He didn't shift from his position next to me and in front of Simone.

'How's it going back there, John?' I shouted over my shoulder.

'Haven't had this much fun in a long time,' John called back without losing his rhythm. He destroyed the demons with effortless ease; his ponytail didn't even move. He raised his voice so that everybody could hear him. 'Be aware, people, there are more on the way, and they are bigger than these. Clear these out quickly so that we have room to work; they are just to soften us up.'

'Any Princes on their way, John?' I said.

'At this stage I couldn't say. But I can take him anyway.'

The two Masters Liu had finished the demons around them and returned to me.

Michael used the second-last demon as a weapon and smashed it into the last one, making both explode.

Jade, Gold and John finished off the last few stragglers. We returned to position around Simone.

'Jade,' John said.

'My Lord.'

A cloud appeared above us and drenched us in a brief, intense shower of warm water, washing the black demon stuff off us.

'My jacket will run,' the Shaolin Master said cheerfully.

'Just take it off if you don't like it, sweetheart,' Meredith said.

'Oh, please don't,' Jade said with distress. 'Anyone want to dry off?'

We nodded. The cloud disappeared. A small whirlwind of warm air gave us a quick blow-dry.

'Here they come,' John said. 'Nice and big. Stay very still, Simone. Michael, don't try to take on these ones.'

'What do we have here, people?' I said.

'Bugs,' John said cheerfully.

I ran my hands through my damp hair and retied my ponytail. 'Oh no, I hate bugs.'

'What, the way they spray disgusting brown sludge everywhere when you smash their shells?' John said with relish.

'I think I'm going to be sick,' I said quietly.

'You can stand behind us if you like, dear,' Meredith said. 'You don't have to face them if you don't want to. It would probably be a good idea if you don't take on these ones. We don't want to put you at risk.'

'Good practice for me,' I said.

'You're quite right,' John said. He stiffened. 'Here they come. Weapons.'

'Coming,' Gold said.

The demons materialised at the entrance to the alley, about fifty metres away. There were about twenty giant insects altogether. Ten were spiders that had poisonous fangs. Another five or so were cockroaches that would bite at anything within reach, releasing their venomous saliva. Another five were beetles that sprayed toxic green slime out of their back ends. Their jointed legs clicked on the concrete. Each must have been nearly three metres long and two high. They were huge.

'God, I hate these things,' I said.

'You go berserk if there's a tiny cockroach in your shower, and I have to kill it for you every time,' John said, teasing. 'You won't even kill a little cockroach with a minuscule bolt of chi.'

'I'll kill bug demons with a big bolt though,' I said. 'But you know physical is the way to go with these things.'

'Weapons, *now*,' John said sharply.

'My Lord,' Jade said.

My sword appeared in front of me. I nodded to Jade and picked it out of the air. Michael took the White Tiger. The Shaolin Master summoned his staff. Meredith also had a sword, a long straight tai chi-style weapon. John raised his Celestial Seven Stars sword; it was enormous, nearly six feet long, and he carried it without difficulty. Jade and Gold didn't need weapons. Jade's claws were razor-sharp and deadly. Gold's whole body was a lethal hammer of stone.

'Make your sword sing, Emma,' John said. 'We'll see if we can't blow them up before they're too close.'

The demons were about ten metres away. I pushed some chi into the sword and made it sing.

'Oh no, Lord Xuan, you didn't give her *that* sword, did you?' Meredith said over the noise. 'I was hoping it didn't survive the Attack.'

The demons kept coming. The pinging ring of the sword covered the sound of their feet clicking on the concrete.

They kept coming. They were nearly five metres away.

'Give up, Emma, it won't work,' John said over the noise.

I stopped the sound and my ears rang in the sudden silence. The insects stopped.

'Me on point,' John said. 'Liu, Meredith, beside. Jade, Gold, Emma. Michael, Simone, behind. Now.'

We quickly moved into position, a V-shape, with John at the top and the children behind us.

The insects hesitated.

'I will spare you if you turn,' John said loudly.

They attacked.

A spider came at me. All I saw were fangs and big black hairy legs; it towered over me. It lowered its head to bite me, its enormous fangs extended and dripping venom.

I ducked and shot through underneath it, ripping its abdomen open as I went between its legs. I spun to face it as it turned. It didn't seem to notice that its insides were hanging out. I ducked through again, this time diagonally, and took off a couple of legs as I went. It spun more clumsily with fewer legs. It reared up on its hind legs, and the disgusting stuff hanging from its open abdomen smeared on the ground.

It fell sideways, twitched, and curled up. It dissolved into a puddle of revolting brown goo that dissipated quickly. One.

Next was a cockroach. I hated these things: their shells were a good two centimetres thick and almost impossible to crack. Its razor-sharp mouthparts quivered, bubbling with venom. I ducked beneath its head, and its mouth just missed me on the way through. I shoved my sword up into the soft shell of the joint between its leg and its abdomen, then loaded the sword with chi and sent it right into the monster, frying it from the inside out.

The smell was indescribable. Good thing I hadn't had too much for lunch. I ducked out from underneath it before it fell. It dropped vertically and didn't move, then exploded into black feathery streamers. Two.

Another spider. I tried to move around the side to take its legs off, but it spun and quickly followed me. The venom dripped off its fangs and bubbled where it hit the ground. Its face grew an expression of insectile shock: Michael was cutting its legs off at the other end. The spider spun to face him, and as it did I took more legs off. When it was facing Michael and had its back to me I jumped onto its back and rammed my sword right into the top of its head, through the middle of its circle of eyes.

It crashed vertically. I leapt off. It dissolved. Three.

'Well done, Michael,' I said.

'Behind you!' he shouted.

I leapt sideways and the spray of venom missed me. I somersaulted backwards and landed on the beetle's back. I ran my sword into the gap between its wing cases and sent a blast of chi into it. Its wing cases flew open, throwing me off without my sword. I landed lightly near its head. It didn't move, it just watched me. Then its head fell off, it folded up sideways and dissolved. My sword fell to the ground and I collected it. Four.

Only two remained. John was having some fun with a spider; he moved so fast he was a blur. He was taking pieces of leg off one at a time, quite evenly, so that the spider was still able to walk. It grew shorter and shorter.

'Finish it, you silly old man!' I shouted.

He grinned over his shoulder, flashed over it in a huge somersaulting leap, and cut it completely in two from above.

Liu ran his staff through the last one's head and it dissolved.

None left.

We regrouped. I was the only one panting; the rest of them just grinned at each other. Blasted Immortals, they were having a good time and I was fighting for my life. I grinned too. Damn, but this was fun.

We checked Simone and Michael. They were fine. Simone wasn't fazed by the insects; she didn't seem to be frightened by any demons except Wong.

'Again, Jade,' John said. 'Anyone poisoned?'

Everybody shook their heads as the warm shower washed us clean.

John smiled at me. 'Well done.'

'I hate those things.'

The warm wind dried us off.

His smile froze. All of them froze.

'Move Simone and Michael over near the wall and stay there with them,' he said, his eyes unseeing. 'This is it.'

'Is it him?'

'Believe it or not,' he said, his face expressionless, 'it isn't him at all.' He gestured. 'Go.'

CHAPTER TWENTY-TWO

The noise of the traffic outside stopped. There was complete silence. Once again there was the silent rush of sound and a huge vibration.

All the Immortals turned as one to face the entrance to the alley.

The sound of traditional Chinese music came from the end of the alley. Someone was playing pipes, and there was a drum and a gong. Marching feet, and a wet slithering sound. I'd heard that sound before, and a chill went through me as I remembered. A Snake Mother.

A small band of very low-level demons came first, in True Form, tiny, skinny and black with big ears and grotesque faces. They played the musical instruments and looked like a little naked marching band.

A huge sedan chair followed. It was the colour of dried blood with gold trimmings. Four very high-level demons carried it; these demons had the bodies of huge men.

They were about three metres tall, wore brown trousers, and were naked from the waist up. The two carrying the front of the chair had the heads of horses. The two at the back had the heads of bulls. John had mentioned these demons before but I'd never seen them.

Apparently these particular ones spent most of their time in Hell.

John had referred to Hell once or twice in the past but wouldn't elaborate.

Eight Snake Mothers slithered in formation around the sedan chair. Their front ends looked like men with the skin taken off; veins stood out over the muscles and the blood was clearly visible moving through them. From the waist down they were black snakes, oozing toxic slime.

John nodded and the two Masters Liu moved back together to protect Simone, Michael and myself as we stood against the wall.

'I have never seen so many Mothers in one place outside the nests,' Meredith said with wonder. 'Liu, how about you? You have about six hundred years on me. Ever seen so many?'

'Nope.' Liu spoke to me over his shoulder. 'Emma, did you bring a camera with you today?'

'No need to when we come here. We all know this place inside out and have seen absolutely everything we need to see.'

'Would have been nice to take a photo of this though,' Meredith said. 'He hardly ever comes out of Hell, and this is the second time this year.'

'Who?'

'The King of the Demons.'

'Oh my God, no. John,' I wailed softly. 'No.'

'He'll be fine, my Lady,' Shaolin Master Liu said. 'The King is probably just here on a courtesy call. I think he wants to parley.'

'But what about is anybody's guess,' Meredith said. 'I can't see what he would want to discuss with the Dark Lord. It's only been a few months since he nearly destroyed the Mountain.'

John transformed into Celestial Form, nearly four metres tall. His hair was long and black and wild around his head. His face was square and dark and fearsome, with a long, thin black beard. He wore traditional Chinese black lacquer armour. He slid his Seven Stars sword into its scabbard on his back, then took a couple of enormous paces forward to face the sedan chair and crossed his arms over his chest.

Jade and Gold took Celestial Form as well. Each was around two and a half metres tall, slim and elegant, wearing long, flowing old-fashioned robes of embossed silk. Jade's robes were green and Gold's were tan. Jade's shining dark green hair cascaded down to her knees, with elaborate buns and braids decorated with gold and jade on top of her head. Gold's long flowing hair, tied on top, was snowy white with golden streaks through it, similar to the colour of his stone. They took up position as Retainers behind John.

Simone took a couple of staggering steps towards me. I quickly grabbed her and pulled her into me, burying her little face into my stomach. 'Don't worry, sweetheart, you know it's only Daddy.'

She didn't say anything, she just clutched my clothes with both hands.

The demons gently lowered the sedan chair. One of the horse-headed ones turned, went to the side of the chair, bowed, and opened the red fabric curtains.

Meredith and Liu moved very slightly closer to us. John, Jade and Gold didn't move at all.

The King stepped out. He was about the same height as Xuan Wu, but where John was black, he was blood-red and gold. His young, fair face had a fine, ethereal beauty that was a stark contrast to Xuan Wu's dark ugliness. His blood-red hair stood up at the top and swept in an enormous mane down to his waist behind him. He had blood-red bushy eyebrows but was otherwise clean-shaven. His maroon lacquer armour had gold trimmings, and he wore scaled boots of red and gold.

All of the Snake Mothers transformed at the same time. They turned into beautiful tall graceful women of all races, wearing identical blood-red cheongsams. They didn't move a muscle otherwise.

The Demon King bowed and saluted John crisply.

John saluted back.

An enormous Chinese-style outdoor ceramic table appeared, large enough for them to sit. Six ceramic stools appeared around it. The Demon King walked stiffly to the table, held out one arm, bowed slightly, and gestured towards it.

John moved forward, bowed slightly, and gestured as well.

The Demon King nodded to John, flicked his robes under his armour, and sat gracefully at the table. John did the same thing. They sat on opposite sides of the table with their hands on it and studied each other calmly. Jade and Gold moved back and to one side to give them space to talk.

The Demon King turned his head to look me straight in the eye. A charming smile lit up his face and he nodded to me.

John stiffened very slightly.

The Demon King turned his attention back to John and said something. John replied. They spoke to each other calmly.

'They're just exchanging pleasantries right now, Emma,' Meredith said. 'Families, what they've been doing, meaningless conversation. It will take them a while to come to the point.'

The Demon King said something and John went still.

'He is here to make an offer,' Meredith said. 'He knows about the activities of one of his sons.'

John said something in reply, his voice rumbling.

'Lord Xuan said that this particular son has been — to use his own words, Emma — a right royal pain in the ass, and he would like to see the back of him any way possible,' Meredith said with a touch of amusement.

The Demon King smiled as he said something and all of the Immortals stiffened.

'No,' Meredith whispered.

John remained unmoving. The King turned and smiled straight into my eyes again.

Another Immortal in Celestial Form appeared behind John. This one was white with gold trim on his armour. His hair was a huge mane of gold-streaked white that flowed wildly down his back and was tied loosely with a gold ribbon. White and gold. Bai Hu.

He stiffly saluted John and the Demon King, who both nodded formally in return. He sat next to John.

'The Dark Lord has summoned the White Tiger to witness,' Meredith said softly, her voice full of awe.

'Holy shit,' Michael said very softly under his breath.

'What was the offer, Meredith?' I whispered with frustration as I clutched Simone at my waist. 'Tell me!'

'I have been strictly ordered not to tell you, dear,' Meredith said. 'It wouldn't be worth my job. All of us have been ordered most severely not to tell you.'

Then the offer must have been about me. Oh my God, I knew what it was. I saw the way the King looked at me.

I gently pushed Simone away, then gathered myself and made a huge leap from behind the protective pair of Immortals to land beside John at the parleying table. I could barely see over the table, it was so huge.

'Please go back to the others, Emma,' John said without looking at me. His voice sounded exactly as it always did.

'No, no, the Lady is most welcome,' the Demon

King said, smiling broadly. 'Would you like tea, my Lady?'

'No, thank you.' He was too high; I couldn't see him properly. I climbed to sit cross-legged on the table, feeling like a leprechaun at a giants' tea party. 'I'd like an answer instead. Did you just offer a trade? Me for your one hundred and twenty-second son?'

John stiffened beside me. 'Whoever told you that is out of a job and off my Mountain,' he said, his voice a low rumble.

'Nobody told me, old man,' I retorted. 'Nobody needed to. It was absolutely obvious.'

'I must have her,' the King said with a wide grin. He thumped the table with his fist. 'Anything you want, Turtle. Anything at all. Just name it. I must have her.'

'She. Is. Mine,' John said very slowly and calmly.

'No. I'm. Not,' I said, matching his tone. 'Right now, I belong to me. And if I decide to go with him, to keep Simone safe, then it has absolutely nothing to do with you.'

'Anything,' the King said softly.

'If I go with you, and stay with you, and don't attempt to escape,' I said to the King, 'will you promise to keep Simone safe for the rest of her life?'

The King shot to his feet. 'If you come with me and stay with me, I vow that Princess Simone, daughter of Xuan Wu Shang Di, will be perfectly safe for the rest of her natural life.'

'How long is that vow good for?' I said.

'Forever,' he said matter-of-factly as he sat again.

'Is his word good, John?' I said without looking at John by my side.

He didn't reply.

'Answer me!' I still didn't turn to him. '*Is his word good?*'

'Yes, it is, my Lady,' Bai Hu said from the other side of John, his voice full of awe.

'Please do not do this thing, Emma,' John whispered.

'I won't. Don't be ridiculous. Right now you can defeat Wong. Why should I go with this guy? There's really no point.' I glared up at the Demon King. 'Understand?'

He nodded. He smiled again, and his beautiful face lit up. 'You are extremely remarkable.'

'You owe me a gold coin,' I shot back. 'Listen to me, all of you.' I felt ridiculous laying down the law to these giant fearsome deities. 'I have made a promise to Xuan Wu to wait for him until he returns. Do you understand, Your Most Loathsome Majesty?'

The Demon King sat back, aghast. 'How did you know my correct title?'

'Look at yourself. Did you actually hear what I just said? Or are you too busy drooling at my tits to take any notice?'

'You promised to wait for him.' He grinned at John. 'Of course she will keep her word to you. She is a woman of honour.' He leaned back slightly, looked at me, then looked back at John and his grin widened. 'But she didn't say what she'd do while she waited!'

A shot of pain stabbed me right through. My throat thickened and I tried to swallow it. I looked down.

'I will never love anyone else the way that I love you, Xuan Wu,' I said softly to the table, 'but I would do anything for Simone, you know that.'

The expression on John's face matched my emotions, even through the Celestial Form.

'Anything,' I said.

He glanced away.

'And I know you would too.'

I looked back up at the King. 'Can you give me

something so I can call you if I change my mind and decide to go to you?'

His beautiful face lit up and he nodded.

I put both hands in my lap and looked down at them. 'Would you only hold me until Xuan Wu returns, so that I can keep my promise to him?'

'I swear,' he said.

I glanced up at him. 'You could have a full-on try to convince me to stay with you. You could go for it. You're very attractive, you know that? I could grow to like you.'

His smile widened. 'I could give you more than you could ever possibly desire.'

I folded my hands together in my lap. 'Do you solemnly vow not to give anybody any assistance in going after us? That you'll stay out of this in the meantime?'

He nodded.

'Stand up and do it right,' I said sternly.

He rose and put his hand on the table. His face went hard and fierce. 'I solemnly vow that I will not assist anyone in their efforts to harm the Dark Lord, Xuan Wu, or any member of his household. I hereby swear that if the Lady Emma chooses to come to me of her own free will, I will ensure that the Princess Simone remains safe for the rest of her natural life. If the Lady Emma comes to me of her own free will, I will only hold her until the Dark Lord returns, if that is her wish.' He smiled kindly at me. 'Will that do?' He sat again.

'What do you think, Bai Hu?' I said without looking at the men on my side of the table.

John remained perfectly still, but it was obvious he hadn't missed the significance of me not asking him.

'I think you've covered all your bases there, my Lady,' Bai Hu said softly. 'Remind me to have you in next time I have to negotiate a treaty with one of my neighbours.'

'*I'm* one of your neighbours,' John said.

'Sure, Tiger.' I felt pain; my hands were held so tightly together my fingernails had drawn blood from my palms. I shook them to loosen them up, then looked up at the Demon King. Bastard. 'Why do you want me so badly, King? I'm just an ordinary human female.'

'He wants everything I possess,' John said. 'He wants all that I love. He wants my Mountain, he wants my Lady, he wants my daughter.'

'One out of three already, Xuan Tian,' the Demon King said. 'I hear it will take you years to fix the damage we caused with our little party on top of your Mountain. Do you have any idea how many of my children are after your head?'

John stiffened very slightly. 'I have caused him a great deal of grief over the centuries, and he would love to make me suffer.'

'I love you dearly, Turtle.' The Demon King smiled right into John's eyes. 'I would particularly love you stewed with vegetables in a hotpot. Right after,' he smiled gently at me, 'a large tureen of shredded snake broth with sliced pig's ear. And,' he looked at the Tiger, 'braised tiger penis on yin-yang rice.'

'You won't be eating my dick, you'll be sucking it,' the Tiger said, very calm.

'By the Ten Levels of Hell but I adore you, little pussy cat,' the Demon King said with a gentle smile. 'Eaten any unborn children lately?'

The Tiger didn't reply.

'Give me something so that I can call you,' I said, ignoring them.

The King grinned and handed me a perfectly normal mobile phone. I checked the phone book: only one number stored.

'Now piss off,' I said. 'Go away and leave us alone. Stay out of this. If I call you, I call you. I don't ever intend to. But now you can't stick your ugly red nose into our business.'

The Demon King threw his head back, roared with laughter, then rose. John and the Tiger stood as well. I remained sitting cross-legged on the table.

The King saluted John and the Tiger. They returned the salute perfectly politely. I ignored them.

As the King returned to the sedan chair I unfolded my legs and hopped down off the table to stand next to John.

The Demon King turned back before he entered the chair. 'Oh,' he said casually. 'I forgot about this. This happened before I gave you my promise not to interfere, my Lady Emma, I do apologise. But my Ladies insisted, they said they had a score to settle.'

He gestured, and one of the Snake Mothers took full huge, ugly True Form. It slithered to the back of the sedan chair and opened a large trunk there. It reached in and pulled out Leo by one arm. He was unconscious and hung limply from its grip. Blood covered his face and his clothes.

I moved to rush to him but John held out his arm to stop me.

'Don't make any sudden moves,' John said quietly. 'Stay very still, and let it give him back to us.'

The Snake Mother slithered to us, still dangling Leo. It dropped him in front of us, and he crumpled. The Snake Mother grinned viciously into my eyes.

'We had a lot of fun with this little Lion,' it hissed loudly. 'But we did not kill it, because the King would not permit it. He said that you love it.' The Snake Mother lowered itself on its coils so that its red eyes were level with mine. 'Please do come and join us in Hell, my Lady. We have so many *wonderful* plans for you.'

It raised itself, then changed back to a slim, beautiful European girl with bright red hair. She smiled tightly at me and returned to position.

The small demons began to play the music. The Demon King gave me a friendly wave and boarded the sedan chair. The animal-headed demons picked it up, and the whole procession turned back down the alley and disappeared.

The silence continued for a few moments, then the noise of the cars and the people outside restarted.

John, the Tiger, Jade and Gold took human form. We all knelt around Leo. The other Immortals, with Simone and Michael, rushed to us.

Leo started to regain consciousness. He cast around, eyes wide, then saw us and collapsed back. He grimaced with pain.

'Quickly, Leo, if you can tell us any major injuries you've sustained it will save us a great deal of time,' John said urgently.

Leo winced. He shook his head, then turned away and spat out blood.

I became very calm. 'Meredith, Liu, Michael, take Simone away where she won't be able to see Leo, and turn her around. I don't want her to see this. Michael, you too.'

'No, Meredith, stay,' John said. 'Everybody else, do as Emma orders.'

I heard them move but didn't look at them. I studied Leo and looked right into his eyes. 'Oh dear Lord, Leo, they didn't. No.'

'Tell me, Leo,' John said.

'He can't. He ripped out the Snake Mother's tongue and killed it when you were on the Mountain, John.' I turned back to Leo. 'Did they take it completely out?'

Leo shook his head. He turned and spat out more blood, gagging. I knelt closer to him and took his hand;

it was like ice. He grasped my hand fiercely and gazed into my eyes. I put my other hand on his bloodied cheek and whispered, 'Show me.'

He shook his head, his mouth clamped shut.

'Show me, that's an order,' I whispered again, my heart breaking.

He opened his bloodied mouth and showed us.

They had sliced his tongue in half right down the middle. He had a forked tongue exactly like they did.

'No,' John said quietly.

Meredith gasped behind me. 'Oh, dear Lord.' She moved quickly. 'Turn him over, I need to reach the points on his back.'

Leo helped us to tip him over onto his stomach. Meredith ripped his shirt to reveal his back, then put her fingers over some of the energy points on the meridians down Leo's back.

'Over again,' she said, and pulled the remains of the shirt from him after we'd turned him over. She concentrated on the energy points on his chest, up his neck, and across his face.

Leo relaxed and smiled with his eyes closed. Then he looked up at her and nodded, smiling, mouth still firmly shut.

'You're most welcome,' Meredith said softly. 'The anaesthetising effect will last for a few hours.'

'Well?' John said.

'I can't do this by myself,' Meredith said, 'and none of the others has enough experience with energy. I'm sorry, my Lord, without another energy expert I simply can't do it.'

'Try Emma,' John said.

'She's not Immortal,' Meredith said. 'You let your love cloud your judgement.'

'No, I don't,' John said. 'Try anyway. She can do shen work and she can use her Inner Eye. Try.'

Meredith stiffened and glanced sharply at me.

'Please, Meredith, for Leo,' I said. 'Please.'

'First we need to move him back to the house and somewhere comfortable,' Meredith said. 'This will take a while.'

John raised his head and spoke loudly. 'Immortals, carry. Jade, Emma. Gold, Simone. Tiger, Michael. Meredith, Leo. I will walk. Back to the house. Liu, dismissed. Report.'

CHAPTER TWENTY-THREE

The world blinked out, then I was next to the bed in Leo's room. I fell over, but strong arms hoisted me into a chair. The world stopped spinning and I saw Meredith holding me.

'It will go away very quickly,' she said. 'It was just a short distance.'

Somebody pushed a glass of water into my hand but I shoved it away. I threw myself up, ignoring the dizziness, and stumbled to Leo's bedside to hold his hand. He smiled at me, his mouth carefully closed. His expression went strange.

'Somebody get him a bowl, very quickly,' I said, but Meredith was already shoving one in front of him from the other side of the bed. He spat out blood. He gagged on it, and more came out.

'How much healing energy work have you done, Emma?' Meredith said softly without turning away from Leo.

'Apart from using the phoenix feather on Leo last time a demon injured him, none at all.' I shook my head with remorse. 'I wish I'd brought it with me.'

'Waste of time.' Meredith put the bowl on the bedside table. 'You'd need at least two feathers to fix this.'

'Damn.'

'Let's see if we can do this. You will be a receptacle.' Meredith took both of Leo's hands. 'You don't really need to do anything, just be able to hold enough *chi*.' She put her hand on my shoulder and studied me closely. 'You'll do.' She turned back to Leo. 'Has anybody ever done energy healing on you before?'

Leo shook his head without opening his mouth.

'Then you will find this a most interesting experience. Don't panic, it won't hurt. If you feel like you're suffocating on your tongue at all, just breathe. That's normal. You won't suffocate, I promise. Do you understand?'

Leo nodded, perfectly calm.

'Right, then,' Meredith said crisply, sounding like an English matron. 'Let's get started. Emma, hold my hand.' She took my left hand in her right. 'Stay very still and keep your mind clear. Feel free to follow along; you might find this enlightening. You may learn something. Leo.' She took Leo's right hand in her left. 'Just breathe. You won't suffocate, despite what it feels like. Relax. Don't worry if you feel sleepy, just let yourself doze off, it will make the procedure go faster for you. Okay, people, let's do this.' Her voice softened as she reached inside Leo and his energy meridians lit up like Christmas tree lights. 'You are in a great deal of serious trouble, young Emma.' She moved the energy through Leo. 'I don't want to be anywhere around when Lord Xuan finally sits you down; he is going to go quite spare.'

John and Gold were waiting in the hall when we came out of the room. Both of us were exhausted. John had a face like thunder; rigid with control.

'Don't bother getting stuck into her right now,' Meredith said to John. 'She won't hear you, she's absolutely exhausted, and so am I. Both of us are going to our rooms to collapse and sleep for a week. When we come round we will be starving, so be ready for us with a great deal of fresh food. After that you can feel free to kill missy Emma if you like.'

She was right. I was too exhausted even to say something cutting.

'What about Leo?' John said.

'Leo will live. I did my best. He has lost an awful lot of blood. You were right about Emma. She is remarkable.'

'You owe me a gold coin,' I whispered.

Meredith continued, ignoring me. 'But Leo will have a serious speech impediment. He will sound like he is profoundly deaf. And when I wake up again, I am going to go out and kill something.'

John looked like he was about to say something, then changed his mind. He gestured down the hallway. 'Go.'

I was asleep before my head hit the pillow.

I woke up. I was paralysed. I knew this: sleep paralysis. It happened when you were exhausted but something woke you. Your body was still asleep. It was still paralysed, like when you were asleep. But your mind was awake.

Wonderful. I hoped nothing was there to get me, 'cause I really couldn't move.

My consciousness struggled upwards. My body was made of lead.

Oh my God. Turtle hotpot with vegetables. Roast tiger penis on yin-yang rice. *Shredded snake broth with sliced pig's ear*. He looked at *me* when he said that. I needed to *remember* that.

My consciousness drifted back down again.

* * *

277

I waited for John in his office on the first floor of the Kensington house. He came in, quietly closed the door and then stood with his hands clasped behind his back. He strode over to the desk and stood behind his office chair. He leaned his arms on the back of the chair. The sunshine streamed through the first-floor window behind him and lit up his dark hair.

I sat silently. I took a sip of the tea. I was perfectly calm.

'Sometimes, Emma, I think you *want* to take a trip through the Ten Levels of Hell,' John said. 'What's the big attraction?'

'Don't be ridiculous. Simone is the reason I do everything I do.' I stopped and glared up at him. 'I'll make a trip through there anyway. I'm well aware of that.'

He seemed surprised. 'How come you know this?'

'You people don't keep your activities too much of a secret from the world at large, Xuan Wu,' I said. 'All I had to do was some research. There's a great deal of misguided claptrap, but a lot of truth out there. I've been reading. I know.'

'And you would still face that by choice?'

I shrugged. 'For Simone.'

'He would try to win you over, you know,' John said, looking me in the eyes, his voice still very mild. 'But when he sees it is a waste of time, he will throw you to the Mothers.'

'Simone would be safe.'

'I would return to a gibbering husk of a woman with a mind pummelled into imbecility by their torture. What they did to Leo was just a tiny taste of their capabilities.'

'Simone would still be safe,' I said. 'Look me right in the eye and tell me you wouldn't have done exactly the same thing.'

He sighed and sat across from me. He reached into his pocket, pulled out a gold coin, and slid it across the desk to me. He put his head in his hands, then rubbed his hands over his face. He leaned back to retie his hair.

We were both thinking: I love you so damn much. One day this will all come together for us.

'None of this would ever have happened if I had never married Michelle,' he said. 'If I had met you first, it could have been completely different. I would have been at full strength, able to train you and defend you. In a short time you would have had the capability to handle any demon. We would be Dark Lord and Dark Lady together on the undamaged Mountain. We would not be in this situation.'

'How *dare* you!' I shouted, furious. I leaned forward and thumped the table, making the tea slop out of the cup onto some of his papers. 'If you had never married Michelle you would have never had Simone. I can see what Michelle was like, there's a lot of her in Simone! She must have been a remarkable woman!' My voice thickened. 'You are such a bastard sometimes. How could you say such a thing?'

He watched me silently for a while. Then he slid another gold coin to me.

He smiled slightly. 'You know, *I* am the one who is supposed to be cross with *you*.' He leaned back and put his palms on the table. 'Well, now you have this pact with the King, I suppose we both just have to make sure that you never use it.'

'But it's nice to know that it's there just in case. And to know that red-headed bastard will keep his ugly nose out of this.'

His face was still expressionless. 'Will you still be this impossible after we're married?'

'Probably,' I said, matching his even tone. 'Will you?'

He smiled slightly. Words weren't necessary.

'Gold has appeared outside. He says there is something important he needs to discuss with us.'

'Tell him to come in, if you're finished with me,' I said, still very calm. I stopped. There was something I needed to talk to him about as well, but for the life of me I couldn't remember what it was. Oh well, it would come to me. Couldn't be that important if I couldn't remember it.

There was a tap at the door and Gold came in with a sheaf of papers under his arm. He was back to his normal human form, sharp tan suit and everything. He sat down next to me and dropped the papers onto the table. 'My Lord, my Lady.'

He knew what I'd done. I certainly didn't look like I'd just been chewed out; I was sitting there calmly drinking tea. He saw the gold coins on the desk in front of me and smiled slightly.

'My Lord, you have put this house in Kensington on the market. I suggest that you withdraw it immediately, because you can't sell it.'

'Why not?' John said.

'How long have you owned this house, my Lord?' Gold said.

'About a hundred and fifty years,' John said.

'The house has been in your name the entire time?'

John stopped. We shared a look.

'As long as I paid the rates, nobody looked very closely at the deeds,' John said. 'The house hasn't changed hands in that entire time. Not even passed down. Damn.'

'I suppose you didn't need to,' I said. 'You probably never had any intention of selling it, ever.'

Gold glanced down at the papers. 'It's too late now for me to hack into the system and fix this, my Lord. I can't do historical documents. They would be paper. I'm afraid you can't sell this house right now. It will take me a long time to fix this for you, there will be legal implications.'

'I'll spare some tame demons from somewhere,' John said. He sighed. 'Oh well, I don't have to sell the car now either.'

'You still owe me a drive in that car,' I said.

'I promised my nanny a ride in the car. I didn't promise my Lady anything.'

I smiled grimly. 'That's because the Lady's driving.'

'By your leave, my Lord,' Gold said, and John waved him away with one hand, still glaring at me. Gold shook his head and grinned as he disappeared.

Then we heard shouting downstairs. It was Michael and Bai Hu, shouting at each other very loudly. I heard some of the language and winced.

John rose and went to the door.

'We should stay out of it,' I said. 'This is between father and son.'

'They are both my Retainers,' he said, his voice calm and firm. 'And as their Lord I have the right to intervene. I think we had better get down there.' He cocked his head and listened, then his voice became more urgent. 'Before they come to *blows*!'

He threw the door open and rushed downstairs. I ran to follow him, he was right.

'...why I should go with a fucking *bastard* like you after what you've done, when Lord Xuan and Lady Emma have taken me into their home and treated me like a *son*!' Michael was yelling as we went down the stairs.

'You're *my* son and you'll fucking do what you're told!' Bai Hu bellowed back. 'You'll come with *me*, boy, and that's an *order*! Now stop giving me this shit and get over here!'

'Don't worry about Simone, she's upstairs with Leo in the nursery,' John said to me. 'He saw this coming a mile off.'

'Leo has the most brains of all of us,' I said.

'Oh, I don't know. Look what he puts up with.'

I shrugged in reply. He was right.

We went across the black and white tiled entry hall to the living room. James hesitated at the kitchen door, and John waved him inside.

Bai Hu and Michael had gone quiet. They faced off in the living room. Michael was rigid with fury and panting. Bai Hu was in human form and just as rigid. When they saw us enter they both saluted. Bai Hu just shook his hands up in front of his face; he was too distraught to salute properly. Michael, on the other hand, dropped to one knee and took his time, saluting John and then me very carefully.

When Michael was back on his feet he bowed slightly to us so that he could have the first word. 'My Lord, my Lady, please inform Lord Bai Hu that I wish to remain in your service and do not wish to leave.'

'He should go with me to the West, Ah Wu,' the Tiger growled. 'He is too young for this. This is getting really heavy. He doesn't have the experience to handle it.'

'Come. Sit.' John gestured to the comfortable fabric-covered sofas in the living room. It had been decorated in a delightfully relaxed cottage style. Large windows overlooked the quiet leafy Kensington street.

They sat on the sofas as far apart as they could. John and I took one each. I sat next to Michael. John sat next to Bai Hu.

'Now that the Demon King is out of this, Ah Bai,' John said, 'we will not be attacked by anything bigger than about level fifty. Emma and Leo can handle nearly up to that level alone. Michael will be there soon.'

'I want to stay!' Michael said loudly.

'What about that fucking bastard One Two Two?' the Tiger said.

John stiffened and his face became fierce. 'You mind your mouth in front of my Lady, or your tail will be in serious trouble.'

I nearly smiled. Weren't no ladies here, just us demon-killing bitches with swords that made dogs howl with terror.

Bai Hu threw himself up out of the sofa, quickly went to the middle of the rug next to the coffee table, and knelt. He saluted. 'Please accept my earnest apology, my Lady.'

'Rise,' I said wearily.

The Tiger nodded, rose, strode over to the sofa and threw himself back onto it next to John. He flung his arm over the edge and stretched his long legs out in front of him. He grinned at me ruefully. 'Sorry.'

Michael had remained perfectly still during this entire exchange. All he wanted was to stay with us. He didn't care about anything else that happened.

'I will deal with the Prince in my own good time,' John said evenly.

Oh dear Lord. I knew exactly what he meant. No.

John continued. 'He can only rally small demons around him; Leo has already killed his Mother. It won't be long before Michael is able to easily handle anything he throws at us.'

Bai Hu leaned forward, put his elbows on his knees and spoke softly. 'This kid is really talented, Ah Wu. I think when he reaches maturity he may be able to Transform. His mother is,' he hesitated, 'astonishing. A league of her own. The only one who's ever left.' His voice dropped. 'I don't want to lose this one.'

'Don't I have a say in this?' Michael said loudly.

'No!' the Tiger shot back. 'You do as you're told, boy!'

'Go to hell,' Michael said.

John and I were both hard pressed to conceal our amusement. Michael was more than a match for the Tiger.

The Tiger went rigid with fury. He opened his mouth to let loose another tirade at Michael but John raised his hand. The Tiger subsided, still furious, and glared at Michael. Michael glared back.

John studied Michael appraisingly. I knew what he was thinking.

'Ah Bai,' John said, 'for the first time in I think about six hundred years I am pulling rank on you. The kid stays.'

Bai Hu threw himself back into the sofa and flung his arm over the edge again. 'Eight hundred years,' he said softly. 'I want this kid, Ah Wu. You can see the potential.'

'That is why he would be better off with me,' John said. 'I am the best. You know that. Let me teach him. When I go, the pair of you can decide what to do. I would prefer he guard Simone. I can't think of anybody better for the job, apart from yourself, and you don't have the time. Tell me I don't speak the truth.'

The Tiger stayed very still for a long time. Then he shifted slightly. 'One condition. He spends his time off with me. One day a week, Western Palace. He needs to learn the skills of a Horseman. I won't have a son of mine unable to ride a horse.'

'Until Lord Xuan leaves, Bai Hu, I think Michael can probably spend some of his school holidays in the West as well,' I said. 'How about that? Is that acceptable? Michael?'

Bai Hu was about to say something but he thought better of it. He glowered at Michael.

'*Dak han le*. Can do.' Michael's handsome face lit up. He smiled shyly at me. 'Thanks, Lady Emma.'

'Is he old enough to go to the Celestial Plane without his mother?' I said.

'Yes.' Bai Hu shook his hands in front of his face without moving on the sofa. 'My Lord. My Lady. By your leave.' He disappeared.

I sighed and relaxed. John and I shared a look. Another disaster averted. We smiled.

'My Lord,' Michael said, 'he said that I may be able to Transform. Did he mean that I could turn into a tiger?'

'It is a rare gift. Only about one in a hundred of his children inherits the ability. To answer your question: yes,' John said. 'Once you have reached adulthood and your powers are set. It will be interesting to see. You may also be able to manipulate metal.'

'Way cool,' Michael said under his breath. 'I could be a were-tiger.'

'Are you sure you're all right to be spending your Sundays with him, Michael?' I said.

Michael grinned. 'Child custody arrangements.'

I laughed softly at that. 'You're the product of a broken home.'

His grin broadened. 'Little pieces.' He sobered. He looked from me to John. 'I just want to say thanks. You are the best. Lord Xuan, thank you. I really appreciate this. I want to stay with you guys. Both of you.'

'Just don't get yourself killed, lad,' John said, amused. 'If you do I'll never hear the end of it. From either of them.' He pulled himself up. 'I'm summoning Jade. She'll have to help reorganise the demon staff. This will take a while.'

'Take your time,' I said to his back. I turned to Michael. 'Up for a spar?'

His whole face lit up. 'Yes, please, ma'am.'

CHAPTER TWENTY-FOUR

The weather the day of Charlie's funeral was perfect: warm and mild without a single cloud in the seamless blue sky.

We followed the hearse in a van, and took Charlie's mother with us. Mrs Bradford was delightful; as wonderful as her daughter. She insisted on me calling her Elizabeth. She was over eighty years old, but still active and bright.

Simone and Michael were perfectly behaved throughout the entire proceedings, quiet and respectful. It wasn't obvious how much of it Simone understood, though.

The Chen family plot was in a cemetery on the outskirts of London. It was in the centre of a wide expanse of lawn with towering ancient oak trees not far away. There was a small iron fence around the area. Some of the graves were obviously very old, but the plot was immaculately cared for with small hedges and a few rose bushes.

The sun shone brightly on us as Charlie received an old-fashioned farewell. I was introduced to a large number of nieces and nephews by her sister and brother, who were all as lovely as she and her mother were.

Afterwards, John took Charlie's mother over to a park bench and sat beside her. He held her hand and spoke to her for a long time. She wept, but she smiled and nodded through the tears at some of the things he said.

'Stop,' John told the driver as we drove towards the exit of the cemetery. We stopped at a small, ancient, ivy-covered stone cottage next to the cemetery gate. It looked like a medieval garden shed. It had a microscopic, fastidiously neat garden around it and a picket fence.

'Emma, there's someone here you have to meet. Leo, Michael, Simone, you stay here in the car and wait. This won't take long.'

As soon as we approached the cottage door a tiny middle-aged European man with a shock of black hair and very pale skin dashed out with a huge grin on his face. He bobbed obsequiously a few times to John, smiling with delight. Then he pointed the grin at me and I felt it.

I couldn't pick him. He wasn't a demon, although he did have something demonic about him. He also wasn't a normal human being. He was definitely some sort of supernatural creature, but I hadn't seen his like before. I inwardly compared him to Jade; nope, not a dragon. Not a stone, either.

He noticed my regard and his grin widened. John waited patiently for me to work it out, amused.

I opened my Inner Eye to examine the creature internally and he froze. His face became a mask of horror.

'That is extremely bad manners, Emma,' John said quietly. 'You can destroy lesser creatures by doing that to them. Unless the creature attacks you, turning your Inner Eye on them really shouldn't be necessary.'

'Sorry,' I said to the creature. 'I didn't know.'

John gestured towards the little man. 'Apologies, Franklin. That was only the second time my Lady has done that, and I didn't know she could do it with such ease. I don't think she'll do it again.'

The little man bowed crisply and smiled again. 'Have you worked me out yet, my Lady?' he said. 'The Dark Lord says that you have not been in Europe for any length of time, and so would not have encountered anything like me before.' He studied me carefully, his eyes sparkling. 'So this is her, eh?' His voice gained a hungry edge. 'Powerful. Sweet. Delicious.' He turned and gestured. 'Come inside, I have tea.'

'You vowed to stay off the hard stuff, Franklin,' John said as we went through the tiny picket gate to the little cottage.

'I have not had a drop of anything stronger than bull in over twenty-five years, my Lord,' the little man said. 'I swear.'

'I can smell white bull on you,' John said meaningfully. 'Are you sure?'

'All bought and paid for, I assure you, my Lord,' the little man said with glee. 'I have been exceptionally good.' He turned and held out his hands. 'Look at me! In the sunshine.'

'I suppose that speaks for itself,' John said. 'Come on in, Emma, and meet Franklin. He has been looking after the Chen family plot for ...' He hesitated. 'How long, Franklin?'

'About two hundred and thirty years now, my Lord,' Franklin said with satisfaction. 'I can remember when this was far out on the edge of the city.'

We entered the cottage. Franklin obviously lived in it. It had a tiny bed, a little table and a stove. A door led out the back of the cottage. It was Spartan but spotlessly clean. A checked tablecloth covered the table, with a small vase of daisies in the middle.

'Please, my Lord, my Lady, sit,' Franklin said, gesturing to a couple of chairs at the table. 'So sorry to hear about the Retainer, my Lord. Circumstances are very difficult right now, aren't they.'

John didn't say anything, he just motioned for me to sit. Franklin turned and filled the kettle, then put it on his tiny stove.

'All right, I give up,' I said. 'What are you?'

Franklin busied himself pulling tea cups and a teapot out of the cupboard. He turned and put the cups and saucers on the table. He stopped and smiled at me over the checked tablecloth. 'Old-fashioned Eastern European vampire, my Lady. Not surprised I'm the first one you've ever met,' he said cheerfully. 'Been given a second chance by the Dark Lord here, and doing my best.'

John leaned back slightly and put his hand on the table. 'Tell the truth, Franklin. You are neither old-fashioned, Eastern European, nor a vampire.'

Franklin's smile didn't shift. 'Uzbek is close enough, my Lord. My dietary habits ... well, you know. And I'm very old now.'

'When Marco Polo returned to Europe, there was some interest shown in his tales. The demons here in Europe knew that the ones in China existed, but hadn't had much contact. Franklin here,' John gestured across the table, 'is one of the first products of experimentation.'

'Last one of my type in existence, too,' Franklin said without rancour. 'Those were the days, eh, my Lord?'

'That particular part of history was very unpleasant here in Europe and you know it,' John said grimly.

'Not for us.' Franklin's grin didn't shift. 'More of a golden era for us, my Lord.'

'Experiments?' I said.

John's face was still grim. 'Demon Lords are constantly looking for ways to improve the stock

289

produced by the Mothers. Some of their recent activities are rather disturbing. Franklin is one of the first products of interbreeding. Bad idea. The results were high maintenance, fragile, unable to hold their shape for very long, unable to tolerate bright light, and easy to destroy. Their metabolisms were so fast and their digestive systems so delicate that they could only ingest plasma.'

'You actually have a digestive system?' I asked Franklin. 'What level are you?'

'Oh, very good, madam,' Franklin said. 'You have been studying us. I am level seventy equivalent.'

'Whoa! You don't look that big. You're *huge*!'

'Big but weak,' John said. 'Interesting abilities, but easy to destroy. I don't think they tried Eastern–Western hybrids again.'

'Eastern–Western?' I said.

John nodded. 'They don't normally have much to do with each other. Professional rivalry. Western demons don't have anything to do with me; I'm an Eastern Shen.' He smiled slightly. 'Your home has Southern Shen, very old, very powerful. Much older than me. Never met a single one. We are strongest nearest to our centres; the demons are as well.' He gestured towards Franklin again. 'Interbreeding between the types is always a bad idea; the results are usually extremely weak.'

'I am lucky to still be here,' Franklin said as he passed a tea cup across the table to me.

'Vampires,' I said. Franklin nodded, but John looked impatient.

'Demon hybrids,' John said. 'Most of them don't survive. Some are disastrous malformed atrocities. Others emerge new and powerful. There have been some recent experiments where the results have been appalling.'

'Experiments?' I said as I picked up my tea cup and studied it suspiciously. Perfectly normal tea. I took a sip. Very good quality Ceylon too.

'Experiments?' Franklin echoed, his smile disappearing.

'Not just animals can be engineered,' John said, his voice very grim. 'The King doesn't approve. He's a traditionalist. But there are some activities out there that are causing us a great deal of concern.'

'That is very bad news, my Lord,' Franklin said faintly. He flopped into a chair across the table from us. 'Very bad news indeed.'

'Vampires. So Western supernatural creatures are just as real,' I said.

'Of course,' John said. 'Each region has its own.'

'Better give me some tips on the different types then,' I said. 'Just in case Simone wants to study overseas.'

'Good idea,' John said. 'I don't know how they'll react to her.' He leaned back. 'The world is becoming a very small place. Five hundred years ago, contact between China and the West was rare and intermittent. Two hundred years ago, it would take months to travel from one place to another. Now, it only takes a matter of hours. We Shen are starting to travel around. More powerful Shen such as myself can even spend extended periods of time in different areas. The bigger demons do too. I think sometimes they materialise in the holds of aircraft and ride them from one place to another.'

'Wouldn't that take them too far from their centre?' I said.

Franklin broke in. 'Sometimes being far from your centre is better than not existing at all, my Lady, when you have angered the one you serve.'

'Your own little demon was too small to do that, Emma,' John said. 'Her only hope was to join one of us.'

'You are taming demons already?' Franklin said with disbelief. 'Has she attained the Way already, my Lord? She does not appear to have.'

'No,' John said. 'She is just a human being, but a most remarkable one.'

'You owe me a gold coin,' I said.

'A gold coin?' Franklin said.

'Every time someone says she is extraordinary, they have to give her a gold coin,' John said. 'It started with Kwan Yin. Now everybody has to do it. How many do you have now, Emma?'

'Six,' I said.

'Dear me, but she is enough to make even the most well-behaved vampire fall off the wagon,' Franklin said with awe.

'Try me,' I growled. 'I could probably take your head off with my bare hands.'

'Delicious,' Franklin said, looking me in the eye and grinning evilly. He held out a plate. 'Biscuit?'

I wrapped my black silken coils around the eggs. I stroked them with my hands. They were so beautiful. My eggs.

I used my hands to polish them gently. I could see them through the shells. There, the first one: tawny brown hair. Fine pale skin. Exquisite. The second: a blonde mop, golden skin. So beautiful. I sighed with bliss. And there, the most perfect of all, the third one: golden light brown hair and skin like porcelain, clearly visible through the shell.

I stretched my fingers over them and rolled them gently. The nestlings inside shifted as I moved them, bright eyes unseeing. They were all so perfect.

I pulled my black coils around them more tightly, so that I could lean on myself. I carefully groomed my scales, making sure that the gaps between them were spotlessly clean. It felt good.

I looked up. The ceiling was invisible in the darkness of the chamber. I didn't care; I was safe there, miles below the surface, with my gleaming, transparent eggs. I could see another Mother on the other side of the chamber, around her eggs as well.

Stay away, bitch. These are *mine*.

I curled over my beautiful cool coils and sighed. I dangled my arms. I was *bored*. I wished the King would bring me a toy to play with. I smiled to myself. I thought about what sort of toy I would like to play with. And exactly what sort of game I would like to play.

I shot upright with horror. I threw the covers off my legs to make sure.

Then I ran down the hall to the upstairs bathroom and was violently sick.

Ms Kwan appeared almost immediately as I held my hand on the pearl and concentrated. She knew that there wasn't a problem with John; she could probably sense it. She saw my face and came to sit next to me at the Kensington house's dining table.

'I had a dream,' I whispered. 'I dreamed I was a Snake Mother. And in the eggs ...' I choked. 'Were Simone. And Michael. And someone else, I don't know.'

She didn't seem at all concerned. 'Did the eggs hatch in the dream?'

'No.' I could barely breathe.

'It was just a dream, Emma,' she said softly.

'Ms Kwan, when a demon attains perfection, and they can live a human life, what happens to them? Are they born as a human child?'

'I cannot answer that question, I am sorry, Emma. It is not our place to tell you what lies beyond. You all must find that for yourselves. You wonder if it is possible that you are a Snake Mother that has attained perfection. My answer is: I cannot tell you. You must discover this for yourself. But even if you are, it is irrelevant for what you are now.'

I folded my arms on the table and dropped my head onto them. I looked up at her miserably. 'Would a demon remember being a demon?'

She just shook her head sadly.

'Am I a snake demon?' I whispered.

Ms Kwan held her hand out and concentrated. A live white mouse appeared on her palm. 'Take it,' she said gently.

I took the mouse. It had adorable white whiskers. Its little nose wiggled as it smelled my hand. Its tiny feet were cold. I ran my other finger over the top of its head, bending its translucent pink ears. I'd forgotten how much fun mice were. I'd always felt guilty about feeding them to my pet snake.

'Eat it.'

I glanced sharply at her, then collapsed over the table laughing, carefully holding the mouse so that I wouldn't hurt it. I laughed so much that tears sprang from my eyes.

I gently passed the mouse back to her. She concentrated again and it disappeared.

'Sorry,' I whispered into my arms.

'Not a problem.'

I looked up. She was gone.

I shot upright in the middle of the night. If it had been nothing more than a dream, then why had she asked me *if the eggs had hatched*?

CHAPTER TWENTY-FIVE

I had been hoping that if I didn't bring it up, he wouldn't remember. No such luck. The morning before we left London, John gathered the three of us — him, Leo, myself — into the dining room to discuss the logistics of a visit to my sister.

'You will need a guard,' John said. 'Who would you prefer? Who would cause the least difficulty with your family?'

'We should both ...' Leo said and then stopped. He'd heard himself again. He did sound profoundly deaf. The vowels were flat and the consonants were mushy. His voice was a slurred hiss. It would take some getting used to. My heart went out to him.

'Yes?' John said impatiently.

Leo just shook his head, his mouth clamped shut.

John sighed. 'Wear your scars as symbols of valour, Leo. You have been injured defending your family. There is no higher honour.'

'Leo.' I took his hand over the table. 'We can't hear it. We just hear *you*. I don't hear any impediment; I just hear an incredibly annoying guy who's always playing nasty tricks on me.'

'I think I'll learn sign language,' Leo said under his breath. 'At least then I won't sound like a moron.'

'Go right ahead,' I said. 'Then I'll have no trouble hearing you over a crowd.'

'You're on.' He turned to John. 'We should stay together, my Lord. Both Lady Emma and Simone are targets. They should be guarded by both of us.'

I nodded. 'He has a point.'

John sighed his acquiescence and tied back his hair. 'We'll need to have our stories straight.'

'Actually, you're quite right, and this is great,' I said. 'The kids can use my sister as a dry run for school. Simone can try to be normal and not give anything away. I don't know why I didn't think of this before.'

'What a good idea,' John said. 'We'll all pay your sister a visit as a normal family.'

'Even if you weren't a reptile, an Immortal and the North Wind, my Lord,' Leo said, 'we still wouldn't be a normal family.'

'Heaven forbid,' John said placidly.

I had a horrible thought. 'John,' I said urgently, 'forget it. She's my *family*. She's a *target*. They all are.'

'No, they aren't,' John said. 'No demon would dream of going after those who are not involved. Much too dishonourable.'

'What about Michelle's family?' I said. 'And Charlie?'

Both of them went very still.

'There's one demon who has no honour whatsoever,' Leo said.

'Damn,' John said, perfectly calm. His voice gained a very slight fierce edge. 'This will *not* happen again. Your family are not a target, Leo, don't be concerned. You are still a Retainer. But Emma is now my Lady, and she is quite correct.' He sighed. 'You're the smart one, Emma, what are we going to do?'

I nearly laughed at the 'smart one' comment, but this was too serious. I had the sudden urge to call all my family and make sure they were okay.

'I might be the smart one, John, but you're the expert on demon behaviour,' I said. 'He hasn't rounded up my family yet and used them as hostages. Why not?'

'I think he wants to be sure to have a good hold on me, and not waste his time trying to control me through a third party. I think your family are safe. Besides,' he said, leaning back, 'both your sister here in the UK and your family in Australia are a very long way from his power centre. He would much prefer to attack on his home turf.'

'You'd better be right,' I said.

'This can be a test both ways then,' he said. 'We'll see if he makes a move for your sister after he finds out where she is.'

'Does he know where my family in Australia are?'

'Probably.'

I ran my hands through my hair. 'I don't want my family to know about this. It would freak them out. I don't think my mum would be able to handle it. We *must* keep them safe and in the dark.'

'We may only be able to achieve one out of two, love,' John said.

We sat silently. Leo looked particularly morose. He was worried about his family. They didn't know about his mouth yet. He wouldn't want to tell them. But he'd have to call them soon, and it would all come out about his injury. Damn.

'How will we know if he makes a move against Jennifer?' I said. 'After we're gone?'

'I'll put Gold in their house somewhere and he can stand watch for a few days,' John said. 'He'll enjoy the opportunity of taking True Form for a while.'

'And you say *I'm* the smart one,' I said. 'Can you find any more sentient rocks and post them around the place to guard our families?'

'You *are* the smart one,' he said with wonder. 'I never thought of doing that before.' He put his hands on the table and his voice became businesslike. 'I'll see what I can round up. Gold can help me.'

'If it pleases you, my Lord,' the stone in my ring said, 'I request permission to assist you. Some of my children may be able to aid you. It would be the least I can do.'

'Permission granted,' John said. 'You have some making up to do.'

'I only spoke the truth, my Lord,' the stone said, 'but I apologise for my arrogance.'

'Provide us with the services of four or five of your children to assist us, and I may consider recommending that the Lady Emma not throw you down the toilet after all.'

The stone's voice was full of remorse. 'My Lord.'

Leo made a soft sound of amusement.

'Where's your sister, Emma?' John said.

'South-east. Just out of London; she said it's about a forty-five-minute drive. She married a solicitor, and apparently they have a huge house just out of town there. I've never seen it.'

'Leo.' John didn't look away from me. 'While Emma calls her sister, go and find Simone and Michael. We'll give them some final coaching before we go down.'

Leo didn't say anything; he just nodded, rose and went out.

'That was an unusual show of disrespect, coming from Leo,' John said, glancing at the door. 'Normally he would address me before he went out. He didn't say a word. Most odd. He didn't seem upset about anything, why would he do that?'

'Get used to it, John,' I said. He really didn't understand people very well sometimes. 'He'll only talk when he absolutely has to, from now on. And if he learns sign language and others can understand him, I think he'll prefer to use that. He hates sounding like an idiot.'

'Even to the point of disrespect?' John was astonished. 'Even to me?'

'Even to you.'

I called Jennifer to warn her.

'Hi, Jennifer, it's Emma.'

'Emma!' Her voice was bright on the other end of the line. 'So good to hear from you! Where are you? Are you still in Hong Kong?'

'I'm in London right now, Jen, and I was wondering if I could come and pay you a visit.'

'Sure, go right ahead, it's not far.' The smile in her voice was clearly audible. 'Plenty of room. Bring the boss.'

Good God, Mum and Dad had told her. I shook myself. Oh well, I was planning to ask her if it would be okay to bring them anyway. This was just my toe in the door for what I wanted.

'I'd love to bring my boss, Jen,' I said, trying to be as cheerful as possible. 'Can I bring his daughter as well?'

'Sure, the more the merrier.'

'Well, how about his nephew and the driver too?' I said, pushing it. 'The driver will drive us down, and Mr Chen's nephew is staying with us, so he'll have to come too.'

There was a short silence. 'He has a driver?'

'He's really nice, he's American.'

'Oh well, no trouble fitting five extra here, we have loads of room, our house is huge. How long will you stay for?'

'Just for the day. We're flying out tomorrow, so we need to be back here to pack.'

'You can stay over if you like. We can take all of you. We have buckets of room.'

'No thanks,' I said firmly. 'No need.'

'Oh, okay then. When do you think you'll be here?'

'After lunch. Two-ish. We'll stay a couple of hours, and then head back up here.'

'Sounds good,' she said, the smile still in her voice. 'See you then. The kids can't wait to meet you.'

'I can't wait to see them either.'

I nodded to John. His eyes sparkled at me. He was enjoying this far too much.

There was a tap on the door. Leo came in with Simone and Michael. He guided them and they sat at the table. Family meetings with all of us together weren't common and they were both very serious. Dear, but they were adorable. From the look on John's face he was thinking the same thing. We shared a smile. He gestured slightly to me and I nodded. I would take over.

'Do you need me?' he said quietly.

'I think you'd better stay, we need to work on our story,' I said. 'You can help.'

He shrugged. 'Good idea.'

Leo sat next to Simone and Michael without saying a word.

'Simone, Michael, I have a sister here in England and we're all going, as a family, to visit her today. After what happened a couple of days ago, we don't think it's a good idea for us to split up right now. So we'll all go together.' I turned to Simone. 'This is also a good chance for you, Simone,' her eyes went wide, 'to try out being ...' I searched for the right word. I didn't want to use it, but it was the only one that would do the job, '... a *normal* person.'

300

'I *am* a normal person, Emma,' Simone protested, eyes still wide.

'I'm sorry, sweetheart, but your dad is a Shen, and a Wind, and ...' I stopped there. I didn't want to say it.

'Say it,' John said quietly.

'No,' I responded, just as quietly. Not in front of Michael. 'Let it go.'

He didn't move.

'You're half Shen, Simone,' I said sadly. 'What is perfectly ordinary for you is really weird for other kids. You already know that ...' I hesitated. 'But now you're going to look it right in the face, 'cause you're going to meet some ordinary kids.'

'Can I make friends with them?' Simone said softly.

My heart ached for her.

'If you don't do anything really weird and freak them out,' I said as gently as I could, 'I'm sure they'll be glad to be your friends.'

'I'd like that,' she said in a tiny voice.

Michael glanced at her sharply. Then he looked down at the table and some of the emotion leaked out.

Yes, that's right, Michael, I thought at him. She doesn't have a single friend her own age in the whole wide world.

'We're going to visit my big sister. Her name is Jennifer. You call her Mrs Black. Okay?'

Both of them nodded.

John smiled. I wondered what was so funny, then I understood. My sister's name was Mrs Black. I shrugged. 'Hopefully one day there'll be two Mrs Blacks in the same family.'

John and Leo didn't move but it was obvious what they were thinking.

'Okay. Simone, she has two little boys. One of them is the same age as you, six, the other is smaller, four. I honestly don't know what they're like, but the little one is Andrew and the big one is Colin. Okay?'

Simone nodded.

'This is the hard bit, Simone, listen carefully.' She nodded again. 'You want to hear something really weird? They've probably never heard of martial arts.'

Leo moved to say something and I raised my hand to stop him. 'It's quite possible, Leo, children that young may not have had any exposure to it. Think about it. They've only seen children's television, and that's all.'

Leo subsided. He thought about it. He nodded without speaking.

Simone's eyes were wide. 'Never heard of the Arts *at all*?' she said, breathless. 'Not even tai chi?'

I shook my head. 'And if you show them anything, you'll probably completely freak them out. So as far as we are concerned, as long as you're with them, you can't do anything. Nothing physical, and *definitely* no energy work. If you do any sort of energy work at all, it will scare them to death and they won't want to be your friends. Okay?'

Simone was obviously overwhelmed. She nodded, eyes wide.

'It will be the same at school, sweetheart. None of the kids there will know much about it either. Next thing ...' I saw Michael's face. 'Bear with me, Michael, okay? You're next, and we all need to have our stories straight.'

Michael nodded.

'They won't know what a Shen is, and even if they did we wouldn't tell them that your dad is one.'

Simone glanced at her father. He smiled encouragement.

'Don't tell them he can change his form, don't tell them he can do things with the weather, don't tell them he can do things with water. In fact, it might be best if you don't mention your dad at all.'

You make me sound like an embarrassment, Emma, John said silently.

I rounded on him. A great many inappropriate comments jumped onto my tongue and I swallowed them all. Not in front of the kids. His face lit up with a broad grin and he leaned back to smile sideways at me.

'Your dad works for a company in Beijing, and we live in Hong Kong. That's all you need to tell them. Okay?' I turned to Michael. 'You're her cousin and your dad works in the same company. Your parents are divorced and we look after you while your mother's travelling for business, and you came with us to see London and Paris. Okay?'

Both of the kids nodded.

'Have I missed anything?' I said.

'Simone,' John said, still smiling encouragement, 'if you are concerned that you may say something wrong, or if you don't know the answer to a question, just call me silently and I will tell you the answer silently. I'll be able to help you.'

Simone studied her little hands. 'Thank you, Daddy,' she whispered. 'I hope I can do this right, Emma. What's a cousin?'

'It's when your dad and his dad are brothers. That means that Michael is your *family*, not a Retainer.' I made my voice more stern. 'So don't you go ordering him around in front of people, okay?'

Simone glared at Michael. 'I don't order you around anyway.'

Michael glowered at her. The animosity between them made them appear perfectly normal and would be the icing on the cake if they could pull it off.

'Michael,' I said, 'please try to refrain from calling me "my Lady", or any other honorific term, while we're there. If you do slip up accidentally, make it sound like a private joke between us. Got it?' Michael nodded and his blond hair flopped over his forehead. 'I'm the *nanny*, guys. Leo is the driver. Michael, call Lord Xuan "Mr Chen" or "Uncle John" the entire time we are there. But don't worry too much, I'd never heard of Xuan Wu before I met him.'

Leo smiled. I smiled too. I remembered as well.

'*Now* have I missed anything?' I said.

'Simone,' Leo lisped. He winced and continued. 'They don't think demons are real, as well. Okay?'

'Why do you talk funny, Leo?' Simone said innocently. 'You're doing it all the time.'

'The Snake Mothers hurt my mouth. I can't talk properly now.'

'They're really mean,' Simone said. 'Those Snake Mothers are really bad.'

'Yes, they are.' His face softened. 'You have no idea.'

CHAPTER TWENTY-SIX

A small yard at the front of the house had been covered with gravel to accommodate visitors' cars. Leo parked the van, we all hopped out, and I led the way up sandstone steps to the front door. Simone was very stiff and her eyes were unseeing. John was silently coaching her.

I rang the doorbell. There was silence for a moment, then the sound of feet coming. The door flew open and there was Jennifer.

I hardly recognised her. My sister had always been a little drab and dowdy, but now she looked like an English lady. Her hair was blonde instead of brown and she sported expensive make-up and gold jewellery. She wore a pencil-thin pale blue skirt and matching cashmere twin-set. She looked fabulous.

'Emma!' she exclaimed. 'Finally! I thought you'd never get here.' She reached out to hug me, her fingers glittering with bright red artificial nails and a great many gold rings. She pulled back to beam at me. As usual, I was wearing a tatty old shirt and a pair of jeans and loafers, my hair tied back in a rough ponytail. Her smile widened. She moved back and gestured broadly with one arm, inviting us in.

We all went into the hallway, Jennifer leading. She guided us into the living room. 'Please, sit,' she said, smiling at all of us. 'And who do we have here, Emma?'

The living room was elaborately decorated in cream and blue, with fancy pictures and expensive porcelain. She'd done very well for herself. I was glad.

A couple of little boys dashed in, their shoes thumping on the wooden floor of the hallway. They stopped dead when they entered the living room. One of them jumped backwards slightly with surprise.

'This is Andrew.' Jennifer grabbed the smaller one around the shoulders and dragged him forward. 'And Colin.' She gestured towards the bigger one. 'Say hello to Aunty Emma, boys.'

'Hello, Aunty Emma,' the boys said mechanically, in unison.

'This is my employer, my boss, Mr Chen.' I gestured towards John and he nodded to Jennifer.

'Bout time you acknowledged me as boss, John said right into my ear. *But I think you should have said it the other way round.*

I shot a warning glance at him. He smiled at me serenely, then smiled at Jennifer.

Jennifer's smile froze.

I did not believe this.

'This is his daughter, Simone. I look after her,' I said.

Simone looked like she was about to rise and bow, then stopped. I quietly breathed a sigh of relief. He was forgiven for that last crack.

Jennifer warmed up again when she saw Simone. She went and crouched in front of her. 'Hello, Simone, you are very pretty.'

Simone hesitated, then, 'Thank you,' she said softly.

I gestured towards Michael. 'This is Simone's cousin, Michael, who came along for the trip to Europe.'

Michael nodded without smiling at Jennifer. She

studied him appraisingly from where she was crouched in front of Simone, then smiled and rose.

'And this is Leo,' I said, gesturing towards him. 'The driver.'

Leo nodded without speaking.

'Leo doesn't talk much,' I said, and Leo nodded almost imperceptibly in thanks.

Jennifer's smile went even more ice-cold.

I really did not believe this. I didn't know she had changed so much.

'Would you like the boys to show you their rooms and their toys, Simone?' Jennifer said.

Simone hesitated. 'That would be very nice, thank you, Mrs Black,' she said very carefully.

'Andrew, Colin.' Jennifer's bright smile didn't shift. 'Would you like to take Simone upstairs and show her your rooms? I'm sure she'd be interested to see how we do things here in England.'

'Can I leave my shoes on?' Simone said.

Jennifer hesitated at the unusual question. Then she shrugged it off. 'Of course, dear, don't take your shoes off, there's absolutely no need.'

Simone nodded and rose. Andrew smiled at her and took her hand. He and Colin led her out.

Michael jumped as if he had been stung. 'May I go and see the boys' rooms too, please, Mrs Black?' he said politely. 'I'd like to see what houses are like in England. It's very different to Hong Kong.'

'You don't want to stay here with us?' Jennifer said.

Michael shook his head.

'If you like,' Jennifer said. 'Just follow the boys, they know where to go.'

Jennifer sat next to me and put her arm around my shoulders. 'Would you like to come and have a look around the house, dear?' she said maternally. 'I'd love to show it to you.' She smiled at John. 'Would you like to see?'

I think you would probably like to spend some time alone with your sister without us men in the way, John said silently into my ear. *Nod if you would. We can go outside and wait.*

I nodded very slightly without looking away from my sister.

'I don't think so, if you don't mind, Mrs Black. I have some calls to China to make. Do you mind if I go back out to the car and get my phone?' John said.

'Of course, no problem, get your phone, come back inside. I'll have the housekeeper make you some tea,' Jennifer said. 'Would you like tea? Oh, and call me Jennifer.'

'That would be very nice,' John said. 'Jennifer.'

Jennifer grabbed my hand. 'Come and have a look, Em.' She showed me through the dining room. John and Leo went out the front door.

'This is the kitchen.' She dragged me through. It was expensively appointed with luxurious European appliances. She waved deprecatingly at a smiling round English woman in a maid's uniform. 'That's just Tess, the housekeeper.'

Tess nodded without saying anything and I nodded back.

Jennifer pulled me back into the hallway. She opened a door. 'Here's the garage,' she said proudly. She pointed down the stairs at the car below us. 'That's my car, Leonard bought it for me.' It was a shiny new silver BMW. 'His Jag isn't here, he'll be home soon. He'll take some time from the office to come and see you, don't worry.'

'I look forward to it.' I tried to remember what he looked like. I couldn't. I had spoken to him about three times nearly ten years before, at their wedding, and that was all.

We walked along the hallway to the bottom of the stairs that went to the next floor up. She opened another door. 'Leonard's study.' Like the rest of the house, it had been decorated by a professional, and had a bay window overlooking the front yard. John and Leo stood next to the van. John *was* on the phone and I wondered who he could possibly want to talk to.

If you're wondering, he said into my ear when he saw me at the window, *your sister's children are making my daughter's life miserable and she is in constant contact with me for help. Please get up there and rescue her. Even Michael is getting a pummelling.*

'Are the bedrooms upstairs?' I said brightly. 'I'll bet the boys' bedrooms are even nicer than this.'

'I'll show you.'

The boys were shouting as we went up the stairs. They sounded very angry. I didn't hear a sound from Simone or Michael.

'They're in Colin's room,' Jennifer said cheerfully. She opened the door.

The boys were screaming and hitting Simone with a pillow. Michael tried to block their blows. Simone sat with her hands over her head, her little face a mask of torment. I rushed to her, pulled the boys off, and grabbed Simone. She buried her face in my neck. 'Thanks, Emma,' she said quietly.

'The little tinkers. Is their play too rough for you, petal?' Jennifer said to Simone without a hint of compassion. 'They go to a boys school and they don't really know that girls are a little more *delicate*.'

'I'm okay,' Simone choked. 'Can I go back downstairs now, please?'

'You'll be fine, Simone, I'll look after you,' I said into her ear. I picked her up with one arm, put her on my hip, and she clutched me.

Jennifer gasped.

'What's the problem, Jen?' I glanced around, there didn't seem to be anything wrong. Michael's face was rigid with control. The two little boys glowered at me.

Jennifer stared at me, eyes wide.

'Can I see the rest of the bedrooms?' I said, trying to snap her out of whatever daydream she had drifted into. Then I realised I'd just lifted a five-year-old girl one-handed. Way to go being normal, Emma!

Fortunately, Jennifer shook herself out of it. 'Let me show you,' she said, and went to the door. I followed her, still holding Simone with one arm.

The master bedroom was enormous. Jennifer took us onto the balcony. It overlooked the rear garden, which was formally laid out and beautifully landscaped with a small fountain.

Simone was fascinated. 'This is your garden?'

Jennifer smiled. 'Yes it is, pet.'

'You don't share it with anyone?'

'It's like the house in Guangzhou, Simone,' I said. 'It has a garden.'

Simone nodded, understanding. She wriggled a request and I lowered her. 'Can I go out there?'

'Let's take you out so that you can see, pet,' Jennifer said kindly. 'You don't need to see the next floor up, it's just guest rooms and storerooms. Let's go and see the garden.'

Michael quietly followed us down the stairs. Jennifer didn't appear to notice him. We went out to the back garden. An expensive outdoor table sat on the lawn next to some play equipment.

Simone says thank you, John said into my ear. *But*

she didn't want to say it herself, she's a little ashamed that she couldn't handle them.

Poor Simone, what a baptism of fire. She clutched my hand. She stopped when she saw the play equipment.

'This is *yours?*' she said with wonder. 'You don't share it with *anybody?*'

'Go and play, dear,' Jennifer said generously.

Simone glanced enquiringly up at me and I nodded. She ran to play on the swings. Michael followed her and posted himself nearby, guarding.

Jennifer sat at the table and beamed at me. 'So, tell me all about it. You're a nanny for this Chinese man, are you?'

I nodded. 'I care for Simone.' Simone's face was full of delight as she played. Probably one of the first times in her life she didn't have to share. 'Her mother's dead, had an accident when Simone was very small. It's a lovely family. Mr Chen is a wonderful man, and Leo is great.'

She waited for it. Go on, Emma, give her what she wants.

'I can't get over your house, Jen,' I said with wonder. 'And you have this great car and everything. Your house is fabulous. I am *so* jealous.'

Jennifer's smile broadened. 'Oh, it's nothing really. I must have Mum and Dad over to visit. Leonard will pay for their tickets for me.'

'He's a solicitor?'

'Senior partner,' she announced with pride. She leaned forward over the table and tapped her long red nails on the surface. 'He does work for *royalty*,' she said conspiratorially, her eyes sparkling. 'I've met some princes and kings and *everything*.'

'That is *so* impressive,' I gushed, thinking of some of the princes and kings that I'd met.

'Come inside. The housekeeper made tea, we can have it in the dining room.' She rose and gestured for me to follow her. I shot a glance at Michael. He went into military at-ease position to indicate that he was guarding. I nodded. Jennifer missed the exchange completely.

We sat at the dining table and the housekeeper brought out a tea tray of expensive china. 'Have a look at the table, Emma, it's an antique,' Jennifer said. 'Cost a fortune, but Leonard said that we have to have the very best. We bought the table, and a few other bits of furniture, at an auction in London. It was great fun.'

'Wow, I am so impressed,' I said, wide-eyed. 'You've done so much incredible stuff. How old is the table?'

'About two hundred years old. Doesn't look like it, does it.'

'Gee, it doesn't.'

The boys raced down the hallway towards the back door, their shoes clumping on the floorboards. The back door was thrown open and then slammed shut.

'I hope Simone will be okay with them,' I said. 'She's not really accustomed to playing with boys.'

'Oh, she'll be fine, the boys are good.' Jennifer looked around. 'Why haven't your boss and the driver come back in? They should come in and have some tea. We can't have them standing out in the front yard like that, it just won't do.'

She rose, smiled at me, and went out. She spoke to John and Leo as she brought them back in. She guided them into the dining room and sat them down, then poured tea for John. She slopped some tea into Leo's cup as an afterthought.

I really did not believe her. She had changed so much.

The back door opened and Simone and Michael came in. They stopped when they saw all of us sitting at the table. I put my arms out to Simone and she crawled into my lap.

They threw me off the swings, Emma, she said silently.

'Not all children are like that, sweetheart,' I whispered into her ear. 'You'll make lots of friends with some lovely children when you start school.'

She nodded into my chest. Then she turned, hopped off me, skittered to Leo, and climbed into his lap. He wrapped his huge arms around her and she put her head on his chest. Probably felt safer in his arms; I would have to remember that for later. She might feel safer with Leo nearby when she first started school.

'Come and sit, dear,' Jennifer said warmly to Michael. 'Would you like a soft drink?'

'A cola?' I added, explaining.

Michael waited, but nobody helped him. He smiled. 'That would be great, thanks.'

Jennifer rose and leaned through the door to the kitchen, ordering the housekeeper.

A car engine rumbled in the garage. 'There's Leonard,' Jennifer said. 'He said he'd love to see you, Emma.'

The door banged in the hallway and Leonard came in.

He was tall, dark-haired and in his mid-forties, about ten years older than Jennifer, with an intelligent, friendly face. He wore a smart pin-striped suit. He smiled kindly at all of us; then he saw John and froze.

John shot to his feet. 'Of course! *Leonard* Black! I didn't realise until just now. Good to see you!'

Leonard bowed very deeply from the waist to John. 'Your Celestial Highness.' Then he rushed to John, grabbed his hand, and pumped his arm until it was about to fall off, a huge grin on his face. 'Lord Xuan! What are you doing here?'

'It seems,' John said, 'that your wife is the sister of my Lady.'

Leonard was bewildered. 'Emma? *You're* the Dark Lady that everybody's been talking about?' His face

313

cleared. 'Oh my God, Emma. Of course. I didn't know.' He looked from John to me and he grinned broadly. 'What an amazing coincidence.'

'Leonard,' Jennifer said as Leonard charged over to pull me up and give me a huge hug, 'what *are* you talking about? Emma is just the nanny, to this man from Hong Kong.'

'No,' Leonard said, 'Emma's the Dark Lady of Lord Xuan Wu, sworn to marry him when he returns. Didn't you *know*?' He grinned widely at me. 'I hear you can throw fireballs, Emma, you must show me. Come into the backyard. The boys have to see this.' He saw Simone sitting in Leo's lap. 'Is that who I think it is? Princess Simone?' He saw Leo. '*And* the Black Lion. My, but the house is fairly bursting at the seams with notables today.'

'Now hold on a minute!' I shouted, pushing Leonard away. I studied him closely. Nope, perfectly normal human. 'What the hell is going on? How come you know all this, Leonard?'

'I told you this was to stay in the office, Leonard,' Jennifer said fiercely. 'I want none of this business brought home.'

'It was your idea to have Emma over, dear,' Leonard said. 'Didn't you *know* she was the Dark Lady?'

Jennifer looked daggers at me. She was ready to rip my throat out.

'She has her singing sword, Leonard,' John said. 'You may see it after all.'

Leonard gasped. 'Could I? Please, my Lord, I've heard so much about it.'

John gestured, and Leo popped Simone out of his lap. She went to John and held his hand. Leo went out to the van.

'I cannot believe that my own sister-in-law is the promised of the Dark Lord. I always knew you came from an exceptional family, Jen,' Leonard said. 'Come on out to the yard. I really have to see this.'

We all tramped out to the garden. Leonard gestured for us to sit and we did. Leo came out the back door, sat, and placed my sword on the table in front of him.

The boys chased each other through the yard, obviously no longer wanting the swings now that Simone didn't. They ran inside, both banging the door as they went through it.

'May I play on the swings again, Mrs Black?' Simone said.

'Call her Aunty Jen, Highness,' Leonard said. 'Dear God, what an honour. Call me Uncle Leonard. Go and play if you like, Princess, the house is yours.'

Simone hesitated. I smiled reassurance, and she went to play.

'How come you know all this, Leonard?' I said.

'He's my London solicitor,' John said. 'The firm of Black and Black has handled my affairs for, what ...?'

'Nigh on two hundred years, my Lord,' Leonard said. 'I'm about the sixth in the line to handle the Dark Lord's affairs here.'

'What about Gold?' I said.

'Gold is a recent acquisition, you know that, Emma,' John said, then his face went strange. He pulled Gold out of his pocket and put him on the table. Gold had made himself about a centimetre long.

'Your people made a huge mistake, Black,' Gold said in his usual voice. 'The Dark Lord's Kensington house hasn't changed hands in a hundred and fifty years. It'll take me ages to fix that.'

'We thought he'd never want to sell it,' Leonard said, looking around for the source of the voice.

'Permission to stay in True Form for just a *little* longer, my Lord,' Gold said. 'And if you could put me in the sun for a while, that would be delightful.'

'Leo.' John gestured, and Leo obliged, moving Gold to a sunny spot in the garden. Gold sighed with bliss.

'You are extremely lazy sometimes, Gold.' I explained for Jennifer: 'Gold is our solicitor in Hong Kong.'

'I don't want to know about it,' Jennifer snapped. Then she burst into tears.

Leonard rushed to console her. 'It's all right, darling, it's just your sister. Sometimes strange things happen when you deal with Immortals, you know that.'

Jennifer rounded on me, furious. 'Are you an *Immortal* as well, Emma?'

'No, of course I'm not, Jen,' I said, as kindly as I could. 'I'm nothing really special at all.'

John made a soft sound of amusement across the table and I glared at him, then thought better of it and turned back to Jennifer. 'I'm still just Emma, Jen. I'm just the same person.'

'It never connected, Leonard,' John said. 'Emma even told me her sister's surname was Black, but she didn't tell me her brother-in-law's name. It didn't occur to me that it could be you.'

'That explains it,' said Leonard, his arm still around the sobbing Jennifer. 'What a coincidence, eh, Emma? I can't believe how honoured we are. After you marry, my wife's own sister will be Dark Empress of the North. Unbelievable.'

'I'm just taking one day at a time, Leonard,' I said.

The boys charged out the back door, slamming it behind them. They stopped dead when they saw all of us sitting at the table.

'Ah, here they are, my own two little demonic sons. Please don't run them through, Emma, they are quite human, I assure you,' Leonard said.

Jennifer started to sob more loudly. Leonard squeezed her around the shoulders and spoke softly into her ear. 'Come on, dear, don't be like that, it's a great honour to have a *god* in our house. Lord Xuan is about as big as you can get, Jen, and he's going to marry your own sister.'

The older boy, Colin, screwed up his face and ran to the swing set, obviously ready to tip Simone off. Michael quickly moved between them.

Leonard jumped up, leaving Jennifer, and went to the boys. He pulled them aside and hissed angrily at them for some time. The boys scowled at John and Leo, then they looked at me with newfound respect. They both shot their heads around to their father. Then they nodded. They came quietly to the table, cowed.

While Leonard was up I sat next to Jennifer and put my arm around her. She still sobbed quietly. 'Come on, Jen, it's not that bad, it's really just me.'

'Who is this impressive young man?' Leonard said, gesturing towards Michael.

'Michael MacLaren. Trainee bodyguard. Son of the White Tiger, the West Wind.' I waited for it. Yep: Jennifer started sobbing again.

Leonard glanced at his wife and then obviously decided to leave her to it. He grinned at me as he poured some tea for us. 'Well, come on, Emma, show the boys. I'm sure they're dying to see.'

Jennifer went quiet and watched. She pulled a tissue from her pocket and wiped her eyes. She seemed to be okay, even interested. I nodded to her and smiled. She smiled back slightly.

'Are your neighbours home?' I asked Leonard, looking around. There was a high fence, but there was a chance somebody next door would see me.

'Do it low and nobody will see you,' he said. 'Come on, show us.'

'Go on, Emma, show them,' John said. 'Leonard is the only Black who has never been shown energy work, and he deserves to have his chance. I used to make Guy Fawkes night extremely special for the entire firm.'

'I still hear tales, my Lord,' Leonard said.

I rose and moved away from the table to make room for the *chi*. 'You didn't just walk into their office off the street a couple of hundred years ago because of the name on the brass plate, did you, John?'

He didn't say anything, just grinned.

'Thought so.'

I generated a small ball of *chi*, about the size of a tennis ball. I floated it off my hand towards Leonard. 'Don't touch it; it will burn you badly if you do.'

Jennifer froze completely.

I moved the *chi* until it was near the boys. They watched it like two little rabbits frozen in headlights. I whizzed it over their heads, then reabsorbed it.

'How much damage can you do with that, Emma?' Leonard said, fascinated. 'Can you blow things up with it?'

I nodded.

'Can you show me? Could you blow up ...' He looked around, '...the little statue there?' He pointed at a concrete cherub holding a bunch of grapes.

'Are you sure?' I said.

'Don't you dare touch that. It's *mine*!' Jennifer threw herself up and stormed back into the house.

'Don't mind her, Emma. She's always been talking about how great it will be to show her little sister Emma how well she's living,' Leonard said. 'And now she's found that her little sister Emma will be lording it over *her*.'

'I don't want to lord it over anybody,' I said, and I meant it. 'I just want to be her sister.'

I followed Jennifer inside.

CHAPTER TWENTY-SEVEN

Jennifer sat on one of the couches in the living room, looking out the bay window towards the street. She had another tissue in her hand. She wasn't crying; she just stared out the window.

I went in and sat across from her.

We watched each other silently for quite some time.

'I'm sorry, Jen, I should have told you,' I said softly. 'But the whole thing is so weird ...'

'When's the wedding?' she snapped.

'I have no idea,' I said. 'There may not even be one, ever.'

'And he's a *king*, is he?'

'No.'

She glanced sharply at me.

I sighed. 'Yes. No. To tell the truth, he's more like a god.'

She turned away. 'I suppose I should be glad for you.'

'You know what, Jen? I don't care if you're glad for me or not. Frankly, I don't think there's much to be glad about. But I am glad for *you*. You have a wonderful husband who adores you, two healthy little boys of your own, and a fabulous life here in England. I would give anything to have what you do,' I sighed at the stab of pain that went through me, 'because I will probably never have anything as good as this.'

'Oh come *on*, Emma,' she said. 'What did Leonard call you? Dark Empress? And that's not better than this? You'll be leading this jet-set lifestyle, rubbing shoulders with anyone you want, as much money as you want —'

'You know what it's really like for me right now?' I let it all out. All of the pain. All of the frustration. All of the anger at the situation that I found myself in. 'All right, let me tell you. I love that man,' I pointed towards the back door, 'and we can't touch each other at all, because he could kill me.'

Jennifer opened her mouth to say something but I cut her off. My voice went fierce. 'It's because he's not a human being. He can't touch me. He's going to leave both Simone and me in about two years. He'll be gone for a very long time. Maybe more than a lifetime. He's promised to come back for me but there are no guarantees. Even if he does come back, it will be *years* from now.'

I dropped my head. It felt good to be letting it out.

'There is a constant stream of monsters attacking us, *all the damn time*. That fireball stuff? That wasn't for fun. I use it all the time to kill the monsters that want to hurt that delightful little girl.'

I looked at my hands, then back up to glare into her eyes. 'The black guy, Leo? The one you don't like the look of? He's my best friend. The monsters got him the other day and *cut his tongue in half*. That's why he doesn't talk much. He'll die soon anyway, you know? He's terminally ill. He'll leave us all alone as well.'

My throat thickened. I didn't want to be left alone; I wanted those wonderful men with me.

Jennifer's expression started to change from anger to anguish.

'Jet-set lifestyle? I spend most of my time teaching, looking after Simone, and doing budgets on damn spreadsheets that I hate the sight of. And all of this, Jennifer, for the love of a man who *can't even touch me*, and will *leave me* in a couple of years, perhaps *never to return*.'

I slapped my hands on my knees and turned away. The street was deserted. I pulled myself together. I didn't have time for this. I looked at Jennifer. I don't know why I'm wasting my time on you, I thought. And then I felt a pang: yes, I do.

I moved to sit next to her and put my arm around her. 'Jen, you're family. You're the most important thing in the world to me. Please forgive me. I'm sorry I didn't tell you.'

'Why can't he touch you, Emma?' she said quietly, her face expressionless.

'It's a very long story. That energy stuff I threw around? He's drained. He'll suck it all out of me and kill me if he touches me, because of the love between us.'

She snorted. 'Yeah, right. You sure that isn't a story he's spun?'

'It's true, we have to be very careful.' I ran my hands through my hair. 'Do you have any idea how lucky you are?'

She didn't say anything. She put it together in her head. She smiled slightly. I breathed a quiet internal sigh of relief. I'd done it.

'I'll tell you what, Jen. When his palace is rebuilt, I'll see if we can arrange for you to see it. I haven't even seen it myself. The monsters broke into it at the beginning of the year and destroyed most of it. Burnt to the ground. Come over to Hong Kong some time — I'll take you shopping, go around to see the sights, take your boys out with Simone. Would you like that? We could go to some social things, charity functions. I could introduce you to some of the big names in the movie industry, things like that. We could have fun, and now you know about John — Lord Xuan, I mean — I can let my hair down. I can take you places that I wouldn't take ordinary members of the family, like our Academy, where we teach kung fu.'

'I haven't really had much of a chance to talk to him,' she said. 'I really should get to know him better. What's he king of?'

'The entire Northern Celestial Heavens of China. He's also the Chinese God of Martial Arts — that's why we teach kung fu. He also has a Mountain in China that belongs to him, that used to hold the Academy before it burnt down.' I decided not to mention the fact that he was a Wind and a Turtle without its Serpent. One thing at a time. I rose and held out my hand. 'Come and meet him, he's a terrific guy.'

'I heard about the kung fu from Mum and Dad,' Jennifer said as we went back outside. 'They said it wasn't anything too exciting.'

'I didn't show them any *real* stuff,' I said.

'Can you show us?'

I laughed. 'If you want, I sure can. And Leo has my stupid singing sword out as well, I'd better show that to Leonard.'

'The sword sings?'

I laughed even more. 'More like it whines. It's really annoying. Everybody hates it.'

We went through the back door. Leonard was listening to John, rapt.

'And then she told him to *piss off*!' John finished with delight. 'I don't think anybody in a thousand years has said that to the King. You should have seen the look on his face.'

They both turned to us as we went out. Jennifer approached John and studied him closely. He rose, took her hand and smiled kindly down at her. 'Are you okay? You're all right with this? I'm sorry we didn't tell you straightaway, but generally it's better if people don't know about it.'

Jennifer looked from Leonard to John. 'You're really a god?'

He nodded. 'I really am.' He patted her hand. 'Sit down. I think Emma had better show Leonard the sword before he explodes with impatience.'

'All right ... Lord Chun?'

'Xuan. But just call me John. You too, Leonard. We are all family.'

'You are really most gracious,' Leonard said.

John grinned broadly. 'This is a perfect opportunity. I would like to teach Emma something that can only be taught outdoors, and our apartment building in Hong Kong is too public. Can I use your yard to teach her? I'll ensure that nobody sees her, but this is the ideal location.'

'What sort of thing?' Jennifer said.

'A wushu technique,' John said.

'Kung fu. What technique?' I said.

'Wall running. Roof running. We may even have you flying for short distances.'

'No *way*!' I exclaimed with delight. 'You think so?'

'Flying?' Jennifer said with wonder.

Before we did anything, I took Simone to one side and explained. 'You did really well, Simone, they had no idea we were any different. But my sister's husband knows your dad, and knows who he is, so we don't need to pretend any more.'

Simone let out a huge sigh and her little shoulders sagged. 'Did I do okay?'

'You did really well. You did better than me.' I crouched to hug her. 'You'll be fine at school, I'm sure.'

'What are we going to do now? Can we go back to the house?'

'Your dad wants to teach me wall running and roof running on this house, and I have to show ...' I hesitated, but what the hell. '... Uncle Leonard my singing sword and some other energy stuff. Do you want to show them some energy work and physical stuff as well? They'd like that.'

'Emma, is it okay if I keep practising while we're here? Pretend to be normal? I need to practise.'

I hugged her again. 'You are very special. That's a great idea.' I pulled away to smile at her. 'Go and play on the swings.'

Colin stayed with his father, but little Andrew went and talked to Simone. Michael rose and joined them to ensure that Simone wouldn't be hurt.

I returned to the table. 'How will you stop us from being seen, John?' Although the neighbours didn't seem to be home, there was a chance that I'd be spotted on the wall of the house.

'Gold,' John said loudly.

'My Lord?' Gold said from somewhere in the sunshine.

Leonard and Jennifer looked around for the source of the voice.

'I will be extremely generous and permit you to stay in True Form if you can hide us,' John said.

'My Lord,' Gold said.

Everything around us went completely silent, as it had when the Demon King had appeared.

'Done,' Gold said. 'Most appreciated,' he added softly.

'How long do we have?' John said to the air.

'About an hour, my Lord, that's all I can manage,' Gold said.

'Should be enough,' John said. 'But we'll need a safety net, just in case Emma falls.' He turned to

Jennifer and Leonard. 'Don't be concerned, but I need the help of somebody who can catch Emma if she falls off your roof, and she just happens to be a dragon.'

Jennifer's eyes went wide, but Leonard grinned broadly. Little Colin shifted closer to his mother.

'Don't worry, Jen, her name is Jade, she's the family accountant, and she's really nice,' I said. 'Don't think of her as a dragon, she's just a person. John, tell her to arrive in human form and transform after.'

Jade appeared in human form and Jennifer shot to her feet with a gasp. Colin clutched his mother. Leonard's grin didn't shift.

Andrew and Simone were busy talking near the swings and didn't notice.

Jade fell to one knee and saluted John, then did the same to me. She bowed from the waist to salute Jennifer and then Leonard.

Jennifer stared at me, eyes wide, then gave Jade a similar look.

'Jen, would you be okay if Jade turns into a dragon?' I said. 'She's only three metres long, and I can assure you that she's perfectly harmless.'

Jade fell to one knee in front of Jennifer. 'I swear I will not hurt any member of your family, my Lady. I am a sworn servant of Lord Xuan and Lady Emma. By your leave, Lady Jennifer.'

John smiled quickly at me. I shot a fleeting smile back: he had her picked; that was exactly the right thing to do.

'Go ahead,' Jennifer said.

Jade nodded and rose.

'I'll do the sword first, then we can work on the technique,' I said.

'Yes, let us see, Emma,' Leonard said. 'I've heard about this sword of yours. I want to hear what it sounds like.'

'You'll want to throw it in the garbage after you've heard it.'

I went to Leo, and he handed me the sword, hilt first. I pulled it from its scabbard, held it in front of me and made it sing. I ran it through a slow scale. Fortunately no dogs started to howl, but Jennifer put her hands over her ears and winced.

I pulled the chi out of the sword and it went quiet.

'And that will blow up demons?' Leonard said.

'Low-level ones, yes,' John said. 'Higher-level ones are unaffected.'

Please don't do that again, Emma, Simone said straight into my ear and I laughed.

'Don't worry, sweetheart, I won't,' I called, and she nodded. She and Andrew were playing on the swings together. Looked like she may have made a friend after all. Without his big brother to egg him on, Andrew seemed to be a nice kid.

Jennifer glanced from me to Simone. 'What was that about?'

'She can talk to me silently, right into my ear,' I said as I put my sword back into its scabbard. I gestured towards John as I returned the sword to the table. 'Both of them can. It's a pain in the neck.'

'Telepathy?' Leonard said with wonder.

I stopped at that. 'I suppose it is.'

'Of course it is,' John said. 'That's what it's called, anyway. The Monkey King once went to the CIA in America and told them he could do it. He demonstrated it to them. They were sure they had a new secret weapon. The little bastard played along with them, pretending to be American and patriotic, the whole works. When they started field testing, he destroyed the entire testing centre and left the place in a complete shambles.'

'Next time he challenges me I will take him up on it,' Leo lisped softly, almost to himself.

'I would like to be there. I think you could take him, if he didn't have that blasted staff of his. Enough story-telling. Emma,' John said more briskly, 'let's get you wall running.'

He gracefully pulled himself to his feet and gestured for me to accompany him to the house.

Leonard, Jennifer, Colin and Jade all followed at a respectful distance.

John stood back from the house about three metres, then ran to it, took three steps up the wall, leapt off somersaulting, and landed on his feet where he'd started, facing the house. He gestured to me. 'Now you.'

'You told me that was the most useless move in the entire suite,' I said. 'While you're in the air, your opponent has plenty of time to set themselves up to hit you hard when you land.'

'It's not a practical move by itself,' John said, tying his hair back. 'It's a base for working with more complicated stuff.'

'Oh, okay.' I did the same thing; I stood a couple of metres away, ran to the wall, took a couple of strides up the wall, flipped, and landed on my feet.

Jennifer's family all stared at me with awe.

'Spectacular but useless,' I said with a shrug.

John waved for me to move back. He turned so that he was nearly parallel to the house. He readied himself, then ran to it, took a few steps along the side of the house, and flipped off.

'Harder,' he said. 'You have to remain sideways on the house. More than that I can't do right now; you'll have to do the rest without demonstration. Give it a try.' He raised his hand. 'Wait. Jade, move away from the Blacks and transform, we may need you.'

'My Lord.' Jade moved away from Jennifer and Leonard. 'Don't worry, I'm perfectly harmless,' she said with a small smile.

She transformed into her dragon form: three metres long, gleaming green, with gold claws and fins behind her legs, and a gleaming gold fin on her tail.

Jennifer gasped and her eyes went wide. She went completely stiff. Jade stood very still and waited for her to get over it, her green eyes glowing.

'Are you okay, Jen?' I said.

Leonard moved closer to Jennifer and put his arm around her. He spoke quietly in her ear. She nodded.

'Okay, let's see you do it, Emma,' Leonard said.

Jade positioned herself under me. I was glad that she was there.

I ran as fast as I could at the wall and attempted similar momentum to the flip. I managed about two steps along the house, but I was losing it. I was falling off. The ground somersaulted to meet me and I readied myself to hit, but Jade was there and she caught me easily with her front legs.

She tipped me gently onto my feet and I nodded to her. She smiled her dragon smile, all gleaming gold teeth.

'You have more gold teeth than a little old Chinese lady,' I said quietly.

'I *am* a little old Chinese lady,' she said.

I turned back to the wall and faced it appraisingly. 'What did I do wrong, John? Not enough momentum?'

'That's right,' he said, sounding pleased. 'Give it a little more of a push. Hit the house hard. Try to push it over.'

'Please don't push my house over, Emma,' Leonard said.

I laughed. 'I'll try not to.'

I made another run at it, really pushing myself. I hit the house very hard; I could feel the force through my feet, enough to crack the brickwork. I took three strides along the side of the house. When I felt myself coming away I flung myself off it, somersaulted, and landed lightly on my feet. I quickly checked the brickwork to make sure that I hadn't damaged the wall but it seemed to be all right.

'Perfect,' John said. 'Now let's add energy.' He gestured for me to approach him. Jade came as well.

'That was really cool, Daddy,' Simone said behind me. 'Can I try that too?'

Simone and Andrew were watching me with Michael behind them.

'You can't do things like that yet, Simone,' John said. 'Your bones are too soft, you'd hurt them. You can do this sort of stuff when you're bigger.'

'Oh, okay,' Simone said. 'Can we go to Andrew's room to look at his cars?'

'I wanna show Simone my cars,' Andrew said.

'Sure, go.' I nodded to Michael and he followed.

Leo rose to go with them.

'Stay, Leo. Rest,' I said.

He grimaced impatiently. He actually opened his mouth to argue with me, speech impediment or not.

'You need to rest, Leo,' John said gently. 'You are still recovering.'

Leo looked from John to me and then nodded sadly and sat. He was still very weak from the blood loss.

'Why does the other boy follow her around everywhere?' Jennifer said.

'He's guarding her, Jen,' I said. 'She could be attacked any time. She needs someone next to her to defend her every minute of the day.'

Jennifer watched them go back to the house. 'The front door's locked, Emma. Nothing can get in.'

'They won't come in the front door,' I said. 'Remember how Jade came here?'

Jennifer's face was unreadable.

'Right,' John said briskly, 'we only have a limited time, let's have you doing this. Adding energy. Focus on the three *dan tian*. You will need to lift the energy and raise all three of them at the same time. That will raise the rest of you. You need to be moving already, with good momentum, otherwise you won't be able to pull it off.'

'Will I injure myself if I fail?' I said.

He understood; I wasn't talking about hitting the ground. 'If you fail spectacularly you may explode,' he said cheerfully, and Jennifer gasped. 'But I don't think you are that much of a novice. You have good control. You should be able to pull it off. If you lose control of the energy centres, then just let go and fall off, and recentre them. Try to run up the wall, using the energy centres to pull you. Got it?'

I nodded. I faced the wall and concentrated. This was extremely difficult. I needed to have enough physical momentum and focus on moving the energy centres at the same time.

'Try running halfway up and then letting go,' John said. 'We really need to find a place in Hong Kong where the Disciples can practise these skills. There's not a single place I can think of where we can do it.'

'Field trips to Guangzhou,' I said, still concentrating.

'Good idea,' he said. 'Getting there?'

I nodded. I just about had it. I focused. I went very still as I concentrated.

Then I launched myself at the wall as fast as I could. My feet hit the wall very hard. I used the momentum to push me the first few steps, then grabbed my energy centres and lifted them.

'Evenly,' John called, and I heard him, but he didn't need to tell me. If I did it unevenly I would become unbalanced and lose control of my energy. All three types. The results could be disastrous if they all moved around too much at once.

The energy centres moved and lifted me from the inside out. It was spectacularly euphoric; I was carried from the inside by my own energy. I managed a couple more steps up the wall, lifted by the energy.

The energy began to get away from me, so I immediately dropped it. I let go of all the energy centres, centred the energy, and fell off the wall. The ground spun to meet me. Jade caught me in mid-air.

'Well done, my Lady,' Jade said quietly as she tipped me back onto my feet.

'Thanks, Jade.'

John shrugged. 'You have it. You just need to practise the skill now. See if you can have yourself on the roof before Gold's charm wears off.' He returned to the table. 'Come and sit and watch, Leonard, Jennifer. This should be fun.'

'Would you like a beer, my Lord?' Leonard said.

'Off the hard stuff right now, Leonard, but if you have some tea that would be tremendous,' John said, falling into a very English accent.

'You sound like my ring,' I said as I leaned forward and concentrated on the wall, readying myself.

'Heaven forbid,' John said.

'Ewe wan may tah sun Strine?' the stone said.

Both Jennifer and I laughed.

'I do *not* sound like that,' I huffed.

'Who said that anyway?' Jennifer was still giggling. 'That was the worst fake Australian accent I've heard in ages, and you definitely find some here in England.'

'You will be in serious trouble with the Grandmother of All the Rocks if she hears you sound like that, Dad,' Gold said.

I gestured behind me without turning. 'I'm busy. Explain for them.' I concentrated on the wall. Then I stopped and straightened. 'Who's the Grandmother of All the Rocks?' I understood. 'Uluru. Of course.' I readied myself and concentrated.

'Remember the stone I put on the table, then Leo put on the grass?' John said as I focused on the wall and ignored them.

'Emma said it was your lawyer in Hong Kong,' Jennifer said.

I launched myself at the wall. I took three huge strides, then lifted myself with the energy. I managed another four strides up the house before I lost it. Jade plucked me out of the air and lowered me gently.

I concentrated on centring the energy.

'Good,' John called. 'You should be on the roof next one.' His voice went quieter. 'Anyway, the stone in the ring woke up, and it's been sending Emma berserk with its cryptic comments since then. And it has an English accent that drives her nuts.' His voice changed slightly. 'Couldn't have thought of a better gift.'

He would definitely keep. When I was able to touch him again, I really would beat the living crap out of him. I faced the wall and concentrated.

I launched myself at the wall, took three strides up, and used the energy to lift me. I managed a few more strides and felt a shot of delight: I had it. The energy moved evenly through me and I was still going up the wall. I heard yelling but ignored it, I was concentrating too hard. As I passed one of the windows I glanced in and saw a demon materialise in the room. Simone and Michael had put Andrew behind them and stood ready to face it.

'Jade, come and get me!' I screamed as I allowed myself to drop off the wall. 'Demon! In the room with the children! For God's sake, get *up there*!' I yelled down to John and Leo, but they were already inside the house.

Jade flew up and caught me. 'That window,' I said, and she nodded and carried me to it. She flipped me out of her arms through the window and I raced towards the demon. Jade flew in the window behind me.

Simone, Andrew and Michael faced it with their backs to me. Michael had pushed Simone behind him as well as Andrew, and stood ready.

'Let me handle it,' I said to Michael as I rushed past him. I stopped and studied the demon. It was a small red humanoid in True Form, about level fifteen.

I generated a ball of *chi* and blew it up. The door flew open just as it exploded and poor Leo was covered with black stuff.

John was behind him. He spun and raced straight back out, his feet thumping on the landing. Leo stood motionless in the doorway.

'There's more coming. They're downstairs, Emma,' Simone said breathlessly. She froze, her eyes wide. 'Everywhere.'

'Leo.' Jade gestured with one gold-taloned claw. 'Come with me, I'll clean you up. We'll take them on downstairs.' She dashed past us through the door and Leo followed.

'Leo,' I called, and he turned back. 'I'll make a stand here with the children.' My voice changed as my throat filled. 'For God's sake, don't let them hurt my sister or her family.'

Leo nodded then charged down the hallway.

CHAPTER TWENTY-EIGHT

Gold appeared next to me and handed me my sword. He transformed into his stone self: a human shape all of stone.

Another red humanoid demon came up the stairs and raced towards us. I blew it up.

'I can only handle a couple more before I run out of *chi* space,' I said. 'Then I'll have to go physical.'

'I'm with you, Lady Emma,' Gold said. 'We can take them.'

'What's it like downstairs?' I said.

'Bad.'

Two more red demons came up the stairs. 'Let me,' Gold said. He went out to meet them. His hands grew into giant hammers and he squashed the demons flat with a sickening wet crunch.

Gold moved back to stand beside me. He held his hands out and made them vibrate quickly, shaking off the black stuff. It dissipated into feathery streamers as it flew into the air off his hands.

'Is my sister okay?' I said softly.

'I defended them until the Dark Lord arrived. They are fine.' Gold froze and his eyes turned inwards. 'Shit.' He disappeared.

'If you know what's happening I'd appreciate an update,' I said softly. 'It's okay, kids, I'm not talking to you,' I added more loudly. I spoke quietly again. 'If you can just tell me without letting them know, I'd really appreciate it.'

'Birds. Fire elementals.' The stone in the ring hesitated. Its voice went very soft in my ear. 'A Demon Prince.'

'Shit,' I said, so quietly that the children couldn't hear. 'Have they stopped coming up here?'

'The way from downstairs is blocked by Gold,' the stone said. 'Both physical and direct. They cannot come to you any more. All of you here are safe, unless the Dark Lord is defeated, which is highly unlikely.' Its voice became fierce. 'Get those children away from the window! *Birds*!'

'Get away from the window!' I yelled to the children, pushing myself between them and the window frame. Michael spun to face the window and put Simone and Andrew behind him. A crow flew in, and Michael plucked it out of the air and snapped off its head with a flick of his wrist. It made a small explosion of black stuff onto his hands.

Two more crows came in; I took them out with the sword. They dissipated.

'Close the window,' I said to Michael.

'No, don't!' the stone said loudly. 'They will just come through the glass and you will be cut. Better to leave the window open and take them as they come in.' Its voice calmed. 'Make the sword sing as they come.'

'How are they doing downstairs?' I said.

'They are holding their positions and waiting for One Two Two,' the stone said. 'At this stage nobody has been injured.' Its voice softened. 'Jade is checking on us for the Dark Lord as I check on them for you.'

I breathed a sigh of relief. 'This attack is awfully close on the heels of the last one, stone. That was only two days ago. The attacks are closer together all the time.'

'That was the King. This is the Prince. You will not see the King again unless you decide to call him. If you defeat the Prince this time, he will probably stay quiet for a while,' the stone said. Then, 'The Tiger is downstairs.'

'He has a personal score to settle with Wong,' I said. 'He made us promise to invite him along to our next little party.'

'Birds!' the stone said.

I spun to face the window and made the sword sing. Five birds exploded before they reached the house.

'How many more birds?' I said.

'Ten. Eight. Jade is chasing them down in the air. Six. Three. At the window!' the stone hissed. I made the sword sing. The three birds exploded.

Jade appeared at the window. She didn't say a word; she nodded, turned, and snaked down through the air.

'She is making it rain to take out the last few fire elementals,' the stone said. 'Gold was required to handle them; humans cannot physically face them, they are too hot.'

There was complete silence, only the sound of the rain pattering gently on the roof. The rain stopped.

'Stone?' I said softly.

'Nothing,' the stone said. 'They are waiting. The Prince has not yet arrived.'

I waited. There was still complete silence.

'We're okay, Emma,' Simone said.

'Good,' I said without turning away from the window.

I heard someone coming up the stairs.

'Who is coming?' I said.

'The Dark Lord. Alone,' the stone said.

'Really him?'

'Yes.'

John appeared at the doorway. Simone raced to him and he picked her up. He smelled strongly of smoke.

'He changed his mind, Emma, when we took out his thralls. We were obviously too strong for him, and he did his usual cowardly thing. It's finished.'

'He's not coming at all?' I said with relief.

John shook his head. He held out his other arm and smiled.

I raced to him and he wrapped his free arm around me. I buried my face into his chest, still holding my sword in my right hand at his back. He smiled down at me. His free hand came behind my head and held me. He closed his eyes and kissed me.

'Yuck,' Simone said loudly.

We laughed into each other's mouths, and turned our heads together to see her. Simone leaned the side of her head against his shoulder and her eyes sparkled at me. 'You two are *so* gross,' she said happily. 'Move away, Emma, I want to look at the cars.'

John pulled away. He gently lowered Simone, then gestured for me to follow him onto the landing. As he closed the door behind us, Michael nodded inside the room.

'We are in big trouble,' John said. 'Fire elementals are supposed to belong to the Red Lady. I'd like to know how One Two Two had control of them. I have summoned the Phoenix and she is on her way. There is a fire elemental bound in the backyard. I am surprised I was able to bind it, that is most unusual. Oh,' he added almost as an afterthought, 'your sister is having hysterics in the living room, and your brother-in-law is ready to rip our throats out for putting his family in danger.'

'Is everybody okay otherwise?' I said.

He nodded, still smiling. 'Emma,' he said, and the smile disappeared, 'I hope you understand what we will have to do eventually. This cannot be permitted to continue. As soon as Simone is ready —'

'As soon as Simone is ready, we will hunt this little bastard down and you will take True Form and give him exactly what he deserves.'

'How did you know?'

'It's what we have to do,' I said. 'I also know that if it comes down to him or us, you'll do it. You'll take True Form and rip his nasty little guts out. I only hope we have Simone up to speed before it comes to that.'

'In True Form I can take him easily,' John said, 'and I don't need to worry about going too far and losing it. Even on the land, I can take him. But you must understand: afterwards I will be gone.'

'I know.'

His eyes turned inwards. 'The Red Lady is here. Let's talk to her first. Jade and Gold are trying to calm your family. It might be a good idea to leave them for a while.'

'Do you think we should move them to the Western Palace?' I said as we went down the stairs. I could hear Jennifer raging loudly in the living room and I winced.

'I will arrange for seals to be set on this house. I will post guards. They will be as safe here as they could be anywhere on the Earthly Plane. It will take a while for the demons to regroup. I do not expect another attack for a while. And it will be directed at us, wherever we are, not at them.'

I nodded. That was enough to keep them safe. The attack had been against us. All of the attacks had been aimed at John, Simone, or me; except when they had taken Charlie as second prize.

'This must end soon,' I said desperately. 'It's worse every single time.'

'He's stronger every single time too, love,' John said sadly. 'Our time is limited.'

We went into the yard. The fire elemental was a creature of flames: roughly man-shaped and about normal human size, but its entire form was writhing fire. It didn't move but the flames danced, making luminous shadows on the grass in the fading afternoon sun. Zhu Que stood in the yard and examined it from about a metre away. When she saw us she waited until we approached and then saluted, bowing to each of us. 'My Lord. My Lady.'

'Madam.' John gestured towards the table. Zhu Que nodded and sat. She put her hand on the table and waited patiently, similar to the way the Demon King had. John sat across from her. I sat next to him.

'Fire elementals. Birds. Explain,' he said.

'Not me. This is not one of mine,' she said calmly, her beautiful long face expressionless. She gestured dismissively with one hand and the colours on her robe rippled. 'It is the bastard son of a Snake Mother and something unspeakable.' She eyed it with contempt. 'It is a corruption of the pure flames. When I discover who is creating these things, I will ensure that they have a taste of the distilled fire themselves.'

'One Two Two,' John said.

The Phoenix stiffened and her face went taut with anger. 'That one is not clever enough to fashion something as powerful as this.'

'The King has sworn to stay out of it. Who else could be helping that little piece of shit?' John said without emotion.

She made a soft sound of amusement. 'Anyone helping it is as stupid as it is.' She leaned her arms on the table. 'We need intelligence, quickly. Do you think the Lady would help us?'

'Ask the elemental first,' John said. 'I do not want the Lady to risk herself for us.'

'It is not an elemental!' she spat. 'It is a vile demon hybrid.'

'Can you control it?'

She eyed it appraisingly. 'I don't know, Ah Wu,' she said softly. 'Let's see. Maybe Lady Emma should move back; it may attack when we unbind it.'

I moved away slightly to watch.

John and the Phoenix moved closer to study it. 'It has a most interesting structure,' she said softly. 'There is a demon in there somewhere, hardly visible to the Inner Eye. Look inside.'

He looked at her pointedly.

She bowed and saluted. 'I apologise, my Lord.' She turned back to the elemental. 'That may be why these have been produced. Can you sense them coming?'

He shook his head without saying anything. His face was rigid with restraint.

'What?' I said. Both their faces were expressionless.

John sighed. He gestured with one hand towards the Phoenix. 'I am North, she is South. I am Water, she is Fire.'

'And?'

The Phoenix explained. 'Although Water is not vulnerable to Fire, it is still not his element. There is no water essence in it at all. He is unable to see inside this creature, because it is composed of fire. He cannot sense it coming. It has the advantage on him.'

'Holy shit,' I said softly. 'And you think Wong made this just for you?'

His face closed down even more. He nodded sharply. Then his expression softened. 'If what the Phoenix says is true, it is a rather unpleasant development. I have never seen anything like this before. Can you see inside it?'

I shrugged. 'I can try.'

I opened my Inner Eye and studied the fire demon. It

340

wasn't pure fire. Black demon stuff writhed like ribbons through the flames.

'I can see the demon stuff,' I said. 'I can see that it's not pure fire. Is a true elemental pure flames?'

Zhu Que nodded. 'You are quite impressive, my Lady. Here.' She raised her hand and another elemental appeared next to the demon. It looked identical for a moment, then I saw that it was the real thing and not bound.

'Will I hurt it if I look inside?' I said.

'No,' she said with a small smile. 'Go right ahead.'

I looked inside it. 'It's really beautiful.' The flames were pure and bright and shot through with gold and silver. At its heart was a core of clean, blistering heat. I could sense its awareness; it returned my gaze with amusement. It had a rather wicked sense of humour and was quite intelligent.

I examined the other one again. It was sullen, stupid and evil and wanted to destroy everything around it.

'The difference is very obvious when you look closely at it. Thanks for showing me,' I said.

'You are very welcome,' Zhu Que said with a smile and small bow. 'I am impressed. Most humans cannot do that.'

The real elemental disappeared.

'I will unbind it. We'll see if you can make it talk,' John said.

'Don't count on it,' she said grimly.

He unbound the fire demon, but it didn't move. Zhu Que's face went taut with effort. She stared at it. She raised her hand towards it. She walked to it and grabbed it by the throat, completely unharmed by the flames. Her red eyes flashed. Her scarlet hair floated around her head. The demon exploded into feathery red and black streamers. Zhu Que lowered her arm and sagged.

'Anything?' John said.

Zhu Que shook her head. 'Nothing. It had a self-destruct mechanism.' Her voice became fierce. 'What a despicable piece of work. Whenever I find who made this, I will make them suffer.' She raised her arms. 'I suggest you contact the Lady. She may be willing to sortie for you. Otherwise ...' She smiled sadly. 'Otherwise you will just have to take each day as it comes.'

'How are the eggs?' John said. 'Are they close?'

She smiled and her face lit up. 'They are very close. I should return to them, they will be getting cold. I have fire elementals on them, but they are not warm enough.'

'Let me know when they hatch,' he said. 'I'd love to see the little ones.'

She saluted him. 'My Lord. By your leave.'

'Go South, little Sparrow,' he said gently.

She saluted me. 'Lady Emma. I believe that I owe you a gold coin.'

'A look at the babies would be enough, I think,' I said.

She smiled kindly and disappeared in a flurry of red.

I went to John. 'Would Qing Long be the father?'

'Her business is her business. Her eggs are her eggs.'

'I'd still like to see the babies.'

'They are usually adorable,' he said. He looked at me. He didn't say anything.

'Negative,' I said. 'Probably for the best anyway. You won't be around.'

His smile didn't shift but I saw the disappointment in his eyes. 'You're quite correct. Probably for the best.'

I changed the subject. 'Do you have water elementals?'

He nodded. 'Right now I cannot summon them. They miss me terribly.'

I dropped my head, then shook myself out of it. 'Let's go and talk to Jennifer and Leonard. I would have thought Leonard would be taking this better. He knows who you are.'

'None of my staff has ever been this close before,' John said. 'This is the first time any of them have been in danger. They have been brought up with the assurance that, as long as they serve me, they are safe.'

'This will be very hard,' I said as we went through the door. 'I'd rather face a battalion of demons.'

'Me too, love.'

The return flight was uneventful. We were all subdued, even Simone. We only had a couple of weeks until school started. The demons would probably have another try at us then.

John and I were in agreement. We refused to let this demon spoil our lives. We could handle him. Simone would go to school like a normal little girl. We would be careful.

But we did lock the security down tighter around ourselves. We tried to avoid feeling that we were under siege.

CHAPTER TWENTY-NINE

The interior of the Science Museum was dark and deserted. The airplane exhibit loomed around me. The propellers on the huge engines to one side looked like grinning teeth against the dimly glowing windows.

'I don't like you,' Simone said in the darkness. I moved to follow her voice.

'I don't care,' he said, and my blood went cold.

'I'm coming,' I said loudly.

'Emma?' Her sweet voice was full of hope.

'Oh good,' he said. 'Now I have you all.'

'Touch one hair on her head and I will make you suffer horribly for the rest of your short existence,' I said loudly.

'Oh, do come, Miss Emma,' he said, his voice full of encouragement. 'I guarantee there's enough of me for both of you.'

'What are you doing?' Simone said. 'I don't like that.' Her voice raised in pitch. '*Stop it*!'

'*You get your filthy hands off her*!' I roared, running towards her voice.

'Help! Emma!' she shrieked. '*Stop it*!'

'Shut up,' he said grimly. 'Keep still.'

I couldn't move fast enough on legs. I changed.

I slithered forward on my black coils. Good. I could see better this way. The ground felt absolutely wonderful beneath my belly. I'd missed that so much. I could see them in the dark. I could taste them. Yuck. I could taste him. He tasted like shit.

There they were. A large group of low-level demons stood between me and them. He stopped when he saw me. She saw me too. She screamed.

I didn't have time to reassure her. I took out the demons around me. They were easy. I bit some heads off, then took one in my mouth and shook it wildly, using it as a club to destroy the others. Great fun. They were much too slow for me.

No more. I raised myself on my coils and carefully approached One Two Two and Simone. Good; it looked like he hadn't gone very far with her. If he'd done anything to hurt her I would not make this quick.

Simone stopped shrieking and sobbed.

'Holy shit,' he said, staring at me, stunned.

I didn't give him a chance to say anything more. I opened my mouth and my fangs sprang out with a spray of venom. The venom hit him in the face and he screamed. Good.

I struck him right in the middle of the chest. My fangs went through the skin and into his chest cavity. Damn, it felt good. But he really did taste like shit.

He fell. He convulsed under my head, making weird choking noises. Dead. Easy. I pulled my mouth free of him and checked Simone. I lowered my head to reassure her, but she had fainted. I nudged her with my nose.

I shot up to sit upright in bed. I looked around. I was back in my room in Hong Kong.

I was drenched in sweat. I checked my hands in the glow of the lights from the city coming through the crack in the curtains. Completely normal.

I rose and quietly went through the door into Simone's room. She was sleeping, her little face angelic. I sat on the bed and touched her face. She grimaced slightly but didn't wake. She turned over. I stroked her hair.

I went back into my own room and sat on the bed. I put my head in my hands.

I heard them arguing as I approached the training room. They went silent when I entered.

'Sifu,' they all said, and saluted.

'What's up, guys? Why the big argument?'

Alvin, the local kid from Guangdong Province, and Julie, a young American, shared an exasperated look.

Finally it was Lai who broke the silence. 'Alvin and Julie are arguing about how Master Leo was injured. We finally gathered enough nerve to ask him in the lesson we just finished, and he wouldn't talk about it.'

'I heard a *Snake Mother* did it,' Julie said. 'One of the fifth years told me that.'

'Not possible,' Alvin said. 'Snake Mothers never leave Hell.'

'Okay, guys, sit.' I sat on the mats as well. 'It took you two weeks to ask him? Most of the other students have already been ignored by him. Revision: Snake Mothers. Lai, you're a Shen, you start.'

Lai grimaced. 'I'm a very small Shen, you know that, ma'am. And my mother won't talk about Snake Mothers. It's really strange. The minute I turned sixteen she's telling me what to look for in a mate —'

Julie swallowed a huge gulping laugh.

Lai rounded on Julie. 'It's all very well for you to laugh, but do you have any idea how embarrassing it is? She's such an *old-fashioned* old hen.' She made her voice thin and wheezy. 'Make sure he has a fine tail, and a good comb, a good comb is important in a cock —'

Every English speaker in the class collapsed in laughter. Lai appeared bewildered. 'What did I say?'

'It's the language charm,' I said. 'Cock. *Cock*. Two different meanings, depending on the way you say it. You heard the two meanings?'

Lai thought about it, then she collapsed laughing as well.

I spoke again when they'd regained a semblance of control. 'Why won't your mother talk about Snake Mothers? Everybody needs to be aware of them; they're so dangerous.'

Lai dropped her head. 'I think one broke into my mother's nest once and ate all the chicks. That's why she won't talk about them.'

The class went wide-eyed and silent at that.

'That's awful,' Julie whispered.

'Snake Mothers,' I said, bringing them back to the point. 'Anybody know what level they are?'

'Anything from fifty up,' Alvin said. 'The biggest ones are as big as the King himself.'

'Good,' I said. 'They occupy the nests, and they bear all the demon spawn. The smaller ones mate with ...? Anyone?'

'The smaller ones can produce spawn with any male demon,' Julie said. 'But the biggest ones will spawn only with the King — they produce the Demon Princes.'

'Good,' I said. 'Do they leave the nests?'

'No,' Alvin said with certainty. 'They stay in Hell.'

'No, that's not right,' Lai said patiently. 'Lady Emma herself faced a Mother when the Mountain was attacked.'

'That's right, Alvin.'

'But if they leave the nests ...' Alvin began, his face filling with horror. 'Then they could come out and attack any of us.'

'They come shopping here all the time,' I said. 'Watch for groups of gorgeous young women, all wearing clothes the colour of dried blood.'

Bunny, a young local girl from Sha Tin, gasped. 'I don't believe it, I've *seen* them in Pacific Place!'

'They won't go for you if you don't go for them,' I said.

'But what about Leo?' Alvin said. 'What happened to him?'

I dropped my head and ran my hands through my hair. 'They kidnapped him and took him to the nests to play. The King wouldn't let them kill him because I'm so fond of him.'

'Dear God,' Julie said softly. '*Play?*'

I grinned at her without humour. 'Yep. They like to amuse themselves with a variety of games in the nests. The victims are usually low-level demons, but sometimes the King will give them a human or Shen to play with, and they regard that as a special treat. They try to make the toy last as long as possible.'

They remained silent for a while, digesting this.

'They cut Leo's tongue in half. Master Liu was able to heal it, but he'll never speak properly again.' I checked my watch and snapped out of it. 'Lunchtime. Off you go. Don't worry, this building is thoroughly sealed, nothing can get in. You're safe here and in the surrounding district. Anywhere the language charm works, you're safe.'

'Come with us, ma'am,' Julie said. 'I want to hear about this pact you made.'

'How do you know about that?'

'The fifth year has a big mouth.'

I opened my mouth to say I had to work on my thesis and then closed it again. To hell with it; the students needed reassuring. I pulled myself to my feet. 'Sure. Let's go to the Seven Brand downstairs, I feel like some ho fan.'

The students grinned and saluted.

As we passed the display rack of the Eighteen Weapons in the lobby, Alvin and Julie had another whispered argument.

I stopped to speak to them. 'What now?'

Julie gestured towards the weapons. 'Alvin says they're wrong, that the mace should be replaced by a spade. I say the trident should be replaced by a spade.'

I laughed softly. 'Guys, Lord Xuan himself selected that set. I think they're the right ones, even though every single student that comes through the door seems to think that they're wrong.'

'Oh,' Alvin and Julie said together.

We filed into the noodle shop and took a table. The owner of the shop thought that we were an English school and was pleased at the business we brought him. We knew him quite well, and he always made sure we had preferential treatment. We had preferential treatment at a few of the eating places around the area, and never had to take a number for the yum cha across the road.

'Shame I have to be vegetarian,' Alvin said. 'Now the cooler weather's coming, the snake shop will be open. I used to like a bit of snake soup in the winter.'

'You eat snakes?' Julie said with disbelief.

'If its back faces Heaven you can eat it,' Alvin said with a grin. 'Snake is yang. Heats up your blood. Makes you warm in winter.'

'Alvin,' I said grimly, 'remember the nature of your Grand Master.'

They all went silent at that. They knew about John's true nature.

'Sorry, ma'am,' Alvin said.

'I still don't believe that you eat *snakes*,' Julie said. She turned to me, concerned. 'Do you mind me asking about it, ma'am?'

I sighed with resignation. 'Share your cultures, guys. Just don't mention this in front of the Dark Lord, or you'll be sharpening every single weapon on the first floor.'

The first floor was the armoury. There were well in excess of eight hundred bladed weapons stacked in there, neatly arranged. John could keep his weapons tidy, but his office was always a disaster area.

'The snake soup shop down the street will open soon,' Alvin said. 'They close over the summer and open during the winter. They only need to open for a few months of the year, they make enough money.'

'How do you eat it?' Julie said.

'Usually we eat snake in soup,' Alvin said, enjoying his rapt audience. 'Sometimes ...' he began, then changed his mind about what he was going to say. 'Usually in soup. They shred the snake, and add other stuff to it, like fungi, or chicken, or pig's ear, and boil it up. It's actually quite ...' He didn't finish. He tilted his head and smiled. 'I won't go into too much detail in front of the Sifu.' He froze when he saw my face. 'I apologise, ma'am, I've offended you,' he said, alarmed.

'No, Alvin, I'm not offended,' I said absently. 'I just remembered something.' I snapped out of it. 'I just remembered, I have something I need to do. I need to go back to the Academy. I'll see you later.'

I rose without checking to see if they'd heard me and went out. I walked into someone coming in, but ignored them. I went straight back to the Academy, went into my office, closed the door and fell into my chair.

I sat quietly for a long time.

There was a tap at the door.

'Come in,' I said without thinking.

John walked over to the chair across from my desk. I didn't really see him. He sat without speaking for a while, but I didn't notice.

'Emma,' he said brusquely, and I snapped out of it. He smiled slightly. 'You just walked right into Meredith at the door of the Seven Brand Noodle Shop and didn't even see her. What's the matter?'

'Shredded snake broth with sliced pig's ear,' I said.

His face went expressionless. He leaned back and folded his arms over his chest. 'Took you a while. You seemed to block that one out.'

'You've known all along?'

He stretched his long legs in front of him. 'You were upset enough as it was after what the stone said.'

'He said he wanted to eat all three of us. You, turtle hotpot. Bai Hu, braised tiger. And me, shredded snake soup.'

'Are you concerned?' John said, his arms still crossed over his chest and his eyes burning.

'Yes,' I choked quietly.

'Then he has won.'

'He said I was a snake, John.' My throat was thick. 'He said I was a *snake*.'

'He wants to eat you, same as he wants to eat me and Ah Bai,' he said evenly. 'And besides, he may be saying that you're a pig's ear, anyway.'

I turned away. 'You are no help at all.'

He rose gracefully. 'Come and let me buy you lunch downstairs. If you don't have anything to eat, your blood sugar will be so low that the next class you take, you'll pass out.'

'Don't go near my second years,' I said. 'You don't want to hear what they're talking about.'

'They're talking about eating you,' he said mildly. 'Pig's ear soup.'

CHAPTER THIRTY

A week before school started, John called me into his study. 'School won't start on time unless I do something,' he said. 'Typhoon.'

'This late in the year? We've already had a monsoon.' I dropped my voice. 'Is it a natural typhoon?'

He nodded. 'It happens sometimes. The wind changes. The circulation can happen over the sea, even after a monsoon. A very big typhoon will form east of the Philippines, and it will be a direct hit. The eye will pass right over us on the morning of the first day of school.' His eyes turned inwards as he concentrated. He could see the weather patterns. 'Really big one.' He snapped back and shrugged. 'I'll make it miss us so that Simone can start school on time.'

I shot to my feet with fury. 'Don't you *dare*! Try anything like that and you will be in serious trouble. *Leo*!' I yelled without moving.

Leo skidded down the hallway and charged in. 'What? What?' He saw John sitting at the desk, arms crossed and relaxed. He saw me standing on the other side of the desk, leaning on it with one hand, furious. 'What?'

'This ...' I hesitated, then, with emphasis on the insult, 'Turtle ...'

John made a soft sound of amusement.

'...wants to divert a super typhoon coming this way, purely because it'll hit us on his daughter's first day of school.' I threw myself back from the desk and stood rigid, glaring at John.

Leo glanced at me. Then his expression darkened. He folded his arms over his chest and glowered at John. I did the same.

'Over our dead bodies,' I growled. 'You do any weather manipulation *at all* in the next three weeks and your shell will be in serious trouble.'

'What she said,' Leo rasped.

John appeared ready to argue with us for a moment. Then he grinned broadly and spread his hands, palm up, over the table.

Both Leo and I sagged with relief.

'I think I must be the luckiest old Turtle in the whole wide world,' John said, his hands still out.

'You're definitely the stupidest,' Leo growled quietly, then stalked out, shaking his head.

I pointed at Leo's enormous receding back. 'What he said.'

I warned Ah Yat to buy extra food at the market. If the typhoon was a direct hit, then we could be stuck at home for at least a whole day; but it would quickly dissipate once it hit the land. The storm would be intense on the coast, and then clear as it moved inland.

School was supposed to start the first Tuesday of September. On the Friday before, the Number One standby signal was hoisted by the Hong Kong Observatory. The symbol appeared in the corner of the television screen when Simone watched her children's shows.

On Sunday afternoon, the Number Three signal was raised. This was the strong wind warning. I watched the typhoon coming towards us on the international weather bureau websites. It was huge. It cut a swathe of destruction across the Philippines. Six people in the northern Philippines were killed in the flooding.

The sky grew very overcast. The clouds came down, thick and grey and low. They swept across the sky like a heavy roiling soup, moving unnaturally fast. The weather made John irritable. He locked his feelings down tight. Hong Kong's spectacular electric storms made him cheerful to the point of euphoria; his eyes would go very bright and hard. But he didn't enjoy the weather patterns around typhoons at all.

I suddenly realised that in the previous three years there had been unusually few typhoons that approached the Territory close enough to warrant the raising of a Number Eight signal. There had even been comments made on television about the low number of typhoon hits. He must have been moving them away because he didn't like them.

The Number Eight was raised on Monday afternoon. Ah Yat and I went through the apartment and put a large cross of tape across every window. If something blew into the window and broke it, the tape would stop glass shards from flying in and hurting us. John had put safety glass in all the windows anyway, but they could still break.

When a Number Eight gale force signal was raised, everybody except vital services stayed at home. Schools, shops and offices closed. As the typhoon approached, bulletins appeared on television informing the people of Hong Kong which buses, trains and ferries were still running.

The noise woke me at about three o'clock Tuesday morning. It was like a rushing freight train directly outside the window. The building swayed gently in the wind.

I hopped out of bed and quickly checked my window. It wasn't leaking, which was unusual. The flat I had shared with Louise in Sha Tin had leaked during typhoons and water damage was a constant part of life. During one particularly bad typhoon we'd stuffed every single towel we owned, and all of our clothes as well, around the edges of the windows to soak up the water gushing in, and had spent the afternoon wringing out the towels into buckets.

I peered out the window. The rain blew sideways. Central District below me was a horizontal blur of lights. The roar of the wind was furious outside the window. No chance of going back to sleep with that, particularly with the building swaying just enough to make me feel seasick as I lay in bed.

I pulled on some clothes and slipped through the door into Simone's room. She could sleep through anything; her little face was angelic in the soft glow of her night light. I quietly checked her window. Not leaking either.

I went into the unlit living room. John and Leo were there already, standing at one of the windows in the faint glow of the city lights, watching the typhoon.

I moved to stand in front of Leo. He threw his massive arm over my shoulder and I leaned back into him. He was like a black boulder behind me, solid and unmoving.

'You are my rock,' I said quietly. 'I can always rely on you.'

He squeezed me gently but didn't say anything.

The building directly below us on the hill had lights on the roof, illuminating the roof garden. The rain hit the building horizontally and then flew directly up in the wind. The roar was even louder on this side of the apartment.

John stood silently on the other side of Leo, wearing his black pyjama pants with an old black T-shirt over the top. He had his arms folded in front of him; dark, sullen and dour.

I leaned around Leo to speak to John. 'How far away is the eye?'

He shifted slightly, but didn't uncross his arms. 'About three hours away. Still not the worst.'

I turned back to the window. 'Any windows leaking?'

John went still and concentrated. 'No.' He shifted slightly again. 'I had the windows resealed after the last one. They did a good job.'

I leaned back into the silent Leo. 'Is it really that unpleasant?'

John's voice was very soft and mild. 'Yes.' He uncrossed his arms and put his hands on his hips. 'Like a strong current. Pulling. All directions at once. Very unpleasant.'

'You used to move them all away, didn't you?'

He didn't say anything.

'If Michelle or me caught him at it, his shell would be in serious trouble,' Leo said, his voice rumbling through my back.

'I have made some very serious mistakes in my life, and employing you was one of the biggest,' John said mildly, still looking out the window.

'Michelle employed me. You never did,' Leo said. 'By the time she was gone I wasn't an employee any more, anyway.'

John crossed his arms over his chest again. 'Employing Emma was absolutely the biggest mistake.'

'Coming to work for you was a huge mistake for me too,' I said.

'And here we are,' Leo lisped softly.

Simone appeared in the doorway, and stopped when she saw us. The three of us turned to look at her. She hesitated. She didn't know which of us to go to. She loved us all.

Nobody needed to say anything.

The storm went quiet as the eye went over. Michael made a fourth leg and we played mah jong in the living room. Over the period of an hour, the roaring slowed, and then stopped. The wind didn't stop completely, but it was greatly reduced. The clouds thinned, but they were still there. The rain eased. John visibly relaxed.

'Eye. Interesting. Double-walled eye,' John said. He grabbed the tile I had just discarded and banged it hard on the table. '*Seung*.'

'Damn,' Leo said.

'You're silly to go for bamboo when Mr Chen is, Leo,' I said. 'It's like it's blown itself out on the coast. If I didn't know better, I'd think that it had passed over and finished.'

John nodded as he sorted his tiles. 'This will be interesting to watch. In about half an hour, the eye will pass over and the wind will pick up to the fierceness it was before. The change will be dramatic.'

'You think people will be stupid enough to go out?' Leo said.

John glanced sideways at him without smiling. 'We have a saying on the Celestial: if there's a stupid thing that can be done, then there's always a human who's stupid enough to do it. Where's Simone?'

'Last time I checked on her, she was in her room playing,' I said. 'She's fine.'

'When the eye passes over and the wind picks up, I will go into the training room for a while and I do not

357

wish to be disturbed,' John said quietly. 'It will be very unpleasant for me when the eye passes over. It will go from calm to furious very quickly. I won't be able to concentrate on anything.'

'What did you do before?' I said softly, wondering if maybe we should have let him move this typhoon after all.

'Go to the Mountain,' he said.

Michael listened but didn't say a word.

'Here it comes,' John said a short while later. 'Give me about an hour. Now that it's hit land it will dissipate quickly. The wind will only stay strong for two or three more hours.' His face went strange. 'Stay away from me. Don't come in.'

He gracefully hoisted himself to his feet and strode out. Leo and I shared a look.

'I agree,' Leo said. 'Next time we let him move it.'

'You can communicate telepathically, Emma?' Michael said with wonder.

I shook my head. 'With Leo, I don't need to.' Leo and I shared a smile.

There was a piercing, high-pitched scream from the hallway that went on forever. Simone.

All three of us threw ourselves up and rushed towards the sound. Both Leo and I knocked our chairs over.

John was hunched inside the door of the training room. Simone curled up against the back wall of the room, clutching her little sword, screaming. She took a huge breath and screamed again.

I squeezed past John, careful not to touch him, and went into the training room. Simone's eyes widened and she went silent. She scurried away from me.

'It's all right, Simone, it's us. What are you frightened

of?' I tried to approach her, but she kept moving away. 'Are there any demons nearby?'

Simone raised her little sword in front of her. 'Stay *away* from me!' She cast around frantically and saw Leo behind me. She dropped her sword, ran a huge detour around me, and threw herself into Leo's arms. 'Get them away, Leo, get them away from me.'

'Get who away, sweetheart? What's the matter?' Leo lifted her and put her on his hip. 'There's nothing here, it's just us.'

Simone buried her face into his chest. 'Get me away. Out. Please, Leo, away.'

Leo carried her out of the training room. John moved further into the room to let them through. Michael stood behind John, looking as confused as I felt.

'What was all that about?' I said.

'Talk about it later.' John's eyes turned inwards and unseeing and his voice became urgent. 'For now, out. Everybody. Leave me.' He pointed towards the door and I quickly went out, taking Michael and shutting the door behind me.

'What happened?' Michael said, baffled.

'I have absolutely no idea,' I said, just as bewildered. 'Hopefully Lord Xuan will tell us later.'

'I thought it would be cool to be able to control the weather,' Michael said. 'Now I'm not so sure.'

'Sometimes I think us ordinary humans have it easy,' I said. 'You want me to include you in the "us"?'

'Sometimes yes, sometimes no,' Michael said good-naturedly as we went to find Simone and Leo. 'I've tried doing things with metal, like he said. Nothing.'

'Don't try to rush it. If it comes, it comes.' We were at the door to Simone's room; she was clearly audible, sobbing inside. 'Michael, could you put the tiles away for me? I think maybe I should talk to Simone alone.'

'Yes, ma'am. Will you need me after that?'

'You can go and play after that, if the net connection is still up.'

'Thanks,' he said and turned back to the living room.

I opened the door to Simone's room and went in. Leo sat on Simone's little pink bedcover. Simone sat in his lap facing him, her head turned to one side on his chest, her eyes wide and glittering. He wrapped his arms protectively around her.

'Are you okay now, Simone?' I said gently. 'What happened? What did you see?'

Simone wriggled around to face me and smiled. She hopped out of Leo's lap and came to me, taking both of my hands in hers. 'Where were you, Emma? Why didn't you come?'

'I came straight here from the training room. Why were you frightened?'

'You weren't in the training room, Emma, there were monsters there.'

'Demons?' I said quietly. 'You know demons can't get in here. Your dad had the seals redone not long ago by a Grand Master.'

'Not demons. *Monsters.*'

'What's the difference?'

Simone went quiet, eyes wide. 'They were horrible.'

'I don't know either, Emma,' Leo said softly from the bed.

I sat cross-legged on the carpet and pulled Simone onto my knee, sideways to me so that I could talk to her. 'Okay,' I said firmly. 'There were horrible monsters in the training room. Is that right?'

Simone nodded, eyes still wide.

'You didn't see us when we came in.'

She shook her head. She gestured towards Leo. 'I saw Leo.'

'Your dad was at the doorway, Simone. He went in there to meditate.'

'My daddy wasn't there,' she said. 'It was a *monster*.'

Leo came and sat cross-legged on the carpet with us. 'Tell us what happened, Simone, right from the start. What were you doing in there anyway?'

'I was bored. You were playing. So I went to do a sword *kata*.'

'Is your dad letting you do that by yourself already?' I said quickly. 'I thought you weren't ready.'

Simone dropped her head and didn't say anything.

'You're not in trouble, sweetheart, we just need to sort this out,' I said, squeezing her around her waist. 'So you went in there to do a sword set. Then what happened?'

'The door opened and there was a *monster* there.'

I suddenly understood. 'Was it big and black and like a huge lizard with a strange body?'

Leo glanced sharply at me.

Simone nodded, and grinned widely. 'You saw it too!'

'Was it a big black turtle, Simone?' I said.

Her eyes went wide again. 'Yes,' she whispered.

I dropped my voice. 'Do you think it's possible that you saw your daddy the way he really is?'

'My daddy is *not* a *monster*, Emma.'

'He is a turtle, though, sweetheart,' I said. 'I think that's what you saw.'

'But what about the other one?' she said.

'What other one?' Leo said.

'After the ... *turtle* opened the door, I screamed. And another monster came in.' Simone gestured towards Leo. 'And then you came in, Leo, and I went to you.'

'What about me?' I said. 'I came in before Leo did.'

She shook her little head. 'No, Emma, you weren't there.' She explained patiently. 'The door opened. There was a big black turtle monster. Then a big black snake monster pushed past it and came towards me. It stopped and said something. Then Leo came in. I went around the snake monster and ran to Leo.'

The bottom fell out of my stomach. 'Did the snake monster say something like "Don't worry, it's only us"?'

She nodded. 'But I wasn't listening very well, Emma. I was really scared.'

My voice sounded dead. 'That was me.'

Leo studied me appraisingly. Then he smiled gently. 'All beyond me, Emma. Wait till Mr Chen comes out; he'll probably have some perfectly normal supernatural explanation for it.'

'For a moment I thought you were about to say "scientific explanation",' I said.

'I've given up hoping that things will make sense around this place,' Leo said. 'You survive from day to day in this crazy house.' He pulled himself to his feet. 'Listen,' he said from somewhere near the ceiling. 'Wind's started again.'

'Daddy hates it,' Simone said. 'He won't say, but it really hurts him.'

'Leo, could you mind Simone for me for a moment?' I popped Simone off my knee and guided her towards Leo. 'There's something I need to do.'

'Sure,' Leo said.

'Okay now, Simone?' I said kindly.

'I'm okay, Emma,' Simone said. 'You're probably right. The turtle was probably just Daddy, and the snake was probably just you.'

Leo stiffened and glanced down at me.

My stomach fell out again. I rose. 'Mind her, Leo,' I said, my voice strained. Leo nodded, but he watched me, his face expressionless.

I quietly went through the door to my room. I sat on my bed. I ran my hands through my hair.

'So I'm a snake, am I,' I said.

There was no reply.

I banged the ring on the end of the bed and the stone squawked. 'I was asleep!'

'Yeah, sure you were,' I said, not believing it for a minute. 'Am I a snake? And if you tell me I'm a perfectly normal human being, you'll do the grand tour of Hong Kong's shiny new sewerage system.'

'Lord Xuan has been waiting for this to happen. The child opened her Inner Eye. She has done it a good year before it was expected. She is extraordinarily talented, even for a half Shen. She brought it about by doing the sword *kata* alone.'

'And?'

'She saw those around her with a heightened vision. She saw her father's true essence.'

'She saw me as a snake, stone.'

'Perhaps she saw your true essence as well,' it said.

'So I'm a snake? I asked you that a moment ago, and you still haven't answered me.'

'That's because you don't want to hear the answer. And I don't want the grand tour, thank you.'

'Okay, let's try this from a different direction. Would it be possible to look at a perfectly normal human being, see their essence, and see it as a snake?'

'Yes, of course,' the stone said. 'Quite possible. Many people have a very strong animal nature. Like a totem. I'm surprised she didn't see Leo as a black lion, and Michael as a gold tiger.'

'About time you made some sense. So I have a very strong snake essence. Like a snake totem. Funny, I don't feel very . . .' I searched for the word, '. . . snaky.'

'You are very cold-blooded,' the stone said.

'Yes,' I agreed reluctantly.

363

'You love a turtle. A reptile,' the stone continued. 'You are a perfect match for each other.'

'Yes.' I could see where this was going.

'You are strong and fast and can be completely merciless when your loved ones are threatened.'

'I yield,' I said softly. 'I see your point.'

'What was your pet in Australia?'

'Now you're just rubbing it in.'

'Have I escaped the Hong Kong tour?' the stone said.

'Tell me when Lord Xuan will emerge and I may think about it,' I said.

'Give him some time. He is in great pain,' the stone said. 'Do not let the storms hit him directly in future, please, my Lady. He is too proud to tell you, but he is suffering greatly. It built up gradually before the eye hit and he could deal with it. But after the eye, it all hit him at the same time and it was excruciating for him. It will take him more energy to withdraw from the tumult than it would have taken for him to move the typhoon in the first place. But he was too proud to admit that he was suffering so horribly.'

'Thank you, stone, you can be really valuable when you want to be. He was just looking for an excuse when he said he'd move it for school, and I should have seen that.'

'You are very wise, Lady Emma, and that is another aspect of your serpent nature,' the stone said. 'Ask Lord Xuan about it. The nature of serpents. There is a great deal of depth to them. Many very positive aspects. Wisdom, healing, great strength and power. Dragons are serpents too, my Lady. To be a serpent is not necessarily a bad thing. Remember that your own true love is half Serpent himself.'

'Now *you* are being extremely wise. Thanks. I feel a million times better.'

The stone shot the question quickly at me. 'Even if

you were a serpent, could you ever hurt Simone, or Leo, or John?'

'Never,' I said firmly. 'And that's all that matters.'

'See? Wise. Ah Yat has made some breakfast. Go and eat, and then I suggest you take a nap while you wait for the other reptile to return. You were up awfully early this morning, and you are very tired.'

'Yes, Mother,' I said with a smile.

CHAPTER THIRTY-ONE

I woke up drowsy and dehydrated. I wandered out to find something to drink. I went into the kitchen; Leo sat at the table with some coffee. His eyes were swollen, making them appear even smaller; he'd been asleep too.

'Is everybody okay?' I said.

He nodded a reply. 'Simone's still sleeping. Mr Chen is asleep too. All the signals have been lowered. Things are starting to get back to normal.'

'Tea, my Lady?' Ah Yat said.

I nodded. 'Sow mei, please, a whole pot.'

Ah Yat busied herself with the teapot.

'Mr Chen said not to worry about what Simone said, it was normal,' Leo said. 'He said that she'd opened her Inner Eye or something like that, and that she could see inside people.'

Ah Yat gave me the tea and I nodded my thanks. I poured for myself. 'The stone in my ring said the same thing.'

Leo glanced at me sharply. 'Then why did Simone see you as a snake?'

'The stone thinks I have a snake totem.'

'What the hell is that supposed to mean?' Leo demanded, his voice slurring more than usual.

'Haven't you ever heard of the concept of a totem?' I said. 'Oh come *on*, Leo, you're joking, right?'

He just shook his head. He didn't smile.

I decided to be brisk and scientific about it. 'Certain cultures believe that people can have animal spirits that either dwell inside them or alongside them, that guide and protect them. They have a special affinity to that animal.' I eyed Leo sideways. 'Black Lion.'

'That's just a stupid nickname the demons thought up, 'cause they don't like the fact that I'm a perfectly ordinary human who can take them down,' Leo said. 'Nothing more. Certainly not one of these totem things.'

The stone in the ring broke in. 'You are courageous in the face of overwhelming odds. You protect your family against any attacker. You travel alone, without a partner. You are without peer as a warrior. And you are as black as night. You are a Black Lion, Leo. You even bear the name.'

'They call me the Lion *because* of the stupid name,' Leo said. 'I wish my mother had never gone through that stupid astrology phase.'

'Your star sign is Leo as well?' I said, incredulous.

'And he was born in the year of the Tiger,' the stone added wryly.

'I know exactly how old you are now, Leo. And I know your birthday to within a month. You're older than I thought you were.' I grinned. 'You're overdue for a really big birthday party from last year. I'm going to find out your proper birthday, and I'm going to buy you a cake.' I giggled with delight and pushed him. 'You're middle-aged. Over the hill. Getting old, Leo.'

Leo ignored my ribbing. 'I'm called the Lion because my name is Leo. I'm called Leo because that's when I was born. It's just a chain of coincidences.'

'There's no such thing as a coincidence, Leo,' John said kindly as he entered the kitchen. His hair was damp from the shower and he looked tired. 'Haven't you worked that out by now?' He plonked himself down at the table. 'Tea, tikuanyin,' he ordered without looking at Ah Yat, and she busied herself with another teapot. 'August fourteenth. Tiger.' He thought for a moment. 'Nineteen sixty-two.' He turned to Leo. 'She's quite right.'

Leo stiffened. 'Thank you *very much*.'

I pushed Leo again. 'Damn, I missed it, it's already September. You were really quiet. You are *still* getting a cake, though, and it'll have forty-one big candles on it.'

John laughed gently and I studied him, concerned. 'Are you all right? We wouldn't have put you through that if it didn't make any difference. You should have told us it would be that bad.'

He shrugged. 'There is very little chance that another of that power will hit us again in a human lifetime.'

'Simone opened her Inner Eye and saw your true essence,' I said, studying him closely. 'You scared her to death.'

He shrugged again, his voice mild. 'I have never seen a human child open the Eye at such a young age. We will turn it on small demons this afternoon and see what level she is capable of destroying.' He glanced sharply at me. 'You will come and try it as well. We haven't done this with you yet.'

'She saw me as a snake, John,' I said quietly.

'Did she see Leo as a lion?' John said, and Leo hissed under his breath. 'That's what he was arguing about, isn't it? That all of his lion alignment is just a coincidence?'

'It *is*,' Leo said fiercely.

'And I will repeat myself,' John said, spreading his hands. 'There is no such thing as a coincidence.'

'She didn't see Leo as a lion, but she saw me as a snake, John,' I said desperately. 'She saw me as a *snake*.'

'And?' John said.

'Just how much snake am I?'

'Probably just enough to be beautiful,' John said. 'Maybe it's the reptile in you that loves the reptile in me.' He smiled. 'We've been through this before, Emma. You know what's important. Don't worry yourself about it; we need to have these children organised for school. And if we can get Simone using her Inner Eye, then she will be even more prepared. I may have Michael there this afternoon as well to do the exercises.'

Ah Yat presented him with his tea and he poured for himself. 'I just thank the heavens that it's all over.'

'You should have *told* me it was so bad,' I said, exasperated. 'If we'd known, we would have let you move it.'

'Oh, I thank you, most gracious Lady. You would grant me your permission.'

Leo made a soft sound of amusement.

I looked John right in the eye. 'You. Me. Staves. Training room. No mercy, no quarter, no rules. No limits; but no touching. I can take you.' I tapped my fingertip on the table for emphasis, the edge of my voice very sharp. 'First one to break their opponent's staff wins.'

'I can take both of you at once,' John said mildly.

Leo shot to his feet. 'Let's go. You're on.'

'Go and warm up and practise to prepare for me,' John said, raising his tea cup. 'I will be in there as soon as I've finished my tea. I will defeat your combined attacks and break your staves within three minutes, unarmed, without a warm-up, and without touching either of you, or I am not Pak Tai, God of Martial Arts.'

Leo and I shared a look. Then we both grinned. 'Excellent.'

It only took about twenty seconds. He was definitely God of Martial Arts.

Later that afternoon Simone and I were drawing pictures together when there was a tap on the door. 'Come on in, Michael,' Simone said.

Michael sidled in. He hated going into Simone's room; too girly for him. 'Lord Xuan is ready for us,' he said.

Simone and I rose together.

'You think I'll see the Turtle again, Emma?' Simone said.

'Are you scared of it, sweetheart? It's just your dad.' I gestured towards Michael. 'You're not scared of his dad in True Form.'

'His dad isn't big and black and scaly and horrible.'

'No,' I said with a smile. 'He's big and white and furry and horrible.'

Michael didn't say anything but I could see that he was delighted.

Simone hesitated at the training room door. She hadn't seen her father since, and was obviously worried. I took her hand and opened the door. Her little hand clutched mine.

John waited patiently for us with his hands clasped behind his back. He studied Simone carefully when she came in, his face expressionless. Simone stopped and gazed at him. They studied each other for some time. Simone's hand still clutched mine.

Then she dropped my hand and ran to her father with her arms up. She hit him hard and he hoisted her. She wrapped her little arms around his neck and held him very tight. He clamped his eyes shut, his face fierce, as he held her.

I moved to guide Michael out and leave them. 'Don't go, Emma,' Simone said, turning in her father's arms. They both watched me calmly. 'I'm okay.'

John nodded. I shrugged, closed the door, and motioned for Michael to follow me into the middle of the room.

'Come and sit,' John said, and we sat cross-legged together in the centre of the training room. 'First we will look at what we will do.' He gestured towards me. 'You can do it already, Emma, you help Michael. I will help Simone.' His voice became brisk. 'The Inner Eye is your vision of the world around you that doesn't require your physical eyes. Once you open it, it is very useful. You can see past obstacles, and,' he looked pointedly at Simone, 'see the inner essence of other creatures.'

Simone nodded, wide-eyed.

'Lady Emma has discovered some other uses; we may try them later. Simone,' he said kindly, 'that's what you did before. You opened your Inner Eye. You could see right through things.'

'I saw you, Daddy,' she said. 'I saw the Turtle.'

'How do you do it, my Lord?' Michael said. 'How difficult is it?'

'You may not be able to do it, you are quite young,' John said. Michael seemed about to protest, then subsided. 'Normally even half Shen must wait until adulthood. We will see what you can do. I think you may be able to. Emma will show you how to do it.' John took Simone's hand. I took Michael's hand. 'Just open your Eye, Emma. Do it in front of Michael, see if he can follow you. I will do the same for Simone when you're done.'

I opened my Eye and Michael watched me attentively. It was an unusual feeling; normally it was me watching somebody else. I turned the Eye on John to show Michael. I didn't see the Turtle at all; I just saw the Dark Lord part of him, like a smaller version of the Celestial Form. Michael gasped. I internally reached out and touched him, comforting, without physically moving at all. It was like there was a second set of people there: our physical beings and our spiritual ones.

'Can I turn it on Simone?' I said softly.

'No, don't attempt that,' John said, and his Celestial Form spoke. 'She's not ready for that yet. Emma,' his voice became more forceful, 'I am going to turn my Eye onto you. Be ready, it will feel very strange. If it hurts, tell me and I will stop immediately.'

I nodded, and the Celestial Form smiled through its thin black beard, still with John's eyes.

'Close your Eye, Emma, and sit very still. Warn me if it hurts.'

I closed off the extra senses and opened my physical eyes. Michael opened his eyes as well. He smiled at me. 'Cool.'

I waited quietly. Simone's little face was rigid with concentration as she watched her father. John's face was serene, his golden skin glowing. He looked me right in the eyes, smiled slightly at me, and I felt it.

It was like static electricity, all the way through me. It was like touching an electric wire, but it didn't stop. A continuous tingling spark ran through me, slightly unpleasant, but not painful.

'Are you all right, Emma?' John said softly, still smiling gently. 'I'm not hurting you? Tell me if I am.'

'It doesn't hurt,' I said. 'It feels weird, but I'm okay.' I hesitated. 'What do I look like?'

'Are you a snake?' John said, voicing my unspoken question. 'Is she a snake, Simone?'

'No, Emma, you're a beautiful lady,' Simone said, her voice full of awe. 'You're really beautiful.' Her voice softened. 'You love us a lot. Me and Daddy.'

'Stay still, Emma, let's let Simone try by herself,' John said, and the electricity snapped off. He let go of her hand.

I remained still, to let Simone see me. She closed her eyes and her face went slack as she concentrated.

Nothing happened.

'You're trying too hard, sweetheart,' John said. 'Just relax. Like you were doing the sword set. Don't try, just do it.'

Still no tingling.

Simone frowned.

John took her hand. 'Let me.' He concentrated, holding her hand.

The tingling went through me, then stopped.

'Now you,' John said, releasing her hand.

Simone's face went rigid with concentration.

The force of the shock knocked me over. My head hit the floor with a smack. I was held paralysed on the floor with the electricity going through me.

'Let her up, Simone,' John said quietly, 'you may hurt her.'

The electricity stopped. 'Sorry, Emma,' Simone said. 'I don't know what I did.'

'Why did that happen?' I said as I pulled myself back up. 'That didn't happen when I came in before and she saw me as a snake. I didn't feel anything.'

'She only had it half-open when we came in, but her vision was clear,' John said. 'This time she had it open all the way, but her vision wasn't as clear. When you are more experienced you will understand. Are you okay? You didn't hit your head too hard?'

I shook my head. 'I'm fine.' Michael watched me with a grin of mischievous delight. 'You will keep,' I said. 'We haven't done it to you yet.'

'She has a powerful Eye and she hasn't any control over it yet,' John said. 'Once we have control over it, we can choose the level of effect we have on you. I could quite easily kill you if I turned it completely onto you.' He smiled gently at Simone. 'I wasn't expecting anything quite so powerful out of you yet, love. It'll be interesting to see what you can blow up with that little Eye of yours.'

'Whoa, really?' Michael said, aghast. 'My dad could kill somebody just by looking at them?'

'Once the Tiger was attacked on the Earthly Plane by a band of robbers in the West. This was a long time ago,' John said, remembering, 'about a thousand years ago. He was riding alone. He was attacked by a whole group of them, about twenty. He turned his Eye on them and killed them all in one go.' He smiled grimly. 'Humans are easy.'

'He didn't give them a chance at all?' I said.

John shook his head.

'You were right, Emma,' Michael said. 'He is a bastard.'

'*Lady* Emma,' John corrected.

'Just Emma,' I said. 'He's family.'

'I suppose he is,' John said. 'And it's his turn.' He gestured towards Michael. 'On me first. We don't want to hurt the ladies.'

'Do you want me to show you again, Michael?' I said.

Michael nodded. I took his hand and showed him again how to do it.

'Try to open it more, Emma,' John said. 'That's a pathetic attempt if ever I saw one. You won't be able to kill anything with that.'

I huffed at the insult, and tried to open the Eye further.

'Try looking deeper inside me,' John said. 'Look for the Turtle. It is in there, believe me.'

I tried hard. I managed a little more. Not very much more, though.

'I suppose that's the best you can do,' John said, sounding slightly disappointed. 'Oh well, humans aren't supposed to be able to do it anyway.'

'Aren't they?' Michael said. 'Then how come Lady Emma can?'

'No idea,' John said. 'We'll find out eventually. No great hurry. We have all the time in the world. Now, Michael, you try. Look for the Turtle in me.'

I closed my Eye and released Michael's hand. I waited and watched him.

His face relaxed as he concentrated. He closed his eyes. Then his face cleared and he opened his physical eyes. 'That is the most incredible thing I have ever seen.'

'*Don't look at Emma,*' John said sharply. 'With an Eye like that you could easily kill her. Don't look at Simone either, I don't think she could handle it. Excellent,' he added with satisfaction. 'Well done. Close it quickly before you hurt somebody.'

Michael's eyes snapped back and he grinned at me. 'He is,' he said, pointing at John, 'the ugliest damn reptile I have ever seen in my life.' His face changed and he looked horrified. He bobbed his head. 'No offence intended, my Lord, forgive my forwardness.'

'No offence taken, Michael,' John said. 'I happen to agree with you.'

'I want to see, Daddy,' Simone said.

'It's a little scary, sweetheart,' he said. 'You may not like it. It made you really scared before, remember?'

She nodded, her face serious. 'I want to see anyway.'

'Go and sit next to Emma while you do it,' John said. 'She can hold onto you.'

Simone nodded, came to me, and sat carefully in my lap. She reached down and took one of my hands, holding it tightly. I wrapped my other arm around her middle and she put her arm on top of mine. She nodded. 'I want to try.'

She went very still in my lap. Then her Eye opened onto her father. She held my hand even tighter. I saw him as he usually appeared; I also saw the small Celestial Form at the same time, through her.

'Open wider,' John said. 'Put more into it. Come on, Simone. Michael can do it, why can't you?'

I nearly laughed out loud at how much that stung her. She stiffened, and threw all of herself into it.

John wavered. He shimmered. He grew and went black.

Simone squeaked and shot to her feet. John snapped back to normal; I could no longer see him through her Eye.

Simone was completely rigid. Her breathing accelerated. I reached to hold her hand again, but she pulled it away. She didn't want to hold my hand. She was concentrating.

'Control, Simone,' John said, watching her intensely.

Simone took some quick, deep breaths.

'Are you okay?' I said.

She nodded, still rigid.

'What does he look like?' I said.

'He's not ugly, he's *beautiful*. You're mean, Michael.' She stiffened even more. She gasped, then screamed very quietly, almost a squeak of despair. '*Why didn't you tell me, Daddy?*' she wailed, then dashed out the door of the training room. 'Leo! Leo!' she yelled, and Leo rushed to comfort her, his deep voice rumbling.

'What?' I said.

'She knows,' John said, his voice full of anguish. His eyes were dark and burning, his face was expressionless. 'She saw. She saw it all.'

'Oh dear God, no,' I whispered. 'No.'

CHAPTER THIRTY-TWO

And there I was again, outside Simone's room, listening to her sobbing in Leo's arms.

John and I shared a look, and I nodded. This time he needed to talk to her. He rapped on the door and went in. I gestured for Michael to leave, and I went to the kitchen. I sat at the table and put my head in my hands.

Leo came into the kitchen and sat across from me. 'This is getting monotonous,' he said. 'You people have to stop torturing that poor little girl.'

Ah Yat presented Leo with coffee and me with tea without being asked, and we both nodded to her.

'What happened?' Leo said. 'She wouldn't tell me. Mr Chen just walked in, and she went to him, and they sent me out. Did he scare her again?'

Michael came in and sat with us. 'What was all that about? She didn't seem scared of the Turtle this time, she said it was beautiful.'

'She saw right through him,' I said sadly, 'and saw that he's leaving.'

Leo inhaled sharply. 'No.'

I explained for Michael. 'She didn't know that he has a limited time with us. She thought she'd be with him forever. She knew he'd leave eventually, but she thought that she'd be able to go with him and live on the Mountain with him. She didn't really understand the situation.' I ran my hands through my hair. 'Now she does.'

Michael threw himself backwards and flung one arm over the back of his chair. 'That really sucks.'

Emma and Leo, come into the dining room. We will tell all.

Leo and I shared a look. We rose and went out without saying a word.

Michael silently watched us go.

Somebody pick up some tissues on the way.

I went across to the living room and grabbed the box on the coffee table for when Simone spilt her drinks. She hadn't fallen down or spilt anything in a while.

Leo held the dining room door and I went in. John and Simone were already sitting at the table. Simone's face was streaked with tears. I put the tissues on the table and sat next to her. She grabbed some tissues and wiped her eyes. She hopped off the chair and climbed into my lap facing the table. I held her close and kissed the top of her head.

Leo sat next to John, his face grim.

John leaned his arms on the table and studied his hands. 'I'm sorry, Simone, we thought you were too young to know, so we didn't tell you. Now that Emma and Leo are here, I'll tell you everything.'

Simone sniffled. She didn't reply.

'You saw that I only have a limited time. That's right. Even with Aunty Kwan filling me with energy, I will lose it all eventually and I'll have to go.'

Simone shook once with a huge gasping sob, then went still.

'I don't know how long I'll be gone, sweetheart, but I promised Emma I'll come back for her. So that means that I'll come back for you too.'

Simone's voice was tiny. 'You don't know how long you'll be gone?'

He shook his head. 'I'm sorry, darling.'

'Why don't you just go to the Mountain and take me with you?'

'I can't. Firstly, most of the Mountain is gone, and it'll take a long time to rebuild. There's no power there for me until I come back and put it there. It's gone.'

She nodded and sniffled again. She understood.

'Second, a child can only enter the Celestial Plane with protection. The protection of the child's mother. You can't go there because your mother is dead. You can't go until you're grown-up.'

'I can go with Emma,' Simone said firmly, grabbing my hand and clutching it. 'She's like my mother.'

John looked me in the eyes and smiled. My heart twisted. He turned back to Simone. 'I wish I could take both of you.'

'I'll have Leo and Emma to look after me when you go. We'll wait for you together,' Simone said.

Leo sighed, then ran his hand over his head and dropped his hand onto the table. 'Do you know what AIDS is, Simone?' he said gently.

Simone nodded. 'Emma told me about that,' she said, her little face serious. 'It's a bad disease. If you catch it, you die. Every time. It takes a long time for you to die, but you always die.'

Leo smiled gratefully and I nodded.

'I have that, Simone. Your dad is keeping me alive. When he's gone ...' his voice thickened and his speech slurred even more, 'I'm going to die.'

'You're both going?'

Leo and John both nodded.

'That's why you got Michael, isn't it?' Simone said. 'I *hate* him!'

'Don't hate Michael, sweetheart,' Leo said. 'I chose him. He's the best person to do my job when I'm gone.'

Simone's voice was cruel. 'I *hate* you, Daddy. I *hate* you, Leo. I hate Emma, I hate Michael, I hate *everybody*!' She started to sob and I turned her around in my arms to hold her. 'I hate the *world*!' she wailed into my chest.

I let her cry for a while. She needed to let it out of her system. Leo and John sat quietly and waited for her as well.

When she had stopped sobbing she sat very still and silent, her head on my chest. 'Are you okay, sweetheart?' I said.

She didn't move or speak.

Do you think I should get her professional counselling? John said silently.

'Get Ms Kwan,' I said.

'I hate Ms Kwan,' Simone said, her voice muffled by my shirt. Her little arms clutched me tighter. 'I hate her.'

Kwan Yin appeared next to me. 'Come with me, Simone,' she said softly. She held out her hand to Simone.

Simone moved away slightly and clutched me even tighter. 'Go away.'

'I have something to show you.' Ms Kwan's hand didn't move from next to me. 'Would you like to see my Garden?'

Simone lifted her head off my chest to look at Ms Kwan. 'No.' She dropped her head again, looking away. 'Go away.'

'Would you like to see my Garden, Emma?' Ms Kwan said kindly. 'Would you like to come and see it?'

'There is nothing I'd like more, Lady,' I said. 'Can an ordinary person like me go?'

'The Garden *is* for ordinary people like you,' Ms Kwan said, amused. 'It's the ordinary people who need it the most.'

'Can I go, Simone?' I said to the little tawny head on my chest. 'Will you be all right with Leo and your dad?'

'If you leave me here without you I will never talk to you again,' Simone said thickly. 'I won't let you go without me.'

'Well then, you'll have to come, won't you?' I said gently. 'Let's go and have a look at Aunty Kwan's Garden.'

Simone nodded into my chest without saying anything. I reached out and took Ms Kwan's hand.

Take your time, John said as we disappeared. The last thing I saw were his blazing dark eyes.

There was no dizziness or blackout. We just went straight from the living room to the Garden.

It was tiny, only about a hundred metres to a side. There was a large pond in the middle, with carefully trimmed flowering shrubs all around it. A couple of open pavilions with benches overlooked the pond, hugging the high stone wall surrounding the Garden.

We were the only ones there: Ms Kwan, Simone and me. Ms Kwan had materialised us at a table in one of the pavilions.

Ms Kwan gestured and some tea appeared in front of us. She poured.

'Are we on the Celestial Plane?' I said.

'No,' she said. 'You are nowhere at all.'

'Good,' Simone said into my chest.

'Your father is a big, black, ugly, mean Turtle,' Ms Kwan said gently.

Simone didn't move or speak.

'He really hates you,' Ms Kwan said, her voice still gentle.

Simone still didn't move.

'He'll go away and leave you all alone,' Ms Kwan said.

Simone shifted slightly in my lap. Her little hand moved on my arm, then held it tightly again.

'Leo will get sick, and die, and then he'll be gone too,' Ms Kwan said.

Simone jammed her head harder into my chest.

'Ms Kwan ...' I said, but she smiled and waved me down. *I know what I am doing.*

'And then Emma will go and leave you as well. You'll be all alone.'

Simone started to sob quietly into my chest and I held her tight.

'Emma will never leave me,' Simone said through the gasps.

'That's right,' I said.

Simone suddenly spun in my lap to glare at Ms Kwan. 'My daddy doesn't hate me, he *loves* me.'

'But he's leaving you.'

'He's staying for *me*. To look after *me*. Because he *loves* me.'

'But he'll be gone in the end.'

'I know,' Simone gasped. 'But he's staying until I'm okay.' She glared at Ms Kwan again. 'Do you know how hard it is for him to stay? It hurts him. He's really weak. He's staying. He's staying *just for me*.'

'He'll be gone for a long time.'

'He'll come back for us,' Simone said fiercely. 'He promised.'

'Yes, he did,' I said.

'Emma has to wait for him too. It's hard for her too. You're *mean*, Kwan Yin,' Simone said.

'Leo will die before your daddy comes back,' Kwan Yin said.

Simone didn't say anything.

'Come with me for a walk, Simone,' Ms Kwan said. 'We need to talk.'

'Is Emma safe if I leave her here alone?' Simone said.

'Yes,' Ms Kwan said. 'She can enjoy the Garden.'

I opened my arms so that Simone could jump down. 'Go, Simone. I'll wait here for you.'

'Have a walk around the Garden,' Simone said. 'I think you'll be surprised. I'm going to talk to Aunty Kwan.'

'Have a walk, Emma,' Ms Kwan said. 'Do not be concerned about becoming lost. We will be able to find you, wherever you are. Enjoy.'

The Garden was tiny. 'I don't think I'll get lost.'

'Come on, Kwan Yin, let's have a walk,' Simone said, taking Kwan Yin's hand and leading her away.

I looked out over the pond, then back to Simone and Kwan Yin. They were gone.

Use this time for contemplation, Emma, Kwan Yin said. *It is the last you will have for a while.*

I rose and walked down to the pond. Some koi that had been hovering near the surface disappeared under the water with a plop. There was a path around the pond and I followed it. A couple of graceful willows straddled the water. Some gravel was strewn at the edge of the pond, making a tiny rocky beach.

I followed the path past a stone lantern under a bush and turned the corner. Some stepping stones led me across a miniature stream that splashed into the pond.

When I had carefully navigated the stepping stones, I looked up to follow the path along the wall, but there was a round opening, a moon gate, in front of me. I followed the path through it.

I was in a dense forest of pines. The wind whispered through the needles high above me. I stopped. The silence was complete, except for the whisper of the needles. There wasn't another living thing for miles; I could sense it. A feeling of absolute calm tranquillity filled me as I walked along the gravel path through the towering pines.

I was on a sandy beach next to a huge, placid lake. Blue mountains softened the horizon on the other side of the lake. A couple of deer came to the edge of the lake to drink, and ignored me as I walked past them. The pines came almost to the edge of the water. There was a small pavilion, set with tea, on a tiny promontory. The tea was still hot. I sat and drank for a while.

I walked back along the beach. The lake became rice fields. I didn't even see it change. The water glittered through the rice stalks. I was still alone. On the other side of the rice fields were the mountains of China; all vertical, straight up and down, thousands of them, just like a traditional Chinese painting.

I walked further and found myself beside another lake, this time with the vertical mountains in the distance. A zig-zagging walkway guided me to a pavilion in the centre of the lake. The edge of the lake was draped with willow trees. Some ducks flew in and landed next to the pavilion. I sat in the pavilion for a while.

I went back along the walkway to the edge of the lake. A couple of storks eyed me warily from the bank, but didn't fly away.

My heart leapt. I was on top of a mountain. I could see clouds halfway down the slopes a long way below me. The brilliantly blue sea glittered at the base of the mountain.

A pavilion with a table and chairs was set for tea. Ms Kwan gestured for me to sit with her.

The sound of children at play wafted from below. Simone played with some other children in a playground in front of us.

'Thank you,' I said softly.

'You are most welcome,' Ms Kwan said. 'Any time.' She watched the children. 'She will be fine now.'

We sat in silence for a while.

CHAPTER THIRTY-THREE

'So your trip to Europe was quite eventful,' Ms Kwan said as she put down her tea cup.

I watched Simone playing and sighed. 'You could say that.'

'Your family were unharmed?'

I nodded. 'But the things that attacked us were apparently very strange.'

She sat slightly more upright. 'Strange? In what way?'

I hesitated. She was obviously concerned. 'Zhu Que said something about asking you to sortie. But Xuan Wu said he didn't want to endanger you.'

Kwan Yin refilled her tea cup, and then mine. 'What attacked you, dear?'

'Red humanoids, about level fifteen. Low-level birds. And fake fire elementals.'

She stiffened as she raised her tea. 'What do you mean, *fake*?'

I took a sip of the tea, trying to remain calm. 'Zhu Que said that they were some sort of new demon hybrid. Created specifically for John.'

'She must have been furious.'

'I'm surprised my sister has any grass left in her backyard. Some parts of it were quite badly scorched.'

'Zhu Que was right. I should go and have a look.'

I suddenly realised that she was talking about visiting the demons on their home turf to gather information for us. 'Wait! What if they catch you?'

She smiled. 'They haven't caught me yet.'

I quickly reached out to grab her hand. 'Please don't do this unless we don't have any other alternative. I hate to think what they'd do to you if they caught you.'

'They've been compiling a list of what they want to do to me for over a thousand years,' Kwan Yin said mildly. 'You have no idea.'

'And if they caught you down there, they would have you?'

She nodded, smiling sadly.

'How do you make sure they don't know you're there, Ms Kwan?' I said, then stopped. 'If it's a secret, you don't have to tell me.'

'I take the form of a demon myself,' she said. 'My demon form has become rather famous. Occasionally I travel the Halls to comfort some of the longer-term residents. I must be very careful.'

I dropped my head onto my hands. 'I should never have mentioned this to you. If I'd known what it meant, I would have stayed quiet. No wonder John was so loath to call on you.'

'I would love to know where the hybrids came from though, Emma,' Ms Kwan said. 'Whoever managed to create a false elemental is certainly worth watching.'

'Zhu Que said that Simon Wong ... that One Two Two wouldn't be able to do it, and that he had to have had help.'

She sighed and took a sip of her tea. 'She was quite correct.'

Simone came to me and wriggled into my lap. Kwan Yin gestured slightly and a cup of apple juice appeared on the table in front of us.

'Thank you,' Simone said and took a noisy slurp.

'You sound like a blocked drain drinking like that, Simone,' I teased.

She lifted the cup and slurped it as noisily as she could.

'You are a little monster,' I said. 'Are we all right to go home now? School will be starting tomorrow.'

'Simone,' Ms Kwan said, 'call me if you need me. Any time you want to talk to me, I am here.'

'Thanks, Kwan Yin,' Simone said, sounding much more mature than her five years. 'But I'll be okay with Emma.'

I squeezed Simone around her waist. 'We'll be just fine together, waiting for your dad to come back for both of us.'

'*And* we'll find a way for Leo to get better too,' Simone said with confidence.

'I don't think we will, sweetheart,' I said sadly to the top of her head. 'I think we should enjoy being with Leo as much as we can now.'

'I cannot say what the future holds,' Kwan Yin said. 'But I can tell you one thing, Ladies of the House of the North, and that is that the Black Lion is truly noble and well on the way to becoming a Worthy.'

Simone put her arms on mine where I held her around her middle and we squeezed each other with delight.

'How can we help him, Aunty Kwan?' Simone said breathlessly, still clutching my arms.

'You already are,' Ms Kwan said. 'Every minute you spend with him, you help him to approach the goal that he has no personal desire to reach.'

'He doesn't want to?' I said.

She shook her head sadly. 'He is a true warrior.' She shifted to silent speech so that Simone wouldn't hear. *He lives as if he is already dead. His life has no value to him, save as a means to serve. He has no desire to live once his Lord has departed. The Japanese have a word for such as he: Samurai.*

'I think you're right,' I said softly, my heart breaking. 'If they found a cure for him tomorrow, he would be delighted, because then he could make the sacrifice of staying on to care for us.'

'I am glad you understand,' Ms Kwan said. 'You have adapted to our ways remarkably well.'

I had to smile at that. 'Oh, I don't know, Ms Kwan. I still won't knock people over to get a seat on the MTR.'

Simone giggled, and wriggled in my lap.

'You're okay now, Simone, aren't you?' I said to the top of her head.

'Can we go back home now? I want to get ready for school tomorrow,' Simone said. 'I want to give my dad and Leo a big hug, and then I want to beat Michael at Monopoly again.'

'You've been beating Michael at Monopoly?'

'Yep.' She nodded under my chin. 'He complains all the time that I'm better than him. He's really bad at it.'

Ms Kwan smiled, nodded, and we were back in the living room. Simone leapt off my lap and raced down the hall to find her father. The training room door opened and Simone squealed with delight. I heard them talking together. I sighed.

Leo came out of the kitchen, saw me and Ms Kwan sitting together in the living room, and smiled. He heard John and Simone talking happily together, and his smile softened. He went quietly back into the kitchen.

Michael appeared in the hall. 'Hello, Ms Kwan.' Then, to me: 'Is everything fixed now?'

'All fixed,' I said, and smiled. 'Are you ready for school tomorrow? Got your stuff together?'

Michael grinned. 'Funny thing, but I'm actually happy about going.'

He turned and went back down the hallway. 'Hey, Simone, want to play?' he called.

'Nah, I'll do some sword with Daddy,' Simone said from down the hall.

'You want to join us, Michael?' John said. 'We'll pull some demons out and do some Inner Eye work as well.'

'Wait for me!' I called to them.

'Okay, Emma, hurry up,' Simone said.

'This is an extraordinary household,' Ms Kwan said. Her expression became wry and she gestured. Five gold coins appeared on the coffee table. 'How many do you have now, Emma?'

'I'm putting them together with red thread and making a lantern out of them,' I said. 'By mid-autumn festival next year, I'll have a lantern made of gold.' I suddenly remembered. 'We still have some moon cakes left over from the festival this year — do you want to take some with you?'

'Are they vegetarian?' she said. 'Many of them have a large amount of animal fat in them with the lotus paste.'

'These ones are nice vegetarian Snowy ones with a soft white crust,' I said. 'Not too rich and heavy at all, and no salted duck-egg yolks in the middle. They're quite good, but as usual John bought too many. We have a couple of spare tins in the fridge. Take one with you.'

Kwan Yin rose and I stood with her. 'Thank you, Emma, that would be lovely.'

We went into the kitchen together. Leo was sitting at the table with a cup of coffee. He rose when we entered. Ms Kwan gestured dismissively. 'No need, Leo, we are family.' He sat again.

I went to the fridge and pulled out one of the moon cake tins. It was made of light metal with a delightful decoration of an ancient painting of the moon on the lid. I opened it to make sure that Michael hadn't attacked it yet. The four moon cakes were untouched; still in their plastic wrap. They were round and about ten centimetres across. The design of the moon was clearly visible on the flaky white crust of each cake.

I checked the side of the tin: these ones had lotus seed paste inside and definitely no egg yolks. John said that he liked the yolks, even though he couldn't eat them: they made a symbolic moon when the cakes were cut. I didn't — the yolks were too salty and rich for me.

In the centre of the plastic tray holding the cakes was a clear pouch with a plastic knife and some cocktail forks for eating the cakes outside under the moon.

I put the lid back on and held it out to Kwan Yin, who gracefully took it, nodding to me.

'Give her two,' Leo said from where he sat at the kitchen table with his back to us. 'Get rid of the damn things. Everybody's sick to death of the sight of them, and they're so rich that you can't eat more than a quarter of one anyway.'

'Do you want another tin?' I said. 'He's right, you know. Simone won't eat any more, and Michael and Leo have had enough. And you know how many calories these things have; if I eat them they go straight to my hips.'

Both Leo and Ms Kwan laughed softly.

'Do these pants make my ass look big?' Leo squeaked in a falsetto without turning around. 'No,' he said in a deeper voice, 'but the big hole in the back of them gives a good view of it.'

I sidled over to Leo and flicked the back of his bald head with my finger.

'Ouch,' he said, and rubbed his head. 'Give Ms Kwan another one.'

I pulled a tin out, checked the side, checked that Michael hadn't attacked it, and handed it to her.

'You have another couple of coins on the table out there for you and Leo, Emma,' Ms Kwan said. 'You'll have more than one lantern for the next festival. Call me if you need me.'

'Wait!' I stopped her before she could disappear. 'Please don't do anything unless we absolutely have to. Right now they're quiet. No need for you to put yourself in danger for us. Okay?'

She smiled sadly, nodded, and disappeared.

Hey, Emma! Simone squealed right into my ear. *I just blew up a level three demon with my Inner Eye! Come and have a go!*

'Bastard,' I said quietly as I went out.

'I heard that,' Leo said behind me.

Both Leo and I took the kids to school on their first day. We went in the big car. They sat silent and intimidated in the back in their new, stiff green uniforms, school bags at their feet.

There were a lot of cars outside the school, and the security guard made sure that each vehicle stopped only long enough to let children out, explaining that if parents wanted to come inside they would have to park away from the school. It was chaos.

As we approached, the security guard waved us on. Leo stopped the car and I opened the window to speak to the guard. 'We have a permanent space in the car park,' I said. 'Let us in.'

He smiled, shook his head, and waved us on.

I looked around for the head guard. Obviously they had put extra staff on for the first day. I couldn't see him, so opened the car door and hopped out.

'Go around the block and come back,' I said to Leo.

He nodded as I closed the door, and pulled away.

The security guard smiled patiently at me. 'Just drop children, no parking.'

I ignored him and went to the guard post. Nobody there. I saw the head security guard, Paul, minding the entrance. He was a very nice Filipino who spoke good English; he'd been informed about us and knew that we had a permanent space in the car park. He saw me and I waved to him.

'Hi, Paul,' I said cheerfully as I approached him. 'Is our space ready?'

'All ready,' he said. 'Where your car?'

I pointed. 'That guard moved us on, wouldn't let us in.' I smiled at Paul again. 'Will you let us in?'

'Sure.' Paul went to the guard and told him the situation. The Mercedes appeared as they were talking, and both security guards ushered Leo into the car park, pointing out the space that they had allocated for us.

'Thanks, guys,' I said to the guards. I smiled, trying to turn on the charm. 'Most appreciated.'

'No problem, Mrs Chen,' Paul said.

I froze completely. My heart leapt into my throat. Of course, that was the name on the paperwork. But it felt so damn *good* to be called that. I shook the feeling off; things to do.

'Just Emma, guys,' I said, 'and I'm not Mrs Chen. Miss Donahoe. But just Emma, nanny.' I pointed at the car. 'Leo, driver.'

'Okay,' Paul said. 'Sorry.'

'Well,' I said, 'better get these kids fixed up. Thanks, guys. See you later.'

They both smiled and nodded as I returned to the car.

I heard shouting behind me and turned. A Chinese woman in the back of a large black Mercedes driven by a Filipino driver had seen us park and was arguing loudly with the guards that she should be allowed to park as well.

Michael and Simone pulled their bags out of the car, assisted by Leo.

'We Retainers will drop the Princess in her classroom and check the area, then we'll drop the on-site guard to his station,' I said cheerfully.

'Yes, ma'am,' both Michael and Leo said, but Simone scowled and put her hands on her hips. 'You're the *nanny*, Leo's the *driver*, Michael's my *cousin,* and I'm *not* a princess.'

'Maybe this will work out after all,' Leo said as he watched the children entering the school.

A large number of mothers were hovering outside the first graders' classroom and I had to fight my way through them with Simone. Leo and Michael hung back and waited. Simone hesitated, intimidated, when we entered the room; the children were all over the classroom. There weren't old-fashioned desks, just small tables for the children to sit at, and a row of hooks along one wall for their bags.

I helped Simone put her bag onto a hook at the side, then we approached the teacher. She handled the chaos with aplomb, cheerfully organising the children to sit at the tables.

'Hello, this is Simone Chen,' I said to her, a young blonde Australian woman with a kind face.

'Hello, Simone,' the teacher said. 'Have you been to school, or kindergarten, before?'

Simone shook her head, her eyes wide with apprehension.

'Okay then,' the teacher said briskly, 'I'll put you next to a little girl who already did a year here in the preparatory class, and she can help you. Is that okay?'

Simone nodded, eyes still wide.

'Do you remember about Simone?' I said to the teacher.

'No, what?' the teacher said, obviously trying to recall any medical problems.

I leaned over to speak quietly in her ear. 'She has a guard stationed downstairs in the car park at all times. Either Leo, who's outside waiting, or myself. She's a kidnapping target; she's already had a few attempts on her. Sorry.' I grinned an apology. 'But while we're downstairs, she'll be fine.'

'I remember,' the teacher said, studying me appraisingly. 'Mrs Nelson told me about you.' She smiled. 'Well, I don't need to worry about any terrorist attacks or anything while you're downstairs. How did you get into the bodyguard business?'

'I can honestly say that I had absolutely no intention of ever being one,' I said. 'I'm really just a nanny with some extra training. When your ward is a target, you learn quickly.'

'I suppose you do.' The teacher glanced down at Simone, who was talking quietly to the girl next to her. 'Who's the other bodyguard?'

I opened my mouth to ask Simone to call Leo in, then stopped and mentally kicked myself. Damn, she was better at this normal stuff than I was.

'You can't miss him,' I said. 'He's huge and black. Really nice guy. His name's Leo. He'll be downstairs in the car park. Simone knows who he is.'

The teacher shrugged. 'Lot of trouble to go to when she has all these kids around her. But if your boss wants to waste his money, that's his business.'

I laughed softly. 'You're exactly right.' I watched Simone briefly. 'I think I'm okay to go now. Can I leave you my mobile number just in case?'

'Sure.' The teacher gestured towards her desk, and I wrote my and Leo's mobile numbers onto a piece of paper.

'Call either of us if anything suspicious happens,' I said, and she nodded.

'You don't look like a bodyguard. You armed?' she said quietly.

'No, and really, I'm just a nanny,' I said and left it at that. If I mentioned the martial arts then I could be roped in to giving a demonstration, or, even worse, teaching children at the school, and I had quite enough of teaching at the Academy.

'Bye,' I said to the teacher, and she nodded and smiled a reply, then rushed to sort out a couple of kids who were arguing over a seat.

Simone didn't notice me; she was busy talking to her new friend about the meals provided by the school cafeteria. I knelt so that I was at her level. 'I'm going now, sweetheart, okay?'

'Okay, Emma,' Simone said. 'I'll be fine.'

'Both of us are downstairs today,' I said softly. 'And Michael is up on the fifth floor.'

'I'll be fine, Emma.' Simone tilted her head and smiled cheekily at me. She waved me away. 'You go.' She turned back to her friend, ignoring me. I went out.

The year tens were clustered around a set of lockers outside one of the classrooms. Inside the room, the teacher was allocating lockers and telling the kids how to open them. There was less chaos here, so all three of us approached.

There was a stunned silence when we entered and everybody saw Leo, but it didn't last long and the loud conversations recommenced.

I took Michael to see the teacher.

'This is Michael MacLaren, he's new,' I said. 'Can you tell us what we need to do?'

'I'm Jason Taylor, the Year Ten homeroom teacher,' he said, shaking my hand strongly. He looked at Michael. 'Weren't you told about dyeing your hair?'

I cut in before Michael needed to. 'I can guarantee that his hair is its natural colour, Mr Taylor,' I said. 'Could you let the other teachers know, please?'

The teacher smiled at me. 'Sure. Are you his mother?'

'No, I'm the nanny. And this is the driver.' I gestured to Leo, and the teacher nodded to him, unfazed. 'Could you sort Michael out for us, please? His little cousin is downstairs in the first grade — it's her first day too and I want to make sure that she's okay.'

'Let me handle everything, I'll have Michael here fixed up in a jiffy.' The teacher gestured to Michael. 'Come with me, young Michael, let's get you organised. Are you half-Chinese?'

Michael and the teacher went out to the lockers, chatting amiably. Leo and I shared a smile.

I quickly checked on Simone again as we went back down to the car. She was with a group of little girls who were comparing pencil cases, and didn't even see me. The teacher saw me, gave me a wave and a smile, and gestured that Simone was okay.

Leo and I settled ourselves in the car. The children were all in school now and it was quiet. Nobody went in or out. The guards sat around the guard station and chatted in Cantonese and Tagalog.

I opened the laptop on the back seat, pulled out the budgeting spreadsheets and started going through the figures. I had two sets: the real ones and the figures for my thesis. The real figures didn't include salaries for most of the staff, who were demons.

Leo sat comfortably in the driver's seat and rustled the newspaper against the steering wheel.

I felt it before I saw it. I jerked up from the spreadsheets and saw it come into the car park. High level, but alone. Not a prince. Looked like an ordinary Chinese workman, in dirty white trousers, a torn T-shirt and filthy canvas shoes.

There's a demon downstairs, Simone said into my ear.

Neither of us could talk back to her. We both swung into action together. Leo threw the newspaper onto the seat next to him, pulled off his reading glasses and dropped them on top of the paper. We slammed the car doors behind us and walked quickly over to intercept the demon. Paul, the head guard, smiled at us. Then he saw us walking threateningly towards the demon and his smile disappeared.

The demon saw us coming and stopped. It faced us. It watched us for a while.

We stopped about two metres away from it. Both of us folded our arms and stood quietly, waiting for it to make a move.

It smiled tightly at us, spun, and walked out of the school grounds.

As we went back to the car, Leo held out his hand and I tapped it lightly with my fingertips.

We returned to our spreadsheet and newspaper without saying a word.

Demon's gone, Simone said into my ear. There was nothing for a while, then, *I'm sitting next to a really nice girl, her name is Helen. She has a new puppy and wants to invite me to her house to see it.*

Leo sighed gently, turned the page of the newspaper, and shook it flat over the steering wheel.

CHAPTER THIRTY-FOUR

Two Saturdays later I was in my office at the Academy when there was a knock at the door.

'Come in.'

Leo came in, holding a piece of paper, his face rigid with emotion. He sat down across my desk from me.

'What's the matter?'

He dropped the piece of paper in front of me. United States Internal Revenue. I turned it around so that I could read it, then glanced sharply at Leo.

'Hasn't Jade been handling this?'

'Apparently she screwed up,' Leo said miserably. 'Look at it, Emma.'

Leo was overdue with his taxes. Seriously overdue. US citizens had to pay taxes to the United States on any overseas earnings.

'Why are you coming to me?'

'Jade's not around anywhere. Mr Chen is teaching.' Leo sounded desperate. 'I got a subpoena. They want me back in the States. I am in serious trouble. What am I going to do?'

'Wait,' I said, and pressed the intercom button.

'Yes, my Lady?'

'Get me the Golden Boy, please, Gamma.'

'He's on his way, ma'am.'

Gold came in and sat with us.

'Look at this,' I said, and slid the paper across the desk.

Gold picked it up and studied it. 'Oh, my.'

'I got a subpoena,' Leo said.

Gold eyed Leo over the paper. 'You are in serious trouble, my friend.'

Leo put his head in his hands. 'Oh my God.'

Gold patted him on the shoulder. 'I should be able to fix it so you get minimal jail time,' he said. 'Don't worry.' He smiled. 'You should have no trouble in a US prison anyway, you can defend yourself.'

Leo's head shot up. 'Prison?' His face went blank when he saw the smile on Gold's face. He turned to me.

I couldn't hold it any more. I tittered.

Leo saw the broad grin on Gold's face. He looked from one of us to the other for a while, speechless. Then he stormed out without saying a word.

Both Gold and I collapsed over the desk laughing.

'Thanks, Gold,' I wheezed.

'Not a problem, my Lady,' Gold said. 'But I'm not getting involved in this any more. I'll end up in two pieces.'

Later that evening John tapped on my bedroom door. 'Emma.'

It was quite late, and I wondered what he wanted. 'Come on in.'

John opened the door carefully, leaned around it, smiled and came in.

'Simone really enjoyed her day at the Academy,' he said. 'That was a great idea to bring her down on Saturdays.'

'It was Meredith's idea,' I said. 'She wanted the chance to teach Simone some energy work, and now all of the Celestials are lining up. They said they don't usually get the chance to teach someone so young and talented.'

I glanced at the computer screen, and sighed.

'You need to take a break from that thesis, Emma, and you need to decide that it's finished. Otherwise you'll be working on it for the rest of your life.'

I ran my hands through my hair. 'I'm not happy with the introduction, and the sheets could be better.'

He sat on the sofa across from my desk. 'Let me have a look at it. I might be able to help you.'

'No *way*! I'm doing this myself!'

He raised his hands. 'Suit yourself.'

I pushed the keyboard to one side and looked at him pointedly. He sat placidly without speaking.

'Do you want something?' I said. 'Or did you just come in here to watch me work?'

'Do you mind?' he said serenely. 'I like to watch others work.'

I pulled the keyboard back to me. 'Suit yourself.'

He laughed gently and ran his hand over his face, then tied back his wayward hair. 'Zhu Que would like to drop by with her chicks. Is Monday after school okay?'

I pushed the keyboard away again with delight. 'That's wonderful! They hatched? How many did she have?' I stopped and stared at him with horror. 'Will they damage the apartment?'

'I hope not,' he said. 'When she brought her last brood they only slightly singed the carpet.'

'Have a fire extinguisher nearby just in case,' I said grimly. I brightened; I was looking forward to seeing the babies. 'Monday will be fine.'

'Good.' He pulled himself gracefully off the sofa and went to the door. He opened the door. 'Oh, nearly forgot.' He smiled slightly and reached into the pocket of his cotton pants. 'Here.' He tossed me a small video camera tape.

He turned to the door, then turned back to me. 'I didn't know you could do that,' he said, his voice full of wonder. Then he flung himself through the door and closed it quietly behind him.

I looked at the tape. It had at least an hour of recording on it. Yes! Time to lock the door of my room and enjoy the company of my man the only way we could.

'*Is Aunty Zhu here yet?*' Simone yelled as we went through the front door and kicked off our shoes.

'We're in the training room,' Leo shouted back.

Simone raced down the hallway and into the training room. She squealed with delight. Michael and I shared an amused look and followed her.

Zhu Que must have materialised the table and chairs that were set up in one corner of the room, covered in tea things. She and John sat there together. Leo sat cross-legged on the floor with the chicks. Simone was on her knees, looking at them with round-eyed delight.

Each chick was as big as a medium-sized dog. All three had little round furry bodies without visible wings, rust-coloured with darker horizontal stripes across their backs. One of them rose to approach Simone, but the other two hung back near Leo.

'Hello,' Simone said softly to the chick.

'Hello,' the chick said, its little head bobbing sideways on its long neck. 'What's your name?'

'Simone. What's yours?'

The chick glanced at Zhu Que. She smiled warmly. It turned back to Simone. 'I'm the Biggest.'

'I'm the Littlest,' one of the other chicks quickly piped up.

'I'm Middle. We get proper names later,' the third chick announced proudly. It turned its head on its graceful neck to face Leo. 'Finish the story, Uncle Leo.'

The Biggest chick that had been talking to Simone returned to sit next to its siblings, bending its long legs underneath it. Simone followed it and sat with them.

'I don't remember where I was,' Leo said with a gentle smile.

'The Big Bad Wolf had just come up to the two little pigs in the House of Sticks,' the Middle chick said. 'What happened next, Uncle Leo?'

I went to the table and sat with John and Zhu Que. John poured some tea for me. Michael hesitated at the doorway, unsure.

'Go and do your homework if you like, Michael. Or you can stay with us if you want,' I said.

Michael nodded without saying a word, saluted us carefully, and went out.

Zhu Que nodded respectfully to me. 'My Lady.'

I waved her down. 'No need for that, Zhu Que, we're all family here,' I said. 'It was a good idea bringing them in here; they won't be able to do much damage if one of them goes off.'

Zhu Que smiled affectionately at the babies. 'This is a particularly good clutch. Not a single one of them has burst into flames at any of the places we have visited.' Her smile disappeared. 'Lord Xuan tells me that apart from a single isolated attack at the school, things have been relatively peaceful in the last few weeks.'

I sighed. 'It's been absolutely wonderful.'

John nodded agreement. 'I just wish I knew what was up.'

Zhu Que nodded as well. 'Why did they attack you twice so far from their centre, and then stop when you returned? Even the King going so far from the Eastern Centre is remarkable. Did you request the Lady?'

John shook his head, his face grim. 'I can handle it,' he said, a very fine, fierce edge to his voice.

'We don't want to put Kwan Yin in any sort of danger unless we absolutely have to,' I said with a similar edge. I changed the subject, gesturing towards Simone where she sat with the chicks, listening to Leo with rapt attention. 'Simone has started weapons. Her energy skills are remarkable. She's only been doing weapons for a few weeks, and she can already use her little training sword to throw *chi*.'

'She can destroy level ten demons with her Inner Eye, and level twenty with her bare hands. She'll be ready for a real sword very soon,' John said with satisfaction.

Zhu Que studied Simone. 'She is your first human child, my Lord, is that correct?'

John nodded silently.

Zhu Que appeared to get the message even though she wasn't looking at him. She turned back to us. 'You should have done this a long time ago. Her skills at such a young age rival those of the Third Prince.'

'They exceed his. I remember. She will be more powerful than Na Zha when she is mature,' he said.

Zhu Que smiled. 'Don't mention his name too much, my Lord. You know how vain he is — he'll be knocking on your front door demanding a test of skills with her.'

'I agree,' I said. 'You know how I feel about the Third Prince.'

'I don't know why everybody has such a problem with him,' John said mildly, and both Zhu Que and I snorted with derision. 'He is the best demon-destroyer on the Celestial short of me.'

'Don't forget the graffiti he sprayed on the roof of Hennessy Road,' I said. 'That took Jade ages to clean off. Has his own tag and everything, the little ...' I swallowed what I was about to say. '... Celestial Worthy.'

Both John and the Phoenix laughed softly.

'Now I know how some of that graffiti gets in such unusual places,' Zhu Que said. 'I thought that they would have to fly to spray it there, and now I know: they do.'

'How old is he anyway?' I said. 'He always looks so young.'

'He was present during the Shang-Zhou, was he not?' Zhu Que said.

'Yes,' John said. 'Probably about three thousand, give or take a century.'

'Why does he look like a teenager then?' I said.

'His essence is youth,' John said.

'Will he ever grow up?' I said. 'He hasn't pointlessly killed anything recently, he's mostly stuck to demons. Why did he kill that Dragon Prince anyway?'

'He was young. It was there. He could do it. Usually that's enough for him,' John said.

We all paused to watch Leo finish telling the story. Simone and the chicks sat wide-eyed and rapt. Zhu Que sighed with contentment.

'Can they take human form yet, Phoenix?' I said.

Zhu Que nodded. 'For short periods. Biggest and Littlest are boys. Middle is a girl.'

'I'll go and find some Lego for them to play with when Leo finishes his story,' I said. 'If they can take human form, it will be easy for them to handle.'

'Good idea,' John said.

I went into Simone's room and selected some Lego pieces, then returned to the training room. The chicks had never seen Lego before and they studied it curiously. Simone showed them how to put the bricks together. Leo sat to one side, the fire extinguisher at hand just in case.

The chicks transformed into little round Chinese children of about three years old, wearing old-fashioned cotton jackets and pants. They dug their chubby hands into the Lego and talked cheerfully with Simone as they made things together.

I rose and returned to the table. 'Are they house-trained, Phoenix? They're very advanced for chicks of only a couple of months old.'

'They should ask, but we still occasionally have accidents. I'll take them out soon anyway.' Her smile became wry. 'Don't know how to use human toilets yet.'

I laughed softly. 'They're adorable.'

Simone shot to her feet and came to us. 'Can the chicks have a sleepover with me?'

We all shook our heads. 'They're not big enough yet, Simone,' I said gently. 'They're still only tiny babies.'

'When they're bigger and they won't burn things, they can come and sleep over if you like,' Zhu Que said. 'Middle is a girl, like you. I'm sure the two of you would have a lot of fun.'

Simone looked at the chicks then turned back to us. 'That would be nice,' she said cheerfully. She returned to the chicks and flopped down with them.

'How is she at school?' Zhu Que said. 'No problems?'

'The school staff don't know anything, and it's working out really well,' John said, then gestured towards me. 'Emma arranges everything — she's even volunteered to do some work at the school —'

'Anything to escape those blasted budgeting sheets,' I muttered under my breath.

'— and Simone and Michael have settled in and made friends. Michael goes to a shopping mall near the school with a group of friends now and then, and Simone has even brought little friends home.'

'She knows exactly what to do,' I said. 'She keeps them out of the training room, and talks out loud all the time. She's better at it than I am; I keep asking her to call John for me.'

'None of us thought you'd pull it off,' Zhu Que said with wonder.

We watched the children play in silence. One of the chicks reverted to True Form and its Lego fell. Simone picked the Lego up and held it out for him. He changed back into human form, took the Lego with a smile, and finished building a little car. Simone clapped her hands with delight when he showed it to her. She was being a big sister to them.

'Have you heard of any movements?' John said softly without looking away from the children. 'It is very quiet. Disturbingly quiet.'

'They are planning something,' Zhu Que said, also without shifting her gaze. 'I have sent in agents, but they do not return.' She shrugged. 'I would dearly like to know what they are doing.'

'The King has promised to stay away from us,' John said mildly. 'One Two Two was too cowardly to face me in London.'

'But they're building special demons just for us,' I said. 'They may be planning something big with their new toys.'

Both John and the Phoenix glanced at me, then nodded and turned back to the children.

'The only thing we can do is stay aware, stay ready, and have Emma and Simone up to speed as quickly as possible,' John said.

'I'd like to know where they're making those things,' I said. 'Is it possible that they were made in Europe?'

'Quite possible,' John said.

Zhu Que shook her head. 'If they were, then that raises a very large number of unpleasant implications.' She moved to rise. 'I need to take these chicks outside before they embarrass themselves.' She studied them carefully. 'No, I think I'll take them home. They're tired. Look at Middle.'

She was right. Middle had reverted to True Form and the edges of her feathers smouldered.

Zhu Que turned and saluted us. 'By your leave.'

'Bring them back soon to play,' I said. 'Simone loves them.'

'Let me know if you hear anything,' John said.

Zhu Que nodded and went to the chicks to gather them up. They all disappeared in a flurry of red. Simone and Leo packed up the Lego.

'She forgot her table,' I said.

'The minute we stand it will be gone,' John said without moving.

I poured some more tea. Leo took Simone out to put her toys away. We sat for a while, pondering.

CHAPTER THIRTY-FIVE

I had a pleasant lunch with Rhonda. We discussed Michael's school work; we were both delighted at his progress. He enjoyed school, and I told her about some of the friends he'd made. We arranged for her to come for dinner at the weekend.

I walked back along Des Voeux Road, through Central, towards John's office, where I needed to collect some documents. It was a nondescript building in Wellington Street. The pollution was particularly bad, the car exhaust fumes were trapped by the highrises. There wasn't a scrap of greenery anywhere along the street, just the cracked concrete pavement. But at least the weather was clear and mild, not humid at all. Hong Kong would have about two weeks of delightful weather now, in late October, and then the humidity would hit again, changing from hot and damp to cold and damp.

I took the lift to the first floor and walked to the end of the corridor where the office was located. The staff didn't know who John was; they thought he was a wealthy businessman from China, and that I was his European nanny who occasionally did some errands for him.

After I'd collected the documents, I called the lift. There were a few people in it already and they glared impatiently at me. Should have taken the stairs since you're only on the first floor, they were thinking at me, and not wasted our time stopping here.

One of them was a high-level demon. She ignored me completely. My heart sank.

As soon as I was out of the lift in the lobby I pulled out my mobile phone. It wasn't working.

I strolled casually to the guard station near the front door and asked the guard in Cantonese for a phone. He pushed one over to me. I picked up the receiver. Not working.

I stood at the guard station and pondered. I was in serious trouble. This was a really big demon, far too big for me to handle alone. To anyone who saw her, she was a perfectly normal young Chinese woman waiting for someone. She even checked her watch occasionally. She wore a lavender suit and her hair was short and trim. She ignored me completely.

Holy shit, what was I going to do?

I pulled out my mobile phone again, pretended to dial a number, and pretended to listen. I held it up to my face with my left hand. It was completely dead.

'I would really appreciate some help right now,' I hissed into the phone quietly. 'For God's sake, wake the hell up!'

Nothing. The stone was more and more useless every day.

I tapped it with my other finger. 'Wake up!'

Still nothing.

I spun around and banged the blasted thing on the wall, *hard*.

Still nothing. Oh my God, it wasn't asleep. She'd somehow managed to turn it off too.

I briefly pondered going back up to the office and asking one of the girls to call John, then dismissed the idea. The minute they were involved in this, the demon would take them out.

Fine. To hell with it. I stormed right up to her. 'What do you want?' I said loudly enough for anybody in the lobby to hear.

She smiled sweetly. 'Do I know you?'

'Where do you want to do this?' I demanded.

Her cute smile didn't shift. 'I'm sorry, I have no idea what you're talking about. Do you mind going away now?'

'Fine.' I spun on my heel. 'See you at my car. I just hope you're more honourable than that bastard Wong, and don't try to stab me in the back.'

The security guards watched me incredulously but I didn't care. They probably didn't understand most of the exchange anyway; only that I had stormed up and abused this girl who hadn't even spoken to me. Typical weird Foreign Devil behaviour.

I stomped out the front door of the office building, turned left, and walked up the steep hill of Wellington Street. I concentrated hard on John. I hadn't tried calling him before; I was sure that I wasn't capable of the skill. But right now I needed it more than anything else. Nothing.

I tried Simone. Still nothing. Leo? Gold? Jade? Nothing. The Goddess that Hears the Cries of the World? I'm really crying here, Lady. Nothing.

Damn, I was in very serious trouble.

I cursed my own stupidity as I reached the escalator and went back down towards The Centre. I hadn't even had the brains to bring my weapon. I was unarmed and facing a demon that appeared to be close on level fifty; much higher than anything I had ever faced before.

Well, this was it. This was where all the training and the work and the suffering and the torture came together. I only hoped that I could fight her valiantly, and lose with dignity if I had to. Then I felt a shot of panic: if she was working for Wong, she could be coming to pick me up. I had no way of killing myself if I lost. Then I immediately went very calm. Yes, there was. If I was losing, I'd hit her with energy, blow her up, and then blow myself up with the backlash. Easy.

And then, suddenly, I felt really good. I was relaxed and serene. I shouldn't have felt that way, but I did. Either way, they wouldn't get their hands on me, and it would be over soon.

I walked calmly and confidently through the water garden and past the large flat screen displaying the stock market prices. I went to the car park lift and pressed the button. The lift doors slid open and I went in. No demons there. She'd be waiting for me next to the car. *Bring it on, bitch.*

And there she was, right next to my car, as expected. She gestured for me to follow her and I did. We went to a cul-de-sac at the end of the car park. There weren't any cars parked there. Lunch was finished. Nobody would be coming in or out. And there were plenty of spaces on the next floor up, closer to the shroff office. We had all the time and privacy in the world.

It was worth a try. 'You wouldn't like to come and work for me, would you?' I said. 'The other demon help say that I'm a good boss.'

She seemed amused. Then she grinned. 'If I bring you back in close to one piece, I'll be promoted to Mother.'

'Whoa, high stakes,' I said cheerfully. And I did feel cheerful. I knew exactly what lay ahead of me for the next half-hour, and possibly for the rest of my short life. 'I won't let you though. If it looks like you're winning, I'll blow both of us up.'

She shrugged. 'Try me.'

I put my hands out in a gesture of welcome. 'No, sweetie, you first.'

She came at me lightning fast. I'd never taken on anything as good as her before, short of John himself. She came at my head and my body so fast she was a blur. Head strike, head strike, body strike, spin kick. I managed to block them all, one after the other. I lost some ground but not enough to worry me. I used the block on the kick, grabbed her foot, unbalanced her and tipped her over. She landed neatly on her feet, spun again, and kicked me right in the middle of the abdomen.

My abdomen was loaded with chi and I absorbed the impact. I was knocked backwards but landed on my feet, unharmed. I didn't hesitate; I went straight back at her and struck at her in return. Head, head, head, body; she damn well blocked them all. I couldn't get through her.

We were evenly matched. She was at least as good as me.

Well then, there was an easy way to defeat her: I just had to be *better* than me.

We paused and studied each other. Neither of us was panting yet. This was just a warm-up. She raised her arms and snapped out her wrists. I did too. I waited.

She came at me with a spinning series of kicks, one after the other, head, head, abdomen. I blocked them all. I hit her hard with the blocks, trying to break through her human shell and get to the demon stuff underneath. Her shell was thick. If I could break it, she would be finished. I just needed to hit her hard enough.

I retaliated with my fists. I struck at her head and abdomen with everything I had. I tried to be as fast as I possibly could. She was just as fast. She blocked it all. She grabbed my hand and pulled me in. I went in as she pulled me and hit her in the face with my other hand. Her face wasn't there. I rolled past her and tried to take out her head with my feet as I went through. No such luck.

I sprang back to my feet and stood panting.

Before I even had time to catch my breath she was at me again. She spun fast. I blocked her foot with my left, but I wasn't fast enough with the block and it hit me awkwardly.

She hit my left forearm hard. I felt the impact. I felt the bone break inside. It was a remarkable sensation. And then the pain exploded and I wanted to tear my own arm off.

I didn't have time. Her feet were in my face, with multiple strikes. I tried to block with my right but I couldn't block them all. She hit my forehead, my cheekbone, my cheek again, and then my jaw. Fortunately she didn't break anything except the skin. Stars spun in front of me. I tried to shake them away, but it made my head spin and hurt. The blood ran down my face, making it hot and slick. It ran into my eyes.

I hugged my left arm in close, somersaulted backwards, and concentrated.

I did not have time for this pain. Come on, Emma, all you have to do is be *better than yourself.* For John. *For Simone.* For *everybody* who loves you.

I brushed the blood out of my eyes. God, I hated the smell of blood.

No, wait … it smelled *good.* I *loved* that smell. Sweet, delicious blood.

And then my veins rushed with ice. I was calm and powerful and I could *do* it. The pain disappeared. I saw her as she really was. I saw her coming towards me. She came in slow motion. I had all the time in the world. I wanted blood. I could taste the blood. I wanted to eat her alive, black stuff and all.

Her fist came towards me in a slow arabesque and I smiled. Her face went slack with horror. I ducked casually under her hand. I tapped her on the face, then again, and again, and again. So fast she didn't even seem to move. Just enough to hurt her without destroying her. Great fun. Her eyes were wide with shock.

Then I spun and hit her in the middle with a devastating butterfly kick that knocked her five metres backward into the wall.

The force of the explosion of demon stuff slammed me off my feet, and suddenly everything was normal speed again. My left arm hurt so much I had trouble holding back the scream. My eyes were full of blood. I couldn't think straight. The ground hit me hard.

Black. Red. Dark.

Gold's boyish face was right in mine, but I couldn't really see him.

'I can't carry you directly, my Lady,' he seemed to be saying. 'It would aggravate the injuries.'

'I am in a *lot* of pain, Gold,' I gasped. 'Can you do anything for the pain? Anything? Anything at all?'

'Wait,' he said softly.

I was about to protest that I didn't want to wait when Jade appeared and put her hand on my forehead.

Lying in the back of the Mercedes. Looking at the ceiling. Jade holding my hand. Every bump on the road exploding into agony. A hand on my forehead again.

Strong hands lifting. Voices, but I didn't understand. Smooth movement. Lights going past above me.

A sharp pain through the suffering. Falling. Falling. Floating down, into a warm cloud of comfort. No more pain. Ease. Sigh. Darkness. John?

God, I was tired. Why couldn't I turn over? I hurt all over. Too bright. Open your eyes, come on, there you are ... you can see. Dark hair. John. Sigh. Let go.

CHAPTER THIRTY-SIX

Movement. Sounds. Soft voices. I snapped open my eyes. It was all blurry. I looked around, trying to focus, but everything kept going upwards. I grabbed the universe and told it to stay put. It did.

A dark shape to my left. I tried to focus on it. Warm dark eyes. John. Another dark shape behind him; I focused. Leo had just come in, bringing Simone. All three of them watched me, concerned.

'Hello,' I croaked. 'What happened to me?'

'Would you like a drink?' John said quietly. 'Do you think you could hold it down?'

I nodded. He grabbed the jug from the bedside table and poured me a glass of water. He paused. 'I can't do it,' he said, his voice full of pain. 'You need someone to lift your head.'

Leo moved around him and gently reached behind my neck, raising my head. It exploded with pain and I winced. He hesitated. He brought the glass to my lips and I took a few sips of the water. It was incredibly sweet. I nodded my thanks. My head exploded again. Leo carefully lowered me back to the pillow.

I looked around. A simple hospital room. Dark blue curtains over the window. Beige walls. Two chairs next to me. John, with Simone in his lap. Simone's little face wide-eyed with concern.

'How's your head?' John said quietly. 'Do you have much of a headache?'

I felt inside my head. My brain was numb and swollen. 'I feel fuzzy but I think I'll live.' I tried to remember what had happened. Nothing. My left arm was in a cast; I must have broken it. I was on a drip. Whoa, but my face felt weird. 'What happened?'

'You collected the files from Wellington Street. You went back to your car. You were obviously attacked by something big. You took it out, but it must have broken your left arm and managed some serious strikes to your head before you did.' John leaned forward over Simone. 'Do you remember anything at all?'

'Level fifty, female,' I said with wonder. 'I saw her in the lobby of the office building. I don't remember anything after that.'

Leo inhaled sharply. 'No *way*.'

'Leave it for now,' John said firmly. 'Rest. Now that you've come around we'll be able to take you home, and you can recuperate properly. The police want to talk to you. What do you want to tell them?'

'I have no idea,' I said helplessly. 'I don't know. I don't remember anything.'

'Well, then,' he said, 'tell them the truth.'

'Are they starting to look at you?' I said.

'Yes, they are. When the time comes you may run into some difficulty. I hope it doesn't happen.'

I didn't say anything. I leaned back on the pillows and closed my eyes.

'Take Simone home,' John told Leo. 'I will follow with Emma as soon as she is strong enough.'

'Emma will need help, my Lord, and you won't be able to touch her. It'll have to be me who stays,' Leo said.

416

'Leo's right, John,' I said without opening my eyes. 'You take Simone home. Leo can give me a hand.'

Simone's little voice, demanding, 'I want to stay with Emma!'

'Go home with your dad,' I said. 'I'm okay, Leo's here. He'll bring me home shortly, and Meredith can fix me up, good as new.'

'I want to stay here with you, Emma.'

I opened my eyes. Her face was set into a stubborn mask.

'Could you go home, choose some nice clothes for me to wear, and ask Ah Yat to bring them down to the hospital for me, Simone?' I said kindly. 'You're the only one I trust to do that for me. The guys have no idea what clothes I wear.'

'I don't know.'

'Your dad can show you where my wardrobe is, Simone,' I said. 'He knows where everything is. You two go and have a look for me.'

'I'll help you,' John said.

'Okay.' Simone hopped down and gently took John's hand. 'Come on, Daddy, let's go and find something nice for Emma to come home in.'

'Thanks, sweetheart,' I whispered and closed my eyes. The door closed behind them.

'Would you like another drink of water?' Leo said.

'Please.'

Leo gently lifted my head and put the glass to my lips. The water was still sweet. I took a few sips. It flowed coolly down my throat. I nodded and he gently let me down. I had a sudden shock of concern. 'What happened to you, stone?'

No reply.

'If you're talking about your ring, they took your jewellery and put it in a safe place,' Leo said. 'It's not here.'

'The demon seemed to have disabled it,' I said. 'I banged it on the wall and everything, and it didn't say a word.'

'Talk to Mr Chen when you get home,' Leo said. 'Rest right now, and I'll take you home when you feel up to it.'

'Leo,' I whispered.

His face moved into view.

'Sorry, mate, but can you help me up? I want to use the bathroom.'

'Mate?' His eyes sparkled with amusement as he lifted me easily. 'Just call a nurse. You don't have to get up.'

'I want to get onto my feet anyway,' I said as he helped me around so that my legs hung over the edge of the bed. 'I want to go home.'

I gently lowered myself onto my feet. Leo held my arm. I couldn't help it, I leaned on him. I was as weak as a kitten. 'All I did was break my arm. How come I'm so weak?'

'Wait till you're in the bathroom, you'll see why,' Leo said.

I pushed him away and tried to stand by myself. I couldn't. He jerked forward to catch me before I went down.

'This just isn't good enough,' I growled under my breath. 'I have to get out of here.'

'What's the big hurry?' he said, gently amused.

'My thesis is due next week.'

Leo didn't say anything. He held me up and guided me towards the bathroom. The IV bag followed on its little wheeled stand.

'You don't have to do this,' I said quickly, realising what he was about to do. 'If you're uncomfortable, we'll just call a nurse.'

'Oh, come on, Emma, you're like a sister to me. I'm a Retainer. What about the attack in Guangzhou when you helped me? Besides,' he said, his grin gaining an evil edge, 'I want to see your face.'

'What?'

He guided me through the bathroom door. There was a mirror directly in front of me. I saw my face and his grip tightened as I nearly fell over with shock.

'Holy shit,' I said softly as I looked at myself.

My entire face was a swollen purple mass of bruised flesh. My eyes were barely visible. I had stitches on my forehead and across my cheekbones that I hadn't even been aware of. Now that I knew they were there I could feel them. They weren't painful, they were more like unpleasant pressure across my face.

'Have to take a photo of this when we get home,' Leo said with amusement. 'What a good job. I think you deserve a special prize.'

'You put a camera anywhere near me and my *chi* is out to get you,' I threatened fiercely. I tried to pull myself free of him. He held me. 'Let me go. I want to see if I can stand alone.'

He gently complied, ready to catch me if I went down.

A wave of weakness hit me as he let go. I fell into his arms. 'Damn.'

He didn't waste any more time. He swept me up and carried me like a child. 'Let's get this over with and get you back to bed.'

'I want to go home,' I said fiercely the next time I came around. The IV was gone; they must have taken it out while I was asleep. 'Meredith can fix most of this, but I can't just walk out of here a hundred per cent. I have to get home first.'

Leo understood. 'Do you think you could walk if I helped you?'

I nodded and my head exploded with pain. 'Ouch.' I turned carefully on the bed and lowered myself. I tried standing. I could do it. 'Whoopee,' I said quietly, 'I'm up and around.'

Leo moved to help me but I waved him away. 'Let me see if I can walk.' I gingerly tried a few hesitant steps. 'Call Ah Yat. Tell her to bring me some clothes. Let's get me out of here.' I turned back to the bed and climbed to sit on it.

Leo pulled out his mobile and called home. 'Tell her to materialise carefully,' I said, and he nodded.

Ah Yat came bustling out of the bathroom like a mother hen. She shooed Leo out of the room and helped me to dress. She was strong enough to hold me by herself. When I had the clothes on, the three of us called a nurse and told her we were leaving.

The nurse looked stiffly at me then turned and walked out without saying a word. Gone to find a doctor.

The doctor came in. He was in his mid-thirties, overweight, cheerful, and smelled of cigarette smoke. 'You should stay overnight for observation,' he said over his small, stylish glasses.

'I want to get out of here,' I said firmly. 'I want to go home.' I thought quickly and gestured towards Leo. 'My boyfriend is a registered nurse, he'll look after me.'

Leo snapped me a quick, astonished glance, then spoke to the doctor. 'I'll look after her. She'll be fine.'

The doctor acquiesced reluctantly. 'Go downstairs and sign out first,' he said to Leo. 'Any signs of altered state, lack of perception, bring her back. You know what to look for.'

Leo nodded. 'Nausea, dizziness, dilated pupils, visual disturbance, altered state, I know.'

The doctor nodded, satisfied. 'Take care.' He watched as I walked out by myself, Leo carefully behind me ready to catch me. Ah Yat wasn't there. Must have already gone back to the Peak to prepare for me.

Leo gently helped me into the car. 'How did you know I was a registered nurse, Emma?'

'What, you *are*?' I cried softly with disbelief. 'I just made that up.' I stopped and studied him appraisingly. He smiled gently. 'How have you managed to do everything you've done in your life, Leo? You are the most remarkable man I have ever met.'

'I think the Dark Lord accumulates remarkable people around him,' Leo said as he closed the car door.

Leo removed the stitches as Meredith healed me. They worked together closely and with care. I didn't feel a thing. John didn't want to watch. When they were finished, Meredith went home with the other Master, Liu, helping her. She wasn't completely drained but needed to rest for a long time. She was the only true very high-level energy worker left in the Academy and we needed her skills.

John came in and sat by me when they'd finished. Leo collected his instruments and went out. He came back with my jewellery in a brown paper envelope.

I sat up on the bed and shook my head: no stars. I was still weak and woozy, but I felt much better. I tipped the contents of the envelope onto the blanket and picked up the ring.

'What happened to you? You left me just when I needed you.'

'I didn't leave you, Emma,' the stone said as I put the ring back on. 'I was trying to talk to you, but you didn't hear me.'

'Oh my God.' I sagged back against my bedhead. 'She didn't disable you, she disabled *me*.'

'Tell me,' John said.

'I saw her in the lobby of the office building. No, wait, she was in the lift, and went down with me. I saw her in the lift. I tried to call you, but my mobile was dead. Then I tried the guard's phone, but it was dead too. Then I tried to talk to the stone, but it didn't answer.'

'Emma,' the stone said patiently, 'the phones were working just fine. I could hear the dial tone.'

'She did something to me,' I said.

John leaned back in his chair next to my bed. 'Quite possible. One of the disadvantages of being a perfectly ordinary human.' He smiled briefly. 'What happened after you saw her? Did she speak to you?'

'No. She ignored me. She pretended to be waiting for someone. So I lost my temper and shouted at her, and went out of the building. I said something like "I hope you're more honourable than that bastard Wong and don't try to stab me in the back", or something like that.'

Leo made a soft sound of amusement.

'Then?' John said.

'Then she met me in the car park, next to my car.' I winced. 'Sorry, Leo, *our* car.'

'Your car, my Lady,' Leo said gently.

'Oh, cut it out. That's all I need. Okay, so I met her next to the car. She took me over to the side, no cars there. She went for me. Then Gold ...' I hesitated. That was the way it seemed to have happened. 'Then Gold was talking to me, I was on the ground, and my arm and head hurt like hell.'

'It was a level fifty?' John said.

'Probably. At least.' I suddenly remembered. 'She said that if she took me back in one piece she'd be promoted to Mother.'

Neither of them said anything.

'I called Gold,' the stone said. 'But he was a long way away and it took him a while to get there. By the time he made it to the building, Emma was gone. And then she was underground, so I couldn't call anybody.'

'Why not?' I said.

'The stone was buried,' John said. 'Underground. Silenced.'

'I didn't know that happened,' I said.

'Sorry,' John whispered.

'Not your fault, my Lord. It's difficult to remember what the Lady knows and what she doesn't. I should have been the one to tell her,' the stone said.

'The stone is right,' I said. 'Not your fault.'

All of them were quiet at that.

'So Emma can ask the ring to call for help if she needs it?' Leo said.

'I spend most of my time asleep, Leo,' the stone said. 'Please don't any of you rely on me. I am very old and starting to fade. I will wake if the Lady hits me, but she may not have the chance. I can only call my children, like Gold. And if she is underground, I am silenced.'

'Damn,' John said quietly. Then he shook himself out of it. 'So you don't remember what happened?'

'No,' I said. 'She faced me, she hit me, Gold was there. I don't remember anything in between.'

'Stone?' John said.

The stone hesitated. I heard it hesitate.

'Don't you dare start this with me again,' I threatened softly.

'All right.' The stone fell silent, and I was about to berate it again when it spoke. 'You fought valiantly, my Lady, but she was much too strong for you. She struck you in the arm. Then she hit you in the face. Then ...' It went silent again.

'What?'

If the stone could have sighed, it would have. 'Then suddenly you were all over her, you were faster than her —'

'Faster than a level fifty?' I said with disbelief.

'Not possible,' John said.

The stone ignored us. 'And you took her out easily, then you fell. You were astonishing.'

John studied me. 'And you don't remember doing it?'

My throat was thick. 'No.'

We were all silent for a while.

'What does this mean, my Lord?' Leo said.

'It means that I'm going to pull out a level forty-five and throw it at Emma next time she's in Wan Chai,' John said with satisfaction. 'No, damn, I can't get anything that big out, I'd start draining everything around me. One of the Masters can do it, and I'll watch. Should be interesting to see.'

'You have demons that big in a jar?' I said.

'Only one or two,' John said. 'May have to make do with a level forty. Don't often come up against them with the chance to put them into the jar. I don't have anything bigger than that.'

'I'm not too sure about this,' I said.

'Don't worry, I'll have someone on hand just in case,' John said. 'But I'd really like to see you take out something that big with your bare hands.'

'I would too,' I said. 'I have no idea how I did it.'

'Stone?' John said.

'No idea either,' the stone said. 'I look forward to watching as well. Should be interesting.'

A couple of weeks later I received a clean bill of health from Meredith and we tried it. I stood nervously next to the wall under the mirrors in the training room on the twelfth floor. I really wasn't sure about this.

Meredith waited next to the demon jar, watching me with quiet amusement. John leaned against the short wall of the room, arms folded over his chest.

'Just do what you did in Central,' he said quietly.

'I have no idea what I did in Central,' I said.

'There's two in here,' Meredith said. 'I'll give you the female one. It's a big humanoid. Should take human form. Was that what the one in Central was?'

'I think so,' I said. 'Stone? Any idea?'

The stone was silent.

'It's spending more and more time sleeping,' I said.

'Wake it up, it wanted to see,' John said.

I pulled the chain out from around my neck and tapped the stone.

'Yes, my Lady?'

'We're going to do it. Big female humanoid. Is that the same?'

'Sounds about right.'

'Okay.' I took a deep breath. 'Go.'

Meredith held her hand above the jar and one of the beads flew up into it. She threw the bead onto the floor at the base of the mirrors. The female demon materialised in human form.

I went into a guard position and nodded without looking away from the demon.

The demon stiffened and straightened to study me. 'What are you?'

'Damn. Why do they keep doing that? Okay,' I said more loudly, 'what am I?'

The demon glared at me with contempt. 'If I knew I wouldn't be asking you.'

'I'm a Snake Mother,' I said.

'Emma ...' John said from the side, but I ignored him.

'No, you're not,' she said.

'I'm a snake hybrid.'

'Is that what you are?' she said, tilting her head. 'You don't look like a hybrid.'

'Emma, don't worry about it!' John said.

'I'm a perfectly normal human being,' I said.

'Good,' she said. 'Then I should be able to take you *easily*!' She went straight for my head with both hands, but I ducked under her and went through her, hitting her in the abdomen with both feet, one after the other, as I went past.

She spun to follow me. 'Trained by the Dark Lord himself,' she said. 'Impressive.'

She came at me, her fists a blur. I managed to block the first three or four strikes, but quickly found myself unable to keep up with her and retreated, losing ground. She saw that I wasn't nearly as fast as her and her face filled with grim satisfaction as she kept the strikes coming at my head. It was all I could do to stay out of the way.

I fell back, dodging and weaving and making feeble attempts to block her flurry of blows.

She hit me on the side of the head with a cracking thump. The floor crashed into me. I couldn't see.

'If she's sustained brain damage, my Lord, I will personally tear your arms off,' Meredith said.

'You should have seen that coming and bound the bitch quicker,' John said.

'That's right, blame the woman,' I said, and opened my eyes.

I lay on my back on the floor where I'd fallen. My head felt like it was stuffed with lead-filled cotton wool. Meredith was above me, her intelligent face full of concern.

'I'm okay,' I said. 'My head feels fuzzy but I'll live.'

'Meredith?' John said.

Meredith took my hand and studied me. 'She's right: mild concussion, that's all.' She helped me sit up. I wriggled back so that I was leaning against the mirrors. My head was spinning but my vision was clear.

John wiped his hands over his face and tied back his hair. 'Damn.' He and Meredith shared a look but didn't say anything.

'So what was the difference?' John said.

Nobody spoke.

'Stone?' John said.

'I honestly don't know, my Lord,' the stone said. 'In Central, the demon hit her and she moved faster. This time, no difference. Similar demon. Similar circumstances. I have no idea.'

'It will come out in the end,' John said. 'We have all the time in the world. Help her up, Meredith, let's get her home.'

Meredith lifted me with one strong hand under my arm. I was slightly woozy, but I would make it.

'We don't have all the time in the world, John,' I said. 'Time is the one thing that we're rapidly running out of.'

'It will happen for us,' John said grimly. 'Live for the present and look to the future.'

'The future is the only thing keeping me going,' I whispered.

'I won't take you directly home, Emma, it'll make your head ten times worse,' Meredith said. 'Let's get you down to the car, and Lord Xuan can drive you.'

'Okay.'

CHAPTER THIRTY-SEVEN

After we returned from the party the following Saturday we kicked off our shoes and I helped Simone drag all of the gear into her bedroom. The treat sack was huge and stuffed full of gifts.

There was a tap on the door.

'Come in, Leo, let me show you,' Simone said.

Leo came in and sat next to Simone and me on the floor.

'Did you have fun, sweetheart?' he said.

Simone studied me, her little face very serious. 'Emma, you said I'll have a party too. Will it be like that?'

'No,' I said with a laugh. 'Nothing like that. We'll invite about six or eight of your friends over, you can all play in the living room, and we won't have an entertainer.'

'What about the food?' Simone said, eyes wide. 'Like that?'

'No,' I said. 'We'll just have some little snacks.'

'Good,' Simone said. She tipped the contents of the treat sack onto the floor. There was a mountain of sweets, some expensive toys and a large amount of costume jewellery.

'It was one of *them*, wasn't it?' Leo said.

'They rented the entire YMCA in King's Park,' I said to Leo. 'The whole centre.'

'Which one is that?' Leo said. 'I don't remember a YMCA there.'

'It's a new one. Behind QE Hospital. It has tennis courts, a few climbing walls, a big roller hockey rink, an indoor sports hall. Huge.'

'And they took it *all*?' Leo said. 'How many kids did they invite?'

'Must have been more than sixty.'

Leo was speechless.

'We went into the gift room to put our gift on the table, but it had overflowed onto the floor. The room was packed full of presents for this little girl.'

'I don't want that many presents,' Simone said without looking up. 'I want to have a party and play with my friends.'

'They had the staff of the Y pull out the roller-skating gear so the kids could have a skate. But they didn't have enough equipment. Lots of the kids missed out. The parents stood around and watched — you know what it's like.'

'Yeah, parents and grandparents bring the kids. You have to look after them too. And the little brothers and sisters and cousins.'

'Then they did rock climbing, but of course they were all too small to make any progress up the wall. And the Y didn't have enough staff, so I belayed as well.'

Leo gestured towards my T-shirt. 'So that's what happened.'

I glanced down. My T-shirt was absolutely filthy on one side, from the rope rubbing as I'd belayed for the kids. 'Yeah. I had to lift them up the wall; they couldn't do it by themselves.' I stretched my shoulders. 'My arms are killing me.'

'What did they eat?'

'It was catered — big professional firm. None of the kids liked the food. And they had *two* entertainers. Magicians. But the kids ignored them — they'd all seen the shows before.'

'I've seen one of those guys do those tricks *three times* now,' Simone said irritably. She took some of the candy and threw it into her little wastepaper basket next to the door. 'He was *boring*. Daddy can do much better things than that.' She had a sudden idea, charged over and threw herself at me. 'Hey! At my party, can we ask Daddy to do some stuff with water? He can pretend to be a magician! That would be *so cool*!'

I gave Simone a huge hug. 'I don't think that's a good idea, sweetheart.'

'So it was a typical Hong Kong birthday party,' Leo said as he pulled himself up from the floor.

'Absolutely the *most* typical one I've ever been to,' I said. 'They must think it's some sort of competition or something.'

'What did the birthday girl think?'

'I don't think she had very much fun at all,' I said. 'She spent most of the time crying.'

'How long to my party, Emma?' Simone said.

'About three weeks, sweetheart,' I said. I gave her a squeeze. 'We need to make invitations.'

Simone jumped up and threw her arms above her head. 'Yay!' she squealed. She jumped around the room. 'Party for *me*! Friends for *me*! I *love* having friends!' She threw herself at Leo and he hoisted her to sit on his hip. 'When's your birthday, Leo?'

'I'm too old to have birthdays,' Leo said, grinning and holding her close.

'Remember? We had a cake for Leo, and he was all cross with us, and we had to get your dad to order him to stay and blow out the candles?' I said.

'And then we made him go out with all of his silly friends?'

'Some of your friends are funny, Leo,' Simone said into Leo's grinning face, 'but I liked them.' She turned to me, still in his arms. 'When's your birthday, Emma?'

'Not telling,' I said.

'October twenty-third,' Leo said. 'Next Thursday.'

'Don't you *dare*,' I said fiercely.

Leo grinned. 'No idea what you're talking about.'

'Leo, can we go into your room and talk for a minute, please?' Simone said, suddenly serious.

'Don't either of you *dare*!' I shouted at them.

'Still don't know what you're talking about, Emma,' Leo said as he lowered Simone and took her hand. 'Come on, Simone.'

Simone glanced over her shoulder at me. 'I don't know what you're talking about either, Emma.' She tugged Leo's hand. 'Come on, Leo, we need to talk.'

I got out of the lift on the eighth floor to go to my energy work class. It was unusually quiet. Normally the first years would be chatting and laughing in the room, but as I walked towards the door the hall was completely silent. I wondered whether I had the time wrong as I opened the door.

Fortunately they had the brains not to jump out and yell 'surprise!' at me; I probably would have taken all of them out with energy without even thinking. They stood around a large table with a monstrous birthday cake on it.

I spun to leave but Leo was way ahead of me. He grabbed me, lifted me completely off my feet before I had a chance to struggle, turned me around and put me in front of the cake.

Then they all began to sing goddamn 'Happy Birthday' to me.

Simone ran to me with her arms up. I lifted her and sat her on my hip. 'Happy birthday, Emma!' she yelled right into my ear.

'You will thoroughly keep for this, Leo,' I growled softly.

'You did it to me,' Leo said with a huge grin.

'Don't put Simone down,' John said, and charged over to me, wrapped his arms around both of us, and gave me a huge kiss right on the mouth.

Damned if they all didn't cheer and clap. Even Simone squealed with delight.

I looked around. My energy work students were there. Meredith, Liu, most of the other Celestial Masters and all of the human ones. Most of the demon staff from the top floor. Michael and Rhonda, standing together. The White Tiger, standing behind Rhonda with a huge grin. Jade and Gold, both of them grinning like idiots.

'You will all keep,' I said loudly.

'*Now* who's over the hill?' Leo said with delight, gesturing towards the cake with the big '30' on top.

'All of us!' I shouted, and squeezed Simone tight.

'Put her down, Emma, I have a gift for you,' John said.

'I have everything I could possibly want in the whole world,' I said as I lowered Simone. 'You don't need to give me anything.'

John gestured, and one of the demons handed him a wrapped cylinder. He presented it to me with both hands, a small bow and a huge grin.

I wondered if I should open it immediately Western-style, or hold on to it and open it privately later, Chinese-style.

'Western-style,' John said, reading my mind. 'Open it. They want to see.'

I carefully pulled off the red wrapping paper. It was a scroll; it had wooden dowels at the top and the bottom, and a red silk ribbon for hanging. I held the top dowel and let the scroll carefully fall.

It was a single character. The character *si*; made of a field above a heart, done in John's elegant flowing hand.

'What does it mean?' Leo said into my ear.

'Thought. Contemplation. Remembrance. I will see it and remember.' I turned the scroll around so that they could all see, and they went quiet.

'Could somebody get me a tissue, please?' I choked.

'That was a bad present, Daddy,' Simone said. 'You made her cry.'

'These are tears of happiness, Simone,' I said, my voice thick. 'I'll have this on the wall in my room for a long time.'

'Good,' John said. 'For a moment there I thought I'd made a huge mistake.'

'You don't have any bad ideas, John,' I said. 'Only good ones.'

Leo helped me put the scroll up in my room later. He banged a nail into the wall, high enough for the scroll to clear the floor.

'Don't know why he didn't wait until next year,' Leo growled. 'It's a big birthday for you, this one. This is a really depressing gift.'

'No, it's wonderful,' I said. 'But don't you realise?'

'What?'

I sighed with exasperation. 'You've been living in China longer than I have, Leo. You haven't learned anything.'

'What?' Leo said impatiently.

'Everything they say and do has hidden layers of meaning. Everything is symbolic.'

'And?'

'And,' I said, 'Immortals are renowned for their ability to see the future.'

'That would explain why they're so goddamned serene all the time,' Leo said. He hung the scroll on the nail. 'They know what's going to happen.'

'It's hard to tell how much they know; none of them will talk about it. You know there's some things that none of them will talk about. But the symbolism of this gift is obvious.'

We stepped back to admire the scroll.

'No, it isn't,' Leo said. 'Not to me, anyway.'

'He thinks he won't have the chance to give it to me for my next birthday,' I said as calmly as I could.

Leo was silent.

'We have to get Simone up to speed.'

Leo still didn't say anything. He turned and went out.

I didn't turn around when I heard the tap on the door a couple of days later, just called out, 'Come on in.'

Michael poked his head around the door. 'A friend of mine's dropped by, Emma, and wants to know if we can go to the mall together.'

'Don't be ridiculous, Michael,' I said. 'You know you won't be safe by yourself and just one other. Go with a group, or take either Leo or myself to guard you.'

Michael sighed. He obviously hadn't wanted to tell me. 'It's Na Zha.'

'Damn.' I pushed myself away from my desk. 'You know how I feel about him.'

Michael shrugged. 'Come on, Emma, he's okay, he promises to behave. We just want to go and look at the new software in the shops. No trouble, promise.'

'Where is he?'

'Outside the living room window.'

I stormed out to the living room. Michael was right: Na Zha floated outside the living room window, poised on his fire wheels. He saw me coming and grinned.

He moved back about three metres, then rode the fire wheels right through the window without doing any damage whatsoever to the glass. He landed lightly on the carpet without the wheels; he'd already been in major trouble once with John for singeing the carpet.

'Yo,' he said briskly. 'How about it?'

He looked about seventeen. He wore a pair of jeans that were more than four sizes too big for him and floated somewhere down around his hips, with his designer underwear plainly showing and the bottoms crumpled and torn. His T-shirt was black, sleeveless and much too small for him. He wore a black baseball cap back-to-front. His sunglasses and sports shoes were the most expensive on the market. An MP3 player was slung around his neck, rap metal blaring loudly from the tiny headphones. He was the image of the rich, rebellious, spoilt Hong Kong teenager.

I swallowed my feelings as I carefully saluted him. 'My Lord Third Prince.'

Na Zha grinned evilly at me. 'Lady Emma.' He shrugged. 'Come on, we'll be fine, no trouble, I promise.'

'You've just given me your word, Na Zha,' I said. 'No trouble.' I sighed with resignation. 'I suppose it's all right. Back by ten, okay? Michael's half human, he needs his rest.'

'Sweet,' Michael said.

'There's a great mall in Bel Air. Wanna go?' Na Zha asked Michael.

'Bel Air Gardens in Sha Tin? There's not much over there,' I said.

'Not Sha Tin, LA,' Na Zha snapped impatiently.

'*No way*!' I shouted, and both of them glanced at me. 'I said back by ten, and I meant ten *tonight*! You two will stay here in Hong Kong where I can call Michael. Do you have your phone, Michael?'

I don't need a phone any more, Michael said, straight into my ear.

'When the hell did you learn to do that?'

The Dark Lord taught me last week.

'That's all well and good, Michael, but you know I can't do it, so I can't call you if I need you. So take your phone, okay? And you two *talk out loud* when you're near me, or there'll be serious trouble.'

Michael nodded. Na Zha put his hand on his hip, exasperated, but didn't say anything.

'Festie?' Michael said.

'Whatever.' Na Zha turned and jumped through the glass of the living room window. The fire wheels materialised under his feet. He summoned a cloud for Michael.

'Michael, please don't get into any trouble. If you do, your mother will kill me,' I said wearily. 'A little restraint goes a long way, you know?'

'Don't worry, Emma, we'll behave. There's a new game out, we just want to check it out,' Michael said. Na Zha gestured towards the cloud. Michael ran straight through the glass of the window and landed on the cloud. 'Hey,' Michael called as they left. 'Thanks.'

'Just don't make me come down there and get you,' I told their backs as they flew away.

I stormed back to my room and returned to the spreadsheets. Oh well, at least I knew there was no chance of a demon getting him when he was with that little ... *gentleman*.

John must have known that Simone and I had arrived for breakfast in the dining room the next morning.

Come and see me in my office after you've eaten, Emma.

I picked up my tea and opened the newspaper. I froze completely.

Simone saw my face. 'What's the matter, Emma?'

I didn't reply. I was reading the front page. There was a huge colour photo and a headline: LOCAL BUSINESSWOMAN ARRESTED. It was a photo of *Kitty Kwok*. My old boss from the kindergarten. She took up most of the frame. She was wearing huge designer sunglasses and scowling away from the camera, obviously being escorted by plainclothes police.

The bottom fell out of my stomach. Walking behind her, grinning right at me over her left shoulder, was our favourite demon, *Simon Wong*.

I read the copy.

Local businesswoman Kitty Kwok Ho Man Yee was today arrested in connection with what police have described as 'illegal activities'. Sources say that she has been arrested as part of a money-laundering cleanup operation. There are suggestions that she has been using her chain of kindergartens to fund underworld activity.

Miss Kwok's husband, Cedric Ho, died in a mysterious boating accident in 1985, leaving her extensive corporate and property investments. A coroner's inquiry ruled the death of the tycoon 'death by misadventure'.

As well as the kindergarten chain, Miss Kwok has extensive agricultural holdings in China, and is a major shareholder in Tautech, a bioengineering company with laboratories in China, Australia, Hong Kong, the US and Europe.

Miss Kwok refused to comment.

I dropped the newspaper and cast around for the Chinese one. It was still on the table. I could only understand about one character in five, but that didn't matter. There were huge glossy photos all over the front page. The Chinese newspapers were always very good about having big, spectacular, and often explicitly gory colour photographs with every story.

The Chinese-language newspaper had large colourful photos of the raids on the biotechnology labs in Dongguan. People in white lab jackets being herded into vans, and cages of animals and birds being loaded into trucks.

The bottom photo showed the interior of the lab. It wasn't the shiny clean laboratory expected in the West; it was a large dirty room with peeling green paint and rusty window frames. It was full of aquariums. The aquariums didn't have any water in them; they were full of *snakes*.

'I have to go and talk to your dad, Simone,' I said absently. 'If you need anything, ask Monica.'

I didn't even knock on his office door. I went in and flopped into a chair opposite him.

'You still have it in your hand,' he said mildly.

He was right. I threw the newspaper onto his desk.

'She gave you my number in the first place,' I said.

He didn't reply, but his eyes blazed.

'She lured you away at that first charity thing, so he could have a go at me,' I said.

He remained silent and unmoving.

'She kept ringing me after you made your pledge, John. She kept asking me to go to her house.'

'Before then,' he said. 'She called you even before we went to Guangdong.'

I remembered. 'Yeah.'

He remained motionless.

'*How can you stay so calm*?' I shouted. 'She was *working for him*!' I ran my hands through my hair. 'She *planted me here*!'

'I don't think so, Emma,' he said. 'I really did ask her if she knew of a good English teacher. She gave your

438

number to other people, didn't she? She was rather proud of your ability. Every time I saw her, she took full credit for your talent as a teacher.'

I leaned across the desk to speak intensely. 'When did they first know who you were?'

He leaned back and retied his hair. 'Michelle let it slip, at a charity function. She complained to Kitty that I always wore black, despite her best efforts to make me wear other colours. I think that's when they put it together. That was not long after we were married and I moved down here.'

'So she knew who you were when she sent me here,' I said. 'She was a total bitch to me at that first concert. Then she turned all sunshine and butterflies, asking me to go and visit her.'

'I like that, "sunshine and butterflies". I must remember that,' he said, amused. 'One Two Two had just left the Mountain after learning there for two years.'

'He knew you had to stay here to care for Simone after he'd killed Michelle, and took advantage of it,' I said.

'Then they saw how close we were becoming. They saw their chance to cultivate a spy. Too bad you had already joined me.'

'Those labs were full of *snakes*.'

'And birds. I wonder if they built the fire things there.'

'Simone saw me as a *snake*, John. What if this has something to do with it?' I sighed with despair. 'I don't know how you can keep me around, knowing what you do about me.'

He shot to his feet and banged his hand on the table so hard that I jumped. '*Don't you even think about leaving me!*' he roared. '*We need you!*' He sat down again, his voice still fierce. 'I know everything there is to know about you. I have seen inside you. I have loved you. I have seen all of your body and all of your mind. I have seen you, shen, ching and chi. There is nothing I don't know about you. You will grow with time, but you will never hurt any of us.' He studied me intensely. 'Trust yourself as much as I trust you, Emma. Look inside yourself.' He smiled. 'Study the nature of serpents, and do not be concerned.'

'God, I hope you're right,' I said.

'Do you want me to call the Lady? You want to throw yourself onto a demon's sword again?'

'No, I think I'd better move and take Simone and Michael to school.'

He checked his watch. 'You'd better go. If they're late for school I'll dock your pay.'

'Try me,' I said. 'I'll dock yours. I have more control of the finances anyway.'

'Good,' he said as I went out.

Halfway down the hallway I froze. Oh my God. *April*. Kitty had arranged for April to have the baby at a clinic in *Dongguan*.

I called April's apartment in Discovery Bay, but the domestic helper didn't know anything. April's mobile had been disconnected. I didn't know Andy's number, and it wasn't in the phone book.

There was no way I could contact April or her family. There was nothing I could do.

CHAPTER THIRTY-EIGHT

That Saturday the intercom on my desk popped and I pressed the button.

'Emma, it's me.' Leo's voice was thin and tinny. 'I need you, I'm in a hand-to-hand on the third floor. Come and help out, please.'

'Okay, on my way.'

When I arrived at the third floor I entered the room quietly. Some of the students saw me and moved to stop working, but Leo ordered them to continue. I stood next to the door and watched them. They didn't talk to each other as they worked; obviously my presence was intimidating. They didn't even give each other tips.

Leo moved silently down the middle of the group then stood beside me at the back of the class and crossed his arms over his chest.

We spoke to each other quietly without looking away from the students.

'You see the problem?' he said, his voice soft and even.

'Yes,' I said. 'What's his name?'

'Nguyen,' Leo said. 'Vietnamese. Really talented.'

'I can see that.'

Nguyen was lightning fast. Incredibly fast. Leo had paired him up with an African girl who was also fast, but he was light years ahead of her. He had an arrogant grin on his face as he blocked her punches with ease.

'Let me show you,' Leo said under his breath without turning away from the students. 'Swap!'

Nguyen and the African girl swapped. Now he punched and she blocked. But he was through her. It didn't matter what she tried to do, his fist always ended up a couple of centimetres from her nose.

'Is he human?' I said.

'One hundred per cent. That's the first thing I checked. Watch him.' Leo's voice remained soft as he studied the young man. 'He's so damn cocky that his moves are all over the place.'

Leo was right. Nguyen was incredibly untidy. He was so fast that he thought it didn't matter that he was doing it wrong most of the time.

'Did you try having Mr Chen sort him out?'

'He knows that he won't ever face a goddamn *god,* so it didn't worry him that Mr Chen is faster,' Leo said, still low enough that the students wouldn't hear. 'He knows I can take him, but that doesn't worry him either. He knows that with more training he'll be able to take me too.'

'I'd dearly like to do this in front of the whole class, but at this stage probably just him and me would be enough to sort him out,' I said. 'Let's do it.'

Leo nodded without moving. 'End it there!' The students stopped and faced us. 'Dismissed!' All of the students saluted us neatly and turned to go. 'Nguyen,' Leo said as the students filed past us, some of them smiling shyly at me.

Nguyen came and saluted Leo and me.

'What class do you have next, Nguyen?' I said kindly.

'Saturday extra study group,' he said with a sly grin. 'Doesn't matter too much if I miss it, my Lady.'

Leo didn't shift beside me but I knew he was thinking the same thing I was: arrogant little bastard actually thought he'd been singled out for special training because he was so good.

'Do you know who I am, Nguyen?' I said, still being very kind.

'I know who you are, Lady Emma, and I'm honoured by your attention,' he said, the sly grin not shifting.

'Good,' I said, and moved forward to the centre of the room, waving for him to accompany me. 'Do you know what I am?'

He seemed confused. 'I'm sorry, ma'am, but as far as I know you're an ordinary human being, just like Master Leo.'

'That is perfectly correct, Nguyen,' I said. 'Leo tells me that you are one of the fastest things he has seen in a long time. Do you think that's true?'

'I know I'm fast,' he said confidently, and Leo made a soft sound behind me.

'Are you the fastest human you've ever seen?' I said.

'I am,' he said with complete confidence.

'Oh, very good,' I said. 'You're faster than Master Leo?'

The kid just nodded.

'Good,' I said. 'Have you heard that I'm fast?'

The kid nodded again.

'Answer the Dark Lady's questions when they are asked of you!' Leo snapped.

For a fleeting instant Nguyen's face screwed up into a grimace of rebellion, then the smile was there again. 'Yes, ma'am.'

'Well, then,' I said, 'let's see exactly how fast I am. Left guard.'

Both of us moved into a guard stance.

'I want a face hit right, chest left, left uppercut, then another right face. Got it?' I said. 'Measure up.'

'Yes, ma'am,' he said, the smile still there as he measured out the length of his reach and moved back into the guard position.

I realised with a shock that he thought he could take me. He must have heard them talking about me. The level of arrogance this kid displayed was disturbing. I hoped we wouldn't have to throw him out; he was really very good.

'Go,' I said.

He moved through the series of punches and I blocked them easily. His grin didn't shift; not going full speed.

'Faster,' I said.

He moved faster. I blocked them. His smile was still there.

'Faster!' I berated, trying to goad him.

He threw himself into it. Obviously the goading worked: he started to move untidily again. Again I blocked his punches with ease.

'Right,' I said after we had done the series a few times, 'I want to see this all out. Go as fast as you can. Come on, I know you can go faster than this.'

His fists were a blur. His grin was still fixed on his face. He was very, very fast.

I blocked his moves easily and his face fell. He tried again; I blocked easily again. He tried to go even faster but he slightly lost control and I blocked him without difficulty.

'Swap,' I said brusquely when I had made it completely obvious that he wouldn't be getting through me.

We measured up again, and both moved into guard stances.

'Ready?' I said, and he nodded.

I moved through the four punches slowly, letting him block me. His grin returned.

'Now,' I said, 'I will do the series slightly faster each time. Let's see how fast you can go.'

When I was up to about half-speed he began to lose it. The third punch was getting through.

I sped up again, and I was through him. I could do all four punches and have them end up less than a centimetre from the end of his nose. His face froze into an expression of disbelief.

I did it full speed. His face shifted to bewilderment. He couldn't even see them coming. All he could see was me readying myself, and then the fist right in front of his nose.

'You're not human!' he choked.

'Yes, I am,' I said quietly as I pressed the advantage home. I did the four punches, but I didn't stop. I kept the punches coming, finishing each one right at the end of his nose.

'Stop anything you can,' I said as I continued the flurry of punches. His face became a mask of horror as he tried to block the punches, always ending up miles behind them.

I stepped back, did a spinning kick that knocked his feet out from under him, flipped him onto his belly, grabbed one arm and twisted it behind him, and put my knee in the middle of his back. I tapped him lightly on the back of the neck.

'You are now officially *dead*, Mr Nguyen.' I released him. 'Stand up.'

He stood and faced me, stunned.

'Am I fast?' I said.

'You are amazingly fast, ma'am,' he said, his voice full of wonder. 'You're the fastest thing I've ever seen.'

'Leo can take me. I can only handle up to about level thirty demons bare-handed. Once you're past level fifteen, demons are faster than any human alive, even me. How many levels of demons are there?'

'One hundred, the King himself is at level one hundred,' Nguyen said with a touch of humility. 'Snake Mothers start at level fifty. You can only take level thirty?'

'What level have you faced so far?'

Nguyen glanced, disconcerted, at Leo.

'None yet, they're too junior,' Leo said.

'Tell me, Nguyen, how far do you think you need to go,' I said, trying not to put any emotion into my voice at all, 'before you are ready to face your first demon?'

'I need to go through the basics again,' Nguyen said. 'I need more than just speed if I want to be able to handle anything at a reasonable level.' He looked up at me. 'I think with a few more weeks of training with Master Leo I may be able to face something at a very low level.'

'Thanks, Emma,' Leo said behind me, and I nodded without turning. Leo moved to stand beside me. 'I can defeat the Lady Emma in hand-to-hand without difficulty,' he told Nguyen. 'I can take up to level forty bare-handed. Speed isn't everything, Nguyen. That was the whole point of this lesson.'

'You are not being singled out for special training, Nguyen, just because you're fast,' I said compassionately. 'Leo brought me up to teach you a lesson, and I hope you've learned it.'

Nguyen saluted us both, the smile gone. 'I have learned a valuable lesson, Masters, and I thank you. I will work harder at the basics and improve my style.'

'Dismissed,' Leo said softly. Nguyen saluted us again and went out.

'Your own style is incredibly untidy and you really need some work,' Leo growled, his brown eyes sparkling. 'You've been concentrating far too much on the energy stuff lately, Emma. When was the last time you did some hand-to-hand with Mr Chen?'

I shrugged. 'Last time we tried, we were only five minutes into the lesson when he had to run out the door. We've given up.' I had a brilliant idea. 'Find time in your schedule to work with me, Leo, we'll brush me up together.'

'Waste of time, my Lady,' Leo lisped softly, and I winced. 'Ask one of the more advanced Masters to teach you; you're already way past me. I lied. You could probably take me now.'

'No *way*! You have always been better than me at hand-to-hand!'

Leo went into a guard position. 'Let's see.'

I raised my hands. 'No, Leo, you can take me, don't waste your time.'

Leo performed a magnificent roundhouse kick straight at my head and I ducked underneath it.

'Chicken,' Leo said.

'Oh, come on, this is a total waste of time,' I said. 'I have things I need to do. I was in the middle of my thesis.'

Leo threw another roundhouse at me. I ducked. He spun and did it again. He kept coming at me, forcing me back as I ducked under the kicks.

'Stop it, Leo!' I said, becoming irate.

Leo stopped, then stepped forward and lightly tapped me under the chin with his fist.

'Ouch. My face still hurts, you know.'

'Come on, Emma, good practice. What's wrong? Frightened you'll beat me?'

'No,' I said as I took a guard position, 'I'm frightened I'll hurt you.' I grinned. 'You'll cry like a little girl.'

'No, I won't,' Leo said as he went for my head with his foot again. 'You will.'

I didn't duck under his foot this time. I blocked his leg with my left, swept it down, gave it a good push in the direction it was already going, and then kicked his other foot out from underneath him.

He jumped with my movement and somersaulted backwards. He was incredibly lithe and graceful for such a big guy. He landed neatly on his feet and came right after me again, this time with his fists.

'Wasting your time, Leo,' I said as I blocked the blows. 'You'll have to be cleverer than that, I really am faster than you.'

He suddenly spun under me and tried to take my feet out, but I leapt right over the top of his head, somersaulted, and landed facing him.

'Whoa,' Leo said. 'Good one.' He came at me again, this time with both fists and feet. He threw everything he had at me.

He was through me. He hit my feet, and I could feel myself falling forwards. I put my hands out, landed on them hard, and then pushed away from the floor with them. I did a handspring, but I didn't stop. I used the energy centres and lifted myself until I hit the ceiling. I bounced off it, somersaulted, and landed lightly on my feet behind Leo. He still faced the other way. I spun and quickly took his feet out from under him.

He fell with a thud. He obviously wasn't expecting it. He didn't even know where I was.

I stopped and stared at him with wonder.

Suddenly a round of applause burst from the doorway. At least two dozen students of all levels were grinning and clapping. There were even a couple of Masters watching as well.

Leo pulled himself up and performed an elaborate bow for the audience. They cheered and wolf-whistled.

I didn't say anything. I went to the door, pushed through the students and took the lift back up to the top floor. I went into my office and fell into the chair behind my desk. I put my head in my hands.

Leo came in after me and sat in the visitor's chair, which protested under his weight. He studied me silently. Eventually he said, 'I thought you'd be pleased.'

'Leo.' I looked desperately up at him. 'I really should not have been able to do that.'

'Why not?' Leo said. 'You're damn good, you know that. I'm not surprised you can take me.' He grinned. 'But I won't cry like a little girl.'

I turned away. 'How long has Mr Chen been teaching you?'

'Nearly eight years.'

'Did you do self-defence in the Navy? And when you were a bodyguard? And a bouncer?'

'Yeah. Sure. I did about six years of martial arts before I came to Mr Chen. But what he's taught me is light years ahead.'

'How long has he been teaching me?'

Leo paused. 'Damn, Emma, you're really talented. Only about ... what? Fourteen months? Is it really only such a short time? You're incredibly good. Damn.'

'I am *inhumanly* good, Leo. Before I met John, I'd never done anything like this.'

Leo leaned back without speaking.

'You are the greatest human warrior of your generation, Leo. Mr Chen told me that himself. It's taken you fourteen years to get this good, and you're almost as good as an Immortal. Look at me. Fourteen months, and I can take you.'

Leo still didn't say anything. I could see what he was thinking.

'Simone saw me as a *snake*.'

Leo flinched.

'Leo, can I confide in you?' I said softly.

'What are you going to tell me? I'm not sure I want to know.'

'I have these dreams. All the time.'

'What, Emma?' he whispered.

I ran my hands through my hair. 'I dream ... I'm a snake.'

'I don't know what to say,' Leo said quietly, looking down at his hands.

'All the damn time. I dream I'm a snake. Killing demons. Fighting. Moving fast. Killing things. I dream I'm a *snake*.'

'I think you should talk to Mr Chen.'

'You know what he says?'

Leo didn't say anything. His face was rigid.

'He says: Good. He says: Don't worry about it. He says: Some of his best friends are snakes.'

Leo was silent.

'And now I can take you. I'm inhumanly fast. I'm inhumanly good.'

I could see what he was thinking.

'You remember Kitty Kwok? The woman I used to work for?'

'Yeah. At the kindergarten. Total bitch.'

'She lured John away from me at that first charity function. Remember? The concert? The first attack by Simon Wong?'

'What's that got to do with it?'

'She was *working* for Simon Wong, Leo.'

Leo inhaled sharply but didn't say anything.

'She owns the biotech company. The one that's been making the hybrids for him. Did you see the paper? The Chinese paper?'

'No.'

'The lab. In Dongguan. Where they were making the hybrids. Had aquariums. Full of *snakes*.'

'Snakes.'

'Yes.'

'Damn, Emma,' Leo said.

'*I'm* a snake, Leo. Simone saw me as a snake.'

Leo shifted uncomfortably but didn't say anything.

I looked down at my hands on the desk. I didn't know what to say either.

'What else?' Leo said. 'What else are you going to tell me? That you're a snake demon? A hybrid? A Mother? What?'

'I don't know what I am, apart from ...' I sighed. 'Apart from this snake stuff.'

Leo studied his hands for a while. Then he glanced up at me and smiled. 'Okay,' he said briskly. 'You're good at martial arts. You have weird dreams, probably brought on by this stupid goddamn thesis that you're doing. You ever gonna hurt Simone?'

'No, of course not.'

'Well then, what you worrying about?'

'I'm something dark and monstrous.'

'I don't disagree with you there,' he said with a small smile.

I put my head in my hands. 'God, Leo.'

'You're turning into an Immortal, Emma.'

'I don't know what I am, Leo.'

'That wasn't a question, sweetheart,' Leo said. 'I was telling you. Now finish your thesis. We're more fed up with it than you are. I'm sick to death of the sight of you in front of that computer, and I want to spend more time sparring with you. I think with weapons I could probably still take you.'

'I sincerely hope so, Leo.'

'Go and talk to Mr Chen.'

I put my arms on the desk and rested my head on them. He patted me gently on the head and leaned over to whisper in my ear. 'This snake stuff is probably just your overactive imagination, fired up by the stress of your study. And when you finish this goddamn thesis, it'll all go away.'

'I hope you're right,' I said into my arms, my voice muffled. But he was already gone.

CHAPTER THIRTY-NINE

Three little russet balls of fluff snuggled together in a nest of warm blankets. I moved quietly towards them, making quite sure that they didn't wake. I flicked my tongue and tasted them. They were sweet, like babies, but with the slight powdery edge of feathers.

I slid my head gently over the edge of the nest and held my breath. My nose was within touching distance of a slender, elegant neck.

I raised my head slightly, my breath still held. Then I struck. I had always loved the feeling of my fangs piercing the skin with a satisfying pop and then pressing through to the soft flesh beneath. The bitter-sweet taste of my venom mixed with the rich salty flavour of the blood. The little bird didn't struggle much; my venom was a neurotoxin and the victims were paralysed almost immediately. Rather like the five-point push, the wry thought came to me. Much the same thing.

I would have preferred it alive; the feeling of its tiny wings and legs thrashing inside my throat would have been exquisite. But I didn't want to wake the other two. I would eat the last one alive and take my time about it.

I unlocked my jaws and pulled the little one in. I wiggled my head from side to side as I sent it slowly down my throat. The feathers were thick and delightful in my mouth. I sent my breathing tube out around it; so clever. My mouth was full of satisfying textures and I could still breathe around them.

When I had it all the way down I closed my neck onto its body and the soft bones collapsed with a satisfying crunch. I tasted the blood as it trickled down my throat and wished that I could close my eyes with relish.

I turned to the next one. Another tiny luscious sleeping ball of fluff.

I reared up and opened my mouth to strike the second one. They were so adorable. And delicious.

I woke with a start, spun onto my belly and banged my head on the pillow a few times.

I *did not* want to eat the Phoenix's babies. I was *vegetarian*.

Maybe I needed to go to the fast food and have a soy sauce chicken leg.

Nope. The idea made me feel quite ill.

I was definitely vegetarian. Definitely.

I glanced at the clock. I'd been sitting for an hour staring at the sheets, unable to concentrate. The numbers seemed to be meaningless hieroglyphs. My thesis was due next week, and there was still so much more that needed to be done. I couldn't let things like this take over my life.

I made a snap decision, and for the first time actually did what the stone wanted me to do.

I threw myself out of my chair and stormed through the door of my office. I thumped down the hall, ignoring the greetings from the demon and human staff in the top-floor administration area. There was a pleasant, constant bustle of work. Normally I enjoyed the sound of the soft conversations and the smell of the tea and coffee brewing, but instead I felt slightly sick.

John had strongly resisted when Gold and I had designed his office. We'd given him a whole corner of the building on the top floor. His office was nearly as big as my old flat back in Sha Tin. Half of it was a normal office with cabinets; the other half was fitted with white training mats. Both Gold and I knew that he liked to be up high, and that he needed the space. He often held meetings with all of the senior Masters over a conjured conference table in his office, and he and I would occasionally spar together in there when the burden of administration was too much for either of us.

When we'd shown him the plans he'd angrily demanded a small office on the first floor next to the armoury. Both Gold and I had easily acquiesced and then ignored him. He needed the space, he needed to be up high, and he needed to be able to shut the door and practise the Arts in private.

Both of us needed to be able to shut the door and wave a sword around sometimes.

When we had finally moved him into his office he hadn't said a word. But Gold and I both knew that it would be a long time before he forgave us for doing this to him.

I stalked past John's demon assistant, a smiling young Chinese girl in her mid-twenties, and slammed John's door open. He was reading some papers on his desk; probably reports on the rebuilding. As I walked in he glanced up and smiled at me, unsurprised. I flung myself into one of the visitor's chairs, then watched him for a while, not knowing where to start.

He didn't give me any help whatsoever. He sat behind his desk waiting silently and patiently for me.

'Tell me about serpents,' I said.

'About time,' the stone said. We both ignored it.

John leaned forward and folded his hands on the desk in front of him. 'You tell me first. Tell me what you know about them. You used to keep one as a pet; tell me about it. What are snakes like?'

'Lousy pets.' I smiled as I thought about the snake. 'Absolutely non-affectionate. Don't care about anything except where their next meal is coming from, and once they've been fed they just sleep until they're hungry again. Rather like men,' I said, but he didn't rise to it.

'What about their nature?'

'Quiet,' I said, pondering. 'Silent. They hide their intelligence.' I stopped and winced but his face didn't shift. 'And they can be very single-minded. Fast,' I winced again, 'and merciless.'

'You're not very quiet,' he said with a small smile.

I didn't say anything and his smile turned wry.

I ran my hands through my hair and gave up. 'I've been having dreams. Last night . . .' I couldn't finish it.

'Go on,' he said. 'Tell me. Let it out.'

'Last night,' I said, 'I dreamed that I . . .'

'What?'

'I dreamed that I ate the Phoenix's babies,' I said. 'I was a snake, and I ate the *babies*!'

'Most snakes eat baby birds, it is the main part of their diet,' he said, looking me straight in the eye over his hands. 'I used to dream of eating babies all the time.'

I stopped, horrified. 'You didn't, you didn't . . .' No. He wasn't like that at all. But when he had the Serpent, maybe?

'Never,' he said, without a hint of emotion in his voice.

'But you *wanted to*?'

'Of course I did,' he said, his tone not changing. 'I would also dream about killing my demon staff, about killing my students, even killing Michelle.'

He shrugged. 'I never dreamed of killing Simone, which is surprising —'

'Oh my God,' I said, my voice very small.

'When I lost the Serpent the dreams stopped.'

'You lost that evil part of your nature and you stopped dreaming about killing things?'

He wrenched his hands apart and slammed them on the table, palms down. 'You have a long way to go, sometimes, Emma!' he spat, his eyes blazing. 'Haven't you learned anything?' He made an obvious conscious effort to control himself, then rubbed his hands over his face. 'You are a Westerner. I suppose it is inevitable that you would have this attitude.'

I felt thoroughly browbeaten and went silent. He'd never reacted that way before to anything that I'd said in the past.

We studied each other over the table. For the first time since I'd met him, I didn't know what to say. I even felt slightly afraid of him. There was a gulf between us.

Well then, bridge it.

'Tell me,' I said softly. 'Teach me.'

'Do you know what you said?' he said, looking deep into my eyes. 'You said something that always makes me very angry when I hear it.'

I was silent. I didn't want to provoke the same reaction.

'You said that the Serpent is *evil*. You said that *I* am evil. The whole concept is abhorrent. And yet still you stamp it onto me. If you still think that there is such a thing as "evil" then you have not learned anything.' He turned away and tied his hair back.

'Tell me about serpents then, Xuan Wu,' I said quietly. 'They eat babies alive, but they aren't evil. Tell me.'

'Have you eaten lamb?' he said without looking at me.

'You know I have.'

'Veal?' he said. 'Roast sucking pig? Even chicken? Only six weeks old, most of them.'

I stopped as I understood. 'Not any more. And never alive.'

He looked me right in the eyes. 'Imagine that you are walking through Victoria Park, and you see a crow. In its claws, held down with its foot, the crow has a baby sparrow. The baby sparrow is struggling; it is in its death throes. The crow is waiting patiently for the sparrow to die. It is watching the sparrow die with interest. When the sparrow is dead, the crow will dismember it and eat it. What would you do?'

I stopped and deliberated.

'Don't think about what you'd do, the answer will be contrived!' he snapped. 'Tell me! You are there! *What do you do?*'

'I'd walk away,' I said miserably, my voice small.

'Good,' he said, leaning back and eyeing me appraisingly. 'Perhaps you are learning. Would you try to rescue the baby sparrow?'

'No,' I said with more confidence. 'It's in its death throes, so it's already effectively dead.'

'Is the crow evil?' he said quickly.

'No,' I said, just as fast. 'It just wants its dinner.'

'Good!' he said briskly. 'But the sparrow is suffering. Would you try to kill it sooner? To save its suffering?'

'If I could, I would,' I said. 'But I'd be likely to have my hand taken off by the crow if I tried, and besides, it would scare the crow away.'

'Excellent!' he said, his voice full of approval. 'Why wouldn't you want to scare the crow away?'

'Because then the crow would go hungry,' I said with wonder. I hadn't even thought of that angle until he asked me. 'The crow has to eat too, and I have no right to deprive it of its dinner.'

'Now.' He leaned forward over the desk and steepled his hands on the papers. 'What is the purpose of the life of that sparrow? What was the whole point of its existence?'

I was about to say 'to feed the crow' but then I stopped. I didn't know enough to say that.

'I have no idea.'

He banged his palms on the desk, his face fierce. 'The stone was right,' he said with finality. 'All you need to do is cast off your prejudices. You are already well on the way there.'

I breathed a sigh of relief and relaxed.

His face remained fierce though. 'Now.'

I straightened, ready for the next koan.

'You said that the Serpent is evil because it dreamed of eating babies. You said that *I am evil* because I dreamed of eating babies. *Am I? Is the Serpent evil?*'

'No, of course not,' I said without thinking. 'You were just dreaming about dinner. That's the food that snakes eat, so of course you dreamed about eating it. It would have been different if you'd actually gone out and ...' I stopped, seeing the whole point. It didn't matter that I'd dreamed about eating the babies. The *important* thing was that I would never actually go out and *do* it. Snakes in nature, animal snakes, didn't have the choice; they weren't *evil*, it was just the way they were made. But I had the choice; and I made the choice not to do it.

'Are either of our Serpent essences evil, Emma?' he said, his voice suddenly very mild and calm.

'I just wonder if there is such a thing as evil,' I said. 'There are always so many sides to the story ...'

He fell back and sighed. 'Took you a very long time. You will get there eventually, I am sure, but sometimes you are very slow to travel. Nothing is evil, Emma. All is yang and yin. Dark and Bright. There *is* no good or evil.'

'What about that bastard One Two Two?'

'It is my opposing force, the *yang* for my *yin*. It is unbalanced; *yang* and *yin* within it are not in harmony. When the two opposing forces are not in harmony, the results are destructive. When the two forces are in harmony, the result is the *One*.'

'I have no idea what you're talking about, John,' I said, bewildered.

'I would be very surprised if you did.'

'Tell me about your Serpent. I want to learn about its nature, I think it would help,' I said, then stopped. 'If you don't want to talk about it too much, I would understand.'

'No, no,' he said, more relaxed, 'you're quite right. Anything to help you understand. My Serpent essence . . .' He paused, thoughtful. 'Well, it is different from the Turtle. The Turtle is mostly vegetarian. It is quite slow, not just in movement, but in thought as well.'

'You're not stupid, you're just cold-blooded,' I said.

He smiled gently. 'The Serpent is fast and cunning. It is a dedicated carnivore and likes the taste of blood. It eats things alive, very slowly, enjoying the sensation of their struggles. It is much more unforgiving than the gentle Turtle. It is clever, and can sometimes be spiteful, but it isn't *evil*, Emma. That's just the way it is. Remember, it is still a part of *me*.'

'That was in my dream,' I said miserably. 'I dreamed that I wanted to eat them alive, because it was more . . .' I hesitated, then plunged on, '. . . it was more fun.'

'It is,' he said. 'For a Serpent, dead food is unpleasant. You understand. It is good to share this. It's not something I could share with many others. I hope that Simone is able to accept it when it finally happens in front of her.'

'Monty would never eat dead mice,' I said, remembering. 'I tried to make him, but he never would. If they were dead he wouldn't touch them.'

'I wouldn't touch anything dead either,' John said. 'Dead food. Not moving, and therefore not *food*. The Turtle will eat dead meat, and sometimes eat *very* dead meat, but the Serpent never would.'

'You have the most totally split personality it's surprising you're sane,' I said with derision.

'Sanity is highly overrated,' he growled dryly. 'But,' he said, sitting straighter, 'when I was whole, it just seemed to work. The two essences were both *me*, and they combined seamlessly into *me*. I was whole. Right now,' he grimaced so slightly it was almost undetectable, 'it is very difficult. I'm not *whole*. I am all Turtle. Without the Serpent, I am not complete, and you only see one side of me.' He smiled. 'The Serpent is the mightiest healer on the Celestial Plane.'

My face must have shown my shock because his smile widened and he nodded.

'All Serpents are healers, and when I had mine I could heal *anything*.' He glanced down at the papers on his desk, not seeing them. 'The Serpent's healing is sorely missed here in the Academy, and by the residents of the Celestial. Take Leo: the Turtle by itself can only keep the virus at bay. With the Serpent, I could clear him completely, I could heal him.'

'Oh my God. Does he know?'

'No. It is your choice to tell him, if you wish. I will not.'

'Is there any chance of the Serpent returning before you go?' I said desperately. This could be Leo's life.

'I have no idea,' he said. 'Nobody has done this before. Nobody else has the same nature as me: two creatures as I am. I am unique, this is a unique situation, and we must just take each day as it comes. I

461

don't think it would be a good idea for me to have the Serpent back before I go, because to merge I would have to return to True Form, and then I would probably be gone anyway.'

'I've never thought of snakes as healers, just as poisonous,' I said.

John's eyes turned inward and he concentrated. Then he snapped back. 'The Serpent is also the most powerful weather maker on the Celestial. The Turtle can call forth rain; the Serpent can call forth floods and deluges. The Turtle can move typhoons; the Serpent can *make* them. I suspect that some of the unusual weather patterns that have occurred in the last few years have been a result of the Serpent out there somewhere flexing its muscles.'

There was a tap on the door and Two Five One, John's demon assistant, poked her head in. She tossed a small white cardboard box into the air on the other side of the room. It floated to John and he picked it out of the air. She disappeared again without saying a word.

He turned the box over in his hand, then held it out to me, pointing to a small mark on the side. I took it. It was a bandage from one of the medicine cabinets.

'The Serpent, as healer, in the West as well,' he said.

The mark was the standard Western medical symbol of two snakes wrapped around a staff. 'I never thought of that,' I said.

'The Serpent is the wiser of the two of me. It is extremely clever; its intelligence is not measurable. We tried to measure it on the Celestial a while ago, but the results of the tests were not meaningful because I just answered everything right. I miss its intelligence; the Mountain was much better run when I had it. I'm glad I have you instead.' He smiled slightly at me. 'It is a powerful healer, it is a powerful weather maker. It is also cunning, fast, spiteful, and dreams about eating babies.' He leaned back and put his hands on the desk. 'And that is the end of the herpetology lesson. In a way, I am looking forward to leaving you ...' He studied me closely to gauge my reaction, and relaxed when he saw that I wasn't upset. '... and having the Serpent back, because I really am not whole.'

I had a horrible thought. 'Will you change when you have your snake back?'

'No, of course not,' he said. 'I am unchanging.'

He concentrated, and the Tiger appeared next to me in the other visitor's chair. He saluted us both casually without a word.

'Ah Bai.' John leaned his elbow on the desk. 'Do remember back to when I lost the Serpent?'

'I remember,' the Tiger said, and his eyes turned inwards. 'That was a tough time for all of us. No idea what brought that on.' He snapped back. 'It was about 1975. He just completely disappeared for about six months. And then he came back as if nothing had happened at all. The first time he took True Form afterwards, he seemed the most surprised of all of us that the snake was gone.'

'Was I different when I had the Serpent? To how I am now?' John said.

The Tiger studied him appraisingly for a while. He appeared to be thinking about it. Then, 'Yeah,' he said with a grin. 'Come to think of it, you *were* different.'

John frowned. 'No, I wasn't. I was exactly the same person.'

'Nah.' The Tiger's grin widened. He shook his head and raised his hand. 'You've changed. Be interesting to see what happens when you have that Snake thing back.' He realised what he'd said. 'By the Heavens, Emma, I'm sorry. Don't worry, he'll still be the same person.'

My blood ran cold. 'How different was he?'

The Tiger turned back to John. John glared under his brows at him, obviously irritated.

'He was much more *yang*, but that's understandable,' the Tiger said. 'Much brighter, much harder, much more ... I dunno ...' He shook his head. 'I'm sorry, my Lord, there's no other way to put this. He was much more of a bastard.'

'Oh, thank you very much,' John said, leaning back and glowering.

'Why is it understandable that he would be more yang?' I said.

'Suppose it wouldn't hurt you to know, Emma, you'll be spending most of your time with this thing, you'd better be aware of the strange nature of its essence,' the Tiger said.

'He's not a *thing*!' I said, horrified.

'Yes, I am,' John said equably. 'Because I encapsulate both essences in one creature. Two creatures.'

'Essences? Turtle and Serpent?'

'Yang and yin,' the Tiger said. 'You know?'

'I know,' I said. 'Yang is bright, hard, life, light, metal, hot, male.' I gestured towards the Tiger. 'You are extremely yang.' He nodded and grinned. I thought about yin. 'Yin is soft, dark, death, black, water, cold, female,' and I gasped. I looked at John. He was all of those things, except for the female. He nodded. I hadn't thought of it that way.

'How female are you?' I said with horror. This was something about him — and something about *myself* — that I wasn't really sure I wanted to look at too closely.

The Tiger chuckled. 'Ever done it, Ah Wu?' he said slyly. 'I know I have.'

I stared at the Tiger, aghast. 'You've turned yourself into a *chick*?'

The Tiger nodded, and his grin widened. 'We choose the form we take. Gender is part of the form. For us, gender is completely optional. Humans seem to have a great deal of attachment to gender, and often seem to find change in gender threatening. No idea why; most of us Shen can't understand this preoccupation. The Phoenix's human form used to spend most of its time male, now it spends most of its time female, and won't tell anyone why.'

'The Tiger will go to any length to get the girl, sometimes,' John said, his voice a low rumble.

I collapsed forward over my knees, laughing silently. I could believe it. I looked up at the Tiger. You *guy*. Living every hot-blooded guy's dream. I shook my head. Even as a chick, he would still have been a full-blooded male. This was *so* weird, and here I was handling it perfectly.

I crossed my arms over my knees and leaned on them. I glanced up at John. He watched me placidly. Gender was completely optional.

'Is the Turtle female?' I said softly.

'That question doesn't really apply to our True Forms, Emma,' he said. 'We are essence.'

'But he's always male in True Form,' I said, leaning back and pointing at the Tiger. 'Extremely male.'

'You noticed,' the Tiger said, grinning evilly.

'Bit hard to miss,' I shot back, 'you're a shocking exhibitionist.'

The Tiger just shrugged, the grin not shifting.

'The Bai Hu's essence is yang,' John said. 'Extremely yang, even though he is the Lesser Yang. Of course his True Form is male.'

'But your essence is yin,' I said. 'Female.'

'I encapsulate both essences, Emma,' John said. 'Yang and yin. I am two creatures. The Turtle is yin. The Serpent is yang. The essence of the Xuan Wu, combined, is yin. I am the ultimate yin creature: I am dark, cold, water, winter, death. But my human form has always been male.'

'He's right, Emma,' the Tiger said. 'He's always been male in human form, despite his yin nature, his dual nature.'

'No wonder everybody keeps saying you're a very strange creature, Xuan Wu,' I said softly with wonder. 'They're right.'

'Both essences, combined into yin. Two creatures, combined into one. His colour is black, his number is one, his direction is North, and he is Master of the Arts of War. And in human form, he has always been male,' the Tiger said softly. 'With perfect alignment.'

'Okay. So you're a very yin guy, but still a guy,' I said.

John nodded. 'And you're a very yang woman, but still a woman. Think about it. Aren't you?'

I mentally stepped back and studied myself. 'I suppose I am,' I said. 'But I'm still one hundred per cent female, all the way through. I've never thought of myself any other way.' I hesitated. 'That explains our compatibility, I suppose. Yang and yin.'

I had a sudden brilliant, wonderful thought.

'Could I be *your* Serpent?' I said quietly with delight.

He wasn't surprised at all.

'You thought that too,' I said. 'You've thought that for a long time.'

He shrugged. 'We don't need words.'

'No, we don't.'

'I'm not sure I'd want that, Emma,' he said. 'Because if you were my Serpent, then when we joined, I would lose you. You would be absorbed into me and no longer exist as a separate entity; you would become part of the Dark Lord, you would become part of *me*.'

'I can't imagine anything that I want more in the whole world.'

'But we have loved, we have shared our minds and our bodies. If you were my Serpent, we would have

466

rejoined. I have often wondered, but it's not really possible.'

'Damn,' I said softly.

'Not possible at all,' the Tiger cut in from where he was sitting, completely forgotten by both of us. 'Because the Serpent's been found. That's probably why he brought it up, he's somehow subconsciously aware of it. I was on my way to tell him anyway.'

'I brought it up,' I said, but neither of them heard me.

'Where is it?' John said, excited. He leapt to his feet, full of energy. 'I must go to it. It would be good to be whole again.'

'You would lose everything, Ah Wu, you forget yourself,' the Tiger said. 'It is better that it stays where it is.'

John rubbed his hands over his face and grimaced. 'You're right.'

'Where is it?' I said. 'What's it doing?'

'It is at the bottom of the Mariana Trench,' the Tiger said, his face expressionless. 'It is hiding in the deepest reaches of the ocean. It sleeps at the bottom of the darkest seas.'

'Who found it?' John said.

'The Lady,' the Tiger whispered. 'She heard its cries.'

'It cries?' I said, my heart breaking.

John's face was expressionless.

'Can you hear it, Ah Wu?' the Tiger said gently.

'No,' John said, his face still expressionless. He stalked out without saying a word.

'Is anyone holding it there, Tiger?' I said. Maybe someone had imprisoned it.

'No,' the Tiger said softly, his face a mask of misery. 'I think. I think ...' He looked down. 'I think that the Serpent may have forgotten what it is, who it is. It only knows that it is missing ...' He hesitated. 'It is missing half of itself. It cries for its lost half.' He looked me straight in the eye. 'So does he.'

'You know what?' My throat thickened. 'Even if he were to be a different person, and no longer loved me, I think it would be worth it to have him whole.'

'It is very hard to see him like this, Emma,' the Tiger said, looking down. He looked back up at me. 'Remind me to give you a gold coin.' He shook his hands in front of his miserable face. 'By your leave.'

I nodded and he disappeared.

I knew what John was doing. He was in one of the training rooms, doing sword katas until he dropped from exhaustion.

I went back to my spreadsheets. Suddenly I wished that I *was* his Serpent and that he could have absorbed me completely. It would be worth it to have him whole, and Leo healed, even if it meant that I would no longer exist.

CHAPTER FORTY

Later that evening somebody tapped on my bedroom door.

'I'll never finish this if you keep interrupting me!' I shouted at the door.

'Emma, it's me.'

'Come on in, Rhonda,' I said. 'Sorry about that. They keep banging on the door. Everything okay with Michael?'

Rhonda came in and sat on my couch, across from where I was sitting at the desk. 'Tell me about this kid. Na Zha.'

I sighed. 'You don't know about him? There was a TV series on the Cantonese channel about him not long ago.'

'He's an Immortal?'

'Yes. One of the biggest,' I said.

'But he looks like a teenager.'

'I know,' I said. 'John says his essence is that of a youth.'

'I'm not sure I want Michael hanging around with him,' Rhonda said, concerned. 'What's his history?'

'Very long. Very old. He's really powerful. When he was only seven years old he killed a Dragon Prince, one of the sons of the Dragon King himself, for no better reason than he could do it. He's always been a chronic troublemaker. He's supposed to have grown up, but I don't think he ever will.'

'Is Michael safe with him?' Rhonda said. 'There are demons after him all the time. And the other guys, the triads.'

'That's the problem,' I said. 'Na Zha is the best demon killer on the Celestial short of Xuan Wu himself, and that's saying a lot. Michael is actually safer with him than he is with John right now, as John is so weak.'

'They haven't been up to anything together, have they?'

'Not as far as I know,' I said. 'Na Zha promises to behave when he's with Michael. They get on really well, they've become very good friends. Surprisingly enough, they seem to have a lot in common. John has absolutely no problem with him. It drives me nuts. I personally don't like him very much, he's very insolent to me.'

'Okay. I suppose I'll just let you guys keep an eye on him then.'

Rhonda didn't move off the couch.

'Something else?' I said.

She put her head in her hands.

I went to the couch and sat next to her. I put my arm around her.

'I don't know what to do, Emma, I'm so torn,' she said.

'What?'

She glanced desperately at me. 'I really do love that stupid man.'

'Oh God, Rhonda,' I said. 'You know we saw you in Paris.'

'He just whisked me away. He gave me the excuse it was to see Michael, but we never did. He's so romantic, you know? He's so warm, and considerate, and wonderful ...'

'And has a hundred wives.'

'I know,' she moaned. 'That's what makes his offer so damn hard.'

'Offer?'

'He says he wants to Raise me and take me as Empress of the West.'

'Holy shit,' I said softly. 'He'll give up the others for you?'

'No. I'll be Empress in the old-fashioned sense. The traditional sense. You know?'

'Yeah. I know. You'd be in charge of the palace and the women. That's the traditional role of the Empress.'

'Will you be like that?' she said.

'No. We've talked about that. Xuan Wu's not like that. His nature is different.'

'That's the problem,' she said. 'It's his nature. How can I stop him from being what he is?'

'Oh God, Rhonda, he'd Raise you. And you are so worthy.'

'What would *you* do?' she whispered.

'For a while I thought that might be my role,' I said, 'until I asked John about it. He said no, for him there was just one. Always, just one. If it hadn't been that way I wouldn't do it. I wouldn't share him.'

We sat together silently for a while.

'Talk to Kwan Yin,' I said. 'She won't tell you what to do. But she will help out.'

'You can call her for me?'

'I'll ask John to call her for you.'

'Thanks, Emma.'

'Come on.' I rose and held out my hand to her. 'I know exactly where you need to go.'

* * *

471

John was in his office. We both sat across the desk from him, miserable.

'You need to tidy up in here, Emma,' Rhonda said.

'Rhonda's right. What's the problem, ladies?' John said.

'The Tiger has asked me to be Empress of the West,' Rhonda said.

John leaned back and didn't say anything.

'He's offered to Raise her and make her his consort,' I said.

'He's never done anything like that before,' John said. 'He's never accepted a woman as his equal, and that's what he's doing with you. Remarkable.'

'Give her a gold coin,' I said.

Rhonda glanced at me.

I shrugged. 'Private joke.'

'I'm the first one?' Rhonda said softly.

'Yes.' John leaned forward over the desk and retied his hair. 'What are you going to do? Will you take him up on it?'

'I don't know,' Rhonda whispered.

'I think she should talk to Kwan Yin,' I said.

'Good idea,' John said. 'Wait.' He stopped and concentrated. His eyes unfocused.

Kwan Yin appeared behind him. She smiled sadly. She came around the desk to us and held out her hand. 'Come with me.'

Rhonda took Kwan Yin's hand and they disappeared.

'What do you think, Emma?' John said. 'You think she'll do it?'

'I think she will, love,' I said.

'Did you tell her what you would do in the same situation?' he said.

I folded my arms on the desk and dropped my head onto them. 'I lied.'

His voice was full of quiet humour. 'You said you wouldn't share me.'

I nodded into my arms.

I heard a soft sound and looked up. He watched me with amusement. In front of me on the desk was a gold coin.

I took the coin, rose without saying anything, and went out.

My viva was in late November. The office of the university was only two blocks away from the Hennessy Road building, which was a convenient stroke of luck for me — until I remembered that there is no such thing as coincidence.

I took the lift to the second-floor offices. The university was an English one that ran distance MBA programs in Hong Kong. They occupied half of the second floor with offices and some teaching areas. Most of the study I had done had been by correspondence, but I had occasionally met with other students doing the program or talked to staff in the meeting rooms.

Just remember, John said into my ear, making me jump, *the piece of paper is the least important thing about this. You have already gained the knowledge. Unless you are planning to resign as Lady Regent of the House of the North in the near future and take a job outside, the piece of paper is unnecessary.*

I smiled. That's what he thought. The piece of paper would give me some closure; and I'd know for sure that the work I did was good enough.

I smiled at the receptionist and she nodded. No words passed between us; she knew what I was there for. I sat down to wait, uncomfortable in my new suit and clutching the slim leather briefcase that John had presented to me that morning.

Kitty Kwok would be thrilled: I finally had that suit. I wondered where she was. She had been released on bail and had promptly disappeared. John had suggested that she may have gone to Hell. It was where she belonged.

I felt a flash of concern as I thought about April. She hadn't reappeared. Her mother in Australia didn't know where she was, but wasn't at all worried. Apparently Andy said that April was fine, and that was enough for everybody. Andy was a Triad member too — April had told me that herself. He had been in on it from the start. I quietly wondered if he was a demon. I hadn't seen him since I'd been able to pick demons, but I'd always had a bad feeling about him. And if Andy was a demon in league with Simon Wong, then April's baby would be *half demon too*.

I'd asked John about it and he'd said it was possible. Half demon, half Shen, the results would be similar. The child could be pure human, pure demon, or something in between.

And there was absolutely nothing I could do about it.

I snapped back when the door to the meeting room opened. The director, Jan, poked her head around the doorframe, smiled, and jerked her head to indicate that I could go in. I rose and approached the room, my stomach fluttering with a million worries.

The three examiners sat around a low coffee table, surrounded by papers. Jan indicated an empty chair for me.

Jan had my thesis in her hand and smiled at me. She was very tall and muscular, almost Amazonian, with short ginger hair, a wide kind smile and bright blue eyes that twinkled at me. She ran marathons in her spare time and could bore everybody to tears with tales of her two young children.

I didn't know the other two. One was a severe-looking Chinese woman with impeccable hair, wearing a very smart tailored suit, and the other was a kindly black-haired European man in his mid-sixties with a friendly smile and reassuring dark eyes behind his large glasses.

I relaxed slightly. They didn't seem so bad.

'This is Miss Lo, Emma, and Mr Knight. They'll be helping me do your viva today,' Jan said, gesturing towards the other two inquisitors.

I nodded to each of them without speaking. My throat was too dry.

'I'll go first,' Jan said firmly, eyeing my papers appraisingly. My stomach flip-flopped. I immediately decided that I should have formatted the thesis better.

'Emma,' Jan said severely, 'why on earth did you choose this topic? You've always said that you're a nanny. How did you get involved in this?'

The other two professors leaned forward, eager to hear the answer. But I was ready for them.

'My employer is a martial arts instructor,' I explained, trying my best to remain calm. 'It was the easiest way to find a business that I could use as a model. He encouraged me, in fact,' rubbing it in, 'he says that I helped him make the whole place run much better.'

Jan nodded, still studying the thesis. She glanced up at me without smiling. 'What was the most obvious and pressing problem that you think they were experiencing when you started?'

That was in the thesis. The real answer was 'a recent attack by demons', but I didn't think that would go down too well. 'Managing the finances,' I said confidently. 'The business owner, my employer, is an expert at martial arts, but when it comes to budgeting he is completely hopeless.'

All three of them nodded in agreement. They had obviously read the paper right through.

Miss Lo took over. Right, two questions each, I could handle this. 'Are you sure that you've budgeted for everything here? What if some unexpected expenses turn up? How will you handle that?'

'Unexpected expenses always turn up,' I said. 'The essence here wasn't managing for the expected, it was managing for the unexpected. So I had to put that in. Do you want me to go into detail about budgeting for the unexpected?'

Miss Lo shook her head. 'I think that's enough of an answer for me.' She nodded towards the third professor, Mr Knight. I sighed inwardly with relief.

I turned to Mr Knight and was shocked right down to the soles of my feet. He was at least a level fifty demon. Huge. As big as a Snake Mother. I'd been so nervous that I'd completely missed him.

Holy shit, what was he doing here, and what had happened to the real professor? I hoped the real professor wasn't found in a Kowloon City dumpster in a million pieces, the same way that pizza delivery guy was.

The demon smiled kindly at me, exactly like a sympathetic university professor helping a talented student along. 'Tell me, Miss Donahoe, on page thirty-five of the thesis you mention "demon staff". Is this a particular term used in martial arts?'

I looked blankly at him, then smiled. No way, he wasn't getting away with that. 'I'm sorry, Mr Knight? Isn't it?' He nodded confirmation. 'I really don't know what you're talking about. Is there a typo in there? Because I don't remember putting anything in the thesis about "demon staff". And the term doesn't mean anything in martial arts, as far as I know. But I really don't know much about it.'

The other two professors flipped to the page he'd mentioned and scanned it. Jan shook her head. 'Not here, Jim. You sure you have the same paper we have?'

The demon passed his copy to me. 'Look, Miss Donahoe, right in the middle of the page.'

I scanned down. It was my writing until about the third paragraph. Then there was a message for me.

I have offended One Two Two. I am desperate.
Help. I am willing to pledge. I have information.
Nod if you are willing to protect me. I will raise
my hand in oath that I will not attack. I will meet
you downstairs. Please take me to the Dark Lord,
I am willing to pledge to both of you.

I glanced up from my thesis. 'This is a copy. Where is the original ...' I hesitated, 'Mr Knight?' I carefully chose the inflection so that the real question would be obvious to him.

'The original is quite safe and unharmed,' the demon said. 'Nearby. I can get it for you later, if you like.'

I breathed a sigh of relief. 'Thanks. Just making sure.' I nodded. I was willing to take the risk for the information.

He raised his hand in confirmation. I hoped it meant that he had sworn to lay off me.

Both Jan and the Chinese professor looked in bewilderment at their papers. The demon shrugged. It was up to me to gloss this over. Think quickly, Emma.

'I think you have the wrong version of the paper, Mr Knight. The page numbers don't seem to be right in this one, and the words "demon staff" are actually a typo; it should be "demonstrate".'

I handed the paper back to him and he eyed it appraisingly. He flipped it so that he could see the front page. 'Oh, you're quite right, Miss Donahoe, I have an earlier draft that you handed in. The original is in my office; quite unaware of how this happened — I seem to be having periods of memory loss lately, don't know what's wrong with me. So sorry.' He smiled broadly at Jan. 'I don't have any other problems with it.'

Whew, he had the real professor bound and unaware in his office somehow. Must ask how they did that, if that was the case.

'Your graduation ceremony will be in December. Will you be in Hong Kong? It'll be a big occasion,' Jan said, her blue eyes sparkling with amusement.

I nearly let out a whoop of triumph but managed to hold it in. I swallowed my emotions instead. 'Thanks, Jan,' I said sincerely. 'I couldn't have done it without your help.'

Jan waved her hand over the paper. 'Not a problem, Emma, it's been a really enjoyable experience. Most unusual paper I've ever seen, the topic was fascinating. I must come up there one day and have a look, it sounds incredible. Does your employer *really* have three hundred students learning martial arts?'

I nodded a reply.

'What do they all do when they graduate?' she said.

'Go home and teach,' I said, which was almost true. Very few of the Dark Disciples ever returned to the Earthly Plane. If they were good enough, they would be promoted to Master, but only about one in fifty was that talented. Between fifty and a hundred a year were lost to other parts of the Celestial Plane, as elite guards for high-ranking Immortals or Shen; or as training Masters for just about everybody. If they wanted to, they could stay and learn all their lives, moving up through the ranks to teach the younger ones if they had the talent; helping with the management of the Academy if they didn't. Many of them stayed on and cultivated the Tao, attempting to find the Way and become Raised to

Immortality. The very best were sometimes chosen to join the Elite Guard of the Jade Emperor, a very great honour for all of us.

A few of them did return to their home countries on the Earthly Plane to teach, and John encouraged them, welcoming them back if they decided to return. He constantly complained that more of them wouldn't go out into the world and spread the true Arts.

I continued to explain for Jan. 'It's a world centre for martial arts training. They come from all over the world to learn here, then return to their home countries and teach there. The martial arts community is quite small and very well connected, but people who aren't involved generally don't know anything about it.' I had a brilliant idea. 'How about the three of you come up now and have a look? You've seen the paper, why not come and see the Academy? I'm sure they'll be glad to meet you,' I said, looking straight into the demon's eyes.

'I'd love to, but we have one more viva to do, Emma,' Jan said. 'Maybe some other time.'

'I'll wait,' I said. 'I'll call them and arrange it while you do the viva. I don't mind at all. There should still be some people there, it's only four o'clock. I'd love to show you around.'

I willed her to come. If she did, then I would be slightly safer with this enormous demon.

'Sounds like great fun, Jan,' the demon said. 'The viva will only take about twenty minutes, let's go after that and have a look. I'm dying to see all of this kung fu stuff; we don't have anything like that at all back in the UK.'

Now I knew for sure that the demon was sincere. If it wanted my head, it wouldn't invite Jan along.

'Oh, all right,' Jan said. 'Go and wait outside, Emma. When we finish with the next student we'll meet you in the waiting room. Want to come, Connie?'

'I'm not really interested in wushu,' the Chinese examiner said. 'You go without me. I see enough of that on the television; I find it tremendously boring.'

'Well,' Jan said, rising to her feet and towering over me, 'that's that then. Congratulations, Emma, you really are exceptional, and there's a place in the PhD program any time you want to take it.'

'Oh come *on*, Jan,' I wheezed, 'I only just survived this and you want to throw me in again? Give me some time to recover!'

The other two professors rose as well and I shook hands all round. Even the demon. He just smiled, perfectly innocent.

Back in the waiting area, I dragged out my mobile phone and turned away from the receptionist with my hand over my mouth.

'Office.' It was John's assistant.

'This is a major emergency. It's Emma, I need the Dark Lord *right now*,' I hissed into the phone.

'Wei?'

'Oh, John, thank God, this is really big.'

'What? Did you get it?'

'One of the professors for my viva,' I said softly, 'was a level fifty-five looking for sanctuary.'

'What did you arrange?'

'I'm taking them on a tour of the Academy. Jan, the head, asked to see the facilities after hearing so much about them, and he wants to come too. I'll be bringing both of them over in about twenty minutes.'

He was quiet for a moment. Then he spoke. 'I'm sending Liu over there now to escort the three of you back. I'll be on the ground floor here waiting. I'll let it in past the seals. We'll do a low-level tour, show them some of the basic hand-to-hand students, only up to the third floor. Emma, listen. This is very important. When

I greet them on the ground floor, I will shake their hands. Understood?'

'Got it,' I whispered. 'I'll be ready for it.' I hesitated. 'This is a big one, John. Can Liu take it?'

'Easily,' he said. 'Not a problem at all.' He paused. 'I'm assuming you made it anyway?'

'Yeah,' I said, 'but getting this ... person is twenty times better. He says he offended One Two Two and has information for us.'

'Yes!' John said. 'Did you find out where the original professor is?'

'Apparently in his office, bound, with his memory wiped, from what I gathered.'

John was silent. Then he spoke with obvious satisfaction. 'That is extremely good. This is a really big one.' His voice was full of admiration. 'Well *done*, Emma, what a coup. This is the biggest demon tamed in a very, very long time. I hope it lives up to its word; it will be extremely useful. Damn, but I'm impressed.'

'I just hope it really is tamed,' I said. 'If it isn't, we're in big trouble letting it in past the seals.'

'Oh, and congratulations on the MBA as well,' he said.

CHAPTER FORTY-ONE

Liu waited for us downstairs, wearing a pair of tired jeans and a worn-out T-shirt, looking for all the world like a cleaner on his day off. He grinned like an idiot when he saw us.

I introduced him as one of the instructors and Jan was obviously bemused at his appearance. He pretended he was there by accident and we all walked the two blocks to the Hennessy Road building together. The demon was tense and nervous. Jan had absolutely no inkling of anything that was going on with her three companions.

John was waiting for us in the lobby next to the Eighteen Weapons. He met us at the door, and guided Jan and the demon in. The demon hesitated at the doorway, then strode in as if it expected to be electrocuted. It visibly relaxed when it survived the seals.

'This is Mr John Chen, the head of the school,' I said. 'I'm the nanny for his daughter, Simone. He's very kindly offered to show you around.' I gestured towards Jan. 'This is Jan, the head of the university's office here in Hong Kong, and Professor Knight, one of the examiners.'

'Pleased to meet you,' John said. He shook Jan's hand and then held his hand out to the demon.

John, Liu, the demon and I all froze. Time stood still. Liu shifted in the corner of my eye as he readied himself.

'Take his hand,' I said very softly.

The demon stood frozen, his face an expressionless mask. Jan hadn't heard me; all she was aware of was the fact that the demon had hesitated. Bewilderment started to spread across her face.

'Do it, take his hand,' I said under my breath. 'Last chance.'

The demon took a swooping step forward and grabbed John's hand, its face still expressionless. Its eyes widened with wonder as it realised it hadn't been damaged. It was such a high level that John's touch couldn't destroy it, only cause it major damage; but it seemed surprised that it had remained unharmed.

'Welcome, both of you,' John said as he released the astonished demon's hand. 'Let me take you up and show you around.'

Jan enjoyed herself immensely. She loved watching the juniors going through their paces. Liu even had some of the young *Shaolin* Disciples do some circus-style acrobatics for her.

Knight's face was completely frozen in a false grin the whole time. John and I could hardly wait to get him alone, and it was obviously difficult for him too.

When we were back in the lobby the demon had an inspiration. 'Jan, you go on ahead. I need to stop at the pharmacy next door and buy a couple of things. Meet you back at the office, we'll go through the vivas and sort them out. See you later.'

'Okay,' Jan said. 'We can leave most of it until tomorrow morning anyway.' She smiled. 'Good to have it finished, eh?'

'Yeah, we survived,' the demon said. 'Can't believe it,' he added, without looking at either John or myself.

She gave us a cheery wave and went out.

The three of us stood in the lobby looking at each other.

Then the demon fell to its knees before us and touched its head to the floor. 'I pledge. I swear allegiance. Thank you, my Lord, my Lady, you have no idea what this means to me.'

'Get the hell up off the floor, people going past can see you,' John growled impatiently.

The demon didn't move. John breathed an obvious sigh of relief.

'Get up,' I ordered and it immediately shot to its feet.

'Do it again, Emma,' John said quietly, and held out his hand. 'I want to be absolutely sure.'

'Take the Dark Lord's hand again,' I said.

This time the demon didn't hesitate. It strode forward confidently and grabbed his hand.

'I'm finding it hard to retain human form while you have me like this,' it said, its voice straining. 'Either release me, or take me somewhere I won't cause panic in the streets.'

After the demon had returned from releasing the real Professor Knight, we sat together in a meeting room on the third floor. John wouldn't let the demon any higher in the building than that. Tamed was tamed; but trusting was another matter altogether.

In True Form the demon was a huge humanoid and, unusually, it was blue. It only had two eyes, and no scales. Not too bad. It even had a name; for some reason known only to itself, it had chosen the English name of Ralph.

Ralph was minor demon nobility. He wouldn't tell us what he'd done to upset Wong, but we had an idea, knowing Wong's appetites and Ralph's unusual appearance. The demon stayed in human form, big glasses and everything, to talk to us.

'Do you know what he's planning?' John said straight out.

'Something big,' Ralph said.

'All of us?' I said.

'Yes.'

'Are you aware of the details?' John said.

'I know that it is planned for later this year. I know that he has made some very special, rather nasty hybrids that he hopes will take you out. He is bringing in something that will disable you, but I don't know what.'

'Disable the Dark Lord?' I said with disbelief. 'Surely such a thing isn't possible.'

'No,' John said. 'Either you kill me or you don't. You can't disable me.'

'One Two Two seems to think that he has some sort of secret weapon that will ensure your cooperation.'

'Impossible,' John said.

'Well, that's what he's been saying. He's also bragging that he will bring the Dark Lady to his Father, reveal her true nature, and be promoted very quickly.'

My stomach fell out. I was speechless.

'More,' John said.

'No more,' Ralph said. 'That's all I know.'

'Any other word about her true nature?' John said. 'This is vital.'

I suddenly wanted to run out of the room.

'She has caused quite a stir,' the demon said with a small smile. 'She scares the living daylights out of most of the Mothers, they hate her.'

'Throw that phone away,' John said to me.

'No.'

'That was quite a feat in London, my Lady,' the demon said. 'I feel most honoured to serve you. You appear to be an ordinary human, but in action and word, and particularly in battle, you appear very much more.'

'*Why were they both in Europe?*' John demanded loudly.

'Ah.' The demon leaned back and took his glasses off. 'You heard about the Kwok woman? His pussy cat?'

'Kitty Kwok,' I said. 'Agricultural holdings in China. Biotech in China, Australia, America ...' I stopped as I remembered. 'Europe.'

'Europe,' Ralph said. 'Biotech in Europe.'

'Damn,' John said quietly. 'Did the King stop him?'

'The King wanted to,' Ralph said. 'But when he saw the results of the experiments, he decided that it was too good a chance to miss. He has found the activities of this particular son rather diverting. He saw the chance to take both of you.'

I suddenly understood. 'Oh my God, it was all a huge setup.'

'You are quite right, my Lady,' the demon said.

'The King gave me the phone. Then Wong attacked us. They were hoping that they would take out the Dark Lord with the hybrids. If they took out Lord Xuan, I would definitely call the King immediately to ensure Simone's safety.'

'Exactly,' the demon said. 'I was surprised that they seemed to want the Lady more than the child, but that was the plan.' He gestured towards John with his glasses. 'Take him out.' He smiled as he spoke to me. 'You would call the King to ensure the safety of the child. He would have respite from the Dark Lord, and the Dark Lady in his hands. He was willing to pass up the child to have both of you.'

'Shit,' John said under his breath. 'They played us like a *pipa*.' He tied his hair back, then leaned his elbow on the arm of the chair and rubbed his chin. 'Damn, but I miss my Serpent. The snake would have seen this coming.'

'But Wong chickened out at the last minute,' I said. 'He decided not to face the Dark Lord. He must have been in huge trouble for that.'

'No, not really.' Ralph leaned back, quite relaxed. 'He promised that he will have the means to make the Dark Lord cooperate at the end of the year.'

'What happens at the end of the year?' John said.

'I have no idea,' Ralph said.

I had a sudden inspiration. 'The biotech. Were they making snake hybrids too?'

'Yes,' Ralph said.

'No,' John said.

'Did you see any of them?' I asked.

'Yes,' Ralph said.

'Not possible,' John said.

'Did they look like me on the inside?' I said.

'Leave it, Emma!' John said fiercely. 'It's just not possible! I would know!'

'No,' Ralph said, ignoring John completely and well aware of the fact that he was walking a fine line. 'You are something completely different.'

I relaxed. Then I leaned forward to speak earnestly to him. 'Ralph,' I said, 'please answer this next question as honestly as you can. *What am I?*'

'You are a perfectly ordinary human being —' I suddenly wanted to leap up and smack him in the face '— with a great deal of Serpent essence that seems to come and go,' Ralph said.

'It comes and goes?' John said.

'Yes,' Ralph said. 'Right now, she doesn't have much of it there at all. In battle, though, much more of it comes out.'

'That's what happened in Central,' John said to me. 'Your Serpent essence took that demon out.'

'The one that was shooting for Mother?' Ralph said. 'The one that disappeared in Central? You did that?'

'I think I did, but I'm not sure,' I said. 'I can't remember very much about it. I faced her, I hit her, then I woke up in hospital with my face minced.' Shooting for Mother. 'I've dreamed that I'm a Mother. Do I look like a Mother?'

'Something like a Mother —' Ralph said.

John banged the arm of his chair. 'No, Emma!'

'— but not quite. I'm sorry, my Lady, I've never seen anything like you before.'

'I'm unique.'

'Of course you are,' John said. 'And it is a direct result of time spent in constant contact with me, acting as a catalyst for your already present talents and Serpent nature. Remember, Emma, you are the first talented human female I have loved.'

'That's what I think,' Ralph said. 'If you'd been able to sleep together, it probably would have catalysed faster.'

Both John and I stared at him.

'I thought you two couldn't touch,' he said.

'We spent a couple of days in the Western Palace together after John defeated One Two Two in Wan Chai,' I said.

The demon grinned. 'Oh. A dirty weekend.' John's face went stiff. 'Apologies, my Lord.' Ralph chuckled. 'There's a book running on level six.'

'Hell of the Poisonous Snakes?' I said.

John glanced sharply at me, then turned back to the demon.

'Oh, very good, my Lady,' Ralph said, his grin getting wider. 'Well done.'

'A book?' John said.

'Let me see.' Ralph reached into the pocket of his hound's-tooth jacket and pulled out a piece of paper.

He put his glasses back on, then unfolded the paper. 'Ten to one, she's a lost Southern Shen.'

'Rainbow Serpent?' I said.

'Yes,' Ralph said, the grin not shifting.

'I hadn't thought of that,' I said.

'Five to one, she's a lost dragon. Five to one, she's your Serpent —'

John cut him off. 'Excellent!'

'What?' I said.

'That means that they don't know,' John said. 'They won't go after it.'

'Oh,' I said. 'I see what you mean.'

Ralph continued as if John hadn't said anything. He obviously understood. 'Three to one, she's escaped from level six and lost her memory. Also three to one, she's a perfected Mother; but the Mothers deny most strongly that any of them has attempted perfection. But nobody believes those lying bitches anyway.' His eyes sparkled through the glasses at me.

'Ralph,' I said.

'Yes?'

'When the eggs hatch, what do the Mothers do?'

John glanced sharply at me but didn't say anything.

'They must be bound immediately, my Lady, because they will eat the nestlings. Straight away. When the eggs are close to hatching, they must be watched. With the larger Mothers, they usually only salvage one or two nestlings out of a clutch, the Mother is so fast.'

I didn't say anything. I tried to control my face. No wonder John hadn't told me.

Ralph smiled at John and turned back to the paper. 'Two to one on, she's something completely new, a new hybrid that escaped and nobody wants to claim ownership. Also two to one on, she's a hybrid that's been planted with you and is programmed to turn later. There was some argument that those two were the same thing, but the odds are the same anyway, so it doesn't make a difference.'

'Shit,' I said quietly.

'Also two to one on, she's an alien.'

'That is totally ridiculous,' John said.

'We will have our fun, my Lord,' Ralph said. 'There has also been a great deal of money put on the possibility that she's a perfectly normal human, strong snake alignment, activated by your presence. That's where my money is, but at this stage it's ten to one on and really not worth bothering with.'

We all stayed silent for a while.

'You wouldn't care to enlighten me, my Lord? I know where my money is, and it's past the stage of collecting now. But I would like to know, purely out of interest's sake.'

Neither of us spoke.

'Good Lord,' Ralph said incredulously, 'you mean you don't know either?' He stared at me with disbelief. 'You were genuinely asking me the questions, not testing how much I knew? I find that difficult to believe.'

Again neither of us replied.

I had a sudden inspiration. 'April Ho.'

Ralph didn't say anything and the smile didn't shift.

'Do you know what happened to her?'

'Who is April Ho?' Ralph said.

'She's a friend of mine. She married Andy Ho, a relative of Kitty Kwok's. He was probably in league with One Two Two. She was pregnant to him; the child may be half demon. Kitty arranged for the delivery of the baby in China ...' I pulled myself together. 'And now she appears to be missing.'

'I don't know about that particular case, my Lady,' Ralph said, 'but I doubt very much that you'll ever see your friend again. It's obvious they wanted her for the child. With the child in their possession she becomes expendable.'

I knew it anyway but it hurt to hear it out loud. 'Oh *God*.'

We were all silent again for quite some time. 'Anything else for us?' John finally said.

The demon shook his head. He put the piece of paper back in his pocket, then took off his glasses and wiped them on the corner of his jacket. 'That's all I have for you. I'm not holding anything back. I hope I'll be rewarded appropriately, my Lord.'

'What do you want?' I said. 'Do you want to stay with us?'

'I can take you up and do it now,' John said. 'Or later, if you prefer. Either way.'

'Probably the sooner the better, my Lord,' the demon said, still smiling. 'Every minute is a minute spent with them seeking me. Can we do it now?'

'Just be sure that you don't have anything else for us first,' John said. 'If you like you can take some time, make sure you haven't missed anything vital.' He studied the demon intensely. 'You are safe here.'

'You know as much as I do, my Lord,' the demon said. 'Please. Now.' He shrugged. 'Nothing else I need to do, and I'm living in constant fear.'

'I do not believe this,' I said. 'Why don't you try for perfection instead? Come on. You have a chance.'

'You are most gracious, my Lady,' the demon said, 'but I don't have any chance whatsoever. I am too big. Once I walk out your door I am theirs, and it will be slow.' He gestured towards John with his glasses. 'With him it will be quick.'

'Then why did you go through all of this to come to me?' I said.

'For it to be quick.'

CHAPTER FORTY-TWO

Simone was full of bounce as we left the cinema at Pacific Place; she'd enjoyed the movie tremendously. I quietly wondered if I'd ever see a film aimed at adults. I'd seen every children's film released in the past year. John couldn't go with me to the cinema because we'd be too close. We'd even given up on the charity functions.

Simone jiggled happily beside me as we walked through the shopping centre to the food court for some afternoon tea. We bought the food, and then stood and waited for a table to clear. The food court was always full, with standing room only; the only way to get a table was to wait for one.

Simone chatted merrily about the Christmas decorations as we waited. It was only the first week of December but the Christmas hysteria was in full swing, even though most residents of Hong Kong didn't celebrate the holiday. Chinese New Year would be even worse for advertising and decoration, but the coloured lights strung on the outside of the buildings were always entertaining. I particularly enjoyed watching the decorations change from Christmas to New Year; on the sides of many buildings Santa would miraculously transform into the God of Fortune with a slight change of costume. The previous year's decoration changes had been particularly clever, with reindeer suddenly transforming into goats for the Year of the Goat. I wondered what they would do for the Year of the Monkey. I felt a pang as I remembered a cruise on the harbour to watch the fireworks. Only less than a year ago. Probably only two years left.

A table cleared and we sat, Simone still chatting about the decorations. I was roused out of my reverie by my mobile phone ringing. I managed to find it in my bag before it stopped, and flipped it open.

'Emma.'

'Hello, darling, it's me.'

'Mum?'

'Yes. Why aren't you at the airport? Are you running late? We're waiting for you.'

I hesitated, bewildered. 'Airport?'

'Yes, the plane arrived a good half an hour ago, dear. There's a nice young man here. He said that you'd sent him to drive us to our hotel, but I said I'd wait for you. He's right here with us, talking to your dad. Should we go with him?'

My blood ran cold. 'Mum, are you at Hong Kong airport?'

'Yes, dear, of course we are. Why?' She laughed gently. 'It sounds like you forgot we were coming. Come on, Emma, enough joking.'

'Mum, stay right where you are,' I said. 'Don't go anywhere. Don't go with anyone. Move *away* from that young man *right now*!'

'What?'

'Mum, I didn't know you were coming. For God's sake, move to where people can see you —' She started to protest but I cut her off. 'And don't do *anything* until I get there!' My father knew more about the situation than she did, but not much. 'Let me talk to Dad.'

There was silence then I heard my father. 'What's the problem, Emma?'

'Dad, don't hang up. Get away from that young man. Just walk away and go out into the middle, into one of the waiting areas where there are a lot of people around. *Don't go with anybody*! Do you understand?'

'I'm walking,' he said. 'Come on, Barbie.'

'Is he following you?'

'Yes. No. He stopped. He's gone in a different direction.'

I breathed a sigh of relief. 'Listen, Dad, I didn't know you were coming. Somebody brought you here to kidnap you.'

'*What*? You said you weren't involved in anything!'

'Thank God you didn't go with him,' I said. 'Stay on the phone and wait for a second. I'll arrange something.'

'Okay,' he said weakly. 'We're with a lot of people now.'

'Stay. Wait.' I lowered my voice. 'Simone, can you talk to Jade or Gold?'

Simone's eyes turned inwards as she concentrated. 'I can talk to both of them.'

'Simone, listen to me, get them here *right now*. Tell them it's *really urgent*.'

Both Jade and Gold rushed out of the rest room passage and charged over to me. I rose to speak softly to them.

'My mother and father are at the airport. They seemed to think I'd be waiting for them. *Get over there right now*. I'll tell them to look for you and wave when they see you. Stay with them until I can get there.'

They both nodded and raced back down the passageway.

I returned to the phone. 'Are you there, Dad?'

'What the hell's going on, Emma?'

I breathed a sigh of relief. 'Thank God. Listen, Dad, I have a couple of staff out there. You'll probably see them in a minute. Two Chinese people. A girl in green, a young man in a tan suit. Tell me if you see them.'

There was silence.

No.

'Can you hear me, Dad?'

'I see them,' he said.

I sighed with relief.

'Wave to them,' I said. 'Simone, ask Jade if she can see my dad waving.'

'She says she can see him,' Simone said.

'Dad,' I said, 'when they're close to you, give the phone to the girl.'

Silence. Then Jade. 'We have them,' she said.

'Simone,' I said. 'Listen carefully. Ask Jade if she is talking to me on the phone. I want to be sure that it's really her.'

Simone concentrated. 'It's her, Emma, she's on the phone to you.'

I sagged with relief. 'Oh, thank God.' I returned to the phone. 'Give the phone back to my father, Jade. I'll tell him to stay with you until I can pick them up.'

'We can take them directly to the Peak,' Jade said.

'*No!*' I shouted, and a few heads snapped around to me. I dropped my voice. 'They don't know about us! I'll come and pick them up in the car. For God's sake, Jade, listen. This was a setup. I didn't know they were coming. I don't know why they're here. A young man offered to give them a lift to their hotel. Check it out for me. See if he's still there, and *if he is what I think he is.*' I took a deep breath to pull myself together. 'I'll be there as soon as I can, in about an hour. I'll drop Simone back home first, to make sure that she's one hundred per cent safe. Stay with my parents. Understood?'

'My Lady,' Jade said.

'Damn, Jade, I said they *don't know*!' I said. 'I'm just Emma, okay?'

'Sorry,' she whispered. 'Force of habit.'

'Wait for me,' I said, and hung up. 'I have to take you home right now, Simone. Something's up.'

'Why are your mum and dad at the airport, Emma?' Simone said innocently. 'Didn't you know they were coming?'

'I don't know,' I said. 'But I'd better go and find out.'

My mobile phone rang as I was close to the airport and I answered it on the hands-free.

'It's me, Emma,' Jade said. 'We're waiting for you at the cafeteria next to departures. The Western one. You were right.'

'I'm on my way.'

Jade and Gold were sharing a pot of tea with my parents in the cafeteria. Jade and Gold looked grim; my parents were bewildered. I sat down with them.

'Mr Chen didn't come?' Gold said.

'Stayed with Simone,' I said. 'Leo's having the day off.'

Jade and Gold both nodded their understanding.

My father was furious. 'You said you weren't involved in anything!'

'We don't have time to discuss this right now,' I said. 'We have to move you back to the Peak where you'll be safe. We can talk in the car.' I turned to Jade and Gold. 'Which of you is better to come with us, just in case?'

'Me,' Gold said. Jade nodded agreement.

'Come on then. Jade, meet us back at the Peak.' I stopped as I remembered. 'In about an hour.'

Jade nodded. 'My . . .' She stopped and smiled. 'Sure, Emma.'

'I am going to dock your pay, Jade,' I growled.

My mother and father both glanced sharply at me and I banged my forehead with my palm. 'I'm going to dock my own pay as well.'

'Come on, Emma,' Gold said, 'let's get your parents safe.'

Gold sat next to me in the front of the car. My parents were in the back.

'They're not impostors?' I whispered to Gold.

'Ordinary humans,' Gold said under his breath.

'Why are you guys here?' I said more loudly. 'I honestly didn't know you were coming.'

'You sent us a letter,' my mother said. 'You invited us to your graduation. You sent us the tickets. What's going on, Emma? How could you not know?'

My father exploded. 'Damn it, Emma! You said you weren't involved in anything! And here you are, not knowing we were coming and saying that we were brought here to be kidnapped. *What the hell is going on?*'

'This is very bad,' Gold said softly.

'I just thank the heavens that I made it to them first,' I said. 'If my mother hadn't called me, I hate to think what would have happened. If they had gone with that guy, it could have been the end of it.'

My mother moaned. 'Oh God, Emma.'

'*You stupid bitch*!' my father roared. 'What the hell have you gotten yourself into?'

I wished I could run my hands through my hair, but I was busy driving. 'Let's move you up to the Peak where you're safe first,' I said. 'Then ...' I stopped. I decided. 'Then I'll tell you everything.'

'No, my Lady,' Gold whispered.

'You'd damn well better,' my father growled.

'Tell Jade she doesn't need to wait,' I said.

497

Gold concentrated. 'Done.'

'Tell Lord Xuan to be ready.'

'Lord Xuan?' my mother said weakly.

'Done,' Gold said.

'Tell him what happened, Gold.'

'He already knows, my Lady.'

I had a horrible thought. 'Gold, call Leo on his mobile. Check that he's okay.'

Gold pulled out his mobile phone and dialled. 'Leo, it's Gold. I'm just checking — is everything all right with you? No problems? Nothing ...' He hesitated. 'Nothing out of the ordinary?'

Gold stopped and listened as Leo spoke. Leo spoke for a long time. A very long time.

'I think you should come in, my friend,' Gold said gently. 'Something's up.'

My mother moaned again.

'You're safe with us, Mum, don't worry,' I said.

She made a soft sound behind me. I checked in the mirror. She was sobbing silently.

'There are tissues on the back shelf behind you,' I said quietly.

My dad nodded and handed them to my mother.

'Gold, where's Michael?' I said.

Gold concentrated again. 'Festival Walk with a friend.'

'Just *one friend*? How many times have I told him about this? Tell him to call me, I want to talk to him.'

Gold hesitated. 'No need, my Lady, he's with Na Zha.'

I went ice-cold. 'He is grounded for a month.' I glanced away from the road to glare at Gold. 'You knew he was with Na Zha?'

'He is perfectly safe with the Third Prince, you know that, my Lady,' Gold said mildly. 'They are becoming very close friends. They have much in common. They often go ...' he hesitated '... hunting together.'

'You have no idea how much trouble you are in, Gold,' I said. 'The Third Prince is a bad influence and you know it.'

'The Dark Lord said it's okay,' Gold said.

I snorted. 'All three of you will get it very badly when we're home.'

'Dark Lord?' my father said softly.

Gold didn't reply.

'Did you really get an MBA, Emma?' my father said after a long moment of uncomfortable silence.

'I did get the MBA, and the graduation is tomorrow night,' I said. 'They probably thought you'd check. They didn't know ...' I hesitated. 'They didn't know that I haven't told you what's going on.' I banged the steering wheel with my palm. 'Damn!' I glanced at my father in the mirror. 'When did you get the tickets?'

'About two weeks ago,' he said. 'We had to rush to apply for our passports so that we could come. But every time we called you, there was no answer. Your mother was surprised we managed to get your mobile at the airport.'

'What a stroke of luck,' Gold said. 'I wonder why the man who met them didn't try to stop her.'

'He did try to stop her,' my father said. 'She went to the ladies room. She called you on the way back. He went berserk, trying to say she didn't need to call, the phones were down, you were busy, but your mother was already talking to you.'

'Oh God,' I moaned. 'That was so close.'

My mother made another quiet sound behind me.

'Are they gangsters?' my father said.

'I wish,' I said with feeling. 'I'll tell you all when we're home. Mr Chen will talk to you too.' I spoke to Gold without turning away from the road. 'Check Leo.'

Gold dialled again. 'He's at Central Station.'

'Tell him I'll pick him up in Theatre Lane. I'll make a stop there on the way up.'

Gold didn't speak into the phone. He spoke directly to Leo. Leo's voice shouted on the phone. 'He says no, make sure your parents are safe first. He says he'll be fine.'

'Tell him that's an order.'

'Done. He's waiting for you.' Gold hung up.

At Theatre Lane, Gold jumped out of the car and Leo pulled himself in. I nodded to Gold and he nodded back as I drove away.

'What happened, Emma? Who is this?' Leo said.

'These are my parents — my dad, Brendan Donahoe, and Barbara, my mum. Mum, Dad, this is Leo. He's Simone's other bodyguard.'

'Pleased to meet you,' Leo lisped politely. My parents stared at him as if he was from another planet. He turned to speak to me. 'Gold said that they were brought to Hong Kong without you knowing.'

'That's right,' I said. 'It was a tremendous stroke of luck that my mum called me before the demon could stop her.'

There was complete silence.

'*Demon*?' my father yelled.

'Oh *God*!' my mother wailed.

Leo and I both stiffened. Neither of us said anything. Then, 'Let's get you safe,' I said quietly.

My parents sat in silence in the dining room and glared at John with loathing.

'Do you have any questions?' John said gently.

'Yeah. What's the real story?' my father growled.

'You need proof?' Gold said.

'How did you come up here so quickly?' my father asked Gold.

'There's some of your proof,' I said. 'Gold, find me a phone.'

The business day was just starting in London. I called Leonard.

'Hi, Leonard, this is Emma. Could you do me a favour? My parents are here. Could you tell my father exactly who John Chen Wu is? The whole story?'

Leonard wasn't very happy, but agreed anyway. I passed the phone to my father. He listened for a while.

'How long?' he said.

'A *what*?' he yelled.

'I don't believe it,' he said.

He hung up. He glared at John. 'I don't believe it. Tell me the truth, Emma. Are the police after him?'

I gestured towards Jade without looking at her. 'Do it.'

'You are sure, my Lady?'

I wasn't in the mood to mess around. 'Just do it, Jade.'

Jade transformed into her dragon form, her back end still on the chair and her golden claws resting on the table.

My father made a quiet strangled sound and my mother shot to her feet with a gasp.

Jade transformed back. My mother pressed further back into her chair.

My father's face turned ashen and he glanced at John. 'You're a fucking *god*?'

'Brendan!' my mother said. Then she heard. 'A *god*?'

John smiled slightly and nodded without speaking.

My mother glared sternly at me. 'You are coming back to Australia with us right now.'

'No,' I said. 'I have a responsibility to his daughter. And I love him.'

'You always were the stupidest member of the family,' my father said, glaring at me as well. 'Look what you got yourself into.'

'I know,' I said. I ran my hands through my hair. 'I am completely nuts.'

'Why didn't you tell us?' my father said.

'Would you have believed me?' I said.

My mother and father shared a look.

'No, probably not,' my father said with a small smile. He leaned back. 'Okay. So my daughter is engaged to a bloody *god* who can't touch her and is going to disappear in a couple of years anyway. And you have these monsters or demons or whatever after you. And you have,' he said, pointing to Jade, 'a dragon for an accountant. Marvellous.'

'My solicitor is a rock,' I added with grim humour. I gestured towards Gold. 'He's a stone in human form. That is only the beginning of the general weirdness that surrounds this family. Wait till you meet our best friend.'

'Christ, Emma,' my father said quietly.

'Well, now you're here, let us show you around, take you to some tourist spots, and we can all attend Emma's graduation,' John said with satisfaction. 'I've wanted to have you over to visit for a while anyway. I nearly invited you to the graduation, but thought the better of it because it may put you in too much danger.'

'Oh shit,' my father said softly.

'We should send them straight back to Australia, John,' I said. 'It's too dangerous.'

'You are safer here with me,' John said to my father.

'Oh my God,' I said as I understood. '*This* was the secret weapon. They were planning to take my parents.'

'I would love to see the look on that little bastard's face when he finds out that he's failed,' John said evenly. 'Quite a few junior thralls are very likely to turn up on our doorstep in the next few days.'

I had a sudden horrible thought. 'Mum, Dad, please, tell me,' I said. 'Please, tell me the whole truth. Am I your natural daughter? Am I adopted?'

'Why are you asking me this, Emma?' my mother said sharply. 'You think I didn't treat you as well as your sisters? Is that it?'

'No, that has nothing to do with it, Mum. I love you dearly. Please, just tell me. Am I adopted?'

'No,' my mother said fiercely. 'You were born in ward four of Montford hospital at five o'clock in the morning, after I was in labour for seven hours. You were a perfectly normal delivery.'

'Was there anything ...' I hesitated, '... *different* about me? Ever?'

'Why are you asking this, Emma?' my father said. 'What's going on?'

'Emma thinks she's a demon,' John said.

Both my parents glanced sharply at me.

'That's not possible,' my father said. 'You are our daughter. Nothing at all different about you. Except for the fact,' he gestured towards John, 'that you've gone and fallen for this bastard.'

'Snakes,' I said.

'What about them?' my mother said.

'I'm a snake.'

'No, you're not,' my mother said patiently. 'I think you need to talk to somebody if you think that you're a snake.'

I dropped my head and ran my hands through my hair.

'Mr and Mrs Donahoe,' John said, 'would you like me to show you to your room? You should stay with us while you're here. Leo and Emma will be glad to show you around, they can take time off from their teaching and guard duties —'

'I can't afford time off,' I snapped. 'I have three energy work classes on Monday, and I'm on guard duty Tuesday and Thursday.'

'— to take you around town and show you the sights,' John continued, ignoring me completely. 'And tomorrow, we'll all go to Emma's graduation. Her family, celebrating her achievement.' He put his palms on the table. 'I can't think of anything better.'

'Emma, take everybody out, please. I would like to speak to Mr Chen in private,' my father said.

'Of course,' John said. 'Jade, Gold, leave us.' He stood and bowed slightly to my mother. 'My Lady.'

My mother blushed. She was speechless. I gently led her out.

CHAPTER FORTY-THREE

I took my mother into my room while John talked to my father. My mother sat on the couch as Ah Yat brought their suitcase into the room.

'I am so sorry, Mum, I should have told you,' I said. 'But I didn't want you to know about it. I knew it would freak you out.'

'What's done is done, Emma,' she said. 'You actually thought you were adopted? Go and have a look in the mirror.'

'Tell her, stone,' I said.

The stone was completely silent.

'What?' my mother said.

I showed her the stone. 'It talks.'

'Now I know for sure that you need to talk to somebody.'

'No, she's quite correct, Mrs Donahoe,' the stone said. 'But she really should talk to somebody anyway.'

My mother stiffened.

'Maybe that's enough general weirdness for one day,' I said.

'I think you're right,' my mother said weakly.

I sat on the couch next to her and put my arm around her shoulders. 'Jennifer's husband has been Mr

Chen's solicitor for many years. His law firm has acted for John for around two hundred years.'

'I thought you were going to stop with the weirdness,' my mother said.

'Compared to some of the stuff that goes on around here,' I said, 'that's completely normal.'

'Where's the little girl?' my mother said.

'Probably in the training room,' I said. 'Would you like to meet her? She's the reason I do everything I do around here. I love her as if she were my own.'

'What do you mean, "training room"?'

'Oh, damn,' I said, 'more weirdness. You sure?'

'I'm sure.'

'John is God of Martial Arts. Kung fu. You know he's been teaching me — remember I showed you some?' My mother nodded. 'Well, he teaches Simone as well. The training room is like a dance studio, where we do the kung fu. She's probably in there practising.'

'I'd like to see that,' my mother said.

'I'll show you,' I said. 'But just before you go in, Mum, I must tell you, there are weapons in there. Don't be too freaked, okay?'

'Guns?'

'No. Swords. Spears. Things like that. Guns don't hurt demons. We don't have anything to do with guns.'

My mother rose. 'Let's go and meet this little girl that you've thrown your whole life away for.'

I tapped on the door.

'Come in, Emma,' Simone called.

We went in. Simone had been working with a training sword. 'I think I'm ready for a real one now, Emma.' She saw my mother. 'Hello.'

'Hello, dear.'

'This is my mother, Simone,' I said.

'Hello, Mrs Donahoe.' Simone put her little sword back on the rack. 'Don't worry about all the weapons. We won't hurt you.' She came to my mother and held out her hand. My mother shook it gently.

'How old are you, Simone?' my mother said.

'Six,' Simone said.

'She seems older than that, Emma,' my mother said quietly.

'She's half god, Mum.'

'I'm half Shen,' Simone corrected me gently. 'Daddy is a Shen.'

'That's what it's called in Chinese,' I said. 'Get the sword back out, Simone, show my mother some moves.'

'How about you do them with me?' Simone said. 'We can move through a pair set. That would be more interesting to watch. How about,' she stopped and thought, 'how about a level three Shaolin long sword set? That's pretty to watch.'

'Good idea.' I went over to the rack and picked up my sword. I raised it to show my mother. 'Same sword.' She smiled and nodded. I selected the training sword and tossed it to Simone, who caught it easily.

'Move back, Mrs Donahoe. We won't hurt you, but you should move to the side of the room out of the way,' Simone said.

We moved into position and saluted. My mother stood next to the wall and watched with interest.

We went through the set together. I didn't usually do much work with Simone, and it was a satisfying feeling to work with her. She had improved a great deal. We moved in perfect harmony.

'I think you're ready for a real sword too,' I said. 'You should take mine.'

'Oh!' Simone said. 'Make it sing for your mother.' She stopped and gestured. 'Show her.'

'Enough weirdness for one day, pet,' I said kindly.

'I think Emma has a point,' my mother said.

Simone inhaled sharply and her eyes went wide with delight. She danced over to the weapons rack and put her sword away. 'Monica's here!'

I quickly put my own sword away. Then I stopped. 'Oh no,' I said. 'That means the Tiger's here.'

'Uncle Bai's here too!' Simone said. 'Monica'll cook Western food for your family, Emma.' She suddenly went serious. 'Daddy says to explain to your mummy about Uncle Bai first.'

'What form's he in, Simone?' I said.

'Human,' Simone said.

'Oh Lord,' my mother said quietly at the side of the room.

The Tiger stayed and had dinner with us. It was complicated: my parents were served Western food, and the rest of us ate vegetarian Chinese, even Leo and Michael.

I introduced everybody as we sat.

'Everybody, these are my parents, Brendan and Barbara Donahoe. Mum, Dad, this is most of the family.'

My parents appeared bewildered.

'Okay,' I said, 'here goes.' I gestured towards John. 'John you know.' I gestured towards the Tiger. 'This is Tiger.'

'Tiger,' my father said, nodding. 'Unusual name.'

'Not that unusual in Hong Kong,' the Tiger said with a grin.

'Leo you've met.' Leo nodded to my parents. 'The other bodyguard.'

'I'm a perfectly normal human being, one of the few in the household,' Leo lisped. 'Pleased to meet you.'

'Pleased to meet you too,' my father said loudly and clearly.

Leo and I both flinched.

'Please don't talk to him like that, Dad,' I said softly. 'Leo's not deaf.'

'Oh,' my father said. 'Sorry.'

'The Snake Mothers hurt his mouth,' Simone said, helping. 'He can't talk well now.'

'What's a Snake Mother?' my mother said.

Nobody said anything, not even Simone.

'Okay,' I said briskly. 'Next to Leo is Michael. Trainee bodyguard.'

Michael nodded to my father then turned to me. 'Can I go out after dinner, Emma?'

'Who with?' I said.

'Na Zha,' he said defiantly.

'Certainly,' John said, and I glared at him.

'Can Na Zha take anything that Wong throws at him?' I said.

'Na Zha is the best person he could be with in the current circumstances,' John said. 'He is a better demon killer than you and Leo put together.'

My parents shared a look.

'All right then, you can go,' I said. 'Take your phone …' I cut him off before he could protest. 'I *know* you don't need it, but *I* do, so take your phone and be back by ten.'

'My Lady,' Michael said with a grin.

'What do these demons look like?' my father said.

'You've seen them already,' I said. 'The guy at the airport was one.' Ah Yat came in. 'Here's another.'

My parents looked around, bewildered.

'Ah Yat here, the housekeeper, is a demon,' I said.

Ah Yat smiled and bowed slightly. 'I am honoured to meet you, sir, madam,' she said. 'Yes, I am a demon.'

'You look like a perfectly ordinary person to me,' my father said.

'Oh, thank you, sir, you really are most gracious,' Ah Yat said.

'They can take different forms,' I said. 'They can take human form.'

Ah Yat took the teapots into the kitchen with her.

'She's a tame one, she joined us,' I said.

'I see,' my father said.

'That's everybody,' I said.

John and the Tiger focused on one another.

'Oh no you don't!' I said. 'Out loud!'

'What do you mean, Emma? "Out loud"?' my mother said softly.

'I'll explain later,' I said.

'We're discussing what we should do, Emma,' John said. 'Maybe your parents shouldn't be involved in this.'

'We're involved now,' my father said. 'I want to know what your plans are. We're in this now. We have a right to know.'

'He's right, John,' I said.

'People have died, Brendan,' John said softly.

'Even more reason for us to know what you have planned,' my father said.

'We will not let them control us. We are not going to hide,' John said. 'We will go to Emma's graduation, and we will show you around Hong Kong. After that, we will ensure that you are safe.'

'They can stay with me,' the Tiger said.

'But we will eat first and discuss this later,' John said. 'Dinner is not the time to be discussing this. Tell me about yourselves. I want to know everything. Emma is a remarkable woman, and I'd love to know where she gets it from.'

'Me too,' my father growled softly.

* * *

After the plates had been taken away, Monica appeared at the door from the kitchen. 'The Chinese helper will clean up for me, sir, ma'am,' she said. 'May I spend some time with Simone?'

'I was going to ask you to take her anyway, Monica,' I said. 'You two go and do something together.'

Simone hopped off her chair and took Monica's hand. 'I bought some new toys with my birthday *lai see* money, Monica. Come and see.'

Monica nodded and smiled around the table, then let Simone gently lead her out.

Michael rose and saluted around the table. 'My Lord, my Lady.' He nodded to my parents. 'Mr and Mrs Donahoe.' He turned to me. 'By your leave, my Lady.'

'Off you go, Michael, but remember what I said.'

Michael patted his father on the shoulder as he went past him. 'Dad.'

'Three One Five,' the Tiger growled. 'Don't get yourself into any trouble with that little bastard, he can be bad news when he wants to be. Don't go near any dragons with him.'

Michael silently went out.

'He's your son?' my father said.

'One of the best,' Bai Hu said.

'How many children do you have?' my mother said.

'I have absolutely no idea,' the Tiger said with a grin. 'Right now, something in the region of about six hundred, six hundred and fifty — boys and girls. Couldn't tell you the exact number, they keep dying.'

'Dying?' my mother said with a gasp.

'Most of the children are mortal. The Tiger isn't,' I said, explaining. 'They grow old and die. He doesn't.'

My mother's eyes were wide. 'How about you?' she asked John.

'Simone. One. That's it,' John said. 'One human child.'

'Don't ask,' I said.

'I cannot believe you let yourself get mixed up in this,' my father said softly.

'Me either, sometimes,' I said.

'She does it all for Simone,' John said.

'And she's worth it,' I said.

'Okay.' John put his hands on the table and addressed my parents. 'When you came to Hong Kong, there were probably things you wanted to do. Shopping, sightseeing, things like that. Where would you like us to take you? What would you like to do? Stay for a while after the graduation. Let us show you around.'

'Are you sure that's a good idea?' my mother said weakly.

'We will protect you. You'll be safe,' I said.

'I don't think we should be out sightseeing with all of this happening,' my mother said.

'You are perfectly safe as long as you are with us,' John said. 'Please. Take the time — you are here anyway, enjoy the sights. Let us show you. We will protect you.'

'Well, okay, if you're sure,' my father said. 'I saw the tourist stuff on the way in. I wanted to have some suits made, Hong Kong is famous for that.'

'Mr Li,' I said.

'Good idea,' John said. 'I need a new dinner suit. Get him to make it at the same time. Get a couple of new cheongsams made as well, Emma, you're wearing those ones you bought last year to bits.'

'What's a cheongsam?' my mother said.

'Traditional-style Chinese dress,' the Tiger said. 'Suzie Wong.'

John stiffened and glared at the Tiger. Leo's expression darkened but he didn't say a word.

The Tiger grinned at John. 'Black Turtle.'

Leo silently shot to his feet.

512

John's face went completely rigid. His eyes blazed.

'Leave it for later, John, Leo,' I growled softly. 'He'll keep.'

'You are an extremely offensive little cat with a great big mouth sometimes, Ah Bai,' John said softly, his eyes still blazing. 'And you will mind your manners in front of my Lady and her honoured parents.'

Leo sat back down, his eyes not shifting from the Tiger.

'What, Emma?' my mother leaned over to whisper. 'I get the Suzie Wong thing, but the turtle thing?'

'I'll explain later,' I said. 'Or maybe the Tiger will,' I added pointedly.

'Sorry, Emma,' the Tiger said without a hint of remorse. 'Too good a chance to miss.'

I looked the Tiger right in the eye. 'You have offended the honour of myself and my Lord, and if my parents weren't here I would call you out, Tiger.'

'Damn,' the Tiger said softly, his eyes wide with admiration.

'I'd like to see some temples, if I could,' my mother said, changing the subject. 'I'd like to see more of the Hong Kong Harbour too — I've heard about it. Some of those handicrafts you brought back last time were wonderful, Emma, I'd like to see more. I'm very interested in Chinese culture, you can show me while we're here. Things like that.'

'There aren't many temples in Hong Kong,' the Tiger said. 'Not many at all.'

'That's something people say all the time,' I said. 'But there are temples everywhere. You just don't notice them because they're part of the scenery. How many temples on the Island?'

'None at all,' the Tiger said with a grin. 'There's a couple in Kowloon, and a couple in the New Territories, that's all.'

'There's the Man Mo temple in Hollywood Road, and the Tin Hau temple in Tin Hau,' I said. 'And that's just the big ones.'

'How about the Pak Tai on Kennedy Road?' John said.

The Tiger roared with laughter. My parents were bewildered.

'Oh my God,' I said with a huge grin. 'I completely forgot. I go past that all the time.' I explained for my parents. 'It's a temple in Wan Chai. Very pretty. The temple is dedicated to the Dark Lord of the North, the god who can control the water and keeps the fishermen safe.' I gestured towards John. 'Him.'

My parents stared at John, eyes wide.

'Hey, I'm in there too,' the Tiger said.

'One more crack like that last one and I'll have you taken out,' I said.

The Tiger didn't say anything, he just grinned and saluted, shaking his hands in front of his face.

'It's a lovely clear night,' John said. 'How about we go down to the Peak Tower and have a look?'

'If you don't mind, John,' my father said, sounding weary, 'I think we'd just like to settle in, talk to our daughter, and work out what we'll do.'

'I understand completely,' John said. 'We'll need to rearrange the schedules so that Emma can spend time with you. I can do that, don't worry about it. Leo and I will work something out. Go. Spend time with Emma. You probably have questions. She can tell you the whole ridiculous story.'

'Come on, guys,' I said, rising to lead my parents out. 'Let him mess up my schedule, I'll fix it tomorrow.'

'She's right, my Lord,' Leo said softly.

'My Lord, by your leave,' the Tiger said, and disappeared.

'His tail is in serious trouble,' John said. 'Unacceptable level of insubordination.' He sat quietly, musing. 'I think

I may order him to clean out the basement of Wellington Street. Far too many rats in there, despite the best efforts of the pest-control people.'

My parents stood frozen, staring at where the Tiger had disappeared.

'Come on, I'll explain everything. That's a great idea,' I said over my shoulder to John. 'You know he hates the taste of rat.'

'Don't know why,' John said with a grin. 'My Serpent really likes live rat. I used to spend hours in the basement gorging on them. Since the Serpent left we've really had a problem in there.'

'If I start dreaming about eating rats, your shell is in very serious trouble,' I said quietly to myself as I took my parents out.

CHAPTER FORTY-FOUR

The graduation was being held in a large hall in the Hong Kong Polytechnic University, right next to the entrance to the Central Harbour Tunnel on Kowloon side. It was a huge squatting mass of brown-tiled buildings beside the five-lane entrance to the tunnel.

There was no parking on the grounds of the university for us; instead, we parked in the enormous ten-storey affair right next to the Hung Hom KCR railway interchange and the Hong Kong Coliseum. The Coliseum was a towering upside-down pyramid used for canto-pop concerts.

We took the pedestrian overpass from the car park, walking over the entrance to the Central Harbour Tunnel to the university on the other side. The centre of the campus was open space with the buildings flanking us on all sides. John glanced around appraisingly as we walked through the gardens to the auditorium. I knew what he was thinking.

'Just remember,' John said as we parted outside the changing room, 'we'll be able to sense anything coming in, and will send either Jade or Gold right to you.'

'I'll be fine,' I said. 'Go back to the auditorium. Look after my parents. They're the ones that they're after.'

'We are all the ones that they're after,' he said. He smiled into my eyes. 'I am so proud of you.'

'Just go,' I said impatiently.

The changing room was packed with people talking loudly and getting ready. I stopped inside the door and checked carefully. As far as I could tell, everybody was an ordinary human. I lined up, received my robes, and then found a corner to drop my gear.

'Once you are robed, please take your place in the line for the procession. The ceremony will commence shortly,' Jan said loudly from near the door.

I was right after the Chows. There were about a dozen of them collecting awards. Everybody stopped and carefully smiled for the camera as they received their certificate. I made sure that I did too; John had demanded that I stop so that he could take a photo.

When the ceremony was finished, everybody met and mingled in a reception room. John took photos of me with all the members of our family, even Jade and Gold. Leo gave me a huge hug. Simone was over-excited and starting to tire. My parents couldn't stop grinning.

'Time to go home,' I said to everybody. 'Enough. Let me return my robes, and we'll head off.'

I made a quick detour to thank Jan, then went back to the changing room to return the robes. Jade went with me, just in case. Absolutely nothing happened.

We threaded our way back through the gardens to the overpass that would take us back to the Hung Hom car park. There was nobody for miles.

'Stay alert,' John said quietly.

'Can you sense anything?' I said.

'No,' John said, looking around. 'Anybody else?'

'Nothing,' Simone said. Jade and Gold shook their heads silently as they walked beside us, guarding the flanks.

We walked over the Cross-Harbour Tunnel. There were a few people on the overpass, and some hawkers selling fake CDs and designer handbags.

'Nothing,' John said softly.

The other end of the overpass turned left into a long, enclosed walkway lit with glaring neon. There weren't many people there. I began to feel extremely nervous. Our footsteps echoed eerily through the tunnel. It was unusual for the underpass to have so few people. It was normally very busy with people walking from the Polytechnic and Tsim Sha Tsui East to the Hung Hom station.

'Anything?' Leo said under his breath. 'Something doesn't feel right.'

'If anything happens,' John said, 'Jade, take Simone, Gold, take Mrs Donahoe. Get them out of it.'

Jade and Gold were silent.

'What?' I said.

'Simone is already too big for either of us to carry,' Jade said, miserable.

'I suppose I should be pleased,' John growled. 'But this is not exactly the best time for you to tell me this.'

'Don't be silly, Jade,' Simone said. 'I'm much smaller than Mrs Donahoe.'

'On the inside you are already bigger than a human being, my Lady,' Gold said. 'You are a very special person.'

'Oh.'

'Emma's parents, then,' John said under his breath. 'If you have to, get them out.'

My mother made a small gasping sound and I moved to take her hand. 'We'll be fine.'

The entrance to the Hung Hom KCR station was directly ahead. We turned right out of the tunnel into a dead end. It was the lobby for the lifts to go up to the car park. John glanced around the lift lobby. 'Something does not feel right.'

'Can you sense any demons nearby?' I said as John pressed the button for the lift.

'No,' he said. 'Jade? Gold?'

'Nothing, my Lord,' Gold said. 'But something definitely does not feel right. Something feels ...' He hesitated. 'Something feels very wrong.'

My mother clutched my hand so tightly it was painful.

'You'll be fine, Mum,' I said. 'If anything happens, you'll be right out of here.'

'But what about you, sweetheart?' she said. 'I can't leave you here alone.'

'I'll be fine,' I said. 'We can all take care of ourselves.'

The lift doors opened and my mother screamed.

It was definitely some sort of demon hybrid. It appeared to be made of stone, about three metres tall. It had to bend to come out of the lift. It was roughly human shaped, but it had no recognisable features. It was brown and coarse and seemed to have been put together quickly.

We moved to put my parents and Simone behind us. The demon walked casually out of the lift and stood menacingly over us.

I felt them before I heard them. Their footsteps made the ground tremble. More of them. A lot more of them. They appeared on our left, coming out of the tunnel. No wonder John had not sensed them coming. They were earth elementals. Fake ones. Water was destroyed by earth.

'Shit,' John said quietly. 'I can't see them at all. How many are there?'

'Jade, Gold,' I said, 'do it. Get them out of here now.'

'We can't,' Jade said. 'The way out is blocked.'

'Simone,' I said, 'call a Celestial Master. We're getting you out of here.'

'I'm calling a few Masters,' John said. 'Damn!'

'Blocked,' Simone said. 'Can't call anybody.'

'Stone?' I said.

'Sorry, my Lady, they have us silenced,' the stone said. 'There are about thirty of them, my Lord, ranging from about level thirty to level sixty or sixty-five.'

'I killed its Mother!' Leo said desperately. 'How could it make things that big?'

'They are fake stone elementals,' the stone continued. 'They have used sacred stones from circles in Europe to make them; they are extremely powerful Eastern–Western hybrids. The Jade Emperor is going to be monumentally pissed.'

'Not as much as I am,' John growled. 'I can't see them at all. Wait.' He stopped and concentrated. 'Not even with the Inner Eye. Emma, take the others and run. Get out of here. I'll try to hold them off.'

'Nowhere to run, my love. We're trapped.' I gestured towards the tunnel. 'There are at least thirty of them blocking the way.'

'Weapons?' John said.

'Sorry,' Gold said, his voice full of remorse. 'This is it.'

'Mum, Dad, I am so sorry about this,' I said.

'Brendan, Barbara, listen to me,' John said quietly. 'Stay in the corner, stay very still and stay quiet. They don't want you, they want us. They will probably ignore you.'

'Do as he says, Mum, Dad,' I said softly. 'He's right.'

My parents moved into the corner and crouched, clutching each other. Their faces were masks of terror.

'Simone,' John said, 'go over into the corner with Emma's parents. Jade, Gold. Guard them.'

Simone, Jade and Gold hurried into the corner. Jade and Gold transformed and stood guarding.

'Please move behind me and allow me the honour of taking point, my Lord, my Lady,' Leo said, stepping forward. 'I should be able to stop quite a few of them before I go down.'

Neither John nor I moved. Words weren't necessary.

'Granted,' John said.

Leo moved in front of us. We stood ready, waiting. The demons didn't shift.

'What are they waiting for?' Simone whispered.

John and I shared a look. We knew what they were waiting for.

Simon Wong appeared in front of the massed demons.

'Where's your *Wudang* sword?' I said loudly.

Wong scowled but didn't reply.

'The Tiger broke it in Guangzhou,' John said.

Wong strode forward and faced us. He was in human form: an ordinary good-looking Chinese guy of about thirty.

'Where's the boy?' he said. 'I want him too.'

'He's with Na Zha,' I said with satisfaction. 'Go and find him.'

Wong's face twisted into a grimace. 'He'll keep.'

'We can take you,' I said. 'We can all take you. Even Simone could take you.'

Wong leered at Simone. 'She gets prettier all the time.'

John stiffened but remained where he was. 'Try me.'

Wong's leer widened. 'Why would I bother? You can see me. You can't see them. I think I'll just let them have some fun, and then come back later and collect all the prizes.'

'You are such a coward,' I said softly, but he had already disappeared.

I ripped my handbag open and fumbled through it. I found the phone. I shoved it into my pocket and threw my bag to one side.

'No, Emma!' John hissed.

'I won't use it unless you go down, or Simone is in real danger,' I said.

John faced the direction of the demons appraisingly without saying a word. Then he nodded once, sharply, and moved fluidly into a guard position. 'Are you wearing your black jade earrings?' he said without looking at me.

'Yes.'

'Good. I wish I could tell you exactly what I'm thinking right now without endangering you. Don't come too close to me.'

'That's enough for me,' I said, and readied myself too.

'I think this has to be the happiest goddamn moment in my entire life,' Leo said, his voice breaking as he positioned himself in front of us. 'I cannot tell you how pleased I am to be doing this. My Lord, my Lady, thank you so much. Emma, Simone, you guys stay alive, okay?'

'We'll do our damnedest, Leo,' I said softly. 'Fight well, my friend.'

The demons approached us, slowly and menacingly. They probably wondered whether John could sense them. Simone rose from the corner and came to stand between us. She took up a guard stance as well.

'Don't you dare attempt to fight these, Simone, you stay out of this,' I said. 'You are far too little.'

'I want to help. Besides, I have to learn, Emma,' she said softly. 'Daddy's leaving us soon. And I don't think Leo will last long against things this big.'

Suddenly it all bubbled up inside me. All of the rage, all of the pain. I was about to explode.

I glared at the demons. *This is all your fault.* If they weren't there, we could be happy. I could have my man; this wonderful child would be safe; I could share life with my best friend; we could be together on the Mountain; we could be a family. I suddenly hated them all so much I wanted to tear them to bits. The rage turned to power. My *shen* grew until my entire body burned. My *chi* filled my veins with raw fury. My *ching* flooded through me and made me glow red.

My blood was boiling ice. My head was ready to explode. Something tore in my brain. Something shredded in my gut. I clenched my hands into fists and thrust them forward. I wanted to rip the demons apart with my bare hands.

The power grew inside me until I couldn't hold it. My skin was too tight. My eyes were too small. I was huge and dark and merciless and I wanted *blood* and *slaughter* and *death*. *Blood. Darkness. Destruction.*

Something at the base of my skull quietly went *click*.

Ceiling. Lying on the floor.

John's head appeared above me. He smiled. His hair fell over his shoulder and brushed my face.

'Come and help her up, Leo,' he said, still smiling.

There was silence. Simone whimpered. I sat up and looked around. Leo and Simone were curled up together against the far wall. She clutched him. He appeared to be clutching her just as tightly. When they saw me look at them they both flinched away.

'Don't be ridiculous, it's just Emma,' John said matter-of-factly. 'Come and give her a hand up, Leo, she looks dazed.'

'I'm okay,' I said. The demons were gone. John knelt on one knee next to me, still with a broad smile on his face. He looked relaxed.

I must have been knocked unconscious. 'How long have I been out for?' I rubbed my hand over my forehead. I didn't *feel* like I'd been knocked out; I wasn't dizzy and I didn't have a headache.

I pulled myself to my feet and had a proper look around. All the demons were definitely gone. Then I felt a shot of anguish. My parents were gone too. Jade and Gold as well. John rose to stand next to me. He was still smiling.

'Where's my mum and dad?'

John's smile disappeared. 'Worry about them later.'

'No!' I shouted. 'Worry about them *now*! Where are they?'

'They are fine. Jade and Gold took them back to the Peak in your car. It was better not to take them directly considering the state they were in.'

'They're not fine and you know it,' Leo said. 'Her mother was in hysterics and her father was almost catatonic with terror. Gold will probably have to heavily sedate them when he gets them home. I hate to think about the long-term psychological damage of what they just saw. *Nobody* should have to see what we just did.'

'They were terrified by the demons?' I said.

'No,' Leo rasped. 'The demons were *nothing* compared to what they just saw.'

My legs suddenly felt weak. I leaned against the wall.

'You know I can't touch her, Leo,' John said. 'She won't hurt you. You saw what she did. She couldn't possibly harm you. Come and help her.'

Leo's voice was a low growl. 'Is that an order?'

I heard what they said. I felt a shot of panic. Leo glowered at John. He rose and Simone clutched him around his legs. Both of them took a step back when I looked at them.

'No.' I sagged down the wall to sit on the floor. I wrapped my arms around my knees. 'No.' John's face was full of compassion; he obviously wasn't worried. But Leo and Simone were terrified. Of *me*. 'No.'

'We need to go home and help your parents,' John said mildly.

'I am not going in the car with *that*,' Leo said fiercely, pointing at me.

'Simone,' John said. Simone's head shot up. 'Come here.'

'You are completely crazy,' Leo growled, pulling Simone closer to him. 'You saw what that thing can do. You'll let your daughter near *that*?'

'That *thing* is your Lady and you have sworn allegiance.'

I rested my head in my hands. 'Someone please tell me what happened.' I looked up. Leo's face was rigid with a combination of fear and hatred. 'Leo, it's *me*. Please don't look at me like that.'

'You sure that's Emma?' Leo rasped.

'That is one hundred per cent pure Emma, my Lady and my love,' John said calmly. 'And I guarantee that she will not harm either of you. Did she harm you before? When she changed?'

I'd *changed*. I collapsed over my knees. Oh my God.

'Look at her, Leo,' John said. 'I won't order you, but you can see she needs you. Go to her. Simone, go to her. She won't harm you. She's just Emma. You love her and she loves you. She's *family*. She needs you.' His voice was strained with anguish. 'She protected you. *Help* her!'

I didn't see her come but I heard her little feet. Simone threw her tiny arms around me. I lunged forward and grabbed her. She stiffened, then realised that I was just clutching her in a huge hug. I pulled her down into my lap. 'I would never do anything to hurt you, Simone, you know that.' I looked up at Leo. 'You too, Leo, you know I love you both dearly.' I held Simone tighter and buried my face in her hair. 'For God's sake, will somebody tell me what happened?'

John came and sat next to me. He put his arm around my shoulders. 'Do you remember anything?'

I shook my head into Simone's hair.

'We should take you home. You are probably exhausted.'

I shook my head again. 'I'm full of energy. I'm just fine. I don't feel like I blacked out. I *changed*?' My voice thickened even more. 'Dear God, John, please tell me. *What happened to me*?'

Simone's voice was tiny on my chest. 'You turned into a big black snake monster, Emma.'

We went up to the car in silence. Nobody said anything as John paid for the parking ticket. When we reached the car Leo stopped. 'I'll sit in the back with Simone.' He gestured to John. 'You drive and keep that thing next to you.'

My insides twisted as if the demon's sword was inside me. 'It's *me*, Leo. I wouldn't hurt you in a million years.'

Leo glowered at me as he opened the door to put Simone carefully into the car.

'Mercy is waiting at home for you. Don't panic, Emma, you will be fine,' John said.

John drove the car down the ramp and we merged into the tunnel traffic.

'What did I do, John? Did I destroy all of those demons?'

John made a soft sound of amusement. 'You were remarkable. I couldn't have done better myself. You used both energy and physical attacks. You were lightning fast. They didn't have a chance. You took out a level sixty-five with energy and then blasted six level fifties. Then you took out all the others in a physical attack that was so fast that even I had trouble following you. I couldn't see the demons, but I could see what you did to them.'

'Did I at any time threaten to injure any of you?' I

said, my voice small. But I *knew* the answer to that question.

'You knocked Simone off her feet,' John said mildly.

I suddenly found it difficult to breathe.

'A demon went for her. You knocked her out of the way and bit its head off.'

'Yuck.' I wanted to wipe my mouth. 'So I was no danger to any of you?'

He could hear me begging for reassurance. 'Emma, it was *you*. Of course not.' He grinned. 'Leo's just prejudiced.'

I turned back to look at Leo. His face was taut with restraint. He had his arms folded over his chest. I turned back to the road. 'How much me?'

'Interesting question,' John said. 'One hundred per cent of you. But that was less than half of it.' He glanced away from the road to look at me. 'We will perform some tests when we return home. I'll have the Tiger look at you. I'd love to have a look inside you myself, but that may not be a good idea. This should be interesting. Oh.' He stopped and his face filled with wonder. 'You are very powerful. I may be able to touch you after all.' His face lit up with a huge grin. 'Excellent. We must try when we have you home. With Mercy and the Tiger present, we can try under very controlled conditions.' He banged the steering wheel with his palm. 'Excellent!'

'I cannot believe you are pleased,' Leo said from the back of the car. 'She was a goddamn *snake*.'

'So?' John said, glancing at Leo in the rear-view mirror.

I turned to see Leo. He lifted his arms in front of his chest, then dropped them, still crossed, in front of him.

'Some of my best friends are snakes,' John said mildly.

Leo stared out the window and didn't say anything.

'When we return I will accept your resignation,' John said. 'Feel free to pack your belongings and leave.'

Simone shrieked with horror.

I went rigid with shock. 'No!'

Leo stiffened and dropped his arms. He put his huge hands on his knees and leaned forward. His voice was ferocious. 'No *way*! I am *not* leaving you! You try to fire me, I'll camp out at the front door until you take me back in. I am your Retainer and I have vowed to serve you and Simone ...' He hesitated, then plunged on. 'Until the day I die and there is *nothing you can do about it*!'

'Please don't fire Leo, Daddy,' Simone said, her voice small. 'I love him.'

'Who have you vowed to serve, Leo?' John said. 'If you cannot keep your word, you are not worthy to be a Retainer.'

Leo leaned back, his hands still on his knees. He stared out the window.

'Please don't do this to him, John,' I said quietly. Leo studied me, his face expressionless. 'I understand exactly how you feel, Leo, I'd feel the same way if I were you. I'm horrified myself. I *do* know I'd never hurt any of you, regardless of *what* I am. But I understand.' I knew what I had to do. 'When we're home, I'll formally release you. You can continue to serve the Dark Lord and Simone. You won't have to have anything to do with me any more if you don't want to. You can stay with Simone while I'm near, if it makes you feel better. Believe me,' I looked him right in the eyes, 'I understand.'

Leo stared out the window again. I turned back to the front.

'You are entirely undeserving,' John growled. 'You do not trust me.' He gestured with one hand towards me without looking away from the road. 'This is my

Lady. I *know* her. She may have hidden depths, but she is still *her*.' His voice became ice-cold. 'I cannot begin to describe my disappointment. You let your prejudice overcome you. Five minutes ago you were overjoyed at the prospect of giving your life for her.'

He glanced in the rear-view mirror. 'Simone.'

Simone's voice was very small. 'Yes, Daddy?'

'Are you frightened of Emma?'

'Yes, Daddy,' Simone whispered.

My heart twisted.

'Do you think she'll hurt you?'

Simone hesitated. Then, 'No, she won't hurt me,' she said confidently. 'She's *Emma*.'

'Then why are you frightened of her?'

'Because she's scary,' Simone said. 'Like your Celestial Form. I'm scared of that too.' Simone turned to Leo. I couldn't see her, she was directly behind me. 'Emma won't hurt us, she loves us.'

I turned to Leo again. His face was still expressionless.

'Here we are,' John said. 'Let's go up and have a look at the Snake Lady.'

'Please don't call me that,' I said quietly as I stepped out of the car.

CHAPTER FORTY-FIVE

Kwan Yin and the Tiger were waiting for us in the living room.

'I want to check on my parents before we do anything,' I said.

'That may not be a good idea,' John said. 'You scared them half to death. I think your mother nearly had a heart attack. Gold has her sedated.'

'I want to make sure they're okay.'

'I'll go with you,' Ms Kwan said. 'You may need me.'

'Thanks.'

I tapped on the door to my room and sidled in with Ms Kwan's reassuring presence behind me. I tiptoed through my little living room into the bedroom. My mother lay on the bed, staring wide-eyed and unblinking at the ceiling. My father sat beside her, holding her hand. Gold sat on the other side next to the wall. He gave me a brief smile, and I returned it.

My father rose and backed against the window. 'Get out.'

'Dad, it's me. Emma. I'm sorry I scared you.'

'Get *out*!' my father hissed. 'You've done enough damage.' He looked from me to my mother. 'I don't know where the real Emma is, but as soon as Barbara comes around we're out of here.' He glared at Gold. 'I don't know where my daughter is, but I'll find her. I'll have the police onto you people and we'll find her and get her out of here.'

'Oh God,' I moaned. I put my head in my hands, then looked up at my father desperately. 'I'm Emma.'

'Get away from us.'

Ms Kwan glided around me and carefully approached my father as if he were a frightened animal. He stayed completely still and glowered at her.

'Give me your hand,' she said, holding her hand out.

He glared at her without moving. Then he relented and took her hand. His eyes widened and his face went slack. He stared at Ms Kwan in wonder.

'Emma,' Ms Kwan said as if from a great distance, 'come and hold my other hand.'

I did as she said. Her power moved through me and I felt both her and my father. We were joined.

'Brendan Donahoe,' Ms Kwan said gently, 'this is your daughter, Emma. She is unique. She has loved and shared with a creature that is unlike any creature in existence. It has changed her.'

I could sense my father's wonder and Ms Kwan's gentle assurance.

'She is still your daughter,' Ms Kwan said. 'Look.' She showed him how much I loved him and my mother. She showed him my true feelings for my family. 'Now. See.' She showed him my feelings for Xuan Wu and Simone. Then she showed me to him: all the way through.

'Oh my god,' my father said softly. I felt his comprehension.

'Thank you,' I whispered.

Ms Kwan nodded, smiled sadly, and released us. My father looked at me with awe. 'Emma.'

I fell into his arms and gave him a huge hug. He squeezed me tight and pressed his face into my hair.

'We will have to ask this lady to do the same thing for your mum when she comes around,' my father said. 'That was incredible.'

'This lady is Kwan Yin, the Goddess of Mercy,' I said. 'She is the most wonderful person I have ever met.' I turned to thank Ms Kwan but she had already gone.

Come back to the living room, Emma, we want to have a look at you, Ms Kwan said into my ear.

'Let me know when my mother comes around,' Gold,' I said without releasing my father. 'I'll ask Ms Kwan to come back.'

'My Lady,' Gold said.

I pulled away from my father. 'I have to go, Dad, they want to look inside me. None of us has ever seen that snake,' I winced, 'thing before, and they want to do some tests on me.'

'Why were you a snake, Emma?' he said.

'I don't know, Dad. All I know is that I'll never hurt any of you.' I ran my hands through my hair. 'Xuan Wu is part snake. That may be why it's coming out in me.'

'*Part* snake?'

'I'll tell you all about it later. Like Ms Kwan said, he's unlike anything else in existence.'

My mother's face was still blank. 'Let me know when she comes out of it,' I said, and left.

In the living room, John was giving Leo orders. 'A bowl of water. A table knife. A cigarette lighter. If we don't have one in the apartment, then run down to the Seven Eleven and buy one. I'll need a piece of wood with some leaves still on it — go down the drive and find me a small branch. Must be from a large tree. I'll also need a rock. Not concrete, a natural rock. About the size of a fist would be good.' He paused. 'A ceramic bowl, a large one. And some newspaper. That's all.'

Leo nodded. I sat down next to the Tiger. He took my hand and squeezed it affectionately. Leo glared at me, then spun and left.

'I think we should move to the dining room. We can put the elements on the table,' John said.

'Good idea.' The Tiger raised my hand and guided me up. He put his arm around my shoulders and led me into the dining room. 'You'll be fine,' he said into my ear.

'What are you going to do to me?' I said. 'Water? A knife?'

'We will just test your compatibility,' Ms Kwan said gently as we sat. 'We will not hurt you, don't worry. The knife is just for the metal.'

'First the Tiger will have a look inside you,' John said. He leaned his elbows on the table and gestured towards the Tiger without looking at him. 'Bai Hu.'

'No *way*! You didn't tell me you wanted me to look inside her! You said we were just testing her compatibility!'

'What's the problem?' John said. 'Just have a look inside her, see if you can find the snake, have a look at it, tell us what it looks like. You may even be able to get it to talk to you.'

The Tiger glowered. 'I am *not* looking inside Emma.' He gestured. 'Mercy, you do it.'

'You know I cannot,' Ms Kwan said. 'It is not in my nature.'

'I am too drained, even with Mercy's assistance,' John said.

'Get South or East then. Not me,' the Tiger growled.

'What's your problem?' John said. Then his face cleared. He grinned with comprehension. 'I don't believe it.'

'Believe it.' The Tiger glowered under his white brows at John. 'Blind old Turtle.'

'You are very offensive sometimes, Bai Hu,' Ms Kwan said softly.

'Fuckin' A,' the Tiger said, and she snorted delicately at him.

'Watch your mouth,' John growled.

The Tiger shook his hands in front of his face, first to Ms Kwan and then to me. 'Worth it.' He dropped his hands onto the table with a slap. He eyed me appraisingly. 'Don't make me do this, I don't want her to know. You're *going* and you'll be gone for a long time.'

'I know already, Bai Hu,' I said gently. 'I've known for ages. You are a very big white furry fool.'

'You have him thoroughly worked out, Emma,' John said with amusement. 'Only ever wanted things he couldn't have. He has a hundred. I have one. So of course he wants mine.' He grinned at the Tiger. 'Nothing to hide, my friend. Have a look inside her. It will be good for you. You'll see the way she truly feels. Should make you know exactly how big a fool you are.'

'No big ceremony, Tiger?' I said. 'Rhonda said no?'

The Tiger studied me for a while without saying anything, and then obviously gave in. His shoulders sagged and he sighed. 'Okay.' He glared at John. 'You owe me one.'

'I know what to do,' I said.

He put his hands on my shoulders. 'Just relax.'

The Tiger's essence was completely different from John's. John had been smooth and dark when he walked around inside my head. The Tiger was fierce, sharp and bright. I was concerned for a moment that the sharp edges of his consciousness would hurt me, but he seemed to slide through my brain without harming me. I relaxed.

'A good balance of yang and yin,' the Tiger commented quietly as he walked around in my head, his soft paws padding. 'Quite a yang female, but she has learned well.' He shuffled around, and I blocked him out from some of my deeper thoughts despite myself. 'Sorry, Emma, has to be done,' the Tiger said ruefully. 'I need to see everything. Believe me, I would prefer not to be here as well.'

I relaxed and opened up to let him in. But I still wasn't very happy about him exploring some of my darker corners.

'Whoa,' he said, and stepped back. 'Genius-level intelligence.' He grinned inside my head. 'Scary.'

'You have no idea,' John said from the other side of the table.

The Tiger plunged back into me. He came to my feelings for John and skirted around them. 'None of my business. Very strong, very true though.' He chuckled and stole a quick glance. 'Okay, Ah Wu, I see what you mean.' He froze, then stepped back. His Tiger eyes widened inside my head. 'You are one hell of a lucky man, Ah Wu,' he marvelled. 'Whoa.' He was aghast. '*What* a *chick*! How did you two get anything else done in the palace? No wonder you fell asleep in the pool. I *must* get you two back there before you go. Hot damn,' he added with envy, 'none of *my* women are that flexible. And she *likes* it when you let go? Unbelievable.'

'Stop looking at that,' I snapped. 'That has nothing to do with you.'

'You forget yourself, sir,' the Lady said.

'You are walking a very fine line, Ah Bai,' John growled menacingly.

'Sorry.' He grinned wryly and winked at me. I huffed at him in response, and imagined myself putting my hands on my hips and glaring at him. *Sorry,* he said silently to me. He asked me a silent question with a cheeky grin and I imagined myself slapping him *hard* across the nose. He rubbed his nose and smiled.

He went back to the inside of my head. 'Nothing there.' He shuffled around. 'Hold on, what's this?' He started to burrow, and I winced. He really began to dig, and it hurt.

'Ease off, Tiger,' Ms Kwan said. 'You may injure her.'

'There's something down here,' the Tiger said as he burrowed. 'I think I've found it.'

The pain became excruciating. He tore through my brain, making every nerve alive with pain. 'Please hurry, Tiger, you're really starting to hurt me.'

He stuck his claws right into me and I shrieked with agony. I couldn't see anything but I heard John moving. 'Don't touch me!' I shouted. A red veil went across my vision, even though I had my eyes closed. My ears filled with roaring. My head was full of razor-sharp steel knives. Then something went *click*. Everything went quiet. It was perfectly dark and silent.

'Broke through,' the Tiger said softly. 'Will you look at that.'

'Stay very still, Emma,' Ms Kwan said. 'Don't attempt to move, physically or mentally. Just stay very still.'

'What is your name?' John said.

'Emma,' I said softly, and gasped. I heard two voices say the same thing.

'Stay very still, Emma,' Ms Kwan warned me again. 'Try to keep control.'

'You are a Serpent?' John said.

I didn't say anything. Then I had to. 'I'm your Lady, Xuan Wu. I love you.' Those two voices again. Mine and somebody else's. I realised: the snake was talking too.

'Why are you here?' John said.

'To look after Simone, of course, silly,' I said impatiently. I didn't have any control over what I said. It just came out.

'Have you ever seen anything like me before, guys?' the Emma part of me said.

'We are all shaking our heads: no,' John said. He knew I couldn't see.

'What do I look like right now, John?' I said quietly.

None of them answered.

'Make sure Leo doesn't see me then,' I hissed. Both voices hissed.

I had a sudden thought. 'Are you a demon?' I asked myself, and Ms Kwan gasped.

'I said no,' I said.

'Whoa,' the Tiger said, his voice full of awe. 'She really did do that, Ah Wu, I felt it. She asked herself a question, and then answered it truthfully.'

'*Are you my Serpent?*' John said fiercely.

I stopped at that. 'I don't know,' I said. 'I have no idea what I am.'

Suddenly I was filled with such anguish that I felt I would burst. Kwan Yin moaned in sympathy. She felt it too.

'I don't know what I am. I'm not a demon. But,' my heart twisted, 'I'm lost. Can you help me find my way home?'

'I will do my best,' John said gently. 'What does your home look like? Where is it?'

'It's green and crystal and beautiful,' I said. 'It's pure and bright and joyful. It's full of love and kindness. And I miss it so much I want to die.'

'I wish you hadn't done this to me,' the Emma part of me added softly. 'I can see it. It will haunt my dreams until I find it.'

'I'm sorry I did this to you, Emma,' the Tiger said. 'I feel your pain.'

'Simone and John are enough for me until I find it,' I said. 'And poor Leo, who is scared to death of me.'

'Will you leave us if you find it?' John said, his voice full of grief. 'Will you leave us if you find your home?'

'I don't know,' I whispered. I shook myself. 'John, Leo's outside the door. He has the stuff. He's terrified. But he needs to face his fear. He needs to do this. He will have to get used to me, now that I am here. Let him in. Ms Kwan, let him in, and hold his hand. I need to talk to him.'

I still couldn't see anything. But I heard the door open. Ms Kwan moved and Leo bellowed with terror.

'Hold, Leo,' I said firmly, with both voices. I felt him freeze. I saw his face with my eyes closed. I saw right through him. I saw his dread.

'Approach,' I said. 'Don't be afraid.'

He stood still for a long time. 'Kwan Yin,' I said. She nodded, and moved to help him. I blindly sensed them approach me. Every step was a million miles for Leo.

'Touch me,' I said softly. 'Please, Leo, touch me.'

It was the hardest thing he'd ever done in his life. It took reserves of courage that he didn't even know he possessed. He truly was terrified of me. The poor man was more than scared of snakes; he had a phobia. He was mortally afraid of them ... of us. But he reached out and touched me anyway, helped by Kwan Yin, who understood.

'Let go, Lady,' I said softly. Leo flinched. He was sure I would strike him down and kill him.

'You are a stupid asshole, Leo. It's just me.' And I showed him. I showed him right through.

'Holy shit,' Leo said quietly.

'You know, that's the first time I've ever heard you use any sort of bad language?' I said with delight. 'For a Navy guy you really don't fit the stereotype.'

'I try not to fit any sort of stereotype,' he growled. His voice softened. 'What are you, Emma?'

'Apart from what you see, Leo, which I can't see myself right now, 'cause I'm completely blind,' I said, 'I have absolutely no idea.'

'You can't see?'

'Not a thing,' I said. 'You'll have to tell me what I look like later.'

'You don't want to know.'

'Is it one hundred per cent snake?' I said, and turned my head under Leo's hand.

'I wish. That would be a major improvement on what I'm looking at.'

'Do you want me to take a photo, Emma?' John said.

'No way. I'm handling this now, don't freak me out.' I pulled myself together. 'Whoa, I'm okay. I really am. I feel fine.' I turned to Leo. 'Are you okay, Leo, dear Leo?'

I blindly saw Leo nod. 'Yes, my Lady.'

John sighed with relief.

'We have things to do,' I said briskly. 'Parents to reassure, demons to kill, things like that. How will we get me back again?'

'Can I take my hand off?' Leo said.

'Sure,' I said, and his hand moved away.

'I thought you'd be cold and slimy. But you're warm and dry and rather nice to touch,' Leo said.

'Most reptiles are,' John said, across from me. 'What we will do, Emma, is the Tiger will take his claws out of your head.'

'Ouch,' I said. 'That will hurt like hell. You have your claws in my head?'

'Metaphorically speaking,' the Tiger said. 'I'm not actually physically touching you at all right now.'

'Still feel the same way, Tiger?' I said.

'Not so sure now, my Lady,' the Tiger said. 'I think it would take a very special sort of guy to love what I'm looking at right now.'

'Good thing I have one then,' I said, and I felt John nodding. I felt his amused reaction. Then I felt a jolt of shock. 'Wait! Tiger. Hold. Don't do it yet.'

They all hesitated, wondering.

I turned very carefully to face John. I saw him, still blind.

On the other side of the table was a Turtle. Its head was fierce and demonic, with a frilled scaly mane around it; like a cross between a lion's and a dragon's, but much uglier. Its black shell stretched forever. Its enormous shining dark eyes watched me with amusement. With John's eyes. I suddenly wanted to weep with joy, but the snake eyes wouldn't let me. He was the most beautiful and the most horrifying and the most wonderful thing I had ever seen.

'I can see you, John. I can see all of you. My God, but you are ugly. No wonder Simone was scared of you.' I paused. 'Simone should see me, John. She needs to understand as well.'

'What we are looking at now is different from what we saw before,' John said, and the Turtle spoke. The sight took my breath away. 'What we have now is a halfway point between Emma and the Serpent, artificially forced on you by Bai Hu. It would not be a good idea to show this to Simone. I will talk to her later, and explain.'

'Michael too,' I said softly.

The Turtle nodded without speaking. I wanted to smile but I couldn't. 'Damn, John, but you are the cutest thing I have ever seen in my entire life.'

'You're pretty goddamn cute yourself,' John shot back. The Turtle grinned and I wanted to laugh. 'Those black scales are incredibly attractive.'

'Cute is not a word I would be using right here and now,' Leo growled.

I took a deep breath. It felt very strange to be

breathing through both forms. 'Okay, Tiger,' I said firmly, 'do it.'

The world exploded into a haze of agony. He ripped my brain out of the top of my head, pulling my eyeballs with it. He tore the skin on my face from my skull.

And then the pain was gone.

'Open your eyes, Emma,' Ms Kwan said.

I opened my eyes and quickly checked myself. Perfectly normal. The Tiger sat next to me on my right. Leo stood between him and me. Ms Kwan sat across from me. John sat on the other side of her. They all watched me with varying degrees of incredulity.

Leo bent over me, took my hand and kissed me on the cheek. 'I'm sorry, Emma,' he whispered.

I squeezed his hand, then touched his cheek. 'I love you dearly, Leo, you know I wouldn't hurt you.' I looked into his eyes. 'You were really brave. You are the bravest man I know. I saw what that took.'

He smiled down at me and his eyes sparkled. 'Thanks, Emma.'

'You were going to do some other tests? I hope they won't hurt as much as that.' I grinned at the Tiger. 'Those are some serious virtual claws you have there.'

'Can I stay and watch?' Leo said.

'If Emma doesn't mind, I don't,' John said.

'Of course not.'

'Good.' John pulled the bowl of water towards him. 'Watch this.' He put his hand over the water. It quickly boiled. Steam rose from it. 'Now.' The water made a sharp crackling sound as it instantly turned to ice. 'Next.' The water immediately melted, then rose out of the bowl in a glistening lump.

'Whoa,' Leo said.

'Drop it on the Tiger,' I said. 'Wash his dirty mind.'

John and the Tiger both laughed softly. The water went back into the bowl. John put the bowl in front of me. 'Try.'

I concentrated. Nothing happened.

'Put your hand in the water, see if you can warm it,' John said.

I did. I concentrated. Again, nothing.

'Nothing there,' John said, and the disappointment was obvious in his voice.

'If I were your Serpent, I would be able to do that, wouldn't I?' I said quietly.

His face was rigid. He nodded once, sharply.

'You should have tested her while she was that scaly thing,' Leo said.

'You are quite right,' John said, and eyed me appraisingly.

'No *way* is that cat,' I said, pointing at the Tiger, 'sticking his claws into my head again. That damn well *hurt*!'

The knife lifted off the table and moved towards me. 'Catch,' the Tiger said, and it fell out of the air. I concentrated quickly. The knife hit the table with a clatter.

'Try to bend it,' the Tiger said.

I concentrated. Again, nothing.

John grabbed the large bowl, stuffed a piece of newspaper into it, and lit it with the cigarette lighter. He put it in front of me. 'See if you can change its colour.'

I concentrated. Nothing at all.

'Put it out,' John said.

Again, nothing.

John lifted the water from the bowl onto the fire and it went out.

'Not surprising, I suppose,' Ms Kwan said. 'Two more.'

John passed me the wooden branch. It was a large twig with leaves on it. 'Try to make it grow.'

I concentrated. Nothing.

'I think we're wasting our time here, guys,' I said. 'I think in human form I'm just a perfectly normal human woman, and the Snake part spends most of its time hiding.' I stopped. 'I can't believe I just talked about myself taking human form,' I said with wonder. 'That is *so weird*.'

'Try the last one anyway,' John said. 'But it's highly unlikely that you would have Earth; such a thing is extremely rare.'

'You're Water.' I pointed at John, and he nodded. 'You're Metal,' I said to the Tiger, who smiled slightly. 'Qing Long is Wood, Zhu Que is Fire. Who's Earth? There's a Fifth Wind?'

'There is a Centre, not a Wind, Emma,' Kwan Yin said, her voice full of deference. 'Earth is the Middle. It is the Lord of us all. It is the Jade Emperor Himself. He is Earth and Stone.'

'Oh. I sincerely do not want to meet this guy.' They all went rigid the minute the word 'guy' came out of my mouth. 'Just the idea of him scares me to death.'

'I think all creatures know instinctively exactly how formidable the Celestial One is,' Ms Kwan said softly.

John picked up the stone. 'The Celestial will be extremely annoyed the minute he finds out about those hybrid elementals.' He put the stone in front of me. 'Just try to move it.'

I concentrated on the stone. Nothing.

'No elemental alignment,' the Tiger said. 'See if you can nail the snake down when she transforms again and test it then.'

'The Serpent was extremely powerful. I still may be able to touch you,' John said. 'Let's try.'

'You won't,' I said. 'What did Meredith say? You let your love cloud your judgement.'

'Come and stand between myself and Mercy,' John said anyway.

I rose and stood between them.

'Hold my hand, Emma,' Ms Kwan said, and put her hand out. I took her hand in my left. 'Now take his.' I took John's hand in my right.

'Release my hand. Rest yours on mine,' Ms Kwan said. I moved my hand so that it was just resting on hers, palm to palm.

'I will move my hand. Stay perfectly still,' Ms Kwan said. 'Don't move.'

She moved her hand away from underneath mine. Nothing happened.

'Yes,' I said softly.

John moved to say something on my right. A black hole opened up in front of him. I was sucked straight into it. Kwan Yin quickly grabbed my hand. Everything rushed together and I was back between them. I sagged. 'No.'

John dropped my hand, threw himself up, and stalked away from the table without saying a word.

'Come back here!' I yelled. He stopped and turned, expressionless.

'You do not have time to do sword katas right now!' I shouted. 'My parents are in my room, shell-shocked, and we are going to talk to them and sort this out! And then we are going to find out exactly what happened, and go and kick some serious demon ass!'

He put his hands up in defeat. 'All right, all right,' he said wryly as he flopped back into his chair. 'Don't get your scaly tail in a knot.'

Both Leo and the Tiger laughed gently at that.

'I don't have —' I started to shoot back, and then I stopped.

'Damn,' I said quietly and flopped down into a chair. 'I am *not* having a good day.'

'I will be watching you,' Kwan Yin said. 'I will return to help you with your mother.' She disappeared.

'Am I a Shen?' I said to the Tiger before he disappeared as well.

'I don't think so,' the Tiger said. 'Like we said, none of us has seen anything like you before.'

'Am I already Immortal?' I said more softly.

'Most definitely not,' the Tiger said, amused. 'Don't try anything stupid. Right now, you are just an ordinary human female.'

'See?' the stone in my ring said.

'Shut the hell up!' John and I both snapped at the same time.

'Stay and help, if you can, my friend,' John said to the Tiger.

'I am being summoned,' the Tiger said. 'I think I'm about to be debriefed. With extreme prejudice. A great deal of brown sticky stuff is about to hit some swiftly rotating blades. I think you should count yourself lucky that you can't travel very far right now, and that certain Celestials don't like slumming it on the Earthly. I'll be back as soon as I'm finished trying to cover for your worthless shell. Okay?'

'Go,' John said wearily, waving him away with one hand. 'Thanks,' he added sincerely.

'My Lord, my Lady. Dark Turtle, Dark Serpent,' Bai Hu added, rubbing it in with relish. 'By your leave.'

'Piss off, Tiger,' I said, just as wearily. 'Dark Serpent indeed.'

The Tiger grinned at me and winked. He disappeared.

John eyed me appraisingly. 'You think you can do it at will?'

'I did it because Simone said you were going and I was just so mad I wanted to explode,' I said. 'I really don't think I have any control over it at all.'

'Well,' he said, 'with your temper I don't think we'll be waiting too long to see it again.'

Later I sat on the couch in the living room with only a table lamp for illumination. The apartment was dark and quiet; everybody else was asleep. Kwan Yin had shown me to my mother, and my mother had accepted me, but it had been hard for her. Kwan Yin had done something to both of my parents and they'd fallen asleep without trouble.

I heard a soft sound. Simone stood in the hallway in her nightdress, leaning on the doorframe. I held out one arm and she crept onto the couch next to me. She put her head on my shoulder and I wrapped my arm around her.

'Are you okay, Emma?' she said softly.

'Yes,' I said. 'I just can't sleep. What about you, sweetheart? You weren't too scared?'

'I'm okay,' she whispered. 'I know it's you. But why were you a snake?'

I sighed with feeling. 'I wish I knew.'

'You wouldn't hurt us anyway. It's still you.'

'I know,' I whispered.

John appeared in the doorway in his black pyjama pants, his long hair falling over his shoulder. He hesitated, then came to us.

Simone shifted so that he could sit on the other side of her, and he pulled her into his lap. 'Turn around,' I whispered, and he swivelled so that I could braid his hair for him. I braided it tight, enjoying the silken feeling. I threw my arms over his shoulders and held him from behind, then pulled away. He turned so that I could cuddle into him and he wrapped his arm around me. I pulled my feet up and leaned on him.

Simone put her head on his chest, her huge golden eyes turned towards me. 'Your hair smells like the sea, Daddy,' she whispered. 'Why?'

'Because I am what I am,' he said, his voice rumbling through his chest.

Simone didn't move or reply.

'Are you two okay?' he said softly. 'You should be sleeping.'

Simone turned her face away from me, still leaning on his chest.

'You know that Emma loves you,' John said.

Simone turned her face back to me and smiled. She reached out and touched my cheek. 'I know. I think she loves me more than she loves you, Daddy.'

'She would never hurt you,' he said.

'I know that,' she said. 'But why is she a snake?'

'Nobody knows,' he said. 'It might be because I'm a snake too.'

Simone was silent. Then she pulled herself upright, her little arms around his neck, and smiled into his face. 'We'll all be just fine, you know that?'

He wrapped his arm around her and squeezed both of us. 'Yes, we will.'

Simone dropped her head back onto his chest and sighed. 'We're all going to be just fine.'

The Serpent woke.
It raised its head from the silky
soft mud, then slithered forward,
leaving an elegant trail.
It threw itself up into the
freezing black water and whipped
towards the surface.
It cried. There was no answer.

GLOSSARY

A NOTE ON LANGUAGE

The Chinese language is divided by a number of different dialects and this has been reflected throughout my story. The main dialect spoken in Hong Kong is Cantonese, and many of the terms I've used are in Cantonese. The main method for transcribing Cantonese into English is the Yale system, which I have hardly used at all in this book, preferring to use a simpler phonetic method for spelling the Cantonese. Apologies to purists, but I've chosen ease of readability over phonetic correctness.

The dialect mainly spoken on the Mainland of China is Putonghua (also called Mandarin Chinese), which was originally the dialect used in the north of China but has spread to become the standard tongue. Putonghua has a strict and useful set of transcription rules called pinyin, which I've used throughout for Putonghua terms. As a rough guide to pronunciation, the 'Q' in pinyin is pronounced 'ch', the 'X' is 'sh' and the 'Zh' is a softer 'ch' than the 'Q' sound. Xuan Wu is therefore pronounced 'Shwan Wu'.

I've spelt chi with the 'ch' throughout the book, even though in pinyin it is qi, purely to aid in readability.

Qing Long and Zhu Que I have spelt in pinyin to assist anybody who'd like to look into these interesting deities further.

Aberdeen Typhoon Shelter: A harbour on the south side of Hong Kong Island that is home to a large number of small and large fishing boats. Some of the boats are permanently moored there and are residences.

Admiralty: The first station after the MTR train has come through the tunnel onto Hong Kong Island from Kowloon, and a major traffic interchange.

Ancestral tablet: A tablet inscribed with the name of the deceased, which is kept in a temple or at the residence of the person's descendants and occasionally provided with incense and offerings to appease the spirit.

Anime (Japanese): Animation; can vary from cute children's shows to violent horror stories for adults, and everything in between.

Bai Hu (Putonghua): The White Tiger of the West.

Bo: Weapon — staff.

Bo lei: A very dark and pungent Chinese tea, often drunk with yum cha to help digest the sometimes heavy and rich food served there.

Bu keqi (Putonghua) pronounced, roughly, 'bu kerchi': 'You're welcome.'

Buddhism: The system of beliefs that life is an endless journey through reincarnation until a state of perfect detachment or Nirvana is reached.

Cantonese: The dialect of Chinese spoken mainly in the south of China and used extensively in Hong Kong. Although in written form it is nearly identical to Putonghua, when spoken it is almost unintelligible to Putonghua speakers.

Causeway Bay: Large shopping and office district on Hong Kong Island. Most of the Island's residents seem to head there on Sunday for shopping.

Central: The main business district in Hong Kong, on the waterfront on Hong Kong Island.

Central Committee: Main governing body of Mainland China.

Cha siu bow: Dim sum served at yum cha; a steamed bread bun containing barbecued pork and gravy in the centre.

Chek Lap Kok: Hong Kong's new airport on a large swathe of reclaimed land north of Lantau Island.

Cheongsam (Cantonese): Traditional Chinese dress, with a mandarin collar, usually closed with toggles and loops, and with splits up the sides.

Cheung Chau: Small dumbbell-shaped island off the coast of Hong Kong Island, about an hour away by ferry.

Chi: Energy. The literal meaning is 'gas' or 'breath' but in martial arts terms it describes the energy (or breath) of life that exists in all living things.

Chi gong (Cantonese): Literally, 'energy work'. A series of movements expressly designed for manipulation of chi.

Chinese New Year: The Chinese calendar is lunar, and New Year falls at a different time each Western calendar. Chinese New Year usually falls in either January or February.

Ching: A type of life energy, ching is the energy of sex and reproduction, the Essence of Life. Every person is born with a limited amount of ching and as this energy is drained they grow old and die.

Chiu Chow: A southeastern province of China.

Choy sum (Cantonese): A leafy green Chinese vegetable vaguely resembling English spinach.

City Hall: Hall on the waterfront in Central on Hong Kong Island containing theatres and a large restaurant.

Confucianism: A set of rules for social behaviour designed to ensure that all of society runs smoothly.

Congee: A gruel made by boiling rice with savoury ingredients such as pork or thousand-year egg. Usually eaten for breakfast but can be eaten as a meal or snack any time of the day.

Connaught Road: Main thoroughfare through the middle of Central District in Hong Kong, running parallel to the waterfront and with five lanes each side.

Cross-Harbour Tunnel: Tunnel that carries both cars and MTR trains from Hong Kong Island to Kowloon under the Harbour.

Cultural Revolution: A turbulent period of recent Chinese history (1966–75) during which gangs of young people called Red Guards overthrew 'old ways of thinking' and destroyed many ancient cultural icons.

Dai pai dong (Cantonese): Small open-air restaurant.

Dan tian: Energy centre, a source of energy within the body. The central dan tian is roughly located in the solar plexus.

Daujie (Cantonese): 'Thank you', used exclusively when a gift is given.

Dim sum (Cantonese): Small dumplings in bamboo steamers served at yum cha. Usually each dumpling is less than three centimetres across and four are found in each steamer. There are a number of different types, and standard types of dim sum are served at every yum cha.

Discovery Bay: Residential enclave on Lantau Island, quite some distance from the rush of Hong Kong Island and only reachable by ferry.

Dojo (Japanese): Martial arts training school.

Eight Immortals: A group of iconic Immortals from Taoist mythology, each one representing a human condition. Stories of their exploits are part of popular Chinese culture.

Er Lang: The Second Heavenly General, second-in-charge of the running of Heavenly affairs. Usually depicted as a young man with three eyes and accompanied by his faithful dog.

Fortune sticks: A set of bamboo sticks in a bamboo holder. The questioner kneels in front of the altar and shakes the holder until one stick rises above the rest and falls out. This stick has a number that is translated into the fortune by temple staff.

Fung shui (or feng shui): The Chinese system of geomancy that links the environment to the fate of those living in it. A house with good internal and external fung shui assures its residents of good luck in their life.

Gay-lo (Cantonese slang): gay, homosexual.

Guangdong: The province of China directly across the border from Hong Kong.

Guangzhou: The capital city of Guangdong Province, about an hour away by road from Hong Kong. A large bustling commercial city rivalling Hong Kong in size and activity.

Gundam (Japanese): Large humanoid robot armour popular in Japanese cartoons.

Gung hei fat choy (Cantonese): Happy New Year.

Gwun Gong (or Guan Gong): A southern Chinese Taoist deity; a local General who attained Immortality and is venerated for his strengths of loyalty and justice and his ability to destroy demons.

H'suantian Shangdi (Cantonese): Xuan Tian Shang Di in the Wade-Giles method of writing Cantonese words.

Har gow: Dim sum served at yum cha; a steamed dumpling with a thin skin of rice flour dough containing prawns.

Hei sun (Cantonese): Arise.

Ho ak (Cantonese): Okay.

Ho fan (Cantonese): Flat white noodles made from rice; can be either boiled in soup or stir-fried.

Hong Kong Jockey Club: a private Hong Kong institution that runs and handles all of the horseracing and legal gambling in Hong Kong. There can be billions of Hong Kong dollars in bets on a single race meeting.

Hutong (Putonghua): Traditional square Chinese house, built around a central courtyard.

ICAC: Independent Commission Against Corruption; an independent government agency focused on tracking down corruption in Hong Kong.

Jade Emperor: The supreme ruler of the Taoist Celestial Government.

Journey to the West: A classic of Chinese literature written during the Ming Dynasty by Wu Cheng'En. The story of the Monkey King's journey to India with a Buddhist priest to collect scriptures and return them to China.

Kata (Japanese): A martial arts 'set'; a series of moves to practise the use of a weapon or hand-to-hand skills.

KCR: A separate above-ground train network that connects with the MTR and travels to the border with

Mainland China. Used to travel to towns in the New Territories.

Kitchen God: A domestic deity who watches over the activities of the family and reports annually to the Jade Emperor.

Koi (Japanese): Coloured ornamental carp.

Kowloon: Peninsula opposite the Harbour from Hong Kong Island, a densely packed area of highrise buildings. Actually on the Chinese Mainland, but separated by a strict border dividing Hong Kong from China.

Kowloon City: District in Kowloon just before the entrance to the Cross-Harbour Tunnel.

Kwan Yin: Buddhist icon; a woman who attained Nirvana and became a Buddha but returned to Earth to help others achieve Nirvana as well. Often represented as a goddess of Mercy.

Lai see (Cantonese): A red paper envelope used to give cash as a gift for birthdays and at New Year. It's believed that for every dollar given ten will return during the year.

Lai see dao loy (Cantonese): 'Lai see, please!'

Lantau Island: One of Hong Kong's outlying islands, larger than Hong Kong Island but not as densely inhabited.

Li: Chinese unit of measure, approximately half a kilometre.

Lo Wu: The area of Hong Kong that contains the border crossing. Lo Wu is an area that covers both sides of the border; it is in both Hong Kong and China.

Lo Wu Shopping Centre: A large shopping centre directly across the Hong Kong/Chinese border on the

Chinese side. A shopping destination for Hong Kong residents in search of a bargain.

Love hotel: Hotel with rooms that are rented by the hour by young people who live with their parents (and therefore have no privacy) or businessmen meeting their mistresses for sex.

M'goi sai (Cantonese): 'Thank you very much.'

M'sai (Cantonese): Literally, 'no need', but it generally means 'you're welcome'.

Macau: One-time Portuguese colony to the west of Hong Kong in the Pearl River Delta, about an hour away by jet hydrofoil; now another Special Administrative Region of China. Macau's port is not as deep and sheltered as Hong Kong's so it has never been the busy trade port that Hong Kong is.

Mah jong: Chinese game played with tiles. The Chinese play it differently from the polite game played by many Westerners; it is played for money and can often be a cut-throat competition between skilled players, rather like poker.

Manga: Japanese illustrated novel or comic book.

MTR: Fast, cheap, efficient and spotlessly clean subway train system in Hong Kong. Mostly standing room, and during rush hour so packed that it is often impossible to get onto a carriage.

Na Zha: Famous mythical Immortal who was so powerful as a child that he killed one of the dragon sons of the Dragon King. He gained Immortality by unselfishly travelling into Hell to release his parents who had been held in punishment for his crime. A spirit of Youthfulness.

New Territories: A large area of land between Kowloon and Mainland China that was granted to extend Hong

Kong. Less crowded than Hong Kong and Kowloon, the New Territories are green and hilly with highrise New Towns scattered through them.

Nunchucks: Short wooden sticks held together with chains; a martial arts weapon.

Opium Wars: (1839–60) A series of clashes between the then British Empire and the Imperial Chinese Government over Britain's right to trade opium to China. It led to a number of humiliating defeats and surrenders by China as they were massively outclassed by modern Western military technology.

Pa Kua (Cantonese): The Eight Symbols, a central part of Taoist mysticism. Four of these Eight Symbols flank the circle in the centre of the Korean flag.

Pak Tai: One of Xuan Wu's many names; this one is used in Southern China.

Peak Tower: Tourist sightseeing spot at the top of the Peak Tram. Nestled between the two highest peaks on the Island and therefore not the highest point in Hong Kong, but providing a good view for tourist photographs.

Peak Tram: Tram that has been running for many years between Central and the Peak. Now mostly a tourist attraction because of the steepness of the ride and the view.

Peak, the: Prestigious residential area of Hong Kong, on top of the highest point of the centre of Hong Kong Island. The view over the Harbour and highrises is spectacular, and the property prices there are some of the highest in the world.

Pokfulam: Area of Hong Kong west of the main business districts, facing the open ocean rather than the harbour. Contains large residential apartment blocks and a very large hillside cemetery.

Putonghua: Also called Mandarin, the dialect of Chinese spoken throughout China as a standard language. Individual provinces have their own dialects but Putonghua is spoken as a common tongue.

Qing Long (Putonghua) pronounced, roughly, Ching Long: The Azure Dragon of the East.

Ramen (Japanese): Instant two-minute noodles.

Repulse Bay: A small swimming beach surrounded by an expensive residential enclave of high- and low-rise apartment blocks on the south side of Hong Kong Island.

Salute, Chinese: The left hand is closed into a fist and the right hand is wrapped around it. Then the two hands are held in front of the chest and sometimes shaken.

Sashimi (Japanese): Raw fish.

Sensei (Japanese): Master.

Sha Tin: A New Territories 'New Town', consisting of a large shopping centre surrounded by a massive number of highrise developments on the banks of the Shing Mun River.

Shaolin: Famous temple, monastery and school of martial arts, as well as a style of martial arts.

Shen: Shen has two meanings, in the same sense that the English word spirit has two meanings ('ghost' and 'energy'). Shen can mean an Immortal being, something like a god in Chinese mythology. It is also the spirit that dwells within a person, the energy of their soul.

Shenzhen: The city at the border between Hong Kong and China, a 'special economic zone' where capitalism has been allowed to flourish. Most of the goods manufactured in China for export to the West are made in Shenzhen.

Sheung Wan: The western end of the Hong Kong Island MTR line; most people get off the train before reaching this station.

Shoji (Japanese): Screen of paper stretched over a wooden frame.

Shui (Cantonese): 'Water'.

Shui gow: Chinese dumplings made of pork and prawn meat inside a dough wrapping, boiled in soup stock.

Shroff Office: A counter in a car park where you pay the parking fee before returning to your car.

Sifu (Cantonese): Master.

Siu mai: Dim sum served at yum cha; a steamed dumpling with a skin of wheat flour containing prawn and pork.

Sow mei (Cantonese): A type of Chinese tea, with a greenish colour and a light, fragrant flavour.

Stanley Market: A famous market on the south side of Hong Kong island, specialising in tourist items.

Star Ferry: Small oval green and white ferries that run a cheap service between Hong Kong Island and Kowloon.

Sticky rice: Dim sum served at yum cha; glutinous rice filled with savouries such as pork and thousand-year egg, wrapped in a green leaf and steamed.

Tae kwon do: Korean martial art.

Tai chi: A martial art that consists of a slow series of movements, used mainly as a form of exercise and chi manipulation to enhance health and extend life. Usable as a lethal martial art by advanced practitioners. There are several different styles of tai chi, including Chen, Yang and Wu, named after the people who invented them.

Tai chi chuan: Full correct name for tai chi.

Tai Koo Shing: large enclosed shopping mall on the north side of Hong Kong.

Tao Teh Ching: A collection of writings by Lao Tzu on the elemental nature of Taoist philosophy.

Tao, the: 'The Way'. A perfect state of consciousness equivalent to the Buddhist Nirvana, in which a person becomes completely attuned with the universe and achieves Immortality. Also the shortened name of a collection of writings (the *Tao Teh Ching*) on Taoist philosophy written by Lao Tzu.

Taoism: Similar to Buddhism, but the state of perfection can be reached by a number of different methods, including alchemy and internal energy manipulation as well as meditation and spirituality.

Tatami (Japanese): Rice-fibre matting.

Temple Street: A night market along a street on Kowloon side in Hong Kong. Notorious as a triad gang hangout as well as being one of Hong Kong's more colourful markets.

Ten Levels of Hell: It is believed that a human soul travels through ten levels of Hell, being judged and punished for a particular type of sin at each level. Upon reaching the lowest, or tenth, level, the soul is given an elixir of forgetfulness and returned to Earth to reincarnate and live another life.

Teppan (Japanese): Hotplate used for cooking food at teppanyaki.

Teppanyaki (Japanese): Meal where the food is cooked on the teppan in front of the diners and served when done.

Thousand-year egg: A duck egg that's been preserved in a mixture of lime, ash, tea and salt for one hundred days, making the flesh of the egg black and strong in flavour.

Tikuanyin (Cantonese; or Tikuanyum): Iron Buddha Tea. A dark, strong and flavourful black Chinese tea. Named because, according to legend, the first tea bush of this type was found behind a roadside altar containing an iron statue of Kwan Yin.

Tin Hau (Cantonese): Taoist deity, worshipped by seafarers.

Triad: Hong Kong organised-crime syndicate. Members of the syndicates are also called triads.

Tsim Sha Tsui: Main tourist and entertainment district on Kowloon side, next to the Harbour.

Tsing Ma Bridge: Large suspension bridge connecting Kowloon with Lantau Island, used to connect to the Airport Expressway.

Typhoon: A hurricane that occurs in Asia. Equivalent to a hurricane in the US or a cyclone in Australia.

Wan Chai: Commercial district on Hong Kong Island, between the offices and designer stores of Central and the shopping area of Causeway Bay. Contains office buildings and restaurants, and is famous for its nightclubs and girlie bars.

Wan sui (Putonghua): 'Ten thousand years'; traditional greeting for the Emperor, wishing him ten thousand times ten thousand years of life.

Wei? (Cantonese): 'Hello?' when answering the phone.

Wing chun: Southern style of Chinese kung fu. Made famous by Bruce Lee, this style is fast, close in ('short') and lethal. It's also a 'soft' style where the defender uses the attacker's weight and strength against him or her, rather than relying on brute force to hit hard.

Won ton (Cantonese): Chinese dumplings made mostly of pork with a dough wrapping and boiled in soup stock. Often called 'short soup' in the West.

Won ton mien (Cantonese): 'won ton noodles'; won ton boiled in stock with noodles added to the soup.

Wu shu (Putonghua): A general term to mean all martial arts.

Wudang (Putonghua): A rough translation could be 'true martial arts'. The name of the mountain in Hubei Province; also the name of the martial arts academy and the style of martial arts taught there. Xuan Wu was a Celestial 'sponsor' of the Ming Dynasty and the entire mountain complex of temples and monasteries was built by the government of the time in his honour.

Wudangshan (Putonghua): 'Shan' means 'mountain'; Wudang Mountain.

Xie xie (Putonghua): 'Thank you.'

Xuan Wu (Putonghua) pronounced, roughly, 'Shwan Wu': means 'Dark Martial Arts'; the Black Turtle of the North, Mr Chen.

Yang: One of the two prime forces of the Universe in Taoist philosophy. Yang is the Light: masculine, bright, hot and hard.

Yang and yin: The two prime forces of the universe, when joined together form the One, the essence of everything. The symbol of yang and yin shows each essence containing a small part of the other.

Yellow Emperor: An ancient mythological figure, the Yellow Emperor is credited with founding civilisation and inventing clothing and agriculture.

Yin: One of the two prime forces of the universe in Taoist philosophy. Yin is Darkness: feminine, dark, cold and soft.

Yuexia Loaren (Putonghua): 'Old Man Under the Moon'; a Taoist deity responsible for matchmaking.

Yum cha (Cantonese): Literally 'drink tea'. Most restaurants hold yum cha between breakfast and mid-afternoon. Tea is served, and waitresses wheel around trolleys containing varieties of dim sum.

Yuzhengong (Putonghua): 'Find the True Spirit'; the name of the palace complex on Wudang Mountain.

Zhu Que (Putonghua) pronounced, roughly, Joo Chway: the Red Phoenix of the South.